VALLEY OF

Dreams

A HOPE SPRINGS NOVEL

VALLEY OF

SARAH M. EDEN

Mirror Press

Interior design by Cora Johnson
Edited by Annette Lyon and Lisa Shepherd

Cover design by Mirror Press, LLC, and Rachael Anderson
Cover image © Mary Wethey / Trevillion Images

Published by Mirror Press, LLC

ISBN-13: 978-1-947152-74-8

For Andrew,

I've walked the Dublin streets you once called home,
and sat in the churchyard where you were laid to rest.
As I've searched for clues to the person you were,
I've learned more about the person I hope to be.

Chapter One

WINNIPEG, CANADA, 1874

Patrick O'Connor learned three things on the battlefields of the American Civil War: death isn't usually clean or simple, loving someone isn't enough to save him, and music keeps the demons at bay. As he stood in a small shop in Winnipeg, negotiating a price for the fiddle he'd carried through years of battles and a decade of wandering the white north, he knew the demons had won.

"It's in rough condition," the shop owner said, turning the instrument over in his hands. "Battered and gashed and worse for the wear."

"Are we talking about the fiddle or its owner?"

The man eyed him sidelong. "Both."

"How much?" He wasn't enjoying the undertaking; he'd no intention of prolonging the thing.

"Why're you selling it?"

Blast the man. Could he not just name his price? "Why I'm selling doesn't make no nevermind."

"It does if your reason is that the instrument can't keep a tune."

With a grumble of frustration, Patrick snatched the fiddle. He made a few quick pulls of the bow and adjustments to the strings. He played a quick rendition of "Irish Washerwoman," and he played it well, if he did say so. Music had been his refuge through thirteen years of hell.

He forced himself to put the fiddle in the man's hands once more. "How much?"

"I'll give you twenty dollars."

Ten dollars was a fortune to him in the moment, but 'twas a devastating prospect losing his fiddle. He'd played it before battles. He'd played it after battles. He'd played it while grieving his brother. But now he was selling it, and not for anything noble.

"I'll take the twenty."

The exchange was made. For just a moment, Patrick couldn't get his feet to move from the spot. He was leaving behind a piece of himself there in that shop. He was giving up the last thread of happiness tied to his years in battle and the last days he'd spent with his brother. But he needed the money. He needed it because he needed what it would give him: escape.

Like the worthless heap he was, Patrick dragged himself from that shop to the saloon. He made straight to the barkeep.

"O'Connor." The barman eyed him suspiciously. "I ain't in the business of handouts."

"I have money," he mumbled.

"I'll believe it when I see it."

Patrick slapped four dollars on the counter.

"That's more than a glass's worth."

"Four bottles," he said. "Whiskey, not beer."

The usually hard expression the man wore turned to something like worry. "You've been drinking too much lately, paddy. Four bottles'll do you in."

"I'll make 'em last." For a while, at least.

"You've a problem."

He was in no mood for lectures. He knew full well he had a problem. He had more problems than anyone realized. "Are you taking my money or not?"

The man's mouth pulled in a tight line. He set bottles on the counter, one after the other. "Make sure this does last. I won't sell you any more."

"This'll do." He'd move on , go to the next town, start again, manage what he could before he burned more bridges.

He tucked the bottles into the thick canvas bag he'd carried his fiddle in and slumped his way out of the saloon. His trek back to the single room he rented took him past the post office.

The postmaster stopped him. "You have a letter." He held out a beaten and crumpled envelope.

Patrick snatched it with his free hand. It would be from Maura, his sister-in-law. She was the only one who ever wrote him, though heaven knew why she did. He'd cost her her husband, had walked out on her hospitality, and he almost never wrote back. What could he write, "Dear Maura, I'm drinking m'self into the grave, so I'm not likely to receive your next letter. Best regards, Patrick"?

He stuffed the letter into his pocket and kept walking. The weather was never truly warm in Winnipeg. It certainly wasn't that day. The bite of air was helpful, though. It kept him moving even in his lowest moments and gave him a ready excuse for drinking. He could lie to himself and say he was only trying to keep warm.

He knew the truth.

His landlady eyed him with warranted suspicion as he came inside the house and climbed the stairs to his room. He'd been thrown out of enough boarding houses to know it would happen again soon enough. Losing the roof over his head hardly bothered him any longer. Like most things in life, he'd grown numb to it.

He set his whiskey bottles on the bureau and tossed the envelope on his bed. This was an odd sort of boarding house: the residents brought their own furniture. He'd debated selling it instead of his fiddle, but he couldn't convince himself that music was more crucial than sleep.

At the window, he pulled back the strip of scrap fabric he'd hung as a curtain and looked out over the street below. This was a tiny town. Hardly warranted being called a town, really. He might've made something of himself here. Every possibility had seemed to exist here at once. But there'd been nothing more for him here than any other place he'd laid his head the last thirteen years. And his time here was ending the same way the others had: no friends left, no job, no money, no reason to stay, and nothing but whiskey to keep him going.

He'd run out of hope years ago. He wasn't even certain it had ever existed.

The bed creaked beneath him as he sat. Soon enough, he'd pour himself a glass of oblivion, but first he had Maura's letter to read. He'd read every word she'd sent over the years, clinging to the connection he didn't deserve to have.

Last he'd heard from Maura, she'd left New York and gone west to the tiny town where his parents and siblings had settled. Had he found them? Had they welcomed her? He couldn't imagine they would've been anything but overjoyed. Maura was the kind of person who made a place better simply for being in it. And she deserved to not be as alone as she'd been back East.

Patrick snatched up the envelope and broke the seal. He pulled out the letter inside.

My Dear Darling Patrick,

Maura never addressed him that way. His eyes dropped to the end of the letter.

Ma.

Every inch of air spilled from his lungs. *Ma.* The letter was from his mother. His mother, who he'd never written to. Who he'd not seen in thirteen years. Who he'd let believe he was dead.

My Dear Darling Patrick,

 Maura's only just told us that you've not died as we believed. I can't make my mind or my heart understand why you'd not tell us. And I can't make myself not worry over those possible reasons.

 We've grieved you these thirteen years. The whole family feels as though you've risen from the very grave.

 I don't know what's kept you in Canada

for a decade, but if you've a mind to come to Hope Springs, even the merest whisper of thought in our direction, I hope you will.

    You've a home here, lad. You've a family.

    Please come back to us.

    Ma

His breaths came shaky and shallow. His pulse pounded in his head.

Ma had written him a letter. He'd not intended to ever let her know he was still alive; it was better for her not to know. No one was better off for having him around. Not even himself.

His eyes fell on his four glass sentinels, mocking him with their promise of temporary freedom. Liquid numbing was the only escape he ever had from the pain he carried around.

He didn't drink to the degree of excess some did. And he didn't grow angry or violent. He simply couldn't face everything—and there was so very much to face—without something to ease the relentless pain of life. And he had to dull that pain more and more often of late.

I even sold my fiddle. Begor, how had things grown that bad? Luck had landed the instrument in his hands during the war. He'd managed not to lose it over years of marching and battles, and he'd kept it during lean times between jobs. He'd kept his fiddle and it had been an important part of his life.

And he'd sold it.

To buy whiskey.

He dropped his head into his hands, his matted hair and beard testifying to the mess he'd made of so many things. How had he come to this?

Patrick still had some control over this thirst that drove him, but how long would that last? How long before its clutches squeezed the life out of him?

Few people would even notice, and fewer still would care.

You've a home here, lad. You've a family.

He laughed in a short, humorless burst. What family would claim the lump he'd become? He'd caused them heartache enough. What right did he have to cause them more?

Patrick stood and crossed to the bureau. He set Ma's letter next to the line of bottles. How long would they last? And what would he sell next time to buy more?

You've a home here, lad.

He swallowed against the lump in his throat.

You've a family.

He pushed out a breath.

He had an offer of a home and family. There, in that sparse room and town of spent opportunities, he had nothing. He'd simply slip further, drink more, waste away.

He reached for a bottle, but stopped, hand hovering a mere inch away. Life offered few choices now, but one remained he couldn't ignore. He could stay in Winnipeg and drink himself into the grave. Or he could add another mark of guilt to his soul and accept the offer Ma had dangled in front of him.

The choice depended on one crucial question: was his a life worth saving?

His heart dropped to his toes as he realized—he didn't know the answer.

Chapter Two

WYOMING TERRITORY, 1874

After two days in the stagecoach, Eliza Porter concluded that her fellow passenger was either a fur trapper, a man with a deep-seated fear of razors, or a bear that had learned to walk on two feet, mumble the occasional one syllable word, and spend hours pretending to be asleep. She found all three possibilities incredibly intriguing.

Based on the stage driver's estimate, she and her almost two-year-old daughter, Lydia, would be set down at the tiny town of Hope Springs within the hour. Time enough for one more attempt at sorting the mystery of her furry fellow traveler.

"Do you live in Wyoming territory?" she asked.

He shook his head no.

"Are you making a visit or planning to make it your new home?"

He nodded.

"Which one?" she pressed.

"Guess," he mumbled from behind his bushy beard.

Where he hailed from Eliza couldn't be certain, but she suspected her mysterious companion didn't have an American accent. Of course, neither did she.

"New home?" she guessed.

He nodded.

Getting information from someone who offered such brief

answers required creative questions. "Have you been in this country long?"

"Have *you*?"

She smiled back at him as she bounced Lydia on her knee. "Heard my origins in my voice, did you?"

He scratched his dark beard between answers. His long, scraggly hair hung enough over his face so that she couldn't tell where he was looking, though she suspected his gaze had wandered to the stage-coach window.

"Do you look out the window so often because you can't resist the brown, dusty vista, or because you think it'll get me to stop talking to you?" She waited eagerly to see how he would answer that question with only a word or two.

After a moment, he said, "Both."

She couldn't help the laugh that slipped from her. Lydia laughed too—she nearly always laughed when her mother did. There had been a lot more laughing and smiling since they'd left New York City. They were on their way to a new life, a better life. Though Eliza was a little nervous, she was nearly giddy with anticipation.

America had been a disappointment in a lot of ways. Finally, its promises felt within reach, and leaving England felt less like a mistake.

Did her reticent fellow traveler feel good about his decision to leave his home country? And what *was* his home country? The man didn't say enough at any one time for his accent to be obvious.

"England?" She guessed aloud.

His head turned in her direction. "Sounds like it to me."

Five words at once. A new record, and enough to tell that he was definitely from the British Isles. A few more words, and she would have him sorted.

"What brings you to Wyoming?"

"Stagecoach," he muttered.

She laughed. Lydia did as well. "I think you're being grumpy on purpose."

He turned his head toward the window once more. "I like hearing your wee girl laugh."

"Ireland!" There was no mistaking his accent now that she'd truly heard it.

"I-und!" Lydia made a valiant attempt.

The grumbly bear didn't noticeably react. Eliza wasn't certain what to make of him. Instinct told her she had nothing to fear from him. She stayed alert, of course—being cautious was never a bad idea—but during their day and a half on the stagecoach, he'd never given her reason to worry.

As the stage rumbled to a stop, her heart dropped a little. She was excited to begin this new chapter in her and Lydia's life, but a twinge of disappointment flickered through her, knowing she would have no further opportunity to talk to the intriguing man. He'd made her laugh and kept her company, however quietly, and she was grateful for it.

"This is our stop," she told him. "Thank you for being kind to us. Safe journey."

He nodded, and she climbed down with Lydia on her hip. Her trunk and carpet bag had been set down beside the coach. But—she looked around—there was no town. Had the driver made a mistake?

"Over the hill behind you," the driver said, apparently recognizing her confusion. "You can't see the town until you crest the hill."

She turned to look. Getting to the hill alone would be no small jaunt. She would have to come back for her trunk. Surely someone in her new town would fetch it for her.

She heard the coach roll away behind her. There was no turning back now.

"Are you ready to begin a new adventure, Lydia?"

The little girl's eyes were on the sky. "Clouds."

"Lots of clouds," Eliza said. "You'll see a lot more of the sky now that we've left New York."

"Clouds."

Eliza spun back to grab her carpetbag; *that* she could manage even with Lydia. On the dusty ground on the other side of the road from where the stagecoach had been, was another trunk. And standing beside it . . . the grumbly bear himself.

He dragged his trunk across the dirt road toward her.

"Is this your destination as well?" Eliza asked.

9

He nodded, taking the handle of her trunk as he reached it. His own trunk was left behind as he slung hers on his back and began his trek up the hill.

She rushed to catch up with him. "What about *your* trunk?"

"'T'won't run off while I'm gone." He kept trudging upward.

"You didn't say you were bound for Hope Springs." She kept pace with him.

"Never came up."

"Which is surprising," she said. "We talked about so many things."

"Aye, *you* did," he muttered.

Eliza—and Lydia—laughed. "I'm glad you're going to be living nearby."

"Why's that?" The man had too much hair and too wide a hat brim for her to see if he looked as annoyed as he sounded, or if the hint of amusement she heard in his voice twinkled in his eyes. She hoped he was at least not *dis*pleased at the idea of being her neighbor.

"Why?" she repeated. "Because it'll give me time to sort out why you act grumpy when I don't think you actually are."

He stopped and set her trunk down. Had she upset him?

"*Begor,*" he whispered. "That must be the town."

She looked ahead out over the vast valley, a patchwork of farm fields and the occasional building. A river wound through, with a couple of small bridges crossing it. Nearest the hill they stood on was a small group of buildings. *Small,* in this case, meaning three. In total. *Three* buildings.

"Is that all of it, do you suppose?" Her dear friend Maura, who'd sent for her to come west, had told her that the town of Hope Springs was small. But this was shocking.

"It could be hidden under a clover." He sounded as shocked as she was.

"'Under a clover.' You really are Irish."

"I used to be." He picked up her trunk once more.

Eliza adjusted her hold on Lydia, then walked alongside him down the hill toward the town she meant to make her new home. Her hairy companion didn't speak again. Usually when Eliza was nervous, she grew chattier. Approaching the three-building town, however, her tongue was entirely tied.

"Sweet heavens, I hope coming here doesn't prove a mistake," she whispered.

She didn't consider herself cowardly, but now and then her mettle faltered. Fortunately she had a knack for rallying her courage. Her stride was sure and purposeful as she entered the town. She pulled from her pocket the written instructions she'd received, directing her to where she was meant to meet Maura.

"Walk through town to where the road forks. The house at the fork is the Archers', and you'll more likely than not find me there."

She would be "through town" in the blink of an eye. Not too far ahead, near enough to be easily seen, the dirt road did, indeed, fork, and a house sat directly in the middle of the fork.

The bear man glanced her direction, still carrying her trunk.

"I'm meant to go to that house up ahead, at the fork in the road."

"Aye." He continued on.

"Isn't 'aye' more of a Scottish word? Have I guessed your origins wrong?"

"'Aye' is heard more in the north of Ireland." With a multi-syllable response like that, she had no doubt he'd come from the Emerald Isle.

"Are you meeting anyone in particular in Hope Springs?" she asked as they continued on down the road.

He didn't answer, which, she'd discovered, was as unwavering a response as a spoken one. Mr. Bear spoke only when he chose to. Perhaps on closer acquaintance he would be more inclined to talk.

They reached her destination. Eliza stopped at the bottom of the porch steps and turned to her companion. "You can leave the trunk here. I'm certain someone in the house will carry it for me."

He shook his head. "I'll see it to wherever it's meant to be placed."

She climbed the steps and knocked on the door. A moment passed. Eliza bounced Lydia on her hip, grateful the girl was too in awe of her new surroundings to be nervous.

The door opened. Eliza had fully expected to be happy at being reunited with Maura O'Connor—now Maura Callaghan—a friend so dear to her they were like sisters. She hadn't anticipated being overjoyed to the point of immediate tears.

"Eliza!" Maura burst through the doorway and pulled her and Lydia into a tight embrace. Apparently, Hope Springs had brought out Maura's more expressive side; she used to be rather reserved in her shows of emotion.

"Maura!" Eliza clung to her tightly. "Oh, how I've missed you!"

Maura pulled back without releasing her, enough to give her a glance over. "You seem to have survived the journey." Her gaze settled on Lydia, and her eyes widened with amazement. "This can't be our tiny girl. She's grown so much."

"We've been apart a whole year," Eliza reminded her.

Beside them, Eliza's trunk carrier had stiffened. He'd been very distant the first hour or so they'd shared the stagecoach. After a time, he'd grown more at ease. Now, faced with a new set of strangers, he withdrew once more. Perhaps he was shy.

"Do come inside." Maura pulled Eliza all the way in. "I can't wait to introduce you to everyone."

She didn't want to overwhelm the man who'd so willingly offered his help, nor keep him from retrieving his own trunk.

"Where ought my trunk be set?" she asked Maura.

"The house has a room specifically for the housekeeper," Maura said. "We'll set your things there."

The inclusion of room and board had made possible accepting a job in such a faraway position.

Her traveling companion followed her inside, keeping his distance from Maura.

"Back this way."

They passed through a sitting room, then a dining room, and into a kitchen. It was fairly large and neat, but far simpler than the fine home she'd once worked in back in New York.

Maura motioned to a side door. "That'll be your room."

Her trunk was carried across the kitchen. Maura eyed the man, as he passed, then turned a curious look on Eliza.

She gave her friend a quick smile and simple explanation. "He arrived on the stage as well and kindly carried my trunk here." There'd be time enough for all the details—what few there were—when they were alone.

Maura looked over at the mysterious man, who'd just stepped back out of the room, having left the trunk inside. "I hadn't heard anyone else was expecting an arrival on the stage."

Maura studied him. The scrutiny clearly made him uncomfortable. He tugged the brim of his hat in acknowledgement but moved swiftly past her, retracing the path that had taken them into the kitchen.

"Will you wait for a bite to eat?" Maura offered before he could leave. "You've been so kind to Eliza. Allow me this small way to say thank you."

He shook his head no.

Eliza's heart dropped. "Oh, do pause long enough for something to eat as a thank you for being so helpful."

Somehow he scratched at the back of his neck despite the rat's nest of hair hanging there. "I need to be less helpful," he muttered. "'Tis a terrible inconvenience."

"But you'll stay, at least long enough for a bite?" Eliza would feel better if he did.

He pushed out a sigh and nodded.

Maura continued watching him, curious. Between his unkempt appearance and his gruff manners, he *did* make an odd study.

"There's a bit of a spread just in back of the house," Maura said, motioning to a nearby door. "Help yourself to all you'd like."

Again, he tugged at the brim of his hat. "Ladies first."

Maura hooked an arm through Eliza's. "There'll be time and plenty for taking a look at your new room. For now, let's get you a bit to eat as well."

She led Eliza through the back door and directly into a large gathering.

"Who are all these people?"

"My late husband's family. There are a lot of them, and I want you to meet them all. But first, let's feed you. I remember well how long the journey is."

Eliza was pulled into the crowd, introductions tossed at her, even as food was placed on a plate that had somehow made its way into her hands. Maura held Lydia, something she'd once done daily when they'd been neighbors back East.

The sheer number of people as well as their enthusiasm made the gathering both wonderful and a little intimidating. Still, she wouldn't trade the feeling of "family" for all the quiet comfort in the world. She'd had more than enough loneliness for one lifetime. She was ready to finally belong.

Chapter Three

Patrick stood in the kitchen of this unfamiliar home, attempting to decide if he was in greater need of silence or food. He'd passed two days in a stagecoach with the most determinedly chatty woman he'd ever met. But he'd also gone twice that long with precious little to eat. His indecision was real, but it was not the true reason for his hesitation.

Seeing Maura O'Connor again without warning after ten years had upended him. That his sister-in-law, widow of his oldest brother, hadn't recognized him hurt deeply. Coming to Hope Springs where his estranged family lived had been an act of desperation, really. He hadn't anticipated the possibility that they wouldn't even know him.

Maybe he could live among them without having to face them. It would be the coward's way, something more apt than he cared to admit.

He rubbed at his face and beard, weary and worn, but too near his breaking point to simply walk away. The family he'd turned his back on a decade earlier were now his only hope.

"You can never wander so far that there isn't a road home," Ma used to say. He was depending on that being true.

He nodded to himself, setting his jaw and shoulders. Maura would know where his parents were. He'd have to tell her who he was. But, she'd taken him in before, kept in contact with him over the years. She'd likely accept his return better than the rest of the family would.

Patrick stepped out onto the back porch of the home, fully

prepared to see Maura again. Instead, he saw a flood of familiar faces, painfully beloved faces. His *entire* family.

He stopped at the edge of the porch, unable to take a single step closer to them. He'd imagined so many times over the past years seeing them again. Now that he did, it hurt. It hurt in every beat of his heart, every breath he took.

They would hate him; he knew they would. He'd known before he left Canada. But he'd had nowhere else to go.

Maura spotted him, and with the same lack of recognition, she approached. "Do come eat. There's plenty."

He shook his head no. His hunger wasn't enough to push him toward the rejection that awaited him in this sea of family.

Maura glanced back at the crowd. "Mother O'Connor, come help me convince Eliza's Good Samaritan to accept some food."

He wasn't ready for this. Not remotely. "I'll be on m'way."

"Nonsense." Maura waved someone over.

In the next instant, Ma emerged and walked toward him.

Patrick swallowed back a surge of emotion. He'd not seen his mother since he was seventeen, a child, really. She approached, her gaze growing more pointed as she drew near. Her eyes narrowed, studying him. Maura hadn't recognized him, and she'd seen him more recently than Ma had.

He pulled his hat off his head and held it against his chest. Ma eyed him ever closer. Confusion tugged at that achingly familiar face. She didn't look away. Her gaze narrowed. Her brows pulled low. She couldn't place him—he could tell she couldn't—but she seemed to sense that she ought to have been able to.

He couldn't endure it any longer. He couldn't bear the thought of being a stranger to his own mother.

Patrick cleared his throat. Voice quiet, uncertain, he said, "I got your letter."

She gasped, her hand pressed to her heart. "Patrick." Her arms were around him before he could brace himself. "My Patrick. My Patrick."

He kept himself still and breathing through sheer power of will.

Every fiber of him insisted he set her away for her own good. No one was ever better for having him in their lives. No one.

Without warning, Da was there, weathered brow pulled into a mixture of surprise and hope. "Is it really himself?"

"'Tis our boy, Thomas," Ma answered. "Under all those whiskers, it's our boy come back to us."

They'd anticipated the Patrick he'd been at seventeen. That dewy-eyed lad no longer existed, hadn't for years.

Da's firm embrace engulfed both Ma and Patrick. Around them, a flood of O'Connors descended. Though they were older, he recognized them all. His older sister, Mary. His brother Tavish, who bore a painfully striking resemblance to the oldest of the siblings, who'd died at Gettysburg. A woman he felt certain was his little sister, now grown. They were all surrounded by children—his nieces and nephews, no doubt—and people he didn't know but wagered were his siblings by marriage.

He searched their faces, looking for the brother he'd thought of every day of the past thirteen years. He and Ian had been the best of friends. Until the day Patrick stayed in New York while nearly all the others had come west, they'd never been apart, not for a single day in all of Patrick's life. They'd been each other's best friends and closest confidantes. Patrick had been there when Ian met the lass who would eventually become his wife. Ian had offered Patrick the support he needed when deciding what to do with his life.

He'd been lost without Ian. For years he'd needed his brother nearby. He'd've had someone to talk to, someone to help him sort out the mess he'd made of his life. He wouldn't have been so entirely alone.

"Come eat." Ma *had* always considered food the cure for whatever ailed a person.

"You weren't planning on me," he objected.

She waved that off even as the entire clan, questions flying at him from all directions, crowded him off the porch and toward the table of victuals.

"Where have you been?"

"Are you staying?"

"We thought you were dead."

He cringed at that non-question. After Gettysburg, he'd been wrongly reported as killed in battle. He hadn't told his family in Hope Springs that he'd actually survived.

It had been better that way. If Maura hadn't told them the truth, they'd still have believed him dead, and everyone would have been better off.

Eliza stood near the table of food as he was tugged there. She smiled at him, something like laughter in her eyes.

"Enjoyin' this, lass?" he muttered.

"I'm simply glad to have a name to put with you." Her accent marked her as English. He'd spent the hours listening to her talk, attempting to sort her origins beyond that general location. In the end he decided she'd come from whichever corner of England produced the chattiest women. She'd talked ceaselessly through the journey here and now was present for this uncomfortable reunion. And why shouldn't she be? He'd made a fool of himself in front of strangers for years.

"Where will you stay?" Maura asked him.

Before he could admit he'd come hoping to impose on the family he'd neglected for more than a decade, Da spoke. "With us, of course. We'll not hear of him going anywhere else."

How little he deserved such generosity. He'd do far better to find somewhere else to lay his weary bones.

The group parted a bit. From among them came the person Patrick had been watching for. Ian was older—they all were—but Patrick knew him on the instant.

Seeing him again, a lifetime of memories flooded over him with a hint of the hope he'd once had.

Ian. His older brother. His best friend in all the world. After more than a decade apart, there he was.

Patrick hadn't cried in years, but seeing Ian again brought his emotions perilously close to the surface. He wanted to say something but struggled to find the words.

Ian didn't embrace him like Ma had, nor offer words of welcome like Da. He hit him, belted him right in the gob.

The blow left Patrick sprawled on the ground, the metallic taste of blood in his mouth.

Ian's hard, unyielding eyes extinguished the tiny flicker of hope he'd had. Patrick wiped the trickle of blood from his lip.

He ought to have expected this. He certainly deserved it. But, like a fool, he'd let himself believe for one glorious moment that the brother who'd always looked out for him wouldn't hate him.

But he did.

And Patrick deserved it.

Maura held her hand out. Patrick set the wet, bloodied kitchen towel in her palm.

She leaned in close, eying his split lip. "Ian belted you proper."

"Seems he was none too happy to see me." Patrick gingerly touched his fingertips to his lip.

"You shouldn't've let him think you were dead." Maura had always been a very direct sort of person. "If I'd known you hadn't sent the letter you said you had, I'd have told the family myself . . . immediately after belting you so hard it'd make Ian's effort look like a mother's kiss."

"Violence, Maura?" He clicked his tongue as he shook his head. "I'm shocked."

She sat in the chair nearest him. "They've mourned you all these years, Patrick. You shouldn't've put them through that."

He regretted that they'd been pained by his "death," but it had been for the best. He'd done them a favor, really. Maura was the one who'd undone it all, telling them not only that he was alive but where he'd been living.

"Your parents'll insist you live with them," Maura said. "That'll put you nearest neighbors to Ian. Might want to work on an explanation or an apology."

"Or ducking."

She smiled at him. "I've missed that humor of yours, Patrick. It began disappearing right before *you* did."

"Life ain't always funny, Maura."

Eliza flew in through the back door. "I saw Aidan. Heavens, Maura, he's grown so much this past year. I hardly recognized him."

Aidan. Patrick hadn't seen the lad since he was four years old. He'd be fourteen or fifteen by now. *Begor*, so much time had passed.

"Did Aidan see Lydia?" Maura asked

Eliza nodded. "He spun her around and around, saying, 'My little Lydia.' She stared at him as if he was entirely out of his mind." She laughed. "Poor girl doesn't remember him—she was so tiny when you left. She'll love him again soon enough, though." Her gaze shifted to him. "Did the man with the ginger hair knock any of your teeth out?"

"Are you hopin' he did?"

She smiled and, without answering, turned and walked into the room Maura had indicated would be hers once she began working in this house. "This room is so very much nicer than any at the Widows' Tower."

Patrick's heart dropped at the reminder of the building where Maura had lived when he'd found her again after the war. "Eliza lived in that hellhole?"

Maura hooked an eyebrow. "You left Aidan and me in that 'hellhole,' so you must not've thought it too terrible."

It had, in fact, been entirely terrible—falling apart, a hovel in every sense of the word. If he'd had the means to help her escape it, he would have. In the end, he'd done the only thing he could to improve her situation. He'd removed himself from it.

Eliza peeked her head out of the room. "Every drawer in the bureau opens without even the tiniest bit of difficulty. You didn't tell me I'd be living in the lap of luxury." She slipped inside once more.

"I've missed her," Maura said fondly. "I've never known anyone as buoyant."

"Or as talkative," Patrick added in a low voice. "Must've said a thousand words to every one of mine."

"And they were all cheerful, weren't they?"

He nodded. "Is she a little touched?"

Maura laughed lightly. "No. She's simply the most determinedly optimistic person a body's likely ever to meet."

A woman like that ought not to have been trapped in a stagecoach with someone as despicable as he. Fate was sometimes vindictive.

A lad of likely about fourteen stepped inside the increasingly busy kitchen. Patrick's mouth hung open. Looking at the boy was like looking in a mirror, but when he was less than half the age he was now.

"That's not wee Aidan," he whispered in amazement.

"He's nearly grown now," Maura said. "And looks so very like his father."

"He's a good lad? Treats you as he ought?"

She nodded. "And he's so much happier here than he ever was in New York." She reached over and patted Patrick's hand. "This is a fine place to live. It's good that you've come."

He needed it to be far more than "fine." He needed Hope Springs to be miraculous despite the fact that he was never granted anything resembling a miracle.

"Ma, have you seen Lydia?" Aidan was holding the hand of Eliza's little girl. "She's so big, and she can walk now, and Mrs. Porter says she can even talk."

"A child is very different at a few months old than at nearly two years old."

"I'm glad you sent for them," he said, his very American accent at odds with all the Irish voices ringing in through the open back door. "They'll be happier here."

Ma and Da stepped inside next. Would so many O'Connors coming and going ever grow easier to endure? His heart lurched at each arrival. Perhaps coming to Hope Springs hadn't been an entirely wise decision.

"Chores are calling to everyone," Ma said. "We'd all best get back to our work." The tenderness with which she looked at him made him feel guilty as sin. He didn't deserve anything but being shoved away. "We're over the river and a pace down the road. A beautiful farm. The house we all built together. You'll love it; I know you will."

21

"I don't want to take up room."

Da held a hand up to cut off his objection. "Best not argue with your ma about this, lad. She'll not give you the tiniest listen on the matter."

He'd not expected such close quarters. Every town he'd lived in since the war had boasted at least one house that took in boarders. He'd known he'd need his family's generosity for a time while he found a means of supporting himself and renting a room somewhere with space enough to breathe. But in all his imaginings, he saw himself lying in a corner of a barn or some other kind of outbuilding, far enough away from his family to grant them the distance they deserved.

Life didn't merely withhold miracles; it punished him at every possible turn. "I'd need to fetch m'trunk," he said.

"Our wagon's out back o' the barn. I'll drive you out to fetch your trunk."

"*We'll* drive you out to fetch your trunk," Ma corrected.

Da's smile emerged on the instant. Oh, how Patrick had missed that smile, that face, this family.

"She's grown fierce," Patrick said.

"She was always fierce," Da tossed back. "It simply echoes more out West."

Patrick bid Maura farewell, then followed his parents out the back door. 'Twasn't quite as chaotic as it had been before. Some of the family had, it seemed, made their way home again. Still, there were people enough to make him uncomfortable and wary. He kept near the side of the house, hoping not to draw too much attention. He managed to get to the wagon without more questions or embraces or studying gazes.

Even as he kept his distance, he looked for Ian. He knew his brother likely hated him, but found comfort in knowing that man who'd been beside him through so many difficulties in the first seventeen years of his life was nearby again.

But he didn't see him.

Ma didn't stop talking all the way back to where the stage had left him off. Patrick didn't mind. He'd spent two days, after all, with the constant chatter of Eliza Porter. And he'd spent thirteen years without hearing his mother's voice.

When Da stopped the wagon beside Patrick's waiting trunk, he didn't hesitate to hop down, wanting to grab the trunk before his father could. He lifted it slowly, careful not to set the contents shifting around. They were soon situated again, Patrick tucked between his parents on the wagon bench.

He suspected he needed to grow accustomed to the closeness. He wasn't in the wilds of Canada any longer. He'd chosen to join his family here; he couldn't avoid being around them.

If the heavens chose to be kind, something he hoped for but didn't truly expect, he'd find his salvation in this tiny corner of the world and not, as he had for so long, in the contents of that trunk.

Chapter Four

Standing in his parents' home, Patrick couldn't help comparing it to the tiny flat they'd all shared in New York. They'd been packed in tighter than meat in a pie. He and Ian had slept in one corner of the flat behind a quilt hanging from the ceiling. Tavish had slept in another corner, Ciara another. Finbarr, the youngest of them all, no more than six when they'd left, had slept on the floor beside Ma and Da's bed. This house, while far from luxurious, was larger than that flat had been. No quilts hanging. No bedrolls in the corners.

"'Tisn't a mansion," Da eyed Patrick rather than the room. "But we're pleased with it."

Da had misunderstood his scrutiny.

"You've more room than you did in New York."

A hint of relief crossed the man's features. Had he truly thought Patrick meant to think ill of his home, the home they meant to let him stay in? But then, why would he think his prodigal son was anything but heartless and rejecting? He had no reason to think otherwise.

"The whole family lived here for a time until each of the children moved on to their own land."

Patrick couldn't imagine a family as poor as the O'Connors owning enough land for all the brothers and sisters to have their own. That would've been impossible both in New York—there wasn't land to be had—and back in Ireland, where the land was not actually owned by those working it. Da had come west all those years ago chasing this very dream, and he'd found it.

Ma stepped out of a door against the far wall, smiling at him as though he were a full larder in the midst of a famine. She moved quick and sure, her step as nimble as that of a woman half her age. Hope Springs had been good to both his parents.

"You can use the loft," she said. "With Finbarr gone, it sits empty, aching for someone to move in."

Worry gripped his heart on the instant. "What's happened to Finbarr?"

Ma patted his arm. He did his best not to flinch. "He lives with Tavish. 'Tis a better arrangement for the lad."

There was a story there, but Patrick didn't mean to pry into his youngest brother's reasons for not living with their parents. He knew perfectly well how personal one's reasons could be. "Will Finbarr have his own land too?"

"Already does." Da beamed with pride. "Worked for years to purchase it. He's kept at his job, so he'll have money enough for building a house there."

Odd. "Do children often buy land out West?"

Ma and Da exchanged drawn-browed looks. After a moment, Da's expression cleared as if he'd pieced something together.

"Finbarr's grown," he said. "Nineteen now. He's not been a child in years."

Tiny Finbarr. Nineteen? Simple logic told him the little bean sprout wasn't so little anymore, but the reality of it struck him with force. He lowered himself onto a nearby chair. Thirteen years had passed. Thirteen years of his family's lives. Of their struggles. Their joys. Thirteen years, and he'd missed every moment of it. They'd gone on without him, as he'd wanted them to. But facing the reality still hurt.

Ma sat nearby. "I've no doubt he'll come by and offer you his greetings. He remembers you, you know. Not in great detail, but enough. He's a quiet lad, but I think you'll enjoy coming to know him again."

Quiet. Not a word he would've used to describe the little boy he'd once known. "Is Ian still quiet?"

"Aye." A heavy bit of hesitation hung in Da's voice. He couldn't be blamed. After Ian's reaction to seeing Patrick, no one in his family could doubt that these two brothers, once the closest of them all, were now irreparably estranged.

Ian didn't want him there. Finbarr hardly remembered him. The entire family had created lives for themselves that Patrick didn't want to disrupt. He ought to do them all a favor and return to the empty dirt road and climb on the stage when next it passed.

But he knew what would happen if he did. Death had been dogging his heels for years. If he left now, it would catch up with him once and for all. And, though Da and Ma would've been better off if he'd stayed away, making them mourn his death again, as any parent would no matter the worthlessness of their child, would be cruel. He couldn't do that to them.

"I'll be needing a job," he said. "Is anyone hiring in a town this small?"

"Mostly we're farmers here," Da answered. "But the ranches are sometimes looking to take on hands."

Patrick knew nothing of farming or ranching.

"Finbarr and Maura—now Maura's friend, Eliza—work for the Archer family, but I can't imagine they'd be hiring anyone else on just now." Da rubbed at his chin. His stubble, once nearly as dark as Patrick's, was now silver. "The mercantile isn't likely to be taking anyone on, but you might ask. They hire now and then."

None of this was promising. He'd not intended to come and be a burden. More than that, even, he needed to be busy. He had to be. Idle hands, as the saying went. He *needed* to be busy. He had to be.

Again, Ma patted his arm. He couldn't help tensing but didn't pull away. "We'll find you a job, never you fear. You worked so hard at the factory and were always so skilled with those complicated machines. We'll find you something."

He hadn't loved the factory in New York, but he had liked the role he'd had there. Every job he'd had since the end of the war had been similar: repairing things, building things.

"I'll find something," he promised them.

She hugged him. He fought between discomfort and relief. How long had he been grappling with the contradiction? It felt like a lifetime.

He climbed the ladder to the loft, where he had a degree of privacy and room to breathe. He welcomed both. The low bed creaked beneath him as he sat. He'd not had a bed since he sold his furniture in Winnipeg. Light poured in through the small window, illuminating the space.

Patrick felt a brief moment of rare peace.

He pushed out a heavy breath. If he could build a life in Hope Springs, maybe he could finally escape his demons.

But that night, he wasn't strong enough to outrun them. He took one of the bottles of whiskey from his trunk and set a glass beside it. A single sip calmed his worries. A second relaxed him enough to lie down.

He needed to think of a way of supporting himself in this tiny town. He didn't know enough of Hope Springs to have any answers. But Maura had found work for Eliza. Perhaps she'd be willing and able to point him toward employment, too.

When he climbed down the next morning, the smell of eggs washed over him like a welcome rain. The past years, his breakfasts had come from a glass. So had many of his meals. He was trying to change that. Heaven knew he was trying.

"Come eat, lad." Ma waved him over to the large table near the stove and shelves.

"I'll not eat your food until I can replace it."

She popped her fists on her hips, eying him with the look of scolding, which he remembered all too well. "Are you refusin' my cooking, Patrick Duncan O'Connor? And turning your nose up at m'hospitality as well?"

Emotion thickened in his throat—not at the scolding, but at the wave of memories. Rest him, he'd missed his ma. His heart had ached to have her hug him or scold him or laugh with him again. He'd longed to matter to her once more. A fellow couldn't be entirely contemptible if his mother still loved him.

She motioned him to sit. He knew better than to argue.

He sat and, with a word of thanks, tucked into the generous plate of eggs and toast she'd set in front of him. For that morning, he'd indulge in being a child again, letting himself simply accept his ma's fussing and tending. There was time enough for pulling himself up and carrying his own burdens. He needed just a moment to rest his soul.

"Your da's out tending the fields. I'm certain he'd be pleased to have you help him."

"I've not ever done farm work."

"You have so." She tipped her head a bit, eyeing him with confusion. "Back in Ireland."

He could smile at that. "I was eight, Ma. I suspect I've lost most of my no-doubt impressive farming skills these past twenty-three years."

She set her palm against her apron bib, pressing it against her heart. "I forget sometimes how little of Ireland you must remember. Ciara recalls nothing at all of it. And Finbarr, of course, was born here."

Patrick took another bite of his breakfast, his enthusiasm for the meal slowing. Though his stomach begged each morning for nourishment, he found it grew displeased more quickly than it ought, a consequence of too many years filling his belly with whiskey instead of food. Too many regrets hung in his mind; he needed a new topic to distract himself. "You said Finbarr works somewhere in town?"

She nodded as she crossed to the kitchen wash basin. "For Joseph Archer. Finbarr has worked at his farm for years now."

"And Maura worked for Mr. Archer as well?"

"Aye." Ma scrubbed her frying pan. "He's a well-off man, owns most of the valley."

That was promising. A man of means and property might have some work needing to be done. "His was the house we were at yesterday?"

"Finest in the valley."

He'd be the one to petition for work. "Will Maura be there again today?"

"I'd imagine so. Her friend'll be taking on the housekeeper's role, but our Maura'll be teaching her how."

"I've a hope she might have a job in her pocket for me as well," Patrick said.

"She might," Ma said. "And if not, Ryan has connections at the ranches."

"Ryan?"

"Maura's husband."

She'd remarried? How long ago? Did this Ryan treat her well? Was she happy? Grady's death had ricocheted through the family with such force that no one had been spared the agony of it. His death, they knew all too well, could be laid at Patrick's feet.

Patrick finished off his eggs and rose, carrying his empty plate to the basin where Ma scrubbed dishes. "I'll wash it up."

"Nonsense."

He'd eventually have to insist on doing for himself, but he'd not launch into an argument so soon into his stay. "I'm after wandering down the road to see if Maura's heard of any jobs here about."

"You don't mean to stay and gab? Spend the day here?"

The idea of an entire day pretending all was well, pretending his ma's kindness to him was deserved, pretending they hadn't a chasm the size of the Irish Sea between them . . . He couldn't endure it.

A day spent gabbing would unavoidably turn to the topic of separation and war and Grady's death. He hadn't willpower enough for facing that *and* staying sober. He'd promised himself he wouldn't drink during the day. He couldn't break that vow so soon.

"I need a job, Ma. Best if I sort that out now."

"I've not seen you in thirteen years, Patrick."

"Then a few more hours won't seem like much." He moved in a near panic to the door.

"Patrick—"

"I'm sorry, Ma." He pulled open the door. Her downtrodden expression tore at him. But what could he do? "I'm sorry."

He stepped outside and pulled the door closed behind him. For a long moment he stood there, his heavy mind and heart anchoring him to the spot. He pushed his ratty hair out of his face. Living here was proving as uncomfortable as he'd feared. He needed his family's help, but he didn't know how to talk to them or be near them. The least he could do was find work and not be a burden.

The walk back up the road was long. He passed five farms spread out in either direction from the road, none within quick distance of each other. And the valley expanded far beyond these homes. There was so much space here. Distance enough between people that he could, if he found a corner of his own . . .

He shook off the thought he didn't dare finish. Letting himself hope for things only led to disappointment in the end. His family might not want him to stay once they came to know the person he was now. He might find having them nearby was too painful, too full of regret. He'd do best not to build up too many dreams.

He stopped for a minute on the wooden bridge that spanned the river. The past eighteen months, he'd lived near Lake Winnipeg. He'd grown accustomed to the sound of water. This river was a trickle compared to that vast body of water, but it was comfortingly familiar.

He leaned against the bridge railing, taking in the view. The area was dry and leaned heavily toward shades of brown, but it was beautiful all the same. The mountains in the distance had to be enormous. And tall. The tips were white with snow, despite this being the middle of summer. He'd moved around a lot the past years and had learned to appreciate all kinds of scenery.

What he wouldn't have given in that moment to have his fiddle. Music carried over water. Playing now would have been beautiful. Except there was too great a chance of someone stumbling upon him. Playing his fiddle had been comforting, but it was also very personal.

With his hands tucked into the pockets of his trousers, he walked onward, setting his feet in the direction of the Archers' house. He'd not had a drop to drink all morning. Though he felt the tug pulling him back to his trunk at Ma and Da's, he had motivation enough to keep moving toward the hope of a job, an income and, eventually, being less of a burden. In time he might even be an asset to someone, maybe even to himself.

Maura answered his knock at the back door. "Patrick. What brings you 'round?"

"I'm needing work."

She leaned a shoulder against the doorframe. "You spent last night at a large, working farm. There's work and plenty there."

"I know about as much about farming as a cow does about going on holiday."

"You're wishin' I'd offered you the housekeeper's job instead of Eliza?"

He allowed a fleeting smile. "I'm hoping that this Mr. Archer I've heard about has work to hire out. Ma says Finbarr works here as well."

"Even my Aidan has done a spot of work for Mr. Archer now and then."

Promising indeed. "I'd like to ask him what he has on offer just now."

"He's not here," Maura said. "The family returns to Baltimore for a month or so every other year. They'll not be back for another fortnight."

He needed something sooner than two weeks from now.

"Patrick!" Eliza's voice rang out from behind Maura. An instant later, she slipped around Maura and reached out to catch hold of his arm. "Come see the fireplace. It has *three* pot hooks."

How had he come to be this near-stranger's friend of choice? He'd not said more than a handful of words to her on the entire journey from the train station, yet somehow she thought of him as her friend. As he was dragged past Maura, he looked to her, hoping for some explanation. She smiled at him in obvious amusement. He'd get no help from that quarter.

A moment later, he stood in front of an empty fireplace, listening to her explain at length why three pot hooks were such a fine thing. She seemed truly excited to share her enthusiasm with him. Over pot hooks. He did not understand this confusing lass.

"And Maura says the Archers have a little boy almost exactly Lydia's age, so she will have an immediate friend. Is that not perfect?"

He nodded, not bothering to answer. She hadn't yet required him to.

"They have two daughters Maura says are just lovely. I think I'm going to be very happy here."

He suspected Eliza Porter was happy *everywhere*. He'd once been more that way, before life had beaten every bit of joy out of him.

"How is your lip?" she asked, not appearing the least horrified at having witnessed a man getting slugged without warning. "It's so well hidden behind all those unkempt whiskers."

"Fine."

He spotted Lydia toddling toward him, fingers in her mouth. She stopped directly in front of him, wide eyes studying him. He looked to the little chipmunk's ma, hoping for an explanation. Eliza only shrugged.

The little girl didn't look away, or move away, or say a word. He eyed her, very unsure of it all.

"Good mornin', lass."

Still, she didn't speak or move so much as an eyelash. At least she wasn't afraid of him.

Eliza hadn't been helpful, so he looked to Maura next. Blast the woman, she was clearly laughing at him despite not making a sound.

Lydia pulled her fingers out of her mouth and put them, dripping with tiny-girl drool, on the leg of his years-old, work-stained, threadbare trousers. "I-und!"

"Ireland." Eliza offered the unnecessary translation.

He remembered the girl's attempt at the word the day before. He hadn't expected Lydia to remember. Did she think that was his name?

He pointed at himself. "Patrick."

"I-und."

"Pat . . . rick." He pulled the two syllables out long and slow.

She grinned—the brightest, widest smile he had ever seen. "I-und!"

In that moment, the girl claimed a bit of his long-frozen heart.

"I'm afraid you'll be 'Ireland' from now on, Mr. Patrick," Eliza said, scooping her daughter up off the floor. "Lydia does not lose battles of will."

"Splendid," he muttered.

As always, she wasn't the least put off by his grumbling. "I hope your lip is better, and that you didn't lose any teeth."

"I didn't."

She and her daughter both smiled at him as they walked out of the sitting room.

Voices sounded back in the kitchen, one the lower rumble of a man and the other the in-between tones of a boy on the verge of growing up.

"That'll be the lads back from the fields looking for a bit to eat, most likely. Aidan's convinced his schoolteacher to pack his lessons into three days a week instead of five so he can work and learn how to run a farm."

Aidan had found his place in this farming community. Patrick didn't think he'd ever be happy plowing fields and tending animals. Was there any other work to be had in this valley?

"Come offer a 'good day.'" Maura motioned for him to follow her.

It seemed all he'd done since his arrival in Hope Springs was greet people. He'd once thrived in company and conversation. That part of him had long-since disappeared.

They passed through the dining room, but Maura stopped before they stepped into the kitchen, blocking his way. She looked back at him, sudden hesitation in her expression. "Have you seen Finbarr yet?"

He hadn't, so he indicated as much.

"I'll warn you, then."

Warn him?

"There was a fire, and he was burned. Badly. Half his face is scarred from it."

Mercy.

"And because of the fire . . ." Her hesitation indicated something worse. How was that possible? "The lad's blind."

"Saints above."

"He's not as sensitive as I'm told he once was, but his heart's not easy about it. Don't be pitying toward him, whatever you do, but know he has struggles."

Patrick's pulse pounded as they stepped into the kitchen. He recognized dark-haired Aidan from the day before. But even without the scars, he'd have struggled to know that the nearly grown man talking with his nephew was the tiny brother he'd not seen in more than a decade. Finbarr's hair was ginger as it had always been, but that was the only familiar thing that remained. He was now tall, broad-shouldered and decidedly not six years old.

"Finbarr, stop your yammerin' and come say hello to your brother," Maura said.

"Which brother would that be?" That was too low a voice for baby Finbarr. And it held only the smallest hint of Ireland.

Maura looked over at Patrick and motioned for him to answer.

"Patrick," he said.

That turned the young man around to face them. Patrick held back a gasp of shock at the scars twisting Finbarr's face. They weren't gruesome, but neither were they minor.

"Did Ian really belt you?" Finbarr asked.

"Aye."

"And do you really look like a fur trapper lost in the mountains for fifty years without a soap, razor, or washboard?"

"Yes, he does," Eliza answered quickly and eagerly.

The woman was going to be the death of him.

"Ma must be happy to have you back with us," Finbarr said. "She's missed you."

"I've missed her, too." The admission surprised even him—not that he'd missed his ma, but that he'd said as much out loud. A new topic was certainly in order. "I'm told you have land of your own, lad."

Finbarr's shoulders squared proudly. "I do. Someday I'll have a house, too. Building it, though . . . that'll be a trick."

"Houses aren't terrible hard to build," Patrick said. "I've tossed up dozens of 'em."

"With your eyes closed?" The dryness in Finbarr's voice rivaled the grandest desert.

"That'd make it more difficult, yeah."

Aidan tossed a mischievous look at his uncle Finbarr. "Which is why you'll be living with your brother for the rest of your life."

"Aren't I lucky?"

The two of them shoved each other jokingly. Maura watched the exchange with fondness and the smallest hint of worry.

Patrick wanted to contribute something to his family's happiness, to do something that made him less of a burden. Until Joseph Archer returned or Patrick stumbled on some other employment, he hadn't many options. In the meantime, this grown version of the lad he'd known needed a house and wasn't able to build it.

"Have you the means of buying materials for building?" Patrick asked.

That pulled Finbarr's attention to him again. "More or less."

"I build things, lad. I've built mercantiles and depots and more houses than I can count."

One of the lad's brows pulled low. The other, surrounded by scarring, might not have been able to move. "Are you offering to build me a house?"

"Help, anyway." Patrick felt suddenly out of his depth. He was offering something to the family he'd abandoned. It was presumptuous of him. But what else did he have to give? "I don't have many skills. But I can build."

"We'll have to talk to Cecily," Finbarr said. "And to Joseph when he returns."

Patrick didn't know who Cecily was, but if she was the key to him having a purpose in Hope Springs and among his family, then, by the saints, he'd talk to her.

Chapter Five

Eliza felt rather like a sneak thief rambling around the house of a family she'd never met. Maura had spent two days showing her around and explaining what would be expected of her. Now, her third day in Hope Springs, she was on her own in her new position.

Without the family in residence, she hadn't a tremendous amount of work to do. Little of what she did each day was undone the next. That left ample time for settling into her room and acquainting Lydia with her new surroundings.

She walked the little girl to the sitting room for the fifth time that afternoon. "Where's Lydia's room?"

They'd played this game for three days. If the girl could navigate the house easily before the family's return upended her, that would leave one less adjustment for her to make at the same time.

Lydia hooked her finger over her lip and pointed toward the door to the dining room, which they had to pass through to return to the bedroom they shared.

"Let's go to Lydia's room," Eliza said.

She followed the girl all the way back to their shared quarters.

"Lydia's room," Eliza said, motioning around them.

"Woom." That was close enough.

They played "find Lydia's room" from spots both inside and outside the house, even from as far away as the barn. Each time, the little girl easily found her way back. That set Eliza's mind at ease.

The day was lovely, with a pleasant breeze blowing. After they finished the final round of their game, Eliza opened the bedroom window and let in the cool air.

"We're going to make you a bed," she said.

"Bed." Lydia tried to climb onto the bed they'd shared the past two nights. The arrangement was not working well at all. Eighteen-month-old feet kicking her all night was not endurable.

She set Lydia on the bed with a "doll" Eliza had made out of a handkerchief. It was the only toy her daughter had ever had, but she enjoyed it.

"Bed," Lydia said, apparently to her handkerchief doll.

Eliza had a plan for creating a little space for her daughter. She would, in essence, create a three-sided, low-walled box without a top. The bed would sit on the floor, making it safer if she rolled out of bed, and making it possible for her to get in and out on her own.

Working as a housekeeper was not precisely a dream come true for Eliza, but after working in a factory, this new position felt like nothing short of a miracle. She and her girl had a fine room to call their own. Aidan had assured her that the wood she wished for would not be missed by the family she now worked for. And that family, Maura insisted, was even more generous than they were well-to-do. *That* took some effort to believe. Eliza once had a very close connection to a very wealthy family, and "generosity" had not been in their vocabulary.

She sat on the floor beside her pile of wood. Life hadn't been easy and certainly hadn't been fair, but her prospects were improving.

"Doll." Still sitting contentedly on the bed, Lydia held up her knotted handkerchief.

"Yes, sweet pea. That's your doll."

Someday, the girl would have a real doll. Her clothes wouldn't be quite so ragged. She'd have shoes on her feet. Those were the grandest dreams Eliza would allow herself to entertain at the moment.

She laid out the wood to create Lydia's bed. Two sides of the box bed were soon connected. Lydia watched her curiously, a little startled by each thwack of the hammer, but she didn't seem overly bothered by it. Lydia was quite possibly the most contented not-quite two-year-old who'd ever lived, a far cry from the sobbing, fussing, often miserable baby she'd once been.

Building a makeshift bed was a tall ask for one person. Somehow Eliza would manage; she always did. Her hammering mingled with the occasional moderate words of frustration.

After ten minutes attempting to nail the third side of the three-sided bed box in place, she set the hammer down and breathed through her discouragement.

"Are you needing help?" When Patrick O'Connor had come to be in the doorway, she couldn't say, but there he was, as gruff and unkempt as ever.

Why was it she always smiled when she saw him? The shabby grump of a man piqued her curiosity in the most intriguing ways.

"I've built any number of things in my time," Eliza said. It was a bit of an exaggeration, but she didn't want him to think she was entirely helpless. "I'm certain to sort this out."

Patrick nodded but stepped inside rather than leaving. He stopped beside her and bent down, eyeing her haphazard creation. "What is it?"

"A bed for Lydia."

He scratched his neck. "A bed?"

"A . . . *unique* bed." She allowed her amusement to show. She felt certain he was looking at her again.

"Unique in what way?"

Eliza explained her vision for the odd piece of furniture and her need for it. He listened intently, not interrupting. She finished and watched him, unsure what his evaluation would be.

"Are you wanting help?" He'd changed his wording a little. Perhaps she'd convinced him that she wasn't entirely inept.

"I won't say no."

He took up the hammer, holding it quite naturally. He spun it a little in his hand. "What's best for me to be getting on with?"

"If I hold the wood in place, you could hammer."

"Aye." He took up a nail in his hand and waited. That was to be the entirety of the planning, apparently. She didn't mind his prolonged silences. They were part of what made him so intriguing.

"Have you lived away from your family long?" she asked.

"Aye."

"Were you far away?"

"Aye."

He worked as he spoke, though "spoke" was a generous description. "Where were you?"

"Canada." That *was* far away.

"Do they have razors and soap in Canada?"

"Aye."

She suspected he was more entertained by her cheeky questions than he let on. "Is yours a severe allergy to them, then?"

If only the man's face weren't hidden, she could see if he was smiling or his eyes dancing.

He finished the hammering of that piece of wood, then turned toward her. "I'll grant you the state of my hair, lass, but I've no odor hanging about me."

"Have you considered the possibility that you've simply grown so accustomed to your smell that you don't notice it any longer?" Oh, and he was fun to tease. Too many men grew threatening in the face of anything but flattery.

"I've not had any ladies launch complaints about my stench." He spoke with such a comical tone she felt certain that beneath all those whiskers, he was smiling.

She gave her own voice a ponderous tone and asked, "Have you known, then, a great many women without a sense of smell?"

Then something amazing happened: Patrick laughed. Not loudly; if she hadn't been sitting next to him, she wouldn't have even heard it. The sound was magical.

She'd felt certain that sound could lift her spirits on even her darkest days. But how did one go about pulling a laugh from someone determined to be a perpetual grump? Teasing had worked this time, but would it always?

"You're looking at me like you would a slug trying to win a jumping contest."

She *had* meant to stare him into discomfort. "I was only admiring your laugh."

He turned back to his work. "I didn't laugh," he muttered.

"You did so."

"No," he said flatly, taking up the hammer once more.

Why did the idea of having laughed bother him so much? It wasn't a bad thing. He was so difficult to sort out.

As they continued working, he didn't speak. His wasn't an angry silence, or even a frustrated one. She suspected he wasn't upset, but, to her surprise, embarrassed. Embarrassed at what? At a moment of happiness?

They were nearly finished assembling the odd bed for Lydia when the girl herself interrupted the silence between them. "I-und!" She had, apparently, only just recognized the man who'd been in the room for a quarter of an hour.

Eliza looked over at the bed in time to see Lydia crawling to the edge of it. "You'll fall," she warned.

Almost before she finished the two words, Patrick had reached back, scooped up her daughter, and set Lydia safely on the floor.

"Thank you," Eliza said

He simply nodded.

Lydia sat beside her, the handkerchief doll in her hand, and watched Patrick. Was her little girl as confused by this mysterious man as she was? With the last board in place, Patrick spun the hammer around in his hand before setting it beside two leftover nails.

"This'll do, I imagine." He motioned to the floor-level bed they'd created.

"Thank you for your help."

"I suspect you'd've managed." Coming from him, the offhand comment felt like the biggest compliment.

"I appreciate not having to . . . manage. Sometimes it seems that's all I do."

Patrick stood. To her shock, he offered her his hand. She set hers in it, and he helped her to her feet. Her late husband used to do that, a simple gesture of kindness that had always made her feel more important than someone of her birth and circumstances generally ever felt.

Her grief had grown less acute in the two years since his death, but she felt it again in that moment, lapping over her like waves on the shore. Not brutal, not painful, but quiet, an almost gentle wash of sadness.

Other than Maura, no one had seen her grieve for Terrence. Her family was across an ocean. Her in-laws had disowned their son the moment he'd announced his intention to marry her. She was not ready to mourn in front of Patrick O'Connor, let alone in front of anyone else.

She forced a smile. "I'll not keep you."

With that, she turned and picked up Lydia, hiding her discomfort in the busyness of mothering.

Patrick left as quietly as he'd arrived. And in the emptiness of that room and that moment, she did something she'd not allowed herself to do in the year since Maura had left her behind in New York.

She cried.

Eliza Porter was a complication Patrick did not need. He'd learned from a decade of hard experience that people were best kept at a distance. Eliza didn't play by that rule.

Her joyfulness and easy smile kept pulling smiles to his face. She'd even made him laugh. And he never laughed. Not anymore. The sudden tears shimmering in her eyes had tugged at his heart in ways he hadn't expected—and couldn't afford to allow. No one was ever better off for having him in their lives, and the casualties list was already too long.

He'd come to the Archer farm with a task in mind. Allowing himself to be distracted by Eliza had been a mistake. She hadn't really needed his help. The woman was clearly comfortable and capable with tools. Help him if that wasn't intriguing. He'd not ever built anything with a woman before; none had seemed interested. Perhaps she'd allow him to build something with her again.

"It's a dangerous game you're playing," he warned himself as he walked towards the Archers' fields. Enough people in this town were disappointed in him without adding to the number.

He walked through the fields for quite a time before finally hearing what he was listening for: voices.

Finbarr and Maura's boy, Aidan, were working together, an arrangement he suspected was necessary on account of Finbarr not being able to see well enough to get himself about.

"Howdy, Uncle Patrick," Aidan said. The lad didn't sound the least Irish. 'Twas a shame, really. Ireland was as much a part of the lad as it was any of the rest of them.

Finbarr turned toward his nephew, but clearly spoke to Patrick. "Is something the matter?"

"No, lad. It's you I've come to talk to."

Finbarr took off his hat and wiped his forehead with a ragged handkerchief. Patrick was certain that in time, he would grow accustomed to this grownup version of his baby brother, and his heart wouldn't seize every time he saw the burn scars on the boy's face. How long had the rest of the family needed to adjust?

He pushed on. "I'd like to start building your house, lad. But I need you to show me where exactly you want it."

Finbarr shook his head. "I told you, I don't have the money to pay you to build it."

"I don't need you to pay me, boy. I enjoy building things. It'd be a nice challenge."

He popped his hat on his head once more. "Don't you need a *paying* job?"

"I'll keep looking, but I'm wanting something in the meantime to keep me busy and out of Da and Ma's house." He realized after the words emerged how ungrateful they likely sounded. "Not that I'm not thankful for the roof over my head and food to eat."

Finbarr held up his hands. "You don't have to explain. I moved out years ago. There's something to be said for breathing room."

"And for conversation with a brother who doesn't want to hit me in the face."

Finbarr smiled, his scars making the expression a little lopsided. "I don't know you well enough to want to belt you."

"Yet," Aidan tossed in.

Even Patrick had to admit these two were pretty funny.

"Go show him your land," Aidan said. "I can keep working here."

"Who put you in charge?" Finbarr shot back.

"Fate," was the cheeky answer.

Finbarr stepped toward Patrick. "We better go before he declares himself King of Wyoming." And yet, he stopped, seeming to be waiting for something.

Aidan, through hand motions and mouthed words, managed to explain. Patrick guided Finbarr's hand to his arm. They walked out of the fields, Finbarr walking beside him and a bit behind, holding fast to Patrick's arm, Patrick serving as guide.

"When you get to the river," Finbarr said, "you'll go left, in the opposite direction of the Archers' home."

That would also send him in the opposite direction of the road. Finbarr's future farm didn't, it seem, sit near the rest of the family's. "You and Aidan seem to get on well."

"He's the only one who never talks to me like I'm something pathetic."

That hit too near the mark. "Pity is a sour syrup, isn't it?"

"Do people talk to you like that?"

"More often than I'd like," Patrick said.

"They probably *look* at me that way too." Finbarr shrugged. "I'm actually glad I can't see that."

"How much farther?" Patrick asked. "Or can't you tell?"

"Vaguely," Finbarr said. "Just follow the river until you get to a very small pond, but don't go over it. Just past the pond is a big grouping of rocks. That's where my property begins. It borders Joseph's land. We'll eventually get around to fencing it off."

"You seem very close to Mr. Archer," Patrick said.

"He's like family. I don't think I'd want to live here if he didn't."

Interesting that he hadn't said the same about his actual family. What was straining that connection? If this lad, who'd lived among the family his entire life, couldn't seem to fit in with them, what hope did Patrick have?

"I see the rocks you mentioned," he told his brother as they approached the spot.

Finbarr pulled his arm free and made his way carefully to the rocks, then sat on one of them. He kept still a moment, his head tipping towards the river. Listening, perhaps.

Apparently satisfied, he turned and faced away from the water. "That's my land."

"Which bits?"

"The part that's not planted."

Patrick looked out over it. Acres and acres of wild grass rustled in the stiff breeze, butting up next to fields of neatly planted crops. "That's a large swath of land."

"I don't know that I can work it by myself."

That was a complication. "Would Aidan help you, then?"

"Joseph hired him on this summer," Finbarr said. "But Aidan'll need to help his step-da on their farm next year."

His step-da? Patrick had to think on it for a moment before the puzzle solved itself. Maura's new husband would be filling that role in Aidan's life.

"What'll *you* do next year?"

"Keep living with Tavish and his wife and their baby who cries all night."

"Tavish has a baby." Speaking the realization out loud didn't make it any less shocking. "He was about your age when they all went west."

Patrick looked over the area, debating the best spot for a house, which way it ought to face, which side the windows ought to be on, what shape it should take, what size the lad needed. There was a great deal to consider.

"Why didn't you come to Hope Springs with the family?" Finbarr asked.

That was a more difficult question than Finbarr likely realized. It seemed best to give the answer everyone believed. "I liked New York. The busyness of it, the press of humanity . . . It suited the person I was."

Finbarr leaned back on his elbows, face turned up to the sun. "I meant why didn't you come after the war? Maura says you didn't stay in New York. But from what I know of Canada, there's no 'press of humanity' there."

Patrick could laugh a little at that. "Many of the places I lived in were no bigger than Hope Springs."

"So why did you stay away? Everyone thought you were dead."

"Believe me, brother, I was doing everyone a favor," he muttered.

Finbarr pushed out a tense breath. "The fire"—he pointed at his face—"almost killed me. Sometimes I think the family would be better off if it had."

There was sincerity in his words, but not despondency. Still, Patrick didn't like hearing it. Turning the boy's thoughts another direction seemed wise. "I can build you a fine house here, Finbarr. I'd have the door facing the path that lead us here. The house could be laid out in a way that made it easy to navigate."

"Is there a way of building it so there's a lot of light inside? I can see some if there's enough light."

"Aye." Patrick's image of the future home grew more specific. "Windows on the east and west."

"Doesn't have to be big," Finbarr said. "It'll be only me living here."

"Only you *for now.*"

"Only me ever."

Patrick wished he could argue, but he knew how brokenness changed a person's future. "Maybe I'll come live with you, lad. We'll be a couple of bachelors, not minding a bit that we have no prospects."

"Ma'll come by crying," Finbarr warned.

"We'll pretend we're not home."

The lad smiled. "We'll turn into a couple of curmudgeons."

"And wouldn't that be an adventure." Patrick made sure to laugh a bit so his brother wouldn't think he actually meant to impose on him. "What else do you think you'll need in this home of yours?"

Finbarr shrugged. "That's a question you'd do best to ask Cecily."

"I've heard her mentioned before," Patrick said. "But I don't know who she is."

"Tavish's wife."

Ah. "More family."

Finbarr pushed out a breath. "That's something you'll discover about Hope Springs. There's family everywhere."

Chapter Six

Tavish was married to a strong-willed woman, like many O'Connor men before him. Cecily was fiery, intelligent, and a very proper English woman. And, Patrick discovered, completely blind. That explained the oft-repeated insistence that he talk with her before deciding on any details of Finbarr's future house.

"He can see a little when he has enough light," she said. "He'll need a house with an ample degree of it."

She spoke with a refined English accent that made a fellow think he ought to bow or scrape or at least apologize for something. She was also shockingly beautiful, beauty made even more striking by her green-tinted spectacles. How his family had ever grown accustomed to having her nearby he'd never know.

"What else ought I to know about the boy's house?"

Ma had spent the afternoon running about, busy seeing to some unidentified matter of business, but was not, it seems, as distracted as she appeared. She crossed behind Patrick's chair and put an arm around his shoulder. "'Tis a fine thing you're doing for your brother."

Patrick froze, torn between his years-long need for his ma's reassurance and his absolute certainty that if she knew even a bit of what he kept tucked away, it would change everything. And not for the better.

"Sorry lad," she whispered. "I forget you no longer like when I hug you."

How far that was from true. And, yet, Ma wasn't entirely wrong.

He'd longed for her embrace over the years. Wept for it, even. But he'd lost all right to her motherly affection. Receiving even the smallest bit of it was painful.

"I'm just not used to being hugged," he said, wanting to ease some of the sadness he heard in her voice.

His words apparently encouraged her, as she hugged him again, this time more fiercely. "I'll never let you go again, Patrick. I've nearly all m'children with me again."

Nearly all.

"If only Grady hadn't followed you to battle," she sighed. "But, what's done is done."

"Mary?" Da poked his head around the front door. "We've Biddy here looking to set down a stack of plates."

"On the smallest table," she told him. Then, turning to Patrick, she asked, "You remember Biddy, don't you?"

Remember her? How could he not? She'd swept Ian's heart right out of his chest that last year in New York. He and Patrick had still been the best of friends then. Patrick had been witness to all the ups and downs of that love story. His heart had ached for his brother and then rejoiced with him when the woman he loved chose to love him in return. Of course Patrick remembered Biddy.

"Aye," he said, his eyes on the paper where he'd been making notes of Cecily's suggestions.

Ma hesitated a moment before slipping outside. Patrick kept still in the silence she left behind.

"Why did she make you so uncomfortable?" Cecily asked.

How has she sorted that out? He hadn't said anything to her about his discomfort, and she couldn't see his stiffness when Ma came so nearby.

Tavish, standing nearby, rocking his infant son in his arms, spoke before Patrick could. "Don't bother trying to deny it."

"I'm out of practice, is all."

"Out of practice with what?" Cecily asked. "Being a son?"

"It's grown unfamiliar."

"And what about *céilís*?" Tavish asked. "Have parties also grown unfamiliar?"

"I've not been to a *céilí* since we left Ireland."

Tavish smiled. So much like Grady. The three of them had looked nearly as alike as triplets, though years separated them. Tavish was now older than Grady had ever been. So was Patrick, for that matter.

"There's a *céilí* here nearly every Saturday," Tavish said. "Right here at Da and Ma's. We missed last week on account of all the rain."

"Truly?"

Tavish and Cecily both nodded.

The very Irish parties had been a favorite of Patrick's back in their homeland. For a long time, parties of any kind had appealed to him. He couldn't be too careful about them now. In addition to music and dancing, such gatherings always included alcohol. He'd managed the last week and a bit with only a few drinks. He was doing so well. He couldn't bear the thought of backsliding so soon.

"I'm invited?" He wasn't entirely certain what he hoped the answer would be.

"More than invited," Tavish said, "you're expected."

"By who?"

"Everyone," they answered in unison.

Begor. "Any hope of sitting in the shadows unnoticed?"

Tavish, still rocking little Matthew, narrowed his gaze at Patrick. "You used to be the first to jump at any chance for socializing. The promise of company is the whole reason you stayed in New York."

Though Patrick knew his family believed that that had been his motivation, it still surprised him to hear Tavish say it. All the O'Connors must've thought he was the most callous, shallow person on earth.

"I've been living in the wilds of Canada. I've spent more time with horses than people. And horses are terrible dancers."

Cecily grinned and turned in the general direction of her husband. "He has the O'Connor sense of humor."

"Growing up, he was the most comical of us all."

"No." Patrick shook his head. "That was you."

"I was always desperate to make everyone laugh," Tavish said. "You were genuinely funny."

That had once been true. "I've not been *that* Patrick in more than a decade."

Cecily was facing him again. "Is that why you've returned home, to find yourself?"

She could have knocked him over with a feather at that unexpected, astute observation.

"Scary how she does that, isn't it?" Tavish said. "Nothing escapes Cece's notice."

Heaven help him if that proved true.

Every inch of ground in front of Da and Ma's house was filled with people, tables and food, musicians, chairs. These weekly *céilís*, it seemed, were no small thing. Patrick took one deep breath after another as he inched into the middle of the chaos. He knew he couldn't get out of his obligation to attend, so he was going to make the best of it.

A quick glance at the table of victuals didn't reveal a single bottle of whiskey. He felt certain the punch bowl contained only fruit juice. With so many little ones wandering about, they'd not have risked anything stronger in easy reach. He wouldn't be tempted to stray from his fragile sobriety. Now he needed only find the endurance to be around his family for an evening.

He loved them. He truly did. But the years between them were harder to bridge than even they likely realized. If he'd been stronger, he would have stayed away indefinitely. It would have been better for all of them. But he was here now, and he had to find a way to make this work. It was his last hope.

His strategy to keep mostly unseen quickly fell to bits. The very first person he ran into was Biddy. Considering his one brief encounter with Ian, he hadn't the first idea how he'd be received by his brother's wife.

"How are you, then, Biddy?"

"Grand. How is your lip, then?"

He rubbed at it, hidden beneath his whiskers. "It no longer hurts when I talk. But if knowing I'm not suffering would disappoint Ian, you can tell him m'face won't ever recover."

Biddy looked out over the crowd, eyes darting about and her posture stiff. "I'm needing a minute of your time."

"Of course." He'd do anything at all for Biddy. She'd held a special place in his heart from the moment she'd arrived at their New York flat and smiled at his brother as if he were a veritable knight on a white steed.

She stepped aside, and he followed, putting a little distance between them and the partygoers. "Ian's still spitting fire over you, Patrick."

He scratched at his beard. "Can't say I blame him. I should've warned the family I was coming."

She shook her head. "If you think that's what's aching him, you don't know your brother very well."

Not know him? "He's the best friend I ever had."

"And you let him think you were dead for ten years. You let him mourn you. You let him walk about with a crack in his heart and a crushing ache in his soul." More pain than anger was in her words. "You were also the best friend he ever had, and you let him suffer. I don't know if he'll ever forgive you for that, Patrick. The past years have not been easy for him, and you've added to his burdens. Intentionally."

Biddy had grown bold since he'd last seen her. It was good to see. He'd worried about her over the years, wondering if life was treating her well, if she'd found her fire.

"I didn't mean—" He stopped before the lie escaped his lips. He was sick to death of telling untruths. "Would it be better for Ian if I kept some distance between us?"

"Might be," she said. "For now, at least."

He nodded. "I'll do it, then. I'll not press myself on either of you."

She stepped closer and set a hand lightly on his arm. "He's angry with you, Patrick. But he's also glad that you're alive. We all are. We prayed for your soul, of course, but not one of us would've even

51

thought there was any point in praying for the miracle of you returning to us still living."

"I'm—I'm sorry you couldn't have had that miracle with Grady."

Her expression turned sadder, heavier. "He's certainly missed and mourned. If only he and Maura and little Aidan had come west or he'd not fought. Of course, nothing would've convinced him to even consider leaving New York with Maura wanting to stay."

There was so much the family didn't know about that brief time between their leaving the city and Grady and Patrick joining the Union Army. He hadn't meant to open old wounds; he'd caused enough pain.

"Have you been happy here, Biddy? All of you?"

She smiled with quiet sincerity. "We have been. There've been difficulties aplenty. But we've been happy."

They'd not been plagued by the loneliness and heaviness that he had suffered the past years. He'd only ever wanted them to be happy. It seemed they had been. He found a bit of solace in that.

"Do you think there's a place for me here?" he asked.

The tender-hearted Biddy emerged in that moment, the sweet, caring version of her that he remembered so well. "There's always been a place for you."

He looked out over the quickly growing crowd. "And that place, at the moment, is apparently in the middle of this mess of people."

"Oh, just you wait, dear brother. You will be very much 'in the middle of this.'"

His heart dropped. "What're you meaning by that?"

She laughed softly. "No one arrives in Hope Springs quietly."

That was all she told him. Then she simply walked away, pausing only long enough to toss a smile back at him. Oh, he'd missed Biddy. She made a person feel peaceful just by being present. It was little wonder Ian had always described her as an angel.

He popped his hands in his jacket pockets and wandered back into the fray, his heart a little lighter than it had been. He'd worried very little about his appearance the past few years. Ragged clothes and a scraggly beard had suited him just fine in the wilderness. They'd been an easy way to disappear. But here, those things made him stand out.

These people, he suspected, lived in humble circumstances, yet they were neat, and, he'd guess, proud in the best sense of the word.

So many Irish voices filled the space. He'd not heard the like since his days in the New York Irish Regiment. A bittersweet sound. His brothers-in-arms had been precisely that: brothers. One in the most literal sense of the word. So many of them had not survived the war. And yet, he could think back on their nights around the fire, playing the fiddle he worked so hard to master, the long days of marching side by side with a smile and an unmistakable fondness for the friends he'd gained and their time together.

His wanderings took him past an extensive spread of food. Eating hadn't always been a guarantee the past ten years, certainly not the delights he saw here. Turnovers. Sweet biscuits. Cakes. And dessert wasn't the only order of the day. Plates of fried chicken sat next to an enormous bowl of colcannon. At the sight and aroma of it all, his stomach made its years of emptiness known.

And then he spotted, at the very end of the table, his ma's shortbread. She'd always cut it in triangles and sprinkled sugar on top. She'd now and then added cardamom when it was available, on account of Grady preferring it that way. No matter how she made shortbread, Patrick loved it. To him, it was the taste of home.

He'd craved it, even dreamed about it at times. The shortbread was far from luxurious. It would never have been served at the table of the wealthy or important. Yet, he would have chosen Ma's shortbread over anything prepared by the finest chef.

Patrick didn't look away as he moved toward the platter. Ma's shortbread. Right there. After all these years. His place among the family was still shaky, but having a bite of that personal delicacy would give him a much-needed sense of being home again.

"Friends! Friends!" An eager Irish voice broke through the cacophony. "Gather 'round. We've newcomers to welcome."

Newcomers. That included him. They'd all be searching him out, watching him. Being spotted growing sentimental over a piece of shortbread wouldn't help things at all. He stepped away from the table and made his way hesitantly toward the spot where everyone was gathering.

Biddy intercepted him at the edge of the crowd. "I did warn you." With that, she led him through everyone and directly toward the center of the group, right where everyone was facing.

"I'm not wanting to be the focus of attention," he said earnestly.

"You used to love it," she said. "But you'll not have a choice just now. It's tradition."

Ah, saints. "What tradition?"

She abandoned him there in the middle of them all. Another woman's voice filled in the gap she left behind.

"Any idea what we're meant to be doing?" Eliza asked from beside him. She, who never seemed shaken by anything, looked nervous.

"I haven't the first idea, but it seems we're meant to do it together."

Some of the unease in her eyes lessened. "I like the idea of doing whatever it is *together.*"

He shook his head. "You're the oddest lass I've ever known."

She grinned. "We built Lydia's bed together. We're a fine team, you and I. Whatever mischief this town has in mind tonight, doing it together seems a good idea."

The explanation was oddly disappointing. What was the matter with him lately? For so long, keeping his distance from others had been a matter of survival. Why did that distance ache inside him these past days?

"We've a tradition here in Hope Springs." A man standing in front of them all said, his voice carrying. He wore a green bowler and spoke with the unmistakable tones of Ireland. "New arrivals are welcomed with a song."

That wouldn't be so bad.

"And given the task of leading the dancing."

That *was.*

He leaned a little closer to Eliza. "I'm no dancer," he warned.

"You can't dance with each other," Tavish called out from the crowd.

Well, hang that.

Eliza immediately began looking over the crowd. Patrick stood as a man at a mark, unsure what to do. The only women he knew there were family, and he hadn't a strong enough connection with them for something as personal as dancing.

The musicians—there were a great many of them, boasting instruments that were entirely Irish as well as plenty he'd seen only since coming to America—struck up the opening bars of what he quickly recognized as "The New York Reel." Eliza, not surprisingly, had a partner in the blink of an eye: a young fellow, likely only a bit older than she was, and at least five years Patrick's junior.

Everyone was watching Patrick, waiting. Just when he thought he'd be doomed to spend the entirety of the song standing about like a great lummox, he saw the perfect solution. He stepped to Maura but knelt in front of Lydia.

"Would you dance with me, wee lass?"

She pulled her fingers from her mouth and set them on his beard. "I-und!"

He looked up at Maura. "Do you suppose I can consider that a 'yes'?"

Maura nodded with a little laugh.

Patrick swept the girl up in his arms and tucked her close. He took a calming breath. Once upon a time he'd enjoyed being at the center of things. A decade of hiding had beaten that out of him.

With Lydia in his arms, he stepped into the dancing area. Her ma was dancing with the unnamed man she'd chosen, both of them looking rather elegant despite the humble surroundings. He'd not ever look as fine no matter his efforts. Best to let Lydia be the focus.

He spun about and dipped and wove. She held tight to him and giggled with every twirl. He loved the sound of that. There was something reassuring in her pure and unfeigned happiness.

The rest of the gathering soon joined in the dancing. He had the perfect excuse to hand his armful back to Maura and slip away; he'd fulfilled his obligation. But he didn't leave. He didn't even want to.

Hearing Lydia joyfully call out the name she'd given him between her giggles and shouts of "Turn! Turn!" kept him there through the entire song.

He'd long ago abandoned hope of being a source of joy to anyone.

Yet in the length of a single tune, this little girl had given him reason to question some of what he believed about himself.

Chapter Seven

Eliza had been in heaven during the town party on Saturday night. With the music and dancing and storytelling and coming to know her new neighbors, it had been an utter delight. On a whim, she'd asked a stranger in the crowd to be her partner for the required New Arrivals Dance. His name was Dr. Burke Jones. He'd proven kind and friendly, and, though quiet, not unwilling to chat a bit.

He had only arrived in Hope Springs a few months earlier. She looked forward to knowing him better. She looked forward to knowing the entire town better.

A few mornings after the *céilí,* Maura peeked her head inside the kitchen where Eliza was sweeping up the dust blown in by the unending Wyoming wind. "The Archers are in town. They'll be home any moment."

Eliza clamped down the rising worry in her heart. She couldn't help the reaction. Life had taught her all too clearly that the well-to-do were best approached with great caution. She knew the Archers were wealthy because nearly everyone who had spoken about them had mentioned it.

Terrence, her late husband, had come from just such a family. She'd been a maid in the service of his aunt and uncle. She and Terrence met in the corridor of that fine New York City home. She'd been charmed by him and his unassuming air, and lulled into a sense of safety by how immediately accepting of her he'd been. They'd fallen in love quickly and wholly.

The viciousness with which she'd been rejected by his wealthy family, and the cruelty with which they'd completely and irrevocably disowned him, still stole her breath. They'd not even attended his funeral. They'd refused to acknowledge their granddaughter, responding to Eliza's letter telling them of Lydia's birth with venomous insults.

"Leeches are never loved," they'd written. "Weights are never wanted." They'd cast doubt on Eliza's virtue. They'd questioned Lydia's paternity. Then they'd threatened her should she attempt to contact them again.

The wealthy were not to be trusted. Yet there was no avoiding them this time. They were paying her salary.

She leaned her broom against the wall and rushed into her room, where Lydia sat playing with her handkerchief doll. Eliza did her best to tame Lydia's wispy waves. Then she quickly recombed her own hair and pinned it up in a proper and prim knot. Though she was tempted to change into her Sunday dress and Lydia into hers, she couldn't imagine her employer would be pleased with her pausing her work—twice—for an unnecessary change of clothing. Their humble but well-cared-for, everyday clothes would simply have to do.

Even so, Eliza tied on a clean apron before taking up her broom once more, all the while listening for the sound of wagon wheels. When she heard them, her pulse immediately quickened to a worrisome clip.

Lydia stood on a kitchen chair "walking" her handkerchief doll across the tabletop. She was oblivious to the tension quickly filling what had been their private corner of the world.

"Time to scrape and bow a bit, sweet pea." Eliza scooped up Lydia and set her on her bare feet. Until she had some money saved, she couldn't address the matter of Lydia's non-existent footwear.

She held fast to Lydia's hand as she stepped onto the back porch and searched out the newly arrived wagon. Three children were in the process of climbing down from the wagon bed into the arms of a woman she assumed was Mrs. Archer. Finbarr and Aidan were seeing to the horses. Eliza didn't spot anyone who might have been Mr. Archer.

The girls moved toward the front of the house. *The front. Of course.* A fine family would not be entering the house through the back door. How had she forgotten that after only three years away from her time as a maid?

She picked up Lydia and slipped back inside. Careful not to set her hair flying loose in her haste, she moved quickly through the kitchen, the dining room, the sitting room, and into the front entry-way. She set Lydia down once more.

Weights aren't wanted.

She'd make herself useful and not a burden. That was the surest way to survive.

After a quick, deep breath, she opened the front door.

A girl, likely about twelve or thirteen years old, climbed the steps of the front porch, her bearing proper and a little withdrawn. Behind her, a girl closer to nine and very like her in appearance, but utterly different in demeanor, spun in circles as she made her way up the walk. Both were dressed in serviceable versions of fashionable dresses appropriate for their ages. Both, she noticed, wore shoes.

They stopped when they spotted her.

The younger of the two actually spoke. "Who are you?"

"I'm Eliza Porter. The new housekeeper."

With a puzzled tip of her head, the littler girl asked, "Where are you from?"

Her accent, no doubt, had inspired the inquiry. "From England."

"Mama is from Ireland." The girl flitted past, apparently not overset or put out by the presence of a stranger.

The older sister offered a fleeting smile. "You'll grow used to Ivy. She doesn't hold still very long and asks a great many questions."

Ivy. Eliza would remember that.

Mrs. Archer approached, with a child likely Lydia's age on her hip. She, too, dressed fashionably but without the unnecessary lace and ruffles that marked most of the fine ladies back East. Ivy had indicated that Mrs. Archer was Irish. Eliza would have guessed as much. The Irish had a look about them, something in their build and features that, despite the inevitable variations, tied them to their homeland.

59

"This is your mum?" Eliza asked the daughter who remained on the porch.

The girl hesitated only a fraction of a moment before nodding.

Mrs. Archer stepped onto the porch. Though her air was not unfriendly, there was noticeable caution there.

Eliza dropped a curtsy without loosening her grip on Lydia. "Mrs. Archer," she acknowledged.

"You must be Mrs. Porter." Oh, she was most definitely Irish.

"I am, ma'am."

"Please," Mrs. Archer said. "We needn't stand on ceremony here. No need to curtsy or address any of us so formally."

Eliza straightened nervously. Informality with the family of an employer had caused her no end of difficulty in the past.

"I'm Katie," the woman said. "This is Emma, our oldest." Next, she indicated the boy in her arms. "This is our little lad, Sean. And I suspect you've already met Ivy." She spoke with enough amusement to indicate Ivy's utter lack of shyness was a trait of long-standing. "Joseph will be along shortly. He'll want to meet you."

Joseph was, no doubt, Mr. Archer. Eliza didn't let her nervousness show.

"I look forward to meeting him." She stepped to the side enough to allow the family to come in, then followed at a respectful distance. She knew what the family would be wanting. "I can have water heated and ready for doing laundry quick as anything. There's always plenty after a journey."

Katie's head tipped a bit to the side. "You're English."

"I am. Is that a problem?" The English had a long and storied history of mistreating the Irish, abusing and oppressing them. That might be too heavy a history to make *this* arrangement too uncomfortable for Katie.

"Not a problem in the least, I swear to you." Her gaze fell on Lydia. "This is your daughter?"

"Yes. This is Lydia. She's a year-and-a-half now."

"She's of an age with our Sean." She bounced her boy a little. "I suspect they'll be fast friends. And the girls will fall utterly in love with her."

That would be a wonderful thing, and yet . . . "I'll make certain she's not ever a distraction to them or that she prevents me from doing my work."

"We'll sort it out."

Eliza meant to do more than "sort it out." She meant to be the very best housekeeper a family could hope for. Maura had recommended her for the post, and Eliza didn't wish to repay that kindness by undermining the Archers' trust. Further, she needed the income and the roof over her head. Without this job, she'd be in difficult straits.

An hour later, she was seated outside, a large basket of clothes beside her, steam rising before her from a large iron pot on the low-burning fire. The clothesline was empty, awaiting its coming burden. A washtub, washboard, and rinse basin sat at the ready as well.

Laundry was far from her favorite chore, but she was anxious to do it well. First impressions could never be remade.

She glanced at Lydia, making certain the girl was still playing quietly nearby. Handkerchief Dolly was a nearly magical thing; Lydia never seemed to grow bored of the odd excuse for a toy.

Eliza swirled a blue calico dress around in the soapy washbasin, then scrubbed it forcefully against the ridges of the washboard. The clothes in the basket beside her were piled high. Laundry was exhausting work.

Lydia held up her handkerchief. "Doll."

The poor child would likely be confused when she saw an actual doll.

She smiled at the memory of her own younger self thoroughly flummoxed the first time she saw an ordinary house. Her family had run an inn. Their kitchen had served dozens. Their "sitting room" was the inn's public room, always filled with a mixture of local people and strangers passing through. Never did it occur to her that other people's homes weren't like hers.

Mercy, she missed those days. The Charred Oak had been alive with activity. Every day had been different from the last. The challenge of it all had been half the fun. And her family had worked *for* no one. They'd been free in a way few from their station in life ever were.

The memories of that time brought a lightness to her heart despite the aching in her arms and back as she scrubbed one piece of clothing after another against the washboard.

A regular had come to the Charred Oak nearly every day for a thick slice of sprouted-wheat bread and a tankard of ale. He'd told the most diverting stories. She'd loved hearing them as she'd grown up. If only Lydia could've had that same experience.

In Hope Springs, Lydia would hear stories at the weekly town parties; that was something. But her day-to-day life would be in a single room off someone else's kitchen, playing with a handkerchief doll while her mum spent her days in isolation, bent over fires and stoves and floors. Eliza didn't mind the work; she simply would have preferred working for herself, in another inn perhaps, seeing people every day, *new* people regularly. She'd grown up with that and longed for it.

She pulled one of Mr. Archer's shirts from the rinse basin and wrung it out before hanging it on the line. This job had been a godsend. She was truly grateful for it, no matter that she missed her childhood home. She'd seen a lot of her dreams of America fade away over the five years she'd been in this country, and she'd survived each disappointment. More than survived, she'd been happy. At times, she'd been absolutely delighted.

I'll find my feet again. I always do.

And Lydia would have playmates and a safe place to live and—

Lydia. When had she last checked on her daughter? She'd been so deep in her own thoughts that she hadn't glanced over in some time.

Apron damp from the wet laundry, she turned to where Lydia had been. But she wasn't there. Her "doll" was gone as well. Eliza spun slowly, searching the area. No Lydia.

How long had it been since she'd seen her? How far could she have gone?

Eliza moved swiftly to the back porch. The kitchen door was closed, and Lydia couldn't have opened it. She wouldn't be inside, then. Lydia wasn't near the fire, thank the heavens.

The barn, perhaps? According to Katie, Mr. Archer was in there. If Lydia had caused him grief, heaven help them all.

"Lydia? Sweet pea?"

No answer. Concerns about inconveniencing her employer faded, replaced by very real worry. A farm could be a dangerous place for a child on her own, with scythes and axes and any number of dangerous tools. Irrigation ditches she might fall into. Horses that might trample her. Cows that might kick her. Mercy, where was the girl?

"Lydia?" she called a little louder. "Lydia!"

"Over here, lass."

Patrick? She moved in the direction of his voice and found him sitting on the ground on the other side of the laundry she'd hung up. Lydia sat directly in front of him, mesmerized by the Cat's Cradle he'd woven around his fingers. Her handkerchief doll sat on her lap.

Still holding his twine-wrapped fingers out to Lydia, he spoke to Eliza. "She was wanderin' toward the barn. I didn't think you'd want her in there."

Lydia had toddled away, and Eliza hadn't even noticed. What if Patrick hadn't been there? What if Lydia had made for the fields, only to be lost in the endless rows of tall crops? What if she'd fallen into the river?

She pressed a hand to her racing heart. "I looked away only for a moment." That wasn't entirely true. She'd been distracted for several long moments, far more than she ought.

Lydia poked at the Cat's Cradle with one slobber-covered finger.

"I'll trap your finger if you pop it in there, *mo stóirín.*"

Patrick had looked after her. She was safe, no thanks to Eliza. The panic she'd held at bay during the brief moments Lydia had been missing surfaced in a rush of emotion.

"I couldn't find her." She lowered herself onto the ground directly beside him, numb yet aching. "What if she'd wandered into the fire or the fields?"

Patrick pulled gently on the twine, "trapping" Lydia's finger in it. She giggled. While Eliza loved the sound, it didn't ease her worry or her guilt.

"What if I never found her?"

He set his now-free hand on hers, the touch gentle and reassuring. "But you did find her. All's well."

"What about next time? I don't know if I can juggle all of this, the work I have here *and* not be a disaster of a mum."

"My ma lost track of every one of us at one time or another," he said, "and not a soul would accuse her of being a disaster."

Eliza pushed out a breath.

Lydia leaned forward and tugged on Patrick's sleeve. "I-und!"

"Am I neglecting you, *mo stóirín*?" Patrick reassembled the Cat's Cradle and presented it to Lydia again.

What an impossibly confusing man he was, leaping from grumpy and grumbly to tender and kind.

"I don't know how I'm going to tend Lydia and see to my work at the same time." She rubbed her face, weary and overwhelmed. "I cannot lose this job, but neither can I lose my little girl."

He pulled the Cat's Cradle again, earning another giggle from Lydia. "M'ma took Finbarr with her when she cleaned houses in New York. She must've discovered some secret to managing it."

Dare she ask Mrs. O'Connor for advice? "Do you think she'd answer questions or offer ideas?"

"Aye. Ma's a good sort. You needn't be worried about chatting with her."

"But *you* always seem to be."

The silence that followed wasn't long, but it was heavy. It seemed she'd struck at a sensitive spot.

"I'm sorry," she said. "I've a knack for saying things I oughtn't. I can't seem to help myself."

"Maybe if you talked a little less." The muttered response held an unmistakable smile.

"I've tried that," she said. "Didn't work."

"Apparently."

Lydia had fully embraced their version of Cat's Cradle, hooking her finger in a gap between the strings without prompting. Her giggles were so precious; Eliza loved hearing them.

A shout of "Finbarr" from the direction of the porch pulled all their eyes that way. Ivy was running across the yard directly to—Eliza's eyes followed her path—Finbarr, approaching from the barn with Aidan beside him and a man she assumed was Mr. Archer on his other side. Ivy tossed herself against him and wrapped her arms around his waist.

"Finbarr! We're home!"

"So you are." He set one arm around Ivy, hugging her lightly to him.

"Are you still blind?"

"Ivy." Mr. Archer's scold was firm but not heated.

His girl grew instantly repentant. "I wasn't being mean, Pompah. I was just wondering."

"Wonder at Aidan a moment," Mr. Archer said. "Finbarr and I need to have a meeting with his brother."

"Mr. Tavish is coming?" Ivy lit up at the possibility.

"No," Finbarr said. "Mr. *Patrick*."

Ivy popped her fists on her hips. "You're funning me. There isn't a Mr. Patrick."

"Is so." Aidan pointed directly at the man in question. "That's him, sitting right there."

All eyes turned to where Eliza, Lydia, and Patrick sat.

Ivy looked back to Aidan. "That's not a brother, that's a beggar man."

What Eliza wouldn't give to take a razor to Patrick's face. It would be so much easier to sort him out if she could see his features rather than the mass of unkempt hair he carried around.

Patrick stood, tucking his loop of twine in his pocket. He stepped to Mr. Archer and offered his hand. "Pleasure."

Mr. Archer nodded in return. "Finbarr tells me you have offered to begin building his house."

"Assuming he has the means of doing it."

Mr. Archer motioned to the house. "Step inside. We'll sort out what can be managed." But he didn't walk in that direction. Instead, he looked back at Eliza. "I suspect you are our new housekeeper."

Oh, heavens. What an impression she was making. She jumped

to her feet, tucking Lydia up to her. "Yes, sir. I only paused a moment in doing the laundry. I am not shirking my responsibilities, I assure you."

He didn't look upset. "A pleasure to meet you. What would you prefer to be called?"

"Eliza, please." She set her hand on the top of Lydia's head. "And this is my daughter, Lydia."

"Maura spoke very highly of you," he said.

That only added to the weight she felt settling on her shoulders. "I hope I can show myself worthy of her praise."

Ivy kept her arms around Finbarr's waist as the group moved toward the house. Eliza and Lydia remained near the clothesline, but only for a moment. Lydia ran—to the extent she could—toward Patrick.

"I-und!"

He turned back, not ignoring her little plea. Eliza reached Lydia at the same time he did.

"She's delaying you," Eliza said by way of apology.

"I can take her inside with me." The offer was so unexpected she couldn't even respond. "She'll not run off into the fields or the fire while you're seeing to the laundry."

"I can't ask that of you. You're meant to be discussing your building project."

"It'd be no trouble at all to hold her while talking with Finbarr and Mr. Archer. She'll be an angel, I'm certain of it."

In the nearly two weeks she'd known him, Patrick hadn't ever said so many words together at once. And for those words to be ones of praise for her beloved little girl *and* an offer of much needed help? They touched her heart deeply.

"I will sort out a way to manage Lydia and the laundry at the same time next week, but it'd be a godsend if I didn't have to solve that problem right this moment."

"I'm no miracle from heaven," he insisted.

"No. Apparently you're a beggar man."

She hoped he was smiling at least a little.

He scooped up Lydia, who, as always, declared "I-und!"

"Do you like your beard and hair so long?" Eliza asked.

"In Canada it's needed to keep a fella's face from freezing."

"But what is it needed for *here*?" she asked.

"See to your laundry, Eliza Porter. I'll keep watch over your daughter until you're done." He tipped his head, then, with Lydia held easily in one arm, walked inside.

You are a mystery I am determined to solve, Patrick O'Connor.

Chapter Eight

Eliza found her footing among the Archers surprisingly quickly. Nearly all of them, at least. Mr. Archer intimidated her. He'd never said anything unkind or dismissive, and he didn't treat either Finbarr or Aidan with anything other than kindness. But he reminded her too much of Terrence's family for her to ever be truly at ease. His mannerisms, his style of speaking, the way he carried himself, all testified to his being a man of wealth and birth.

He spent most of his time in the barn or the fields. She took her meals in the kitchen with Lydia. They didn't interact often, and that helped.

Emma was utterly sweet. She was tender and motherly with Lydia. Ivy was far more likely to wind the girl up, trying to convince her to play tag or hide and seek, neither of which Lydia really understood. Little Sean was something of a fussy child, forever wishing for his mother to hold him. But in his more content moments, he was all smiles and baby laughter. He fluctuated between the two extremes. His family adored him, even in his difficult moments. That, more than anything else, gave Eliza hope that this house would be a safe place to live with her daughter.

Sunday afternoons were hers to do with as she chose. She'd spent the previous one with Maura and her new husband in their nearby home. Nearly three weeks as a resident of Hope Springs and she was convinced this town was a wonderful bit of paradise.

Lydia had awoken that morning with a hoarse voice and flushed cheeks. She'd been lethargic all day. Her eyes held that look Eliza had seen there before when her daughter was unwell. Half the day had passed with Eliza interrupting her chores to continually check on and soothe her daughter.

One late-afternoon look-in caught the attention of the older Archer girl.

"Is something the matter?" Emma asked.

"She's ill," Eliza explained. "I don't believe she is in any danger, but I don't like seeing her so miserable, either."

"Dr. Jones would know what to do," Emma said.

He most certainly would. She had danced with him at the last two *céilís* and, though he was quiet, he'd shown himself to be personable. He would help; she knew he would. But asking him to do so was not an option she could entertain. She was so newly arrived that she hadn't yet been paid. Without money, she couldn't pay for a doctor's visit.

"If she grows worse, I'll send for the doctor."

Lydia coughed. The sound wasn't overly worrisome, but it did reinforce the fact that the girl was ill. Poor child.

Emma watched Lydia with drawn brow. "Dr. Jones helps Maura with her cough."

Maura's lungs had been damaged during her years working in the factories of New York. The cough Emma referred to was a symptom of that too-often fatal disease. Maura and Aidan had left the city, in large part, to find fresh air and an escape from the work that was killing her. She was doing far better here.

"*Maura's* cough requires a doctor's care. Lydia's doesn't. At least, not yet."

Emma didn't look convinced, though she didn't argue further, either. Instead, she glanced once more at Lydia before slipping silently from the room.

Had Eliza upset her? She hadn't meant to.

Not five minutes later, Katie stepped into the kitchen where Eliza had returned to chopping vegetables for dinner.

"My Emma tells me that sweet little Lydia isn't well."

"She has a touch of a cough is all," Eliza said. "Nothing to be worried over."

Katie sat at the table beside her. "I've no doubt you're correct. Emma likely doesn't *really* either. But, her ma died of a fever when she was just old enough to remember but too young to understand the difference between a fatal illness and an ordinary one. She worries because life has taught her to."

Eliza had a lot to sort in that. First, Katie was not Emma's mum. Likely not Ivy's either. And Emma was still worried about Lydia.

"Would you object," Katie continued, "if we had Dr. Jones look in on Lydia to set Emma's mind at ease?"

"I couldn't. Doctors don't come cheap. If she truly needed—"

The empathetic shaking of Katie's head stopped her objection.

"We will compensate Dr. Jones for his time. He will be coming on Emma's account, after all."

Eliza could hardly object to that. "His visit will likely mean supper'll be a bit late."

Katie wasn't deterred. "You look after your girl. I'll see to the meal tonight."

The suggestion surprised her, and not merely because cooking was one of the things Eliza was paid to do. Her eyes, of their own accord, wandered to Katie's fingerless left hand. The scrutiny didn't go unnoticed.

"I've quite adapted to this"—she held up that hand—"over the years since it happened."

"I'd not meant to cause you any embarrassment."

"You didn't." Katie nodded toward the bedroom. "You sit with your daughter. I'll send the doctor in when he arrives."

Eliza followed "orders" and retreated to the bedroom, grateful for the reprieve. The Archers didn't overwork her. She wasn't mistreated. But the role of housekeeper didn't fully suit her. She didn't find any true satisfaction in her work. Not a day passed in which she didn't daydream of doing something else—almost *anything* else with her life. Yet, she didn't dare risk appearing ungrateful, so she pretended to be perfectly happy keeping house. She needed a break from the playacting now and then.

Lydia was awake, though still sleepy. Her cough hadn't improved, but it also was no worse than it had been. A doctor truly was unnecessary.

She sat on the floor beside Lydia's bed. She took her daughter's warm hand in hers, then leaned back against the wall. Her own eyes drifted shut. A moment's rest was all she needed. She wouldn't fall asleep.

But she did.

Nearby whispers woke her, though it took a moment to even open her eyes.

"The child isn't worryingly feverish," Dr. Jones said. "What other symptoms does she have?"

"I'm not full certain," Katie said.

Eliza sat up straight once more, shaking off her lingering sleepiness. "She's a bit hoarse, and she has a little cough."

That pulled their attention to Eliza. Katie nodded and stepped out.

"Has your daughter eaten anything?" Dr. Jones asked Eliza.

"Porridge. And I've been able to convince her to drink some water even though I suspect it hurts her throat."

Dr. Jones checked Lydia's neck and throat. He studied her eyes and listened to her breathing. "Continue with what you've been doing," he said. "She should feel well again in only a couple of days."

Eliza laughed lightly. "Perhaps Miss Emma will believe your assessment more easily than she did my identical one."

He smiled a little. That was his way, it seemed. He was quiet and a little withdrawn, but he didn't seem unhappy or impersonable.

"Emma tells me you've helped Maura. I worried so much for her when she left New York. The coughs caused by those factories are worrisome things."

"They are," he said, "but the fresh air here is helping."

Lydia watched them as they talked, her cheeks flushed and her eyelids heavy.

"How long have you lived in Hope Springs?" Eliza asked the doctor.

"About a half a year. It's meant to be a temporary position, but I'm hoping to stay."

"Hoping to? Do you think the townspeople will run you out on a rail?"

Again, a tiny smile appeared for a moment. "No. But I can't keep working out of a tiny sod house. I can't see patients there, and it would be easier if I weren't always rushing from one house to another. Sometimes, when I'm needed, I can't be found quickly."

That was a difficulty. "You aren't going to give up and leave, though, are you?"

"I've been looking for a place like Hope Springs all my life," he said. "I'm not going to give it up easily."

Her heart warmed at the sincerity in his voice. "What is so wonderful about Hope Springs?"

"The people, first," he said. "They care about each other, and not in a halfhearted way. I've never known anything like it before. And something about this valley itself is very peaceful. I've needed a reliable measure of peace since I was a child."

His had clearly been a difficult life.

"I'm glad you've found peace and friendship," she said. "I've been looking for a bit of both myself."

"Then you've come to the right town." He stood. "Miracles happen in Hope Springs."

Quick, heavy footsteps pulled their attention to the door. In the next instant, a grumpy bear of a man filled the threshold. "Miss Emma said Lydia's ill." He didn't wait for an answer but moved directly to the three-sided bed and knelt beside it. "Fever? Rash?"

"An ordinary cold," Dr. Jones said, taking up his medical bag. "No cause for alarm."

Patrick touched his fingertips to Lydia's flushed cheeks. "She's warm."

Lydia wrapped her hand around his finger.

He looked over at Dr. Jones. "Anything that ought to be done for her?"

"Rest. Water. Food as tolerated."

Patrick nodded and returned his attention to the little patient.

Dr. Jones stepped to the doorway. "I will let Miss Emma know that she doesn't have to worry."

"Thank you," Eliza said.

"Do you need anything, *mo stóirín*?" Patrick adjusted Lydia's blanket without slipping his finger free of her grip. "A bit of water? Something to eat?"

Lydia coughed, then whimpered a little.

"The poor thing." He turned to Eliza. "Wee ones tug at the heart when they're ill, don't they?"

Eliza slipped a little closer to him. "During our ride in the stagecoach, you did a very good job of hiding the fact that you're tenderhearted."

"I'm no such thing."

She laughed. "You cannot fool me any longer, Patrick O'Connor. You are a pleasant person. Admit it."

"Perhaps you didn't hear, Eliza. I am a beggar man." He could be rather funny when he allowed himself to be.

"It's only your beggar man hair that makes people think that." She eyed him more closely. "Have you considered cutting it? You wouldn't have hair in your face or in the way while building Finbarr's house, and Ivy wouldn't be confused about your occupation."

He shook his head. "I don't have a paying job, Eliza. I couldn't scrounge up even a nickel to pay a barber to hack this mess off my head."

"I don't think Hope Springs has a barber anyway."

"Hope Springs hardly has a town," he answered dryly.

An idea popped into her head and slipped out before she could stop it. "I used to cut my husband's hair. I'm quite good at it, really. I could cut yours."

"I don't need you to—"

"Oh, your hair *needs* to be cut. There's no argument on that score."

He still held Lydia's hand, though he'd turned a little, facing her more directly. "What makes you so certain I don't like my hair just as it is?"

"Those things that bring us joy, we take care of them. But when it's something we're merely hiding behind, it weighs us down."

"So, if I combed my hair, you wouldn't be threatening me with scissors?"

"Let me cut your hair. If you hate it, it'll grow back. And then you can return to pretending you don't know what a comb is."

Lydia stirred at the low rumble of his laugh. Patrick smoothed his hand over her hair, easing her back to sleep.

"I'm coming back with scissors, Patrick," Eliza warned as she stood. "You'll look presentable by the time you leave here. Mark my words."

She slipped out before he could say anything more. Her excitement grew as she gathered what she needed. Somehow, Patrick had become her friend. She couldn't explain it, considering how gruff and off-putting he'd been early on, but she liked him. He'd shown her and Lydia kindness. He was considerate and compassionate. He was funny when he chose to be. He was even friendly now and then.

Eliza grabbed a pair of sharp scissors from the kitchen drawer, a small piece of twine, a towel, and clothes pin. On the way back to her room, she picked up a chair from the kitchen table.

"All ready," she said, stepping back inside. She set the chair in the empty space at the foot of her bed. "Have a seat."

"Has anyone ever told you that you're a bit like a steam locomotive?"

"No." She laughed at the picture he painted. "Why would anyone say that?"

He adjusted Lydia's blanket before standing and crossing to the chair. "This is for me, is it?"

"Sit. I'll have you looking like a person in no time at all."

"A person," he echoed in a mutter. "I don't know why I keep coming back here."

She pulled his hair back and tied it up with a piece of twine. "Because you like me."

"I make a point of not liking anyone."

Eliza pulled the towel around his neck like a backward cape and held it in place with a clothespin. "You like Lydia."

75

"She didn't give me a choice."

She stepped in front of him. "I'm also going to trim your beard. Did I mention that?"

"You're something of a dictator, aren't you?"

"I'm efficient," she corrected. "And I'm applying that efficiency first to your scraggly beard."

He pushed out a near-growl of a breath. "Do what you must, lass."

She very carefully began snipping away at the man's scraggly beard. They talked as she worked, not about anything of consequence, but of little nothings as if they were old friends. The Canadian towns he'd lived in. Friends and neighbors they'd had over the years. In no time, she had his beard trimmed down close to his face, giving him the look of a man who'd neglected to shave for a few days rather than one who hadn't been informed of the invention of razors.

"Do I look like a person?" he asked.

"Very nearly." She eyed the bird's nest atop his head. "Now for the true challenge."

"My hair is not so bad as all that."

She cut off the tail of hair she'd tied back, then, reaching over his shoulder, dropped it onto his lap.

He picked it up the way one might a dead rat. "That *is* a little unpleasant looking."

The appearance of his hair he'd been toting around had ill prepared her for how soft and thick it actually was. And it was a startlingly dark shade of near-black.

"Perhaps if your position here doesn't work out, you could open Hope Springs' first barber shop," he said.

She laughed. "Don't tempt me."

"Do you secretly dream of cutting hair, then?"

"No. I just don't dream of keeping house for a living."

Dark hair dropped all around them, covering the towel and the floor. He had so much that needed cutting off. The transformation would be dramatic.

"What *do* you dream of doing for a living?" he asked.

"I grew up in an inn. My family ran it for generations. I loved living there, loved the work we did." She'd thought about it a lot in the three years since she'd left England. "I didn't realize how much I'd miss it."

"Hope Springs doesn't have one of those, either."

"I know." She kept cutting, decidedly pleased with the improvement. Most of her effort was made from the back and sides of his head, not affording her the best view of his face. But he didn't *sound* displeased. She simply assumed he didn't *look* displeased either. "I don't truly mind being a housekeeper. This is the nicest place Lydia and I have ever lived, and certainly the safest."

"You were in danger before?" He didn't seem to like the idea. Sweet man.

"The Widows' Tower was not in the best area of town, and the building was practically falling down around us. This room feels like the very lap of luxury compared to that hovel."

"I lived there with Maura and Aidan for a time." Now that he mentioned it, she thought she remembered Maura telling her that. "If I could've scrounged up money enough to see them safely somewhere else, I'd've done so without hesitation."

She stepped around him, ready to tackle the front of his hair. "Maura made the Tower a home. When she moved west, it became a misery. I was never so happy to leave a place in all my life."

"Even though it means spending your time giving a haircut to a beggar man?"

She fussed with his hair a little, combing through it with her fingers, feeling for any oddly cut pieces or sections that needed more attention. "Beggar man haircuts are my specialty."

A few snips, and she was perfectly satisfied. She stepped around him and back a bit, wanting to make sure everything looked right from a bit of a distance. He lifted his chin enough to look up at her.

Eliza's breath caught. *Mercy.* The man was . . . gorgeous.

His expression changed from curious to worried. "That bad, then?"

She shook her head and forced her voice to function despite the shock of his transformation. "Your eyes are—They're—"

An angle of mischief tugged at his newly revealed mouth. "The word I've heard the most often is 'piercing.'"

A good word for his ice-blue eyes. They provided a startling contrast to his nearly black hair, which boasted a fair amount of wave now that the weight had been taken away.

Mercy, mercy, mercy.

"Promise me you will never let your hair grow that wild again," she said. "It's a sin to hide behind all of that."

"I will if you promise to fix things if this means Lydia doesn't recognize me any longer."

She laughed. "I hadn't thought of that. I suspect she's going to be confused."

He reached up and tentatively touched his newly cut hair. "This will take some getting used to."

"As, I suspect, will the attention you'll get for it."

His expression sobered. "Attention," he repeated in a whisper. He released a tight breath. "What purgatory have you unleashed on me, Eliza?"

She grinned, but the expression faded as she realized he wasn't joking. He paused only long enough to check quickly on Lydia, then slipped out with all the panic of a criminal on the run attempting to escape capture.

How she hoped he realized how much better he looked this way, and how much better it would be if he'd stop hiding behind the shield he'd so expertly wielded. He was a kindhearted soul, and such a thing was something that ought not be hidden.

Chapter Nine

Patrick stopped on the bridge over the Hope Springs River and leaned over enough to see his reflection in the water below. He'd run his hands over his short, neatly trimmed beard and cut hair and knew how drastic the change was. But he hadn't seen it, and he wanted to.

The face that looked back at him was exactly what he'd feared for years: it was Grady. They'd always looked alike—he, Grady, and Tavish—and he'd feared that his grief would be too acute to bear if he had to see his dead brother's face in the mirror every day.

He rubbed his stubble. Grady had always been clean shaven. That was one difference. And his own hair had a little wave to it, while Grady's hadn't. Maybe if he focused on that, then he could endure the constant reminder of a life cut short.

But could the rest of the family? He'd be seeing them in only a matter of minutes, after all. 'Twas Biddy's birthday, and the O'Connors were gathering to celebrate. He'd not managed to weasel out of it.

He stood straight once more, no longer looking at himself in the water. His family were all at Ian and Biddy's. Ma would be disappointed if he didn't take part. What better time to send the family into a state of shock than while they were all celebrating a birthday? He pushed out a breath. How was it he managed to ruin every happy moment the O'Connor family had?

He stuffed his hands in his trouser pockets and dragged himself down the road. He passed Ciara's house, Maura's, Tavish's. Ian's sat next. Da and Ma's would be after that if he were going that far. Mary's house sat on the other side of their parents'. Finbarr wouldn't be living on the road beside the rest of the family. Was that because there wasn't room? Where, then, would *he* live? There were no more farms available alongside his family's. He wasn't a farmer, anyway.

Patrick stepped up to the door at Ian and Biddy's house. His brother likely wouldn't be very happy to see him, but the rest of the family would at least pretend to be.

He knocked.

A moment later, the door opened. Ian's daughter, nine years old, he'd been told, stood on the other side. Plenty of people moved around behind her, voices echoing throughout the small space. Ian's daughter tipped her head, and her eyes narrowed on him in confusion. He did look a vast deal different.

"Patrick," he told her. "With a haircut."

"Your beard is gone."

Almost without thinking, he reached up and ran his hand over the neatly trimmed whiskers. "Mostly."

From behind her, Biddy's voice called, "Who's at the door, Mary?"

She answered over her shoulder. "Uncle Patrick. But his hair's all gone."

That managed to bring the O'Connor gathering to a halt. All eyes turned to him standing there in the doorway like the beggar Ivy Archer had declared him to be.

"Oh, look at you, lad." Ma emerged from among them, moving swiftly toward him. "What a change in you."

Tavish, standing not too far from the door, grinned over at him. "Seems Ma won't be coming after you with her scissors in your sleep after all."

Ma swatted in Tavish's direction. "*Whisht.* I never said I'd do anything of the sort." She looked back at Patrick once more. "Oh, my sweet lad." She rose on her toes and brushed her fingers over his newly cut hair. "I've missed seeing these waves of yours. I'd hoped you'd cut it, but I didn't want you to think we weren't just pleased as could be having you here no matter what you looked like."

Little Mary, who hadn't stepped away, jumped back into the conversation. "He looks like Uncle Tavish."

"Lucky man," Tavish tossed back.

Putting his family in mind of his *living* brother was a far better outcome than he'd braced himself for.

Biddy slipped up beside him, making hardly a sound. She set an arm across his back. "Come inside, Patrick. No sense standing on the threshold all night long."

"Unless Ian would rather I just go," he whispered to her. He'd no desire to earn more of his brother's wrath.

"He's asked me twice if I thought you meant to turn up." She tugged him all the way through the door. "Now he'll have his answer."

"But is it the answer he wants?"

"Merciful heavens, Patrick. The two of you are like a once-courting couple tiptoeing around each other and making everyone uncomfortable." She pushed the door closed behind them with her foot. To the room in general she called out, "And what do you think I have here, loves? Our Patrick, with that mess o' hair he's been sporting gone, I hope for good."

"Do you know," he said out of the corner of his mouth, "you're not nearly the shrinking violet you used to be?"

"In Wyoming, fragile flowers either grow hardy, or they die. I'm not fond of the latter option." She slipped her arm from his, and, in a bit of impressive maneuvering, set herself behind him and gave him a gentle shove into the horde of family filling the small home.

The nieces and nephews were particularly intrigued by him, declaring again and again how much he looked like Tavish. And Tavish, for his part, took clear delight in telling everyone how fortunate the resemblance was . . . for Patrick.

In the commotion, Maura reached him. She watched him closely, poignantly. Tears shimmered in her eyes. "Saints, you look like him."

His heart dropped to his boots.

"When I first arrived in Hope Springs, I could see that Tavish still resembled him, but you . . ." She swallowed audibly. "Saints." Her next breath shook. "He never did grow out his whiskers." Her eyes skimmed his face again and again. "He would have looked very handsome with whiskers." She pressed her lips together as a tear dropped down her cheek. After a moment, she shook her head and forced a smile. "I'm ruining the birthday with these tears." She wiped them away. "That haircut, though . . . You look so much like him."

He should never have let Eliza cut it. This reaction was one of the reasons he'd kept his distance from his family the past ten years. He was already painfully connected to their shared grief. He'd vowed not to burden them with the constant reminder of what they'd lost. And now here he was breaking that promise because he needed them to fix him. A selfish man he was.

Patrick offered some half-formed excuse and maneuvered away from Maura and the others, determined to slip back out of the house and leave them all in peace. He hadn't counted on Biddy.

She stood at the door, apparently having anticipated his departure. Her arms were folded across her chest. Her expression sat in tense lines.

"Don't you dare," she said. "You've abandoned them long and often enough. You'll not do so today."

"But I'm causing them pain."

"I will make you privy to a secret, Patrick. This family is always in pain. Being together lessens it. Celebrating special days lessens it. Having as many of us here as we can manage lessens it. Loving each other lessens it."

He rubbed at his forehead, pushing his unruly hair back. "It's not right for me to be here. I ought never to've come."

She set her hands on his arms. "Mark me, Patrick. 'Tisn't ever a mistake for you to be in this home."

He shook his head, the all-too-familiar sadness building inside. "'Twasn't what I meant."

If Biddy understood, she didn't let on. "Before you sulk off, will you help with a repair that needs making?"

"Of course." No matter his discomfort, he'd not leave Biddy in need. And being tucked away somewhere with a set of tools was far preferable to watching Maura and Ma cry. "What are you needing?"

"I've a bit of a leak in the roof near m'stove."

"You have a stove?" They'd not boasted such a thing in New York, only a fire to cook over.

Biddy smiled, a laugh in her eyes. "We're living quite high off the hog here. Best accustom yourself to how fine and fancy we've become."

"Fine and fancy doesn't usually have a leaky roof."

She motioned him a bit to the side. He followed all the way through a doorless threshold and in to a built-on kitchen. That alone was fancier than what they'd known in the past. He moved to the stove and set his eyes on the ceiling above it. There was, indeed, a water stain. Not a large one, or one actively dripping, but evidence enough to know the roof *was* leaking.

"Has this been a trouble for you long?" If so, they had reason to worry about the roof rotting.

"Long enough that I'm beginning to fret over the state of things up there." Biddy had always been smart. Her quiet manner may have changed a bit, but her mind had only grown sharper.

"Have you not told Ian about the leak?" He couldn't imagine his always-responsible, hardworking brother neglecting anything about his family's home or his wife's comfort.

"I have, but he can't fix it."

That made no sense. Ian had always been very good with his hands. He and Patrick had been employed at a textile mill in New York, maintaining and repairing the machines and equipment, and they'd been blasted good at it. "It must be something significant to have flummoxed him."

"'Tisn't a matter of the repair being too complicated." A heaviness settled on her.

Patrick didn't at all like seeing her this way. He motioned her closer, and she obliged, sighing as she reached him.

"Talk to me, Biddy. What's the difficulty?"

She spoke more quietly, more strained. "He gets dizzy so easily ever since his head took that beating. We can't risk him slipping off the roof. He'd not recover from another blow to the head. I know he wouldn't. *He* knows he wouldn't."

Patrick's heart sat firmly in his boots. "What beating?"

She met his eye, and the pain he saw there stole his breath. It echoed in terrible ways the ache he'd seen on Maura's face. "We nearly lost him, Patrick. About three years ago. 'Twas a terrible, awful beating. His face and head were bloodied and bruised almost beyond recognition. The banshee filled every wail of the wind for days and days. In some ways, he's not the same man he used to be. He's in pain all the time. He can't do all the things he used to be able to."

Patrick put an arm around her, hugging her to his side. This was one of the few times over the past years that he had initiated contact with someone he cared about. Keeping a distance was almost always better, and always easier. But he couldn't resist in that moment. He loved Biddy. She was as much a sister to him as Mary and Ciara. And she loved Ian so deeply and so entirely. That bonded them.

"The family does their best to help him with his load. But he struggles with needing them to." Biddy wrapped her arms round herself, leaning into his one-armed embrace. "I can't tell you how often these past three years I've wished you were here. You'd've known what to do. You'd've known how to help him without injuring his pride."

"I'm sorry I wasn't here. I truly am."

She pulled back enough to look into his eyes once more. "Then why is it you're still running away from us?"

That was more complicated a question than she likely realized. "I'm no saint, but I've a conscience enough not to make things worse."

"And being part of our family would be worse?"

"Aye." The longer he was among them, the more likely he was to cause them greater pain than he could allow. "But that doesn't mean I don't expect you to tell me anything and everything you need help with." He slipped away to eye the ceiling again, then take a quick inventory of the room. "Any repair, any job around the place, anything I can do. You simply tell me, Biddy. Anything at all."

She took a deep breath. "There's a lot," she said quietly. "He struggles so much, Patrick."

He could hear tears in her voice.

"I wish I'd been here." It was the first time he'd really meant that, and truly regretted staying so far away. "I'm sorry for that."

She used the corner of her apron to dab a tear from her eyes at the same moment Ian stepped into the threshold. His eyes darted from

Patrick to Biddy and back again a few times. His expression, already fierce, hardened further.

"Are you making m'wife cry?" He all but growled the question.

The accusation hurt. No matter the tension created by Patrick's long absence, how could Ian think he would've become the sort of man who would knowingly cause Biddy pain?

"Happy tears, Ian," Biddy said. "Patrick said he'd repair the roof in here."

Embarrassment and defensiveness immediately filled Ian's expression.

Patrick jumped in, offering the first salve he thought of. "I've missed a good many of Biddy's birthdays. Being here for this one brought that firmly to mind. I'm hoping this'll be an acceptable means of paying off m'birthday-gift debt to her."

Ian turned to Biddy. "And repairing the roof would break the two of you even on that score?"

She smiled a little and nodded. "I can't wait to decide what he owes me for all the Christmases he's missed."

A quickly tucked-away hint of laughter passed through Ian's eyes. "Start making a list, love."

She took her husband's hand in hers. "He's missed all those things with you, as well. You had best start making your own list of what he can do for you."

"Do for me?" The hardness returned to his voice. "What he can do is leave me the devil alone." He pulled his hand from Biddy's and left without a backward glance.

His words pierced Patrick. Pierced him. Ian wasn't going to forgive him. And if Ian wouldn't forgive him, there was little chance his brother would reach out and save him.

Patrick had been depending on Ian's help, leaning on the bond they'd once had. Who else would see any value left in the shell of a person he'd become?

"I'll repair your roof, Biddy. And I meant what I said about doing anything else you have need of. And I'll do it without bothering him. That'll be my Christmas-gift debt payment to you: peace in your home, and a happy husband."

He stepped out, avoiding all his family, who were laughing and chatting and making quick work of a cake. He made it out the door without a soul saying a word. If only he had somewhere to go other than Da and Ma's. He'd little privacy there, no chance to sit entirely alone with his thoughts and his grief and his regrets. Sometimes that was helpful. But most days, it was the utter opposite of what he needed.

The weight on his mind was crushing by the time he reached the loft of his parents' house. He sat on the bed, facing the far wall, not bothering with a candle or lantern. The late-evening light coming through the window was sufficient for his purposes.

He can leave me the devil alone. Ian's angry words struck him blow after blow.

"Leave me the devil alone," Patrick muttered.

He'd known his welcome would be a little shaky, but he'd never truly believed Ian would wish him to hades. They'd been partners in mischief. Worries and dreams and joys they'd kept even from their parents, they'd shared with each other. Ian had told Patrick his feelings for Biddy before he'd confessed them to anyone else. Patrick had told Ian of his decision to stay in New York before he'd broken the news to Ma and Da. Their bond had run deeper than brothers. They shared a connection closer to that of twins, though they were born years apart.

Now Ian despised him.

Patrick opened his trunk, and, pushing aside a couple of items of clothing, he pulled out his nearly half-empty bottle of Gooderham and Worts rye whisky. He'd managed to leave it be for a week now. A whole week. That was seven times longer than he'd gone without a drink in more than two years before coming to Hope Springs. He wasn't as needy for it as some he knew. But it still called to him most of the time. He'd get thirsty for it at times when he knew he wasn't actually thirsty. He'd long for it even when the taste didn't appeal to him.

Some men had come away from the War Between the States with a neediness for laudanum. He'd wanted so badly to avoid that trap and had managed to fall into a different one instead.

He held the bottle in both hands, bent forward, head hung. The bottle felt heavy, hard. How was it he could be angry at it and desperate for it at the same time?

The last week had given him a bit of hope. He'd felt a little more comfortable around his family. A little. He'd found the beginnings of a connection with Finbarr. Lydia's sweetness and acceptance had soothed so much of his troubled spirit. Eliza's ready friendship had touched him more than he'd ever admit. Even cutting his hair and beard, though the effect of it wasn't overly comfortable, had proven an act of humanity in its own way. Eliza had seen the person underneath and had freed a bit of the old Patrick.

He'd felt hopeful these past few days.

And that hope had died with five words.

Leave me the devil alone.

Ian—his best friend, his lifelong confidante—hated him. Ian, the one he'd been sure he wouldn't have to convince to take him back.

He pulled the cork from the bottle. He'd take enough deep swallows to numb the pain so he could sleep. It had worked for years. It would work again.

Chapter Ten

"Ian's risk of falling off the roof is almost nothing compared to *mine*." Finbarr stood at the base of the ladder Patrick had leaned against the side of their brother's house. "I think you had best tackle this repair on your own."

"It's not m'wish to see you fall to your death, lad," Patrick said. "I'm after teaching you to help with building so you can do a bit of work on that house of yours. Does a man good to labor on the place he means to call home."

"And that includes a blind boy on a roof?" Finbarr's sarcasm held a noticeable note of self-pity. How well Patrick knew that weight. He couldn't bear to see his baby brother swimming in the same poison he himself had been drowning in for a third of his life.

"I can't say that I'm too impressed with your counting skills, Finbarr."

His scarred face pulled in confusion. "My counting skills?"

"That you think you're a boy makes me wonder if you're able to count past ten with your shoes on." He nudged Finbarr closer to the ladder. "Up with you, bean sprout. I'm behind you."

Finbarr kept stubbornly still. "I can't stay on a roof if I can't see the edge of it."

"I'm planning to tie you to the chimney. And I learned to tie blasted good knots while living in Winnipeg. The place is crawling with seafarers." Again, he nudged his brother. "Up with you. Our sister needs her roof repaired. We'll not fail her in this."

Finbarr made the climb very slowly, very cautiously. Patrick held the ladder still, watching his brother closely.

"Your hand's next spot'll be the roof itself," he called out. "Hoist yourself up and have a seat."

"How steep is it?" Finbarr asked.

"Judge it with your hand," Patrick said. "If you still can't tell, I'll help you sort it."

To his credit, the lad set himself to the task. After a moment, he crawled onto the roof. Hands taking careful measure of the space around him, he sorted out a spot for himself.

Patrick climbed up the ladder, two long ropes looped over his arm. He sat beside Finbarr and began tying the end of one rope into two large loops. "I worked on the viceroy's residence in Ottawa. That pile of stone is far taller than this house. The foreman on that job taught me how to tie off so I'd not kill m'self if I slipped."

"Are you tying yourself to the chimney up here, as well?"

"For sure, for sure. I'll not be up here dancing in the wind." He pulled Finbarr's arms through the loops. "God is good, but—"

"—don't dance in a small boat." Finbarr finished with him, word-for-word.

Patrick let himself chuckle. "Ma still says that, does she?"

"All the time."

Patrick tied the loops together across Finbarr's chest, necessary so that if the lad slipped he wouldn't simply slide out of the harness. He created the same thing with the other rope and put it on himself.

"I'm going to anchor us. Then we can get started."

"I have helped build and fix roofs," Finbarr said as Patrick walked carefully toward the stone chimney. "But that was before—That was when I could see. I don't know how much help I'll be now."

"Don't fret, bean sprout. We'll stumble our way toward some answer or another."

"That's what Cecily says. Well, when she says it, it sounds more like"—he paused for the length of a breath and, when he spoke again, did so with a rather impressive version of their sister-in-law's very proper British voice—"'Do not you fret, Finbarr. We will discover the solution if we put our minds to it.'" The lad then resumed his normal manner of speaking. "She's convinced there's almost nothing I can't do."

"You've quite an ally there, then. A fellow could do worse than have such support."

"It's frustrating, though."

Patrick tested the knots. "How so?"

"There *are* things I can't do. Sometimes it feels like they're all lying to me."

"If I promise not to lie to you, will you promise to try to help me up here?" Patrick set his hand on his brother's shoulder.

"I always try. It's just not ever enough. Cecily and Tavish and Da and . . . well, the lot of them are always pushing me to do more things or do things better." Finbarr, it seemed, wasn't having a much easier go of things than he, himself, was. "Sometimes I just can't, and that's not good enough for them."

"It's good enough for me." He kept his hand on Finbarr's shoulder.

"And you meant it when you said you wouldn't lie to me about the things that are beyond my ability?"

"I meant it." If Finbarr needed honesty, he'd give it to him. "Now, crawl up toward the ridgepole. I'll talk you through where to go from there."

With careful instruction and cautious movement, Finbarr managed to sit directly beside the leak they were meant to repair. A few wood shakes were missing, the reason rain was seeping through, no doubt.

Patrick moved his canvas bag so that it leaned against Finbarr's leg. "I'll be needing four wood shakes. Three maybe. Hand 'em over as I ask for them, will you?"

"I'll keep you supplied and no mistake."

Patrick smiled at the very Irish turn of phrase. The lad sounded so nearly American a body could be excused for forgetting he'd Irish blood in his veins and Irish family constantly around him.

They worked and chatted. Patrick told him of his ideas for building his house. Sod made more sense than wood, owing to its expense. Saving money on building materials would give him extra to spend on glass.

"A lot of windows?" Finbarr sounded more than a little hopeful.

"Cecily said"—Patrick did his most exaggerated version of an upper-class British accent—"do make certain the dear boy has a great many windows in his house. One simply cannot have too many windows. Neglect the windows, and his house will be utterly banjaxed."

Finbarr grinned through the ridiculous "impression." At the final word, he laughed out loud. "I can't imagine Cecily saying 'banjaxed.' Tavish would. All of our siblings and our parents would. This entire half of town would say it."

"We may've left Ireland," Patrick said, "but Ireland's not left us."

"Finbarr!" A voice echoed up from the ground below.

"What's Aidan doing here?" Finbarr wondered aloud.

"Recognized his voice, did you?"

Finbarr shrugged. "When a person can't see, he learns to listen."

"Stay put," Patrick instructed. "I'll see if I can't discover what the boy wants." He moved to the edge of the roof and sat, legs dangling over the edge. "A fine good morning to you, Aidan."

The poor lad jumped in surprise, his gaze flying upward. He recovered quickly. "Tavish told me Finbarr was here."

"Aye. He's up here with me."

"On the roof?"

"Aye."

For a moment, Aidan didn't say a thing. Shock remained on his face even after he recovered his voice. "I'm returning home to help my step-da in the fields. Finbarr needs to take my place at Archers' for the rest of the day."

"Hop over to the ladder." He motioned to it. "I'll walk him over to it."

Patrick stood and returned to the chimney. He untied their ropes, then crossed back to Finbarr and snatched up the now much-lighter canvas bag. "The boss is summoning you."

"Aidan's been promoted, has he?" The lad had a fine sense of humor.

"Promoted to messenger, it'd seem."

He guided Finbarr to the ladder and kept nearby as he turned and inched his way down. Patrick followed him down. Aidan fetched Finbarr's cane and set it in his hand. The two walked off, Finbarr sweeping the ground in front of him, Aidan walking at his side.

Patrick slung his bag over his shoulder, holding the wad of ropes under his arm. The rope belonged in Ian's barn; he'd roll it back up in there. That plan, though, was almost instantly thwarted.

Ian stood not five feet off, looking at him as if he were a cat sporting a hand's worth of tails. "Finbarr was on the roof?"

"I anchored him good and fast. He'd not've fallen off."

Ian didn't answer, but continued simply watching him with an entirely unreadable expression.

"I can't build the boy's house without some help," Patrick pressed on. "Teaching him to lend a hand is necessary."

"You got him to go on the roof," Ian repeated. "None of us have managed anything close to that, and we actually know the lad."

Saints, Ian knew how to slice with a word. Dryly, he tossed back a remark of his own. "Well, one thing I didn't do, I didn't tell him to stay the devil away from me."

Ian's posture stiffened further. "That's not fair."

Patrick moved past him toward the barn. "Life's not fair, Ian. That's how you know you're awake."

Begor, he didn't like being angry with Ian. But he'd learned from his lapse back into the bottle the night before that whether it was anger or indifference or flippancy, he had to pick something other than pain whenever he interacted with the brother who meant the most to him. He wasn't strong enough to let himself feel the grief of losing Ian all over again.

Patrick stopped just inside the barn door and pulled the few remaining wood shakes from his canvas bag. He set them in the woodpile just to the side. He then made his way to an obliging stool a bit farther inside and sat, setting himself to the task of winding up the ropes so he could hang them up once more.

Ian entered. He didn't even look at his brother. Patrick went about his work as if he were the only one in the barn. They'd once shared a tiny corner of the family's small flat. More than once, their parents had needed to shush them, so their chatting didn't keep everyone awake. They'd walked to and from the factory together every day and never wanted for things to talk about.

Patrick had longed for that connection the past ten years. He needed it now. But he didn't have the first idea about how to get it back except for the one thing he was trying. Ian loved his wife; perhaps showing her kindnesses would help.

"Has Biddy thought of anything else I can do to pay off my debt to her?"

Ian stepped from a horse stall, shoving the door closed behind him. "The debt you owe this family can't be mended like a roof, Patrick. You left us to mourn two brothers when we could've been bearing half that burden. That's ten years of pain. You can't make it just go away."

"I know it." He kept wrapping the rope.

"You were with Grady the last couple of years of his life. Do you have any idea the good you might've done if you'd been bothered to share even a bit of that with us? Saints, you're the reason he was in that battle in the first place. Giving us back a tiny bit of him would've helped. But instead you ran away."

"I did what I had to do, Ian," he mumbled. "I don't expect you to understand."

For the first time since coming inside, Ian actually looked at him. "And Grady did what he set out to do: he kept you alive."

And there it was: the reason Patrick had stayed away, and why he couldn't explain any of his past to them. They thought of Grady in terms of noble sacrifice. They set him on a pedestal, one that required Patrick keep mum about far too many things.

He dropped the ropes onto the nail in the wall where he'd found them that morning. "I'll ask Biddy my own self what she wants done, and I'll do m'work out of your way." He made for the barn door.

Ian's voice carried after him. "You should've come back after the war."

Patrick paused in the doorway. "And you should've listened to me before you left New York. But you didn't. None of you did."

He walked out, leaving behind Ian's farm and the pain he couldn't escape. Too much temptation awaited him in the loft of Da and Ma's house, so he set himself in the opposite direction. Patrick refused to drink during the day. He'd started down that path while he was in Toronto. Drinking had cost him jobs, friendships, even a roof over his head. Drinking didn't make him violent or combative. It numbed him, closed him off. It also made him too tipsy to climb up half-finished buildings, saw wood, or do any number of other dangerous things he'd undertaken on a daily basis.

He couldn't let himself return to that. Being around his family had been even more painful than he'd anticipated, but it had done the trick: he'd kept away from the whiskey most of the time. He'd not indulged as much or as often as he had in Winnipeg. But his struggles with his family undermined all that.

He needed to go somewhere he could think. Da and Ma's house wasn't an option. He'd considered dropping in on Maura, but he didn't know her new husband too well yet, and wasn't at all willing to lay all his vulnerabilities on the table in a house filled with strangers.

He needed someone who didn't require him to pretend that he was whole, who liked the person he was even when what he presented wasn't very likeable.

He needed . . . Lydia. Her sweet, ready welcome.

He arrived at the Archer house almost before his mind pieced together his destination. The kitchen door around back was open, as if waiting for him. A wishful thought, but one he let himself indulge in for a moment.

A little girl's voice—too old for Lydia—wafted out to him. Ivy, no doubt. She was talking on and on about people Patrick didn't know. He slipped inside, quiet as he could manage, not wanting to interrupt.

Both Archer girls were at the table, plates of food in front of them. Emma, the older of the two, sat quite peacefully and calmly. Her sister was talking so ceaselessly, she'd need days and days to finish her food.

Eliza stood at the washbasin, scrubbing a pot. She smiled as she listened to the little girl's chatter. Patrick stood there, enjoying the sight of Eliza. She'd made him feel welcome in a rickety stagecoach despite his gruff responses and vagabond appearance. She'd declared him her friend when he'd felt utterly alone. She'd convinced him to cut his hair, something he'd refused to do for years, and she'd cut it without making him feel like a child or a miscreant or a charity project. Little wonder the Archer girls were so comfortable with her. Even he was at ease in her company, and he wasn't comfortable with anyone.

Ivy spotted him, and a squeal pierced the air around them. "You cut your hair off!"

"Miss Eliza cut it," he said. "And m'beard. Am I looking less like a beggar man, then?"

"You look like Mr. Tavish," Ivy said.

Emma, studying him, offered a different assessment. "You look like Aidan."

Ivy rolled her eyes. "Aidan doesn't have whiskers, silly. He's just a boy."

"He's fifteen years old. That's not a boy."

Fifteen was young yet, but to a girl two or three years younger than that, Aidan likely did seem grown up.

"What brings you around, Patrick?" Eliza asked, turning enough to look at him without abandoning her washing. "Would you care for a sandwich? Ask the girls; I make delicious sandwiches."

Ivy knelt on her chair, facing him. "She puts butter on the bread. That's her secret."

"'Tisn't a secret any longer, lass. You've given it away."

Far from looking guilty, Ivy grinned.

"I've come to see how Lydia's faring. Last I saw her, she felt worse than a cat in a room full o' dogs."

Eliza dried her hands on a kitchen towel before stepping away from the basin. "She might be awake from her nap." She motioned him to follow her to the bedroom. He didn't hesitate.

Lydia was sitting in the bed he and Eliza had made for the sweet girl. Sleep sat heavy on her features, but she didn't seem awake enough to venture out.

"You have a visitor, Lydia."

She popped her fingers in her mouth, eying him with palpable uncertainty.

"It's Mr. Patrick, sweetie," Eliza said.

Lydia didn't look reassured.

Eliza lowered her voice, leaning a bit toward him. "You do look quite a bit different."

That did make sense. Patrick knelt beside Lydia's bed while keeping enough distance not to scare her. "Don't you remember me, *mo stóirín*?"

Her face lit up when he spoke. "I-und!"

His heart warmed on the instant. "There you are, love."

Lydia reached for him, and he scooped her up. Before standing, he looked over his shoulder at Eliza, making certain she'd no objections to the girl's nap being over. She only smiled and waved him back toward the kitchen.

He carried his sweet, tiny friend in one arm. She rubbed her little fingers over his neatly trimmed beard. He brushed his hand over her cheeks and forehead. Not a bit of fever. She did cough a little, though.

"She'll need to eat," Eliza said, preparing a sandwich.

Patrick pulled out a chair and sat, setting Lydia on his knee. "I'm glad you're feeling better, sweetheart. I worried about you, you know."

She pointed back at the doorway they'd come through. "Lydia's woom."

"It is that, love."

Ivy switched chairs, sitting directly beside him and his armful. "We're going to play hide and seek, Lydia. Do you want to play with us?"

Lydia giggled at her potential playmate. Patrick hadn't enough experience with children to know how much a girl Lydia's age would understand of what was said to her. Still, it was obvious she liked Ivy.

Eliza put a plate in front of her daughter with a sandwich cut into small pieces. "I truly can make you a sandwich, Patrick."

"I thank you, but m'stomach's not asking after anything just now." He was thirsty, aye, but 'twasn't at all the same thing.

"Would you play hide and seek with us, Mr. Patrick?" Ivy asked. "Mr. Tavish did sometimes, before he had his Miss Cecily and his little baby. And Finbarr did before he got all burned up and grumpy."

"Don't talk about him that way," Emma said. "He's not burned up."

"He *is* grumpy, though."

Emma picked at her sandwich. "Not as much as before."

"He's not as grumpy with *me*." Ivy's voice and expression held a hefty dose of cheekiness. "And Aidan said he thinks I'm going to be Queen of the World."

This kitchen, with these lasses, was precisely what Patrick had needed. They were light and happy and didn't seem the least upset to have him among them. He found he could even join in their chitchat.

"What do you think, Eliza? Would our Ivy, here, do well as Queen of the World?"

"Exceptionally well." Eliza spoke as she scrubbed a plate. "And I certainly hope she'll appoint me Royal Sandwich Maker."

"And Lydia could be Royal Sandwich Eater!" Ivy declared, bouncing in her seat.

Patrick looked across at the quieter sister. "What about you, Miss Emma? What are you hoping to be when you're all grown?"

She blushed a little and answered, characteristically quiet, "I would like to be a teacher."

"Would you, now?"

She nodded, watching him with obvious uncertainty. Did she think he'd disapprove? Would it matter if he did? Poor girl needed a healthy dose of reassurance.

"I'd a teacher of sorts back in New York," he said. "Weren't a formal school, but he kept back at the church after services on Sunday, and any of the poor people thereabouts who wanted to learn to read and write and such could learn how. Changed all our lives. I think teaching's a fine thing. Says a lot about your good heart that you want to undertake it."

Emma's color deepened, and a little smile tugged at her mouth.

Ivy stood up on her chair, bouncing with excitement. "And you could shake your ruler at children who are being bad and say, 'Stop being bad, you bad children.'"

Patrick bit back a laugh and offered, instead, a warning. "I've a softness for bold lasses, sweetie, but I've no love for seeing them topple off chairs."

Ivy plopped down on her bum once more. "God is good, but don't dance in a small boat."

"Where'd you hear that very Irish turn of phrase?" he asked.

"Finbarr used to say it all the time."

"He doesn't any longer?"

Ivy took up her nearly finished sandwich once more. "He doesn't say much at all now. The fire made him quiet."

"Aidan says Finbarr talks to him," Emma said. "And I know he talks to Papa."

"But he doesn't talk to *you*." Ivy's tone was just badgering enough that Patrick half expected her to stick her tongue out at her sister.

Emma didn't answer. She applied herself entirely to the eating of her lunch, pallor making her still-flushed cheeks more obvious. If ever a young lady needed a rescue, this one did. A turn of topic was more than called-for.

"What was it you dreamed of when you were a wee girl?" he asked Eliza as he helped Lydia pick up a bit of sandwich

She set a plate on a shelf near the stove. "My family has run an inn for generations, The Charred Oak. I grew up there, helping cook and clean. Meeting new people. Feeling close to the locals who came by every day. I loved living and working there. I always thought I'd run an inn when I was a grown woman, just like my mum."

"We've been to inns," Ivy said. "One in Ireland had music like Katie used to play, and I danced. The man who brought us the food said that I dance with venom, but Katie said that it was a different word in Irish, and that it was a fine complement."

"It is that," Patrick said. "Means you've energy and fire and fierceness to you."

Ivy looked to Eliza. "Did you have venom when you were at your inn?"

"I was happy as the day was long. We worked hard, but it was the most joyful work in all the world." She bent a little next to Patrick and, with her kitchen towel, wiped something from Lydia's face. "That inn was the happiest place for a child to grow up."

"Why did you leave?" Patrick asked.

She met his eyes with a little sadness, a little longing in her gaze. "America makes a lot of promises. Promises she doesn't always keep."

"Have you been unhappy on this side of the ocean?" He didn't at all like the idea of her being anything but joyous.

"I'm not ever *unhappy*." Such sincerity rang in her tone. "Not for long, at least. Happiness can be found even in the most difficult of situations."

"That's a bit of magic I've not ever managed," he said.

She set her hand on his arm. "Keep coming back, Patrick. Lydia and I'll teach you the trick of it."

If she could manage that, he might start believing in miracles again.

Chapter Eleven

Patrick O'Connor was a delightful sort of mystery. He was still grumbly and standoffish, but more and more, he was showing himself to be tenderhearted and thoughtful. Eliza thoroughly enjoyed the unique combination. But it was not his contradictory personality that most occupied her thoughts. It was their conversation at the Archers' table a couple of afternoons earlier while Ivy and Emma had eaten their sandwiches.

She had always imagined herself running an inn. Even when she and her dearest childhood friend had boarded a boat for America at eighteen, she'd pictured herself finding or founding an inn some-where, or a boarding house, or something similar to her home growing up. That dream had suffocated in New York. There simply hadn't been any such opportunities. Telling Patrick and the Archer girls about that nearly forgotten hope had brought it to the surface once more, and she could not seem to clear her mind of it.

With Lydia on her hip and approval from Katie Archer to slip out for the evening, dinner being served already, Eliza crossed the Hope Springs River and made her way up the road directly to Maura's home.

Aidan answered the door. When his eyes fell on Lydia, his face lit. He'd been such a dear older brother to her when they all lived at the Widows' Tower. He was still so sweet with Lydia. And though she clearly hadn't remembered him from that time a year ago, she'd warmed to Aidan quickly. He held his arms out to her, and she made the switch with a smile. Between Aidan and Patrick, Lydia was most certainly loved.

Eliza followed Aidan inside and was immediately greeted by Maura's new husband, Ryan. She'd come to know him a bit since arriving in Hope Springs, and she truly, truly liked him. He loved Maura and treated her the way she deserved to be treated. His mum lived with them and was a dear woman, clearly fond of her new daughter-in-law and grandson. Theirs was a happy home, and Eliza couldn't have been more pleased for her dearest friend.

Maura, however, did not appear to be present. Ryan's mum wasn't, either.

"Is Maura off chatting with her family?"

Aidan, bouncing Lydia in his arms, answered. "She's in her room with Granny Callaghan and Dr. Jones."

Eliza looked to Ryan. "Is she unwell? Is it her cough?"

He shook his head. "She'll be having a baby nearer the end of the year. Owing to the trouble with her lungs, Doc wants to look in on her regularly."

"A baby!" Her heart pounded an excited rhythm in her chest. "Are you just as happy as can be?"

Ryan smiled broadly. "I am that."

"Ma cries and cries," Aidan said.

"*Happy* crying," Ryan was quick to explain. "She loves babies, my Maura. And she's hoped for more children. It's a dream for both of us."

Eliza closed a bit of the gap between her and Ryan and lowered her voice. "Is she healthy enough?"

"Dr. Jones says she has strength enough. And her cough is worlds better than it was. None of us is afraid for her."

Palpable relief washed over Eliza. How she had worried for her friend. Maura fled New York in a desperate attempt to save her own life. To know her health had not simply held steady but had improved so drastically since her departure did Eliza's heart a world of good.

Aidan sat on the floor with Lydia, pulling faces and making her laugh. Such a sweet boy, precisely the kind and caring young man she'd loved so dearly in New York. The longer she was in Hope

Springs, the more convinced she was that Lydia needed to be here. If only she, herself, felt confident she could live her life as a housekeeper without drowning in lost dreams.

Mrs. Callaghan and Maura stepped out into the room a minute later, neither looking the least concerned. That only added authority to Ryan's earlier declaration.

"Eliza!" Maura's smile blossomed. "Have you come to call on us, then?"

"Lydia missed her favorite brother." She glanced at Aidan. "From what I hear, she'll have to share him soon enough."

Ryan set his arm around Maura and pressed a light kiss to her temple. This was a happy family and a loving home. An unexpected, powerful realization hit Eliza in that moment: she wanted this. She wanted a home of her own, one with Lydia, with space that belonged wholly to them. She would love to have a husband at her side and extended family around her.

She mourned so many things about the time she'd lost with Terrence. That she was alone in such a real and constant way was most certainly one of them. But she hadn't come to cast a pall over Maura's home and happiness. She kept a smile on her face and reminded herself of all the joyful things she'd found in this new home of hers. A roof over her head. Kind people to work for. Lydia's ready acceptance of their new surroundings. Patrick's gruff kindness. Maura and Aidan so nearby again. She had ample reason to be happy.

"Look who's come to visit," Aidan said to his Grandmother Callaghan, leading Lydia over to visit with the dear lady.

At the same moment, Ryan dipped his head closer to Maura's and said quietly, "What did Dr. Jones have to say?"

Eliza didn't have a place in the interactions happening around her. She didn't begrudge any of them their connections. She knew this family well enough to be fully confident that she wouldn't be set adrift for long.

Dr. Jones stepped out of the room where he'd been visiting with Maura and her mother-in-law. He had a way of examining a space quickly and efficiently; no one ever doubted he was aware of every detail around him. That his evaluation led him to cross directly to her spoke volumes about his character. He noted that she was alone and sought to alleviate it.

"Mrs. Porter," he said quietly. "It's nice to see you again. How is your daughter feeling?"

"Better," she said with a light laugh. "I did try to convince Miss Emma that we hadn't reason for worry. You claim greater authority in her eyes, apparently."

"I'm glad I could reassure her." His all-seeing gaze took in her face. "Are you feeling well? You seem . . . weary."

"I am," she confessed. "Not ill or pained or anything of concern. I'm simply a mum with a very young child, working long hours without any extra hands to offer me a bit of a respite."

He nodded. "A wearying proposition for even the most capable of women."

"And I am far from 'the most capable.'"

"I doubt that." A sweetly offered, sincere compliment.

He held his leather doctoring bag in both hands in front of him. When she'd interacted with him at the *céilís* or briefly after Sunday services, he was always quiet and withdrawn like this. But when he'd been doctoring, looking after Lydia, he spoke and held himself with confidence and surety.

"I know all of the O'Connors on this road," she said, "and I know where a few of the families live on the other end of town, but I don't yet know where to find you."

He motioned toward the back of the house. "Out in the fields."

She eyed him sidelong, a smile tugging at her lips. "Are you teasing me?"

"Only a little. There's a soddie not far behind the house. I live there."

"A large soddie?" She knew sod houses could be spacious but usually weren't.

He shook his head. "It isn't. I have no option but to travel to my patients."

"You don't like that." It was obvious he didn't.

"I don't mind. I really don't. But it'd be easier for me, and for them as well, if I had a place most could come to and be seen without having to search me out in dozens of possible places about town."

That made a lot of sense. "But you plan to stay even though the arrangement is not ideal, because Hope Springs is special."

"It is." He was a quiet man. She'd realized that during their very first interaction. But he was a determinedly happy man as well. She liked that about him.

Dr. Jones turned to Ryan and Maura. "Send word if you need anything."

"We will," Maura said.

With only the most cursory of farewells, Dr. Jones stepped from the house.

"I like him," Eliza said. "He's very friendly."

"He chats more with you than anyone else," Maura said. "I don't know how you manage that with these standoffish men."

"Men?" She laughed. "Plural?"

"They don't come more aloof than Patrick O'Connor. At least the version of him walking among us now."

"You mean the version with his hair newly cut and beard neatly trimmed?"

Maura grinned. "I still haven't the first idea how you talked him into that."

Eliza shrugged a shoulder. "I am very convincing."

"Apparently."

"Sit with me." Maura motioned her to the table. "We haven't gabbed in ages."

Eliza wasn't about to say no. She'd come specifically for a gab. They walked to the table.

"How are you faring at Archers'?" Maura asked, pulling out a chair and sitting.

"I adore those girls of theirs." Eliza took the chair directly across from her friend. "That little boy is a handful, isn't he?"

"He is, indeed." Maura nodded slowly and with emphasis. "A sweet, loving, pill of a baby. He's been running his ma ragged since the day he was born."

They talked awhile about the Archer children, about the very fine stove in the Archer kitchen, and about Katie Archer's near-daily fiddle practice. The topic offered Eliza an opportunity to ask a question that had hovered in her mind from nearly the moment she'd met Katie, but which she'd been hesitant to pose.

"What happened to Katie's hand?" she asked.

"The same fire that cost Finbarr his sight cost Katie her fingers. The town doesn't talk about it in tremendous detail, but it was, from all I've learned, entirely terrible. Emma's little friend was killed."

The poor girl. Little wonder she worried for people's well-being.

"How are you getting on with Joseph?" Maura asked.

As always, even a mention of Mr. Archer set a little flutter of nerves tickling inside. "I don't spend much time with him. He's a little intimidating."

"Joseph?" Ryan sat beside Maura, eying Eliza with surprise.

"He doesn't smile much. I've never heard him laugh. And he's clearly quite wealthy." The last bit made her more nervous than anything else. "I haven't the best history with well-to-do people."

"Joseph's a unique sort of rich man," Maura said. "Good to the soles of his feet. And what seems to you as over-seriousness is really just a quiet nature and preference for privacy."

"He *has* always been kind to me. I keep waiting for him to erupt over something or another. But he hasn't so far."

"Are you pleased with your situation, then?" Maura kept asking that. Perhaps Eliza hadn't kept her discontent entirely hidden.

"Housekeeping wouldn't be my first choice, but I don't entirely dislike it. And the room they have for us at their house is nicer than the Tower by anyone's estimation."

"I am certain a garbage heap would be nicer than the Tower."

Ryan set his hand on Maura's. The look on his face was one of concern. Maura shifted her hand enough to thread her fingers through his.

"You're here now, love," he said. "You'll not ever have to go back there."

"Thank the heavens," Maura said. "That journey isn't one I'd wish on anyone more than once."

"Is there a reason there aren't any inns along the stage line?" Eliza asked.

"The stage has only run this way for about a year now," Ryan said. "There's not been much call for one."

"It'd help, though," Maura said. "Breaking the journey sleeping on the ground isn't the least pleasant for anyone."

This area of Wyoming Territory needed an inn. The very thing she dreamed of. She knew how to run an inn but hadn't the least idea how to get one built. She'd repaired any number of things at the family inn. They'd often built tables and simple chairs for the large public room, and she'd helped with that. She'd repaired and even made a few small pieces of furniture for her flat at the Widows' Tower. In all her life, she'd never undertaken anything as complex as building an entire inn.

But—her heart leapt in her chest—she knew someone who had.

Chapter Twelve

How was Eliza supposed to slip away for a private conversation about a half-formed idea she didn't particularly want to be overheard, if the Archers never left home, and Patrick never visited? Four days passed without a single opportunity to ask him about the difficulties and considerations of building an inn.

She couldn't get the idea out of her head. Imagining her own inn gave her something pleasant to focus on during laundry and floor scrubbing. At night, she told Lydia stories of the Charred Oak, inwardly dreaming of raising her daughter in an American version of that magical place. But she knew building such a place would be quite an undertaking. Until she knew precisely what it would take, she couldn't let herself fully hope.

Finally, the Archers left home to spend the afternoon and evening with Ian and Biddy O'Connor. Eliza had her chance. She took off her work apron, plopped on her wide-brimmed bonnet, and set Lydia on her hip.

"We're going to go visit with Mr. Patrick," she said. "You'll like seeing him."

Lydia held tight to her handkerchief doll in one hand and clutched Eliza's sleeve with the other.

"But we have to be quick about it. Miss Emma and Miss Ivy's family will be back in only a couple of hours."

Sometimes having conversations with a not-quite two-year-old was tiring. The Archer girls, at least, could carry their half of it. And though she hadn't had a great many talks with Katie Archer, Eliza had enjoyed the ones they'd had. Even if Patrick had no insights for her, she looked forward to simply talking with him.

Eliza knew the way to Finbarr's future home: follow the river to the small pond, then turn left at the outcropping of rocks. She hadn't visited the site yet, but she'd heard Ivy tell Aidan about "Finbarr's land" more than once.

She made her way there, assuming he would be at the building site. Finbarr's future house was the most likely spot to find Patrick, and the directions proved perfect. She found her way directly to a vast expanse of unplanted land. And very nearby was the start of a comfortably sized house built of sod. The outer walls were knee high all the way around. As she understood it, Patrick had only recently begun the actual building of the house. He'd made fast progress.

He carried an armful of large sod bricks from a wagon to the walls. He wore a broad-brimmed hat, heavy work trousers, thick boots—and no shirt. That stopped her in her tracks for a moment. She felt as if she were walking in on someone in a very private moment, even though he was out of doors and not the least bit hidden.

An urge to apologize seized her. But apologize for what? She was intruding, but not intentionally.

Eliza summoned her self-possession and traversed the remaining distance to the future house. "You've built so much already."

"Aye." He didn't sound the least startled. Apparently she'd not made her approach undetected. "Work goes fast when a fellow's doing what he enjoys."

Which explained why Eliza's days sometimes seemed to drag on endlessly.

A wood frame, the exact size of a doorway, sat in the middle of one of the long walls. Eliza stepped up near it, still holding Lydia. "This will be the door, won't it?"

"It will." He set another sod brick in the wall. "And the walls'll be full of windows. Cecily says it's important for Finbarr to have light."

Eliza stepped over the threshold and into what would be the interior of the house. "He'll have a lot of room in here."

"And when he has money enough for building a finer house, this'll be a good size for a barn."

Lydia rested her head against Eliza's shoulder. The poor thing had missed her nap. She'd be either asleep or fussy in a few more minutes.

"You know a lot about building."

"Aye. A decade spent doing something'll give you a knack for it."

He could help her solidify her currently vague idea. "What do you know about building things other than houses?"

"I've built a great many things. Most *weren't* houses."

She turned to face him again. "I—What do—" She took a breath, trying to collect her thoughts, even as they continually spun back to the upending reality of a very handsome man standing half-dressed nearby. "I was—"

Heavens.

He looked over at her. "Something amiss, lass?"

"I'm sorry, it's only that you—you don't have a shirt on and it's very . . . distracting."

He smiled, his eyes sparkling. "Enjoying it, are you?"

"I'm not disliking it."

For the second time since Eliza met him, Patrick laughed. The sound was every bit as magical as before. So much of her tension, built up over days of pondering her far-fetched dreams, eased.

"Do you mind if Lydia and I stay a minute and talk your ear off while you work? I promise not to keep you from your task."

His smile still hadn't faded. Worse, the troublemaker didn't seem the least inclined to put his shirt on. She could focus if he could. "*Lydia's* going to talk m'ear off, is she? That'd be worth getting behind in my work to witness."

Even if her little girl were fully awake, she wasn't likely to be chatty. A word or two here and there was all she ever offered.

"I'll do the talking for both of us," Eliza said, as if making a great sacrifice.

"Grand." He returned to the wagon and took up another armful of sod bricks.

"Do you have any objections to us sitting inside your house?"

"'Tisn't mine." Though he didn't struggle, the load was clearly a heavy one.

"While you're building it, I think you can claim some ownership of it."

He set his bricks on the ground. "And what do I claim when I'm done? The loft in my parents' house? Quite the fine, successful fellow, I am."

"I live in the kitchen of a family I didn't know a month ago," Eliza answered. "I haven't exactly room for bragging."

He returned to the wagon again but didn't fetch more bricks. He pulled two wads of fabric from the front bench before walking back to the house and through the soon-to-be door. He unfurled what proved to be a blanket and spread it out on the dirt beside her.

"I haven't any furniture for you to sit on," he said. "But this'll be better than the dirt. It's what I sit on when I eat m'lunch."

"Do you know, for a beggar man you're very considerate."

He shook his head, but the gesture was one of amusement.

"And that other lump of fabric?" She motioned with her free hand to the light green cloth flung over his bare shoulder.

"I'm taking pity on you, woman." He pulled it off his shoulder and shook it out.

A shirt.

"Unless, of course, you'd be heartbroken at losing this stunning view you've had."

She offered nothing but a smile before setting Lydia on the blanket and sitting beside her.

Patrick shrugged. "I'll take that as you saying, 'Get on with you, you handsome man, and work bare-chested as you have been.'" He tossed the shirt over the low sod wall and set back to work.

"I think you've a bit of mischief in you, Patrick O'Connor."

He shook his head. "I didn't until you came 'round."

Eliza doubted that. Still, she wouldn't press it. "What is the largest thing you've built?"

"A shipping warehouse in Winnipeg." He lifted a sod brick into place, adjusting it to sit perfectly on the existing wall.

"What was the most complicated?"

He didn't have as ready an answer for that. His hat shaded his eyes, but she could tell he was contemplating her question. A trickle of sweat dropped from his face. "I worked on the viceroy's residence in Ottawa. It was an expansion and renovation, which made it more complicated."

"Did you enjoy building it?

"Aye."

"Even though it was complicated?"

"The challenge makes a job more fun."

Whether it was his breathtaking smile or the fact that he not only had built something large and difficult but had actually enjoyed doing so, her heart hopped in her chest.

"If I told you about an idea—a dream, really—that I have, would you promise not to laugh at me?" she asked.

"Do people usually laugh at this dream of yours?" He sounded sincerely concerned.

"I haven't told anyone about it yet. Well, except for Lydia, but, as you can see, she isn't spilling any of my secrets." The little girl was fast asleep on the blanket, lying on her back with one arm flung outward and her legs bent. When Lydia was exhausted, she could fall asleep in the most uncomfortable-looking positions.

"Still carrying her handkerchief," Patrick said. "I don't know that I've ever seen her without it."

"It's her doll. The closest thing to a doll I've been able to get her, at least." Eliza pushed through her embarrassment on that count. "I realize that's a little pathetic."

Patrick hefted another large brick. "Do you think so low of yourself because you haven't mountains of money at the ready?"

"I'm not looking to have *mountains*," she said. "But enough for a doll and shoes for Lydia would be nice. I want to have a home of our own. To be able to contribute something to the weekly *céilís*."

He looked over at her. "Is that the dream you were speaking of?"

She smiled. "Oh, I dream much bigger than that."

"I don't doubt it." He returned to his efforts. "I'll not laugh."

Eliza stroked Lydia's hair as she spoke. "Do you remember when you were visiting a few days ago and I told you about the inn I grew up in?"

"Aye."

"That's my dream, to have that again."

He grew very still facing the wall he was building. He didn't look back at her. "You're wanting to return to England?"

"No." Even if she'd wanted to, she could never have afforded passage back. "I'd like to run an inn, like my family does, but here."

He resumed his work. "Here in America?"

"Here in Hope Springs."

He didn't say anything for a moment. His posture grew less rigid. He looked over at her. There wasn't any of laughter or mockery in his expression. He seemed content more than anything.

"There's not an inn in Hope Springs." It wasn't a dismissal of her ambitions, simply a statement of fact. She appreciated that.

"One would have to be built." She spoke a little hesitantly, unsure of her footing going forward. "But that's not something I know anything about."

Patrick pulled his hat off long enough to push his hair back off his forehead before replacing it. "I know something about that."

"Could it be built, do you think?"

"Oh, sure. The building of it is the easy part."

She shook her head. "Spoken like someone who has actually built something like this. I wouldn't have the first idea how to begin."

He stood quite nearby, feet shoulder-width apart, hands tucked into his trouser pockets. "You'd want to have access to water and level ground if possible."

Heavens, he was distracting standing there like that.

"You'd need materials, workers," he continued.

She was pretty sure she was blushing a little. She hadn't done that in ages.

"You'd need land you owned or had permission to build on."

"I don't have that," she said, dropping her gaze to her hands.

She could hear him walking around but didn't look up. She needed to focus, and the sight of him was far too distracting.

A moment later, he sat next to her. There would be no avoiding looking at him now, not without an explanation.

She looked up. "You put your shirt on."

He grinned a little wickedly. "Thought I'd take pity on you, stop all that blushing you were doin'."

The warmth in her cheeks turned fiery hot. "You aren't going to tease me about this, are you?"

"Of course I am."

She bumped his shoulder with hers. "Believe it or not, I really did come to talk about an inn, not to gawk at you while you were working."

"I believe you." He tucked Lydia's handkerchief up closer to her. "You do have a difficulty building yourself an inn beyond needing land. I'm building Finbarr's house of sod because timber comes very dear around here. Now, I'm building it better and larger than most soddies. He'll not be living in a shambles, but it's still not considered anything elegant. Eventually he may have enough to build himself a proper house and change this to a barn, but even saving money for as long as he has, he hasn't enough for anything finer."

She hadn't thought of that. "I can't have an inn made of sod. Few people would stay in it."

"You'd likely encounter a lot of hesitation."

"How much money would Finbarr have needed to build a frame house?" she asked.

He quoted a price far beyond anything she could likely ever scrape together, not after years and years of saving. "How am I supposed to come up with that when I can't even put shoes on my daughter's feet?"

"You don't."

She released a slow, deep breath. "It was a ridiculous dream. I suppose I knew that, but I let myself imagine not being a housekeeper or living in someone else's house or—" She swallowed back the emotion rising in her throat.

Patrick set his hand gently on hers. "I wasn't trying to say you ought to give up your dream. Only that you need to find someone willing to invest in your business, someone who has the money you don't."

"Who would invest in an inn out in the middle of nowhere?"

"If I had two dimes to rub together, I would."

She turned her hand enough in his to weave her fingers through his. Having that connection made it easier to endure the disappointment of feeling her tender dream wilt. "You're very kind to try to help me feel less defeated."

"I'm in earnest." He didn't pull his hand away. "Having made the stage ride from the depot, I know the misery of not having a place other than the unforgiving ground to break the journey, of not having a hot meal in my belly. Your inn would provide both."

"I'm as poor as you are," she said. "I can't buy lumber. And a sod inn wouldn't be a comfort to weary and wary travelers."

"Joseph Archer's a businessman by trade. He's invested in any number of things, including quite a few out this way, from all I understand. And when Finbarr and I talked to him about this house, he showed himself to have a good head on his shoulders and to be a man of fairness."

True though that might be, she wasn't reassured. "Well-off people don't have much faith in the poor and unimportant."

"I do think Joseph'll hear you without dismissing you."

She let out another deep breath. That was how she released tension when she felt overwhelmed. "Dismissal I can endure. It's the insults and vitriol and being treated like I'm not even a person . . . I don't want to go through that."

He held her hand a little tighter. "*Again*?"

He'd pieced that together, then. She nodded.

"I'm not a terrible listener, if you're wanting to talk about it."

She leaned her head against his shoulder. "I'm keeping you from your work."

"I'll catch back up. Go on with you, then."

After another deep breath, she began. "I had a job in New York working as a maid in a fine family's home. It wasn't my favorite work, but it was better than the factory I'd worked at before." Lydia moved a bit in her sleep. Eliza tucked the girl up against her with her free hand. "The family I worked for had a nephew who visited them regularly. Our paths crossed quite a bit. He was kind and didn't look down on me the way the others did. We talked often. He began attending Sunday services at the same church I did, and, after a time, he even sat with me and walked me home after services." Those had been happy days. Her heart filled with a quiet sort of warmth when she talked about them. "His family learned of our growing attachment. After dismissing me, they threatened him with disownment if he didn't cut ties with me. Not just a financial disownment—completely cutting him out of their lives."

"So he tossed you over?" Bless him, Patrick sounded offended on her behalf.

"No." She smiled a little to herself. "He married me."

"Ah."

"His family made good on their threat. They had nothing more to do with him. We both found work and a place to live, and we built a life together. But losing his family weighed on his heart. He missed them. Their coldness hurt."

"Of course it did. Hurt both of you, I'd imagine."

She stroked Lydia's hair. Talking about that time was not easy, though the hurt didn't ache as much as it once had. "After he—after he died, I sent word to his family so they could attend his services and know where he was buried. They responded with accusations, saying I was trying to extort them for money, that I had, essentially, killed him, and that I wasn't ever to contact them again."

Patrick let go of her hand and, wrapped his arm around her in a gentle, kind embrace. "And they didn't come to the funeral?"

"No. They said he'd been dead to them from the moment he declared his affection for me." She leaned against him, letting herself rest in his arms. Other than Maura, he was the first person she'd told this part of her past to in any degree of detail. "Lydia was born five months later."

"Oh, lass. I hadn't realized the order of things. What a weight to bear."

"I sent word to his family again, telling them they had a new granddaughter and grandniece. The response I received was, without question, the most hateful, belittling, insulting . . ." To her horror, emotion rushed to the surface. Her breath shook. She truly didn't want to cry, but doing so felt inevitable. "I'm poor and unimportant. The well-to-do consider that a fatal flaw. What my late husband's family said about me was viciously cruel, and I don't want to endure that again. But what they said about Lydia—" Eliza curled into him, not wanting to remember the hateful words they'd written. "I want to believe that Mr. Archer is not like they were, that I've nothing to fear from him."

"But a fear, once learned, is difficult to unlearn." He put her thoughts so perfectly into words.

"I don't dare give the rich man I work for reason to think ill of me—to think *of* me at all, really. Invisibility is far safer for Lydia *and* for me."

"You are a lot of things, Eliza Porter, but invisible's not one of 'em."

His kind compliment offered a salve to her battered heart. She found she could breathe again. She could even jest a little. "With your shirt off, you certainly aren't exactly invisible either."

He shook a little with a quiet laugh. "Are you ready to admit you enjoyed the view?"

"'Enjoyed' is such a strong word."

His laugh returned, louder this time. How she adored the sound of it. The noise, however, woke Lydia. She whimpered. History said the girl would be crying loudly in a few more breaths. She picked Lydia up and held her, gently and slowly patting the girl's back.

"Will it help, Eliza, if I go with you when you talk to Joseph Archer about your inn?"

"You would do that for me?"

His arm dropped away, and he rested back with his elbows on the ground behind him. "I've a vested interest in the success of this endeavor."

"Do you?"

He nodded. "For one thing, I suspect I'd get paid for building the inn, something I can't say for this house. And, being a grown man, I'd prefer not to continue living off the charity of m'parents."

"Fair enough." She kept Lydia in her arms and turned to face him. "What is the other thing?"

"Other thing?"

"You said 'for one thing.' I am curious what else is on your list of reasons."

He leaned on one elbow and reached his other hand out to brush his fingers over Lydia's flyaway hair. His tender kindness to her daughter nearly brought tears to the surface yet again.

"For another thing," he said, "I think Lydia should get to have a doll, and shoes, and a house of her own. And her ma should get to have a dream come true."

"A dream you kindly didn't laugh at."

He got to his feet and offered a quick, friendly smile. "No one should have to dream entirely alone."

Patrick set back to work. She stayed only a few minutes longer. But his words stayed with her. What dream was *he* harboring in his loneliness?

Chapter Thirteen

That Saturday, Patrick listened as Eliza presented her well-thought-out and detailed business proposal to Joseph Archer. He knew she was nervous, but it didn't show. He was glad he could be there, offering what little support he could, but he could tell she didn't truly need him there.

"An overnight stop at Hope Springs, rather than where it is being undertaken now, would change the stage schedule." Joseph made the observation without censure. "But, having a barn in which to stable their horses and a place for their drivers to rest, as well as being able to tell potential passengers about accommodations, would be a boon to the stage company. I have no doubt they'd welcome that."

The hope in Eliza's eyes was tempered with caution. "But I have no connections to anyone at the stage company."

"I do." Joseph's expression was that of a businessman working out complications, not someone boasting. "They might even be willing to put up some of the capital for the project, but if they did, that would grant them control over some aspects of your venture."

Eliza's brow pulled. "I don't fully understand. Are you saying that the stage company would run the inn?"

He shook his head. "Not fully, but they could likely set the cost of your lodgings or meals, or dictate whether or not they pay you for stabling their horses and putting up their drivers."

"They wouldn't pay for those things?"

"They may exchange their initial investment for free accom-modations."

Patrick didn't like the sound of that. He'd mostly stayed out of the discussion, but he'd found neither of them objected to him speaking up now and then. "For how long?" he asked.

"Likely indefinitely," Joseph said.

Eliza steepled her hands in front of her. "They would make back their investment dozens of times over."

"Precisely," Joseph said. "But if that's what gets your inn built, you might decide it's worth it."

She let out a long breath. Patrick had noticed her doing that often. He was nearly certain it was a response to worry. She wove her fingers together and rested her clasped hands on the tabletop. "What would *you* want in exchange for your investment, assuming you decide to invest?"

Joseph leaned back in his chair. "A percentage of profits. We can determine the amount, choose something we both feel comfortable with."

The man was proving to be as fair minded as Patrick had promised he'd be. That was a relief.

"Would I still come up short of what I need?" Eliza asked.

Joseph nodded. "I can't put up all the funds. It wouldn't be prudent."

She sat there, a look of pondering on her face. Joseph waited patiently. Patrick sat beside her, wishing he knew more about business matters and could offer thoughts and information and reassurance.

"I don't know that I want to provide free accommodations to the stage company forever," she said after a long moment. "But I might not have a choice. I can't imagine anyone else hereabouts with money to invest or an interest in doing so."

"You might ask Jeremiah Johnson, the mercantile owner," Joseph suggested. "He's likely in a position to provide you with food and other supplies, which would give him some increased profits over time. And if the road leading past here becomes better and more easily traveled, that will improve his supply line. He may be willing to invest for those benefits."

She wrote that down. "If Mr. Johnson invests, would I have enough?"

"Enough to build, I believe. Furnishing the rooms and filling your larder would require additional funds."

Eliza looked to Patrick. "Would building an empty inn be worth it, do you think?"

A good question. "Nothing can happen without the inn being built," Patrick said. "If I were making the decision, I'd build. And while that was being seen to, I'd work on sorting out the rest."

Another deep, lung-emptying breath. "Do you really think I can manage something this complicated? I may be taking on a taller task than I'm able to do."

"You lived your life in an inn. You know more about what running an inn requires than any of us. And the bits you have to learn—well, I suspect you'll be a quick study."

She nodded. "I can do this. Surely I can. It's my dream."

Patrick looked to Joseph. "How soon do you think we could have building materials delivered, assuming Johnson agrees to invest?"

"His son makes regular trips to the train depot," Joseph said. "I'm certain he'd travel there on very little notice to bring back lumber and nails and whatever else you need."

"I'll make a list of needed building supplies," Patrick said to both of them.

Katie Archer poked her head into the room. "You've a visitor, Joseph."

He looked to Eliza. "If you have more questions, I'll ask the new arrival to wait."

"I think I know how to proceed." She stood; Joseph and Patrick did as well. "I'll try not to bother you with too many questions as I move ahead."

"Ask whatever you need to," Joseph said.

"I will. Thank you." She wasn't as at ease with Joseph as she was with anyone else, but she seemed less intimidated than before.

Joseph turned to Katie. "You can send in whoever's come to call."

"I will," she said.

A mere moment later, a familiar Irish voice filled the momentary silence. "Sorry to burst in on you, Joseph."

Ian.

Patrick stiffened. He'd not really talked with his brother since the day he'd repaired Biddy's roof. They'd awkwardly stepped around each other, keeping to opposite sides of the house during family gatherings, and opposite sides of the crowd during *céilís*. There'd be no avoiding this encounter.

"What brings you around?" Joseph asked.

"I have a door that's sticking. Could I borrow your jack plane?"

"Of course. We'll ask Finbarr where it is; he has that barn memorized."

Patrick, fool that he was, tossed himself into the discussion. "I've planed hundreds of doors. I'll do it for you."

"I don't need you to," Ian didn't even look at him.

"I know it. But I'm offering just the same."

"Why don't you put your effort into helping Da and Ma set up for the *céilí*?" Ian asked. "They've a lot to do and no one to lend a hand."

It was an unfair criticism. He'd helped with every *céilí* since his arrival. He'd helped without question, without hesitation, without needing to be asked. He was hardly an ideal son, and he didn't deserve the love and acceptance his parents had shown him, but he wasn't a terrible person.

"Before I left, I carried out all the tables and chairs and put 'em where Ma asked. I washed all her dishes last night. I helped Da gather what he needed for the fire. This morning I did all Da's chores, so he'd have time to prepare. They *do* have someone 'there to lend a hand,' and that someone lends it all the time."

Far from softened or impressed, Ian's jaw remained set. "Well, bless me, that makes amends for the last ten years, doesn't it?"

Was this to be their relationship from now on? Tension, distrust, accusations? From the moment the reality of Grady's death had settled on him, Patrick had known his connection to his family would be forever changed. But even in his darkest moments, he hadn't fully believed that Ian would toss him aside so completely.

He snatched his hat off the table and, with a quick nod to Joseph and Eliza, stepped out. It was best to keep a distance. He needed to remember that.

He left behind the Archer home and made for the mercantile. He needed a few things there for Finbarr's house. The lad had an account there, something Joseph had suggested, something that had certainly simplified things for Patrick. He had a little money of his own, and meant to snatch up a couple of things for himself on the same trip.

A little bell rang as he stepped inside. The shop wasn't overly busy but also wasn't empty, which Patrick preferred. Crowds were a little exhausting. So was being the focus of attention. A man couldn't hide as long as Patrick had and not be unnerved at the prospect of being so fully seen.

He hesitated a moment near the doorway, telling himself to quit being such a chicken-hearted milksop. Land's sake, he'd fought in a blasted war; he could certainly walk into an empty mercantile. He moved to the counter.

Mr. Johnson greeted him. "What can I get for you, Patrick?" The first few times they'd spoken, the man's southern accent had set him a little on edge. War did that; it made enemies of strangers.

"I'm needing two dozen nails and two spools of twine on Finbarr's account."

Mr. Johnson nodded. "Anything else?"

"I'm hoping you have a spanner."

"On the far table." He motioned toward the opposite side of the shop.

Patrick dipped his head in acknowledgment. It wasn't a large mercantile, but the variety of items was impressive. Fabric. Foodstuffs. Shoes. Buttons and thread. He paused at the table of shoes. A pair likely Lydia's size caught his eye.

"How much are you askin' for shoes?"

From behind the counter, Mr. Johnson answered, "I don't think we have any even close to your size."

He couldn't exactly admit he was shopping for someone else's child. "I mean, generally."

"Two dollars for the children's sizes. Five for adults."

Two dollars. He didn't have an extra two dollars. He didn't know if the shoes would fit her anyway, so it was likely for the best. Still, he was disappointed in himself. He'd let down so many people these past years; he hated having to add the sweet girl to that list.

A shelf on the wall held a few child's toys: carved wooden figurines, a top, and a little doll. How he wished Lydia had something other than a raggedy, knotted handkerchief to play with. A small sign declared each toy was four bits. He couldn't manage that much yet, either.

But the little doll was just perfect—small enough for a child Lydia's age to carry about without difficulty, but not so tiny that it'd get easily misplaced or outgrown too quickly. Eliza had so many pulls on her finances. If she was to make her dream of an inn a reality, she'd not have four extra bits to spend.

He'd do best to focus on what he'd come for. Though he told himself he was looking only for a very particular type of wrench, his eyes swept the store for the same thing they did every time he was inside the mercantile: whiskey. He'd never seen a single bottle, and he was grateful for it. Not having any near at hand was making breaking free of it easier.

The pull was far weaker than he'd seen in some. But he couldn't risk giving his thirst greater power than it already had.

He snatched up a spanner. He'd sold his, along with most of his tools and all his furniture, to pay for the journey to Hope Springs. He'd hoped to replace them all in time. His feet, troublemakers that they were, took him the roundabout way to the counter. Past that little doll.

Four bits. Surely, he could come up with four bits.

He set the spanner on the counter. "Tell me what I owe you."

Mr. Johnson narrowed his gaze on Patrick. "Do you do work other than building houses?"

"Aye. I've done a little of everything. Do you have something you need done?"

Mr. Johnson motioned with a jerk of his head toward what appeared to be a storage closet without a door. "The doorframe split, and now the hinges won't stay screwed in. We can't use the door at all."

That seemed an easy enough fix if a person knew how to do it, which he did. Patrick crossed to the door and eyed the damage. The frame wasn't actually split. The screw holes were worn to too large a size. That could be fixed with hardly any effort. And if Mr. Johnson placed enough value on the repair to let Patrick walk off with an item he didn't have the money for, well, he'd not complain.

Negotiate, certainly. But not complain.

"It'll take a little doing. Nothing too terrible, but a bit o' time." He looked back to the man. "I could fix it in exchange for something I'm wanting."

"That would depend entirely on that something." Mr. Johnson was clearly no one's fool.

"There's a wee child I know who's in terrible need of a doll. The one you have here in your shop would, I'd wager, do the trick perfectly. If I fix your door, here, I'd ask for the doll in exchange. I'll pay you coins for the spanner."

"Have it fixed before tonight's *céilí*, and you'll get both."

Well, then. That was a spot of luck Patrick hadn't anticipated. He didn't intend to let it slip away from him. He held out his hand. Mr. Johnson shook it firmly.

He borrowed the man's tools—sparse but sufficient—and gathered up the few supplies he needed. He adjusted the placement of the hinges and drilled new holes. It was an easy fix, and very doable with the supplies he had available.

Patrick oiled and polished the hinges. He tightened the door handle. With the door hung once more, he tested the glide only to find it stuck a little. He climbed the ladder and planed down the top of the door until it opened and closed smoothly. Ian might not've allowed Patrick to fix *his* door, but by the saints, he got this one working perfectly.

He tested it a few times, just to make certain Mr. Johnson wouldn't have any complaints. He'd wager the door hadn't worked well in ages. That'd be a good trade for Lydia's doll. And it might mean Patrick could arrange additional trades in the future, getting the things he needed when he didn't have money in hand.

Before Patrick finished, Mr. Johnson had closed the mercantile and disappeared into the back of the building, which served as his family's home. He returned, dressed for the *céilí*.

"All done," Patrick told him. He indicated the door. "Go ahead and give her a test. Make certain you're pleased."

Mr. Johnson opened and closed it a few times, eying the door and the frame as he did. "This door's good as new. You did more to it than I'd expected."

"The hinges are tight and oiled. Door swings smoothly. The handle was a bit loose, but it's firm now."

Mr. Johnson eyed him with amused surprise. "I'm getting more than my money's worth here."

"I don't do any task halfway," he said. "And I'm getting from the exchange what I need, so I'd say we're both making off well."

Mr. Johnson nodded. "Fetch that doll you were eying. Your other things are in the crate on the counter. I consider your account settled."

"Let me know if you're needing anything in the future."

Patrick had the doll in hand a moment later. He smiled at the sight of it, easily imagining Lydia's delight when she saw it. He'd had so few opportunities for being a source of happiness in anyone's life; it felt good knowing he could be that for such a sweet little someone.

And to bring joy to Eliza's eyes would be a welcome thing as well. She was, quite honestly, the closest thing to a friend he'd had this past decade. She seemed to like him and feel he had some value. Even *he* didn't always feel that way about himself.

By the time he reached Da and Ma's house, the weekly party was getting underway. He didn't spy Eliza among the still-small crowd. She'd been away from her duties for the length of their discussion with Joseph, so she likely had a bit of catching up to do.

Patrick chose a chair at the far edge of the gathering, where he could spot Eliza when she arrived and be well enough out of anyone's attention, where he felt most comfortable. The position did not prevent Biddy from spotting him, though.

"Ian said you meant to come back and help with final preparations for the *céilí*. Did something happen?"

Ian had likely complained at not seeing him, assuming he was being irresponsible and dismissive of their parents. His brother had no faith in him any longer.

"Mr. Johnson had a repair that needed doing, and he said if I could finish it before the *céilí*, he'd not charge me for the things I'd come to purchase. I haven't more than a few coins to m'name. I couldn't pass that up."

Biddy's gaze dropped momentarily to his coat pocket. "And was that doll poking out of your pocket one of those things you'd gone in to purchase?"

That was a basket of eggs he wasn't ready to crack. "Just picking it up for someone."

"That's good of you." Biddy didn't sound as though she fully believed his explanation.

"Maybe tell your husband that I can be a decent fellow now and then, if given a chance."

"He knows," Biddy said. "He's just afraid to believe it."

"Then what am I even doing here? If Ian, of all people, won't ever think anything but poorly of me, maybe there really is nothing in me worth thinking highly of. Maybe I'm just fooling myself."

"He just doesn't understand. None of us does. If you'd tell us why you've kept away, why you didn't tell us you were alive."

Patrick's lungs tightened. He shook his head. "I can't."

"Don't you think we deserve to know? Don't you think he does?"

He leaned forward, his elbows on his knees. "The explanation isn't mine to give. Large bits of it—" He swallowed. "Secrets are heavy things, Biddy, but when a fellow agrees to carry them, he doesn't toss 'em out just because he's tired."

"Are you tired, then, Patrick?"

He'd been tired for ten years.

He snatched up the crate under his chair. "I'm gonna put these things away. Enjoy the *céilí*."

She likely said something more, but he moved too quickly for conversation. He needed quiet and space and the comfort of being alone. Keeping his secrets distanced him from one brother, but spilling those secrets would tear the family away from another brother. He couldn't do that. He couldn't.

129

He hung his coat on its nail in the loft, then slid the crate of Finbarr's things and his spanner under his bed. His bottles of whiskey were under there as well, the open one emptier than it had been but fuller than he'd expected it to be by now. He pulled Lydia's doll from the pocket of his coat and sat on the bed.

"Can't drink in front of a dolly," he said aloud like a Bedlamite.

He set the little thing on the small table beside the bed. It'd make a decent reminder.

He lay on the bed, looking up at the ceiling. This was going to be a long night, listening to music and laughter outside, fighting the promise of numbness in the brown bottle beneath him and facing the very real possibility that his family would never forgive him.

And if they never forgave him, how could he possibly forgive himself?

Chapter Fourteen

Eliza had far too much to do. She'd missed the *céilí.* The week after that, she was late with the laundry. And on the day she intended to drop in on Jeremiah Johnson to propose investing in her inn, she found herself, instead, rushing up the road to Maura's house, hoping Dr. Jones was in the soddie.

Maura answered the door, a broad smile on her face. Behind her, a bevy of Irish voices filled the air. All women, if Eliza didn't miss her mark.

"Sorry to interrupt, but Dr. Jones said he lives in your soddie, and I need to see him."

Maura's posture grew stiff and alert. "Are you ill?" She looked to Lydia on Eliza's hip. "Or is she?"

Eliza shook her head and held out her other hand. "I burned myself."

"Oh, heavens." Maura motioned them inside. "Mary, sweetie, run out to the soddie and see if Doc is there. Miss Eliza's burned her hand."

A young girl, one of Ian and Biddy's, if Eliza remembered correctly, hurried out the door.

All the O'Connor women were gathered there, along with Mrs. Callaghan and Katie Archer.

Eliza blanched at the sight of her employer. "Emma said she'd look after Ivy," she told her. "I couldn't think what else to do."

Katie waved that off. "The girls'll be grand, and Sean's here with me." She crossed to Eliza. "How severe's your burn?"

131

SARAH M. EDEN

She held her hand up, cringing at how much worse it looked just since leaving Archers'. It was nearly as red as blood. Blisters had formed all over her fingers and hand. And, mercy, it hurt terribly.

Mrs. O'Connor joined them. "How'd it happen?"

"Spilled boiling water."

Mrs. O'Connor set a comforting arm across her shoulder. Maura took Lydia, and Katie pumped water onto a rag.

"Doc'll know what to do." Mrs. O'Connor said. "He's been a gift from heaven, he has."

Katie gently wrapped Eliza's hand in the cool, damp cloth. She was being very kind and understanding. Still, Eliza worried.

"I'll return to the house just as soon as I've seen the doctor. And I'll do my utmost to get dinner on the table on schedule."

"Don't you fret over your work." Katie shook her head. "We're not heartless people."

Eliza had only worked as a domestic servant in one other house. Missing half a day's work, even on account of an injury sustained while working there, would have seen her dismissed. Sleeping late would've cost her the position as well. Not working as fast as they demanded, too. Or ruffling the housekeeper's feathers. Falling in love with her employers' nephew. Somehow, she couldn't see the Archers letting her go on account of that last, unforgiveable offense. Of course, neither Katie nor Joseph had family in Hope Springs of an age to make that a possibility.

Mrs. O'Connor insisted Eliza sit in a rocker near the group. She slipped a blanket over her legs and lap. "Rest your bones," she said. "The doctor'll see you right and tight as soon as he's fetched here."

Eliza laid her rag-wrapped hand on her lap, grateful for the cooling effect and the bit of relief it offered. Lydia was perfectly content with Maura. If not for the pain pulsating in her hand, Eliza would have been in the perfect position to take a much-needed nap. As it was, she closed her eyes and tried to at least rest.

The O'Connor women began their chatting again.

"The harvest looks to be a good one," one of the ladies said. "Puts m'mind at ease. One less thing to worry over."

"Aidan's already talking about making the drive to market," Maura said. "'Twas a grand adventure for him last year."

"That's owin' to Ryan, I'd wager." Mrs. O'Connor's voice was somehow more recognizable than the others, though Eliza didn't know her any better. "Those two took to each other quickly, they did."

"I cannot tell you how pleased I am that Ryan loves my boy like that," Maura said. "He's been without a father so long. Patrick filled that role for him during his brief months with us in New York before he disappeared. 'Tis one of many reasons I wish he'd stayed."

When they'd been neighbors in the Widows' Tower, Eliza had heard Maura speak of her brother-in-law who'd fought in the war and lived with them briefly, but she hadn't ever thought she'd meet the man. Now that she had, she could hardly imagine not knowing him.

"Was he as unhappy living with you as he seems to be among us now?" That was one of the O'Connor sisters, though Eliza didn't know which.

"He was distant at first," Maura said. "He'd a weight on his mind and soul. I always assumed it was the lingering burden of war. But he lightened in time. He was more the Patrick we'd once known, though never quite the same. Then, toward the end, he cut himself off again, more drastically even than at first. There was no reachin' him. He didn't go out with friends or do anything other than work, eat, and sleep. He was never unkind to Aidan or me, but it was clear he was no longer comfortable living with us."

"Did he tell you why he left?" Mrs. O'Connor asked.

"All he said was that he had an opportunity and meant to seize it. I assumed he had a job. But as the years passed, and he kept moving farther and farther away, writing less and less often, I began to suspect what he'd seized was an opportunity to run away."

A heavy silence descended over the group. Eliza didn't open her eyes. She still felt like an intruder, but somehow her guilt abated when she wasn't actually looking at them.

"He and Ian had another row. Patrick said rather sharply that Ian ought to have listened to him when we left New York, but that no one did." Confusion filled Biddy's tone. "Ian and I haven't been able to sort that out."

"I had discussions aplenty with that lad before we left," Mrs. O'Connor said. "I'd hoped to convince him to come with us. But New York had his heart more than any of us did. And, I suspect, the call of war was already beating in him. Determined to save this country singlehandedly, he was. There was no talking him out of it."

"A shame, really," one of the sisters said. "If he hadn't gone to fight, Grady likely wouldn't have, either."

"But if Patrick hadn't stayed in New York, Grady would've had none of his siblings with him," Maura countered. "That, though it was hard on all of you, was a blessing to him, and it eased some of my anxiety at having separated him from the rest of you."

"Life is sometimes one giant mess of a knot, isn't it?" Mrs. O'Connor sighed, weariness deep in her tone. "There's something behind Patrick throwing at Ian's head that he'd not been listened to, but help me if I can figure out what."

The door opened. Eliza peeked in that direction. It was Biddy's daughter returned from being sent to the soddie. "Doc wasn't there, but he put a note up saying he was at the Scotts' house."

Ciara, the younger of the O'Connor sisters, rose and set her sewing on her chair. "I'll ride up there and fetch him."

"Thank you," Maura said. Eliza might've added her gratitude as well, but she still felt a bit like an eavesdropper. She didn't want to draw attention.

"I spoke a bit with Patrick before he abandoned the *céilí* on Saturday," Biddy said. "It didn't set my mind at ease."

All eyes turned to Biddy even as they continued their sewing. Cecily's eyes were hidden behind her green spectacles—Eliza assumed they were needed for something to do with her blindness—but her head turned in Biddy's direction as well. She, too, was sewing, though much more slowly than the others. Her fingers regularly felt back over the stitches she'd made before continuing on. Was there anything that remarkable woman couldn't do?

"He'd not been at the *céilí* long," Biddy said. "I told him we'd struggle less if we knew why he'd stayed away so long." She met her mother-in-law's eye. "He said it wasn't his tale to tell. I keep tossing that around in my mind. Why wouldn't he be able to tell us? And who else could possibly be keeping him mum on something so important?"

Mrs. O'Connor rubbed at her bottom lip. "We've thirteen years of separation between us. A great deal can happen to a man in thirteen years."

"How do we bridge those years?" Biddy asked. "I can't bear to see him and Ian at odds as they are. There must be a way to draw Patrick in enough to start healing whatever wound he sustained during those years, to give him faith to tell us what's keeping him away."

"When he lived with us in New York," Maura said, "nothing tugged him out of himself as fully and easily as Aidan. His heart could be pulled in any direction by that wee little boy. He was that way before the war as well."

"I remember him being particularly tender when Finbarr was a tiny boy," Mary, the older sister said. "It seemed, at times, that Patrick was a born father, looking after children and babies as naturally as breathing."

Eliza had seen that side of him again and again. He loved Lydia, looked after her, took to her as quickly and easily as anything. That part of him hadn't changed from the years his family was recounting

Mrs. O'Connor pressed the tip of her finger against her lip. "We've plenty enough children among the family. That ought to be something of a pull, yet he stays away."

"Perhaps there are too many of us," Mary said. "He may be overwhelmed, being tossed back among such a crowd after so many years away. Most of this family are strangers to him. That can't be an easy thing."

"He seems to be getting on quite well with Finbarr," Biddy said. "The two've been gabbier with each other than either've been with anyone else. He even got the lad to go up on my roof to help with a repair. Can you believe it?"

"Finbarr told me." Cecily's voice was always easy to pick out. She, alone, spoke with a proper English accent, one familiar to Eliza's ears, though her own manner of speaking was far less refined. "I was amazed."

"How did Finbarr get through to our Patrick when the rest of us haven't managed to come even close?" Mrs. O'Connor asked.

Eliza, against her better judgement, jumped in. "He gave Patrick something to do."

They all turned and looked at her. *In for a penny,* as the saying went.

"I've not known Patrick as long as you have, obviously, but these past weeks I've not seen him happier than when he has a project and a purpose. He's a hard worker, and the work lightens him."

Far from arguing, the family all nodded.

"He used to always be that way," Mrs. O'Connor said. "Sometimes, it was exhausting. Never held still, never kept quiet."

Mary laughed. "Heavens, I remember. Patrick always needed a task. That made the sea voyage an utter nightmare—weeks and weeks of nothing to do but sit around and try not to be sick."

"He did agree very quickly to make the repair to my roof," Biddy said. "And he seemed happy about the job."

"I'd wager he was," Maura said. "And he took to the idea of building Finbarr's house without hesitation."

"It was his idea too," Mrs. O'Connor said.

Patrick was also eager to help build the inn. He liked to be useful and helpful and accomplishing something. That seemed an inherent part of his character.

"He's sorted out what I need done for the *céilís,*" Mrs. O'Connor said. "He washes the dishes and sets out the tables and chairs now every Saturday morning without my even needing to ask. He works alongside his da, and they even gab a bit, something they never do otherwise."

Eliza had noticed how quiet Patrick could be. He'd been far more talkative when their conversations occurred while he worked. Something about it set him at ease.

The family kept discussing their brother and son, contemplating what chores he might be able to do, if they could talk him into lending a hand to his brothers and father in their fields, if those brothers and father would accept help from their prodigal kin. While the Irish didn't have sole claim to stubbornness, this particular family seemed to claim it in abundance.

Lydia had grown tired of sitting on Maura's lap and was toddling along the floor. Eliza would fetch her if she got in the way, but having a burned hand still throbbing made the prospect less than pleasant. She breathed through the pain each time she moved her hand. If only Dr. Jones had been in the soddie rather than out visiting. She might already be feeling better.

He arrived more than a quarter-hour later, apologizing and explaining about being pulled all over town to see to patients. She insisted she understood and hoped he knew she did.

"This is a significant burn," he said, examining her hand. "The cool cloth has helped, but you'll need ointment. And the risk of infection will remain until the blisters have healed."

"But I have work to do," she said. "I can't neglect my duties."

"You'll have to make some adjustments. Anything that rubs the blisters open will have to be avoided. Anything that would subject your hand to heat."

She shook her head. "I'm supposed to do laundry tomorrow. That requires dunking my hands repeatedly in hot water."

"No." He allowed no room for discussion. "Exposing this burn to more heat will keep it burning beneath the surface and do significant damage."

Her shoulders drooped. "It's my job," she whispered, hoping Katie wouldn't overhear. "I can't lose my job. I'd have nothing to live on."

Quite without warning, Katie Archer stood. "I don't know what kind of people you worked for before, Eliza Porter, but we don't toss people out because they've a burnt hand that needs mending. M'girls know how to do a lot of things. I certainly do, as well. You do what you can *safely*, and we'll tie up the loose ends until you're well again."

"I can't justify being paid for work I'm not doing." The guilt was part of the reason, but also the way her employer would think of her. She'd be a weight around their necks rather than an employee worth her pay.

A weight is never wanted.

"You've worked hard these past weeks. We know perfectly well that you're not one for being slovenly or idle. We'll not equate your lightened load to laziness or any such thing. We'd far rather you heal."

Eliza shook her head, unable to bring herself to meet Katie's eye. "Servants are replaceable."

"Perhaps in New York City," Katie said. "You'd be amazed the trouble we've had getting and keeping a housekeeper."

"It'd help if they'd quit getting married," Mrs. O'Connor tossed out, earning a laugh from the group.

"You set your mind at ease," Katie said. "We like you, Eliza. You've been a welcome part of our home these past weeks. The girls adore your daughter. Even Sean is better behaved for you than for most people, and with that little lemon, that's something I consider miraculous." She set a hand kindly on Eliza's shoulder. "Follow Dr. Jones's instructions to the letter. We'll not begrudge you the time you need."

"Thank you." Eliza didn't entirely keep the emotion from her voice.

Katie smiled kindly and rejoined the sewing circle.

"Good people, the Archers," Dr. Jones said. "I've been greatly impressed. The O'Connors are fine people as well."

"You seem like fine people yourself, Doc."

He smiled at her. "That is a generous assessment, considering how long you had to wait for me to arrive. The Scotts' difficulty was not something I *had* to travel to them to address, but without an infirmary, I didn't have much choice."

Eliza motioned to her hand. "This likely could have been seen to in an infirmary as well."

"If only Hope Springs had an extra building somewhere that wasn't a tiny, cramped soddie." Having gently applied ointment to her burn, he wrapped her hand carefully. "Keep it clean and, as I said, don't expose it to any unnecessary heat. Give yourself time to heal, or you'll pay the consequences."

A sudden idea popped into her mind. "If there were a new building in Hope Springs built to include an infirmary, would that be something you would be interested in?"

"It would be a miracle, and that isn't an exaggeration."

It might be a *double* miracle. She lowered her voice and leaned a little closer to him. "Joseph Archer has helped me devise a business plan for building an inn out along the stage road. He's investing. Jeremiah Johnson likely will also. Patrick O'Connor is overseeing the building of it. I'll be running it when it's finished."

"Good for you." Though Dr. Jones didn't know of her history growing up in an inn, he didn't seem to harbor the least doubt in her ability.

"We haven't designed the building yet," she said. "What if a wing of it were an infirmary with an attached home for you? It'd be a boon to Hope Springs to not have to always be searching for you. And stage travelers would likely have need of your services now and then."

He paused his gentle wrapping of her hand, clearly thinking over the idea. "And I could easily take the stage to other towns if I was needed somewhere."

She nodded. "And you could design the infirmary and your home in whatever way makes sense to you."

He turned her hand over and adjusted the strips of linen before resuming his expert and careful wrapping. "I wouldn't make the infirmary wing extravagant—that's not necessary—but it would be something functional and easy to utilize." He looked up from her hand and met her eye. "Do you have the funds to add something like this to your project?"

"I'm not entirely certain how it would change things, having only just thought of it. But I'd guess Patrick knows how to make adjustments and likely how to make them with an eye to the cost. And, if you had anything you might be able to contribute to the building of it . . ." She watched him as the suggestion hung in the air.

"I have a little, but it is *very* little." He tied off her bandaging.

She couldn't hold back her smile of excitement and relief. "I think it might work. I'll speak with Patrick and Joseph again. If you'll let Joseph know what money you could toss into the pot, then he can determine what that means for the project."

"I will." He handed her a little vial of ointment. "Keep your hand

139

as clean as possible. Replace the bandaging with clean linen strips regularly and use this ointment to soothe the burn."

"Thank you," she said, taking the vial.

He rose and offered a dip of his head. "Thank *you*, Eliza. Thank you."

Chapter Fifteen

Patrick could build a house quickly when he had nothing else he needed to do and no one clamoring for his company. The outer walls of Finbarr's house were all but done. Another day or two of work, and he'd have the exterior finished. The roof was another question all together. He couldn't manage that part on his own. Maybe Finbarr could make a petition to the family to spend a day getting it up. They'd do it for Finbarr; he knew they would.

Once the roof was up, he could start on the inside: putting up walls to separate the bedroom from the main room, installing shelves for a kitchen space. Glass for the windows was due to arrive in another week. Finbarr would have a house soon enough. Whether he was ready to live on his own, Patrick didn't know.

He sat on his usual blanket, a few yards from the house, taking his time with his lunch, and looking over his handiwork. It'd been a good thing to have something to keep him busy the past weeks in Hope Springs. He'd put in long hours, using up every ounce of sunlight. Once this project was complete, if Eliza's inn didn't come to be, he wasn't sure what he'd do with himself.

"Heya, Patrick." Finbarr's voice caught him so off guard, he nearly jumped.

He hopped to his feet and spun around to face him. "How'd you know I was here?"

"I guessed." Finbarr stood with his cane tip on the ground in front of him. His hat sat tilted forward on his head. "I'm not needed at the Archers', so I thought I'd come ask if there was anything I could do here."

Poor lad sounded as doubtful as he had when Patrick told him he'd be helping with Ian and Biddy's roof repair. "There's work and plenty. I'll accept any help you offer."

Finbarr faced the house. "I can't—I can't tell how much of it is done."

"I've nearly finished the exterior walls. The windows will go in once we have glass, which will arrive soon. I still need to make the door."

Finbarr came closer, his cane sweeping the ground as he walked. "It's not as tall as I expected it to be."

The day was bright enough, it seemed, for the lad to see the outline of it.

"The house doesn't have a roof yet," Patrick said. "That bit I can't do by myself."

Finbarr shook his head. "Repairing a roof was tricky enough for me. *Attaching* one is beyond me entirely."

Patrick wouldn't let him off that easily. "Oh, you'll be helping with the roof, bean sprout. But it's more than you and I can do on our own."

"Who else is going to work on the roof?"

"I'm hoping Da and our brothers and brothers-in-law, but you might have to do the asking. I suspect they aren't all too pleased with me."

"What'd you do?" Finbarr asked.

"I came back."

Finbarr shook his head. "I think the trouble is that you stayed away."

"Sometimes distance is the best gift a fellow can give his family."

"Sometimes a fellow's family doesn't see it that way." Finbarr's tone was not one of a lad talking about anyone other than his own self.

Patrick's little brother had been running away too. He, however, wasn't able to run as far. Patrick felt a deepening connection to him.

"I've just finished my lunch," he said. "Come help me fill gaps in the wall."

"Are they big enough to feel?"

"Sure are, bean sprout."

Finbarr rested his cane against a wall. "Why do you call me that?"

"Because Ma wouldn't let me call you 'lump head.'"

"Did you want to?" Finbarr asked.

"Oh, aye. She gave me such a tongue lashing the one time I did."

"Sounds like I was Ma's favorite," Finbarr said with a laugh.

"Sounds like I *wasn't*." The banter did Patrick's heavy heart good. "I've a bucket of mud a few steps to your left, beside the wall. You'll find a trowel resting against it. That and your hands'll do the trick."

They talked as they worked. Finbarr was glad to hear about the large number of windows. Patrick told him he would, once the sod had time to settle, plaster and white-wash the interior walls. White would reflect more light, so Finbarr would have a well-lit home.

"And there'll be lots of room," Patrick said. "The family could add your house to the Sunday dinner rotation."

"I think I get enough of them as it is." Finbarr filled a large gap with a trowel's worth of mud.

Patrick worked alongside him, using a jointing knife to fill in any spots Finbarr missed. "I don't ever see you at the *céilís*. Too much family? Or too much noise?"

"Just *too much*."

"I can appreciate that."

Finbarr nodded. "No one else does. They're always after me to go, saying it'd be 'good' for me."

"Would it?"

Finbarr shrugged but didn't answer. He scooped another lump of mud from the bucket and slapped it up against the gap his free hand had discovered. The lad was growing a bit more confident with this task.

"Do you still play the pennywhistle?" Patrick asked. "You were learning when we were in New York."

"No, I haven't played in a long time."

Patrick sensed he shouldn't press the issue. He, too, was a bit vulnerable when it came to his own personal music, so he changed the topic. "We brothers used to sing together. Do you lads do that much anymore?"

"No." Finbarr knelt, running his fingers over the lower section of the wall. "We used to, but Tavish stopped singing after Bridget died, and no one wanted to leave him out or push him when he was hurting so much."

Patrick refilled Finbarr's bucket of mud. "Who's Bridget?"

"Tavish was going to marry her, but there was a fever. Killed almost half the town."

Oh, saints.

"And Bridget died?"

"Aye. Tavish was never the same after that. He's better now, though. Cecily has been good for him."

Life hadn't been all flowers and sunshine for the O'Connors.

"So, no one sings anymore?" Why that possibility ached his heart so much, he couldn't say.

"They do sometimes."

"But you don't join them," Patrick guessed.

Finbarr didn't answer. Instead, he entirely changed the subject. "What do you mean to do once this is complete?"

"Eliza Porter and Joseph Archer are scheming to open an inn out at the stage road. If it all falls into place, they're wanting me to oversee the building of it."

"An inn?" Finbarr sounded impressed. "That'd be a change. The stage passengers would appreciate that, I'd bet."

"And the townsfolk might even indulge in a meal in the public room now and then to treat themselves."

Finbarr allowed a scar-marred smile.

"Eliza grew up in an inn. Her family has had the running of it for generations. It's in her blood."

"Maybe that's what she was whispering about with Dr. Jones." Finbarr paused his work, a contemplative look on his face. "Biddy came over last night and was gabbing with Cecily. They mentioned a few times how cozy Eliza was with Doctor Jones earlier in the day."

Eliza had been whispering with Dr. Jones? "Was there some particular reason Doc was hanging about?"

"From what I could gather, he was tending her burn—"

"Her *what?*"

"—and then they were sitting with their heads together real cozy like. According to Biddy and Cecily, there was a lot of smiling. Everyone took note of it."

That was a lot to sort through. But he needed to put the most concerning things first. "She has a burn? How bad is it? Bad enough for a doctor, aye, but did he seem concerned?"

"I don't know," Finbarr said. "Biddy and Cecily didn't sound worried."

Patrick would see for himself the next time he was with her. But the rest of the puzzle might impact how soon that was. "She and the doctor were cozy, were they?"

"I don't know; I wasn't there. Couldn't have seen it anyway."

"Dr. Jones seems like a decent fellow."

"I suppose." Finbarr felt around for another gap to fill. "And Eliza's a good sort. She ought to be happy. She and her little girl deserve that."

The doctor was seen as a source of happiness for Eliza and Lydia. When had they grown that close? *Why* had they grown so close? The strength of his reaction to the doctor's friendliness with Eliza surprised him. He couldn't dismiss it as disapproval of Dr. Jones or protectiveness toward Eliza.

He was feeling one thing, and one thing alone: envy.

Begor. What was wrong with him? He knew perfectly well what happened when he forged a closeness with people. It never ended well—for anyone. He'd left broken connections and broken dreams strewn all over the United States and Canada. He wouldn't leave the same carnage in Hope Springs.

Yet he wanted to make a home here. He wanted Eliza to have the peace her late husband's family had robbed her of. He wanted Lydia to live with joy in Hope Springs.

But the years had shown him all too clearly that peace and joy and home were not things people found when he was part of their lives.

145

Chapter Sixteen

Patrick didn't manage to convince Finbarr to ask their family about helping with the roof of his house. For some reason, the lad was as uncomfortable with their family as he himself was. Despite his shaky standing among them, Patrick had agreed to be the messenger.

Approaching Da at that week's *céilí* seemed his likeliest chance of success; he wasn't likely to toss profanities at Patrick's head when all the neighbors were looking on.

He moved to stand beside his da, pausing to build up his courage. Asking his family for a favor was a bold thing to do. Arrogant, even. He justified it by reminding himself that the favor was for Finbarr, not for himself. That they'd do anything for their youngest brother.

After a drawn-out moment of watching the gathering, Da spoke. "Do you remember the *céilís* in Ireland?"

"Not really. I haven't many solid memories of our homeland."

"You were young when we left. Even Tavish's memories are few and vague, and he's two years older than you are. It's done your ma's heart and mine good to give our children a taste of home."

"And all the town, at that," Patrick added.

A smug smile pulled at Da's weathered face. "We even got our stubborn American neighbors to embrace a heap of our traditions. If you'd asked me five years ago whether they'd ever see value in us or our customs, I'd've struggled to decide whether to laugh or cry."

That was unexpected. "Has the town had troubles?"

"Aye. We had a war on our hands here, and many suffered for it."

Da looked to him. "Did Biddy tell you about Ian taking a beating to the head?"

"She did."

Da nodded slowly. "And you know about Finbarr's burned face and eyes."

"Aye."

"And Katie Archer's fingerless hand."

"Mercy."

A heavy sadness weighed down Da's expression. "We've found peace among us, but it came at a cost, son."

"This country found peace within itself as well," he answered. "But it came at a steep price. Painfully steep."

Da slapped a hand on his shoulder. "War's a brutal thing."

"It is that." He pushed out the words he'd rather have kept quiet but knew needed to be said. "I wish Grady had come back from battle, Da. I really do. And I tried to protect him. But me against the brutality of war was an uneven battle to begin with."

"You came back to us," Da said. "That's more than we thought we'd have. Grady gave us that."

Patrick had made enough confessions for one night. He wasn't ready to make more. He swallowed down any further explanation and switched to the topic he'd meant to discuss from the beginning. "Finbarr and I are nearly done with his house. We're needing to put on the roof next, but we can't do that without help."

Da nodded. "You've a bevy of family ready to assist you. Just tell us when."

"I will."

"Good." Da gave him one more shoulder slap before slipping out amongst the townspeople. He smiled as he greeted them, moving among them easily and happily.

They're at home here. This was how he'd always pictured his family: happy, at peace, together. If only Grady hadn't—He stopped the thought before it fully formed. What was done was done. He'd do better to pick up the pieces rather than bemoan the shattered state of things.

He wandered through the crowd, his feet carrying him where they always did on Saturday nights: straight to Ma's shortbread. He'd not yet been able to justify indulging in it. He hadn't done anything to earn that bit of home. Maybe after Finbarr's house was done, and he had a paying job, and his own roof over his head, and . . . and he could get through a day without his thoughts turning to the bottle under his bed and the relief it would offer, and get through more than a couple of those days without indulging in that relief. He didn't know if he'd ever have strength enough to manage that.

Maura's husband, Ryan, greeted him as he passed with a friendly word and a warm smile. He'd not been part of Patrick's rough history with the family. That likely helped. Maura herself had been welcoming from the moment he'd arrived in Hope Springs, but there'd always been a hint of hurt in her expression and tone. Aidan had kept more of a distance since Patrick cut his hair and trimmed up his beard. Maybe the lad remembered enough of his father to see the resemblance that haunted Patrick every day.

Patrick slipped around a clump of laughing young people and came face to face with Eliza.

She spoke before he could. "I've not seen you in ages, it seems. How are you?"

"Grand altogether." The response wasn't entirely truthful, but it was easy. His gaze fell to Lydia, on her ma's hip as always. "Hey, there, Lydia."

The little one smiled at him, finger hooked over her lip. She had a way of softening his mood no matter how sharp it was. But she wasn't the only one of the Porter ladies who warmed his heart. Ever since his talk with Finbarr and the realization that he'd grown partial to Eliza, Patrick couldn't deny that she was something of a risk, a danger. He wanted to be around her, talk with her, simply embrace the kindness and acceptance she'd offered him from the very beginning.

But that was selfish. He knew it was. A decade of proof lay behind him. He'd not amass more evidence. Not at her expense.

"I love these weekly *céilís*," Eliza said. "Did I pronounce that right? I know it doesn't sound the same as when an Irish voice says it."

"You did fine." She really had.

Eliza looked over at the dancers, spinning about to the music.

"We'll get to do this every Saturday forever and ever. Can you imagine that?"

"Ma says the *céilís* aren't held in the winter. 'Tis too cold for being outside for hours."

She tipped her head. "I hadn't thought of that. And I suppose the church building isn't large enough for holding all of the town plus food and still have room for dancing."

"I'd imagine not."

Her eyes pulled wide in excitement. She grasped his arm with her free hand. "The inn, Patrick. The *céilís* could be held in a public room during bad weather. It'll be bigger than the church building. There'd be space for food *and* dancing."

He hadn't thought of that, but the idea made him smile. "That'd be a fine thing for the town, Eliza."

"We'd be heroes," she said with a laugh.

We. He liked the sound of that, but he shouldn't. The less she connected herself with him, the better off she'd be. She had no idea the demons he wrestled with. Distance was best.

"I'll build it, Mrs. Porter, but it ain't my circus."

She was clearly taken aback. "*Mrs. Porter?*"

It had sounded awkward, but he was desperate. He needed space. She did too, whether she realized it or not.

"I'll be working for you just as soon as the project gets underway. Best begin addressing you properly now."

She did not appear the least impressed by his explanation. "*Mrs. Porter?*" she said again.

"Doesn't it sound like a name of an employer?"

"Of course it does." A hardness entered her eyes, something he'd not ever seen there before. "It's the name of the woman I worked for in New York. The mistress of the house I cleaned. The woman who made my life an absolute nightmare. The woman who said hurtful and hateful things to me about me and my daughter." She took a nostril-flaring breath. Every line of her posture had filled with tension. "I'll accept being called 'Mrs. Porter' by children, but no one else. Certainly not you."

How tempted he was to tell her he'd been mistaken, that they ought to return to the informality between them. "A certain distance ought to be kept between those working and those they're working for. That other Mrs. Porter was right on that score."

Her next breath shook a little. Anger was replaced by hurt. "She wasn't right about anything, Patrick." The pain and fragility in her eyes tugged at him dangerously. He needed to sever that bond now while he still could. He'd be doing her a service.

"Coziness between an employer and employee never ends well," he said firmly. "You ought to know that."

She watched him, silent and still.

"If you're looking for camaraderie, search out the doctor,"—he had to force out the final two words—"Mrs. Porter." With movements he knew were a little stiff, he turned and beat a hasty retreat.

I'm doing her a favor, he reminded himself every time his heart shouted at him to go back and apologize. He kept telling himself the same thing all the way to his parents' loft.

Patrick hadn't made it through an entire *céilí* in weeks. Something always pushed him away. It was the time each week when he was most likely to give in to the promise of oblivion. He sat on his bed, breathing and staying strong. Lydia's doll still sat on the little table nearby, watching him.

"I'm bein' good," he told it.

That didn't make him feel better though. He stood and paced away. How he wished he had his fiddle and a bit of privacy. The instrument he'd sold in Winnipeg had sometimes worked as a distraction from whiskey's siren song. Of course, he couldn't have played it here in his parents' home. He'd not played in front of another person in more than a decade.

Saints, he hated that he'd been harsh with Eliza. He was trying to protect her, trying to protect himself, but he kept getting everything wrong. His own history ought to have taught him how unlikely he was to be a success as a protector.

In the dim, quiet of the house he heard footsteps. That happened off and on over the course of each Saturday night. People came in to fetch things before rushing back out. He just kept quiet so they'd not notice him up there.

This time, however, the footsteps turned into the sound of someone climbing the ladder to the loft. Climbing it slowly, in fact.

Patrick held perfectly still, hardly daring to breathe.

A voice, one straight from the roadsides of England, echoed up to him. "Climbing this thing with an almost two-year-old in my arms is not nearly as easy as you might think. I'd be greatly obliged to you if you'd offer me a bit of help."

He stepped to the ladder and looked down. Sure enough, Eliza was halfway up, clinging to the ladder with one hand and Lydia with the other.

"What're you doing here, woman?"

"Trying not to fall to my death," she answered.

"Saints preserve us." He lay down on the floor of the loft and held his hands down to her. "Hand me the lass."

They managed the exchange, and Patrick twisted enough to set the girl on the floor, keeping an arm around her so she'd not wander away.

"I-und," she said with a grin.

"Patrick."

As always, she didn't even attempt to correct herself. Truth be told, he didn't mind too much. He stood and scooped Lydia up just as Eliza reached the top. The little girl leaned into him, her tiny fingers scratching at his whiskers.

Patrick set his gaze on her ma. "You're missing the party, Mrs.—"

"So help me, Patrick O'Connor, if you call me that one more time, I'll abscond with every piece of long underwear you have up here and sew all the legs shut."

He thought it best to call a truce for the moment, on the topic of how he addressed her, at least. "If I call you Eliza again, will you go back to the *céilí* and leave me be?"

"No. Call me Eliza and I'll leave your underthings alone. I'll go back to the *céilí* when I'm good and ready."

He bounced Lydia a little, eying Eliza narrowly. "Are you certain you don't have some Irish in you somewhere? That was fiery enough for me to wonder."

She arched a brow. "Do you think only *Irish* women can be fearsome?"

"What'll it take for you to return to the party?"

She popped fists on her hips. "The truth."

In his experience, the truth was something best avoided.

"I'd offer you a seat, but I don't have one."

She shrugged. "I can make do." As regal as a princess, she moved to the bed and sat on the edge, quite as if it were a very fine sofa in a very fine house. "Now, what—" Her gaze froze on the little doll on his bedside table. "What's this?"

Embarrassment rushed over him in a wave of heat. "Mr. Johnson needed a repair seen to and made an exchange. The doll was part of it."

She looked at him, gaze hopeful but hesitant.

"I'd not had a chance to give it to her yet." Patrick reached over and snatched the toy up. This was proving more uncomfortable than he'd anticipated.

He offered the doll to Lydia. Her handkerchief doll occupied her one hand, and the other was busy fussing with Patrick's beard.

"We can tuck this in your pinafore pocket," he said, slipping her handkerchief there. Her lip began to quiver. Panic crept over him. He couldn't bear the thought of making her cry. Patrick held the doll out to her. "What do you think of this sweet dolly, huh? Just right for you, I'd say. And she's a pretty thing."

Lydia was hesitant but curious. She poked at the doll a few times. She touched its hair and its dress. He'd not considered the possibility that she wouldn't like it. The silly thing ought to have been so easy for him to dismiss, but the idea of the little girl he'd come to care about rejecting his humble offering tore at his heart.

She looked up at him. What he saw wasn't rejection but confusion. Mercy, did the girl not even know what a doll was? What level of poverty had this tiny family endured if she couldn't even *identify* a toy?

"I'm confusing her," he said. "I'm sorry about that."

Eliza waved that off.

He sat on the edge of the bed and set Lydia on his knee, facing him. He held the doll up in front of her and wiggled it around a bit to seem more alive, more interesting. He moved it to her and let the doll "kiss" Lydia's cheek, before returning to its wiggle dance. On the second repetition, Lydia smiled. That lifted some of the weight on Patrick's mind. Even if the girl didn't know how to play with the doll, she was at least enjoying it.

He began a sing-song repetition of "I love Lydia. I love Lydia," in his best version of a dolly voice while continuing the doll's little dance. After a moment, she reached for the doll and took it in her own hands. She wiggled it around a bit like he had and mimicked his sing-song words, though in little-girl gibberish.

"There you go, sweetie." He folded his hands behind her back, keeping her balanced and safe on his lap. She could sort out what to do with the doll while she sat there. He'd wager she'd have the knack of it in no time.

"Thank you, Patrick," Eliza whispered beside him.

"The lass needed a doll."

She laid her head against his shoulder. "You have a good heart, but you work so hard to hide it. I can't for the life of me understand why."

"Is that the reason you came up here after me? To sort me out?"

"Honestly, I came up here to tell you to quit being such a sour apple. But climbing that ladder hurt so much that I found myself ready to fully forgive you if only I could rest my hand a bit."

He'd been so busy worrying about himself that he'd not even noticed her bandaged hand. "I heard you burned it."

She nodded. "It's feeling better, but it's still very tender."

And he was the reason she'd pained it climbing the ladder. "I'm sorry."

"Do you always apologize for things that aren't your fault?"

"That's a more complicated matter than I think you realize," he said.

"I'm not a dunderhead. I can comprehend complicated things."

"I haven't any doubt on that score," he said. "I only meant to explain why it's hard for me to . . . explain."

She tucked one of Lydia's stray wisps of hair out of the girl's face. "Do your best and take your time. The *céilí* will go on for hours."

This wasn't something he could even consider discussing with his family. But Eliza wasn't connected to that complication. Perhaps he could manage the words with her. He needed to tell someone, he needed someone to know what he carried around every day.

"When my family came to Hope Springs, my brother Grady and I stayed in New York. I loved the city, loved the pulse of it, the enormity of it. I'd planned to stay for a time, figure out what I wanted out of life. I just needed time to manage that. And, knowing Grady was there, neither of us would've been entirely without family. We talked between us about—"

He stopped. He'd never told anyone about this, not even Maura.

Eliza slipped her arm around his without jostling Lydia. "Go on," she said. "I'm listening."

"You have to promise not to share this with m'family. I can't do that to them."

"I'll not whisper it about, but if I think you ought to tell them, I'll probably hound you a bit to do it."

He breathed slowly. "Just promise you'll be gentle about it."

She looked up at him, worry in her eyes. "I'll not push you. I promise."

"Grady and I said that, in a year, or maybe two, we'd see if we couldn't convince Maura to move west. Maybe even talk her parents and sister into making the journey as well. He—He was willing to stay if she absolutely wouldn't go, but he hadn't intended to stop trying. And I'd promised myself that, so long as he stayed in New York, so would I. He'd be heartbroken without at least one member of his family to keep that connection."

"But you would have rather come here?"

"I would've. But they all think I didn't care about them or about being together. It comes up now and then, even though I told them. I swear I did—before they all left, I said that it wouldn't be forever, that we'd be together again. But they didn't—" Frustration and sadness silenced him for a minute. "No one heard me. Sometimes I think they still don't."

"You're here now, though, but you're not happy, and they're not happy. What went wrong?"

155

"They still begrudge me staying behind. It was selfish, they think. Maybe it was, a little, but not listening to me wasn't very giving of them, either."

"Why can't you tell them this?" Eliza asked. "If they knew—"

"I can't." Saints, this was hard to talk about. "When I was living with Maura and Aidan after the war, she'd go on and on about how Grady had stayed in New York on account of her, how he loved her so much to be willing to do that and he never minded and never begrudged her that, how he never even gave it a second thought."

"Oh, dear," Eliza whispered.

"It's proof in her mind that he loved her. Telling her he'd meant to convince her to move west, that he'd given it second, third, fourth thoughts . . . I don't want to be the reason she wonders if her husband loved her, because he did. I don't know many people who loved anyone as deeply as Grady loved Maura. All she has left of him are memories, and if I tell her all the truths I'm carrying around, she might lose even that."

"Truth*s*? Is there more than his not wanting to stay in New York forever?" Eliza had seen the cracks in what he was leaving out.

"A lot of what they believe about Grady isn't true, but it's part of who he is to them, part of who he is to Aidan. I can't take that away. I can't."

"But what they do believe reflects badly on you?" She was whip smart; no one could deny that.

"It's better that they think a little poorly of me. I'll give them that gift, whether they see it as such or not."

"For what it's worth, Patrick O'Connor, I think you should tell them. You should tell them what you've told me, and you should likely tell them whatever else you're still holding back. I suspect even Grady would agree with me."

"And the bits even he didn't know?" Patrick had a lot of secrets.

"Are they so terrible?"

He gave Lydia a little squeeze, then handed her over to her ma. "They are the reason you'd do best to let me call you Mrs. Porter and think of you as my employer instead of—"

"Instead of what?"

He'd told her enough hidden things for one evening. "Instead of my friend." It was as much as he would admit to.

She didn't argue. He helped her and Lydia get down the ladder and watched until they'd left the house before returning to his loft. There was no doll to scold him into behaving, nothing but the guilt of all he'd relived and all he'd refused to admit to.

Sitting there alone and painfully sober, he couldn't face the enormity of his regrets and failures. The sobriety he could do something about.

He bent low and pulled his nearly empty bottle from under his bed. His supply would be down to three bottles by the time he fell asleep. Another failure. Another regret to add to the heap.

The warm burn of oblivion did what it was meant to.

He didn't hear the rest of the party, didn't hear his parents come into the house afterward, didn't have to think about the weight of past years on his heart. He simply escaped the only way he knew how.

Chapter Seventeen

Eliza was truly hopeful for the first time in years. Plans were coming together for her inn. Joseph had a location picked out—a piece of land he owned that he was willing to either lease or sell to her. Jeremiah Johnson had agreed to invest in the inn, seeing it as an opportunity to improve his own profits. Dr. Jones couldn't contribute anything resembling a fortune, but his little bit had placed her dreams within reach.

And she wasn't alone in those dreams. Twice in the past weeks, she'd been held in Patrick's arms, once while she'd told him her heartaches and struggles, and again, last night, as he told her his. He loved her daughter and treated them both with such kindness. He had difficulties and worries a plenty, but the man she was discovering beneath his expertly donned armor was compassionate and thoughtful and seemed to harbor some partiality for her. And her heart was quickly growing quite partial to him.

When Sunday afternoon arrived, the time each week that she had all to herself with no expectation of work, she didn't hesitate to take Lydia and hurry up the road to Mr. and Mrs. O'Connor's home in the hope that Patrick would be there. She was certain she could convince him to take a little jaunt with her.

Their home was overflowing. She'd forgotten that they had family dinners on Sundays. She hadn't meant to interrupt.

Mrs. O'Connor welcomed her inside. Maura rushed over with an embrace and a smile. Her pregnancy was becoming more obvious.

How far along was she? Perhaps this would be an autumn baby instead of a winter one. Eliza really needed to find more time to sit and gab with her friend. During their sojourn at Widows' Tower, they'd never gone more than a day without spending time together. In Hope Springs, days and days sometimes passed without talking together. And this one would pass as well.

"I'd come hoping to talk with Patrick a moment," she said.

A knowing sort of smile tugged at Maura's lips.

Eliza jumped in quickly. "About my inn. I need his input . . . as a *builder.*"

Maura took Lydia from Eliza's arms then turned to face the gathering. "We've a lass here in need of a builder. Anyone interested?"

Aidan crossed to them and took Lydia from his mum. "Patrick's up in the loft."

Under her breath, Maura said, "I swear to you, if that man looked at a pail of milk today, it'd turn instantly to curds."

At the *céilí* the night before, he'd been a bit sour, but his spirits had improved during their more private time together. "I'm willing to risk his bad humor."

Maura sent one of the O'Connor grandsons up to the loft to fetch his crotchety uncle.

"Are you hungry, Eliza?" Mrs. O'Connor asked. "We've plenty."

"I ate before I came over, but thank you."

"You come have Sunday dinner with us anytime."

A generous offer but one she couldn't in good conscience accept. "Thank you, but I'll not intrude."

Tavish passed by in that moment. "Keep Patrick from chewing everyone's face, and we'll feed you every day."

"Is he so surly as all that?" she asked Maura.

"Tavish is making more of it than there is, but Patrick has been difficult. There's no denying that."

If only they all knew what was weighing on Patrick . . . Perhaps some of this tension between them would ease. But it wasn't her place to tell any of them anything.

The man himself climbed down from the loft. Though his family didn't give him a wide berth, no one rushed over to him, either. Eliza could think of no better word for what she saw than "discomfort"—and it sat thick in both directions.

Patrick crossed to her. "How are ya?"

"Grand altogether."

His surprise at her response pulled a broad grin from her. "Where'd you hear that?" he asked.

"Maura says it quite regularly. So does Katie Archer. It's tossed about all over the *céilí.*"

One corner of his mouth tipped upward. "Do you always listen so closely, Eliza?"

Eliza. Not Mrs. Porter. That was a good sign indeed. "I'm a fine listener."

His expression turned soft. "I know it."

"Do you mind if I steal you away for a bit?" she asked. "Mr. Archer suggested a particular location for the inn, and I want your evaluation of it."

Patrick looked back over his shoulder. "Da, may I borrow your wagon? We've a jaunt to make, and I'm not for making Eliza walk all that way."

It was Biddy, however, who answered. "Take our pony cart. It's quicker to hitch up and not so cumbersome."

Though he kept still, Patrick's eyes darted to Ian. Those two brothers' relationship was more strained than any of the others. "I'd best not," he said. "I can manage the wagon."

"Take it," Biddy insisted. "We've not far to go after finishing here. Ours is just the next house."

Patrick shook his head. "'Tisn't a—"

"By the goats, Patrick," Ian muttered. "Take the cart and quit blathering."

Mrs. O'Connor set her hands on her hips, eying her feuding sons. "The two of you are like a couple of cats in a bag. I've half a mind to shake you."

"No need, Ma," Patrick said. "I'll leave the lot of you in peace."

He grabbed the door handle and pulled it open, motioning for Eliza to step out ahead of him.

"Go ahead and hitch up the pony," she said. "I'll just fetch Lydia."

"Let her stay," Maura said.

Eliza shook her head. "You're having family dinner."

"Lydia is like family to Aidan and me. We've thought of you both that way ever since we met you. Aidan misses her. And she's of an age with Ian and Biddy's little one. They're becoming fine friends. We'll look after her."

Eliza tossed her a smile of gratitude. "That will simplify things. Thank you."

Maura gave her a quick squeeze. She whispered in her ear, "Don't endure his sulkiness too long. You deserve better than a grumbly sorehead."

"He's not as grumbly with me as he is with the rest of you," Eliza said.

"You're a witch, then, aren't you? I think that might be the only explanation."

Eliza laughed. "Thank you again for watching Lydia. With a spot of luck, I'll come back with the perfect location for my inn."

"For your dreams," Maura corrected.

"For so, so many of them."

Eliza found her daughter among them, being watched over by Aidan and gave her a hug and quick explanation of her departure. Lydia held her handkerchief doll in one hand and Patrick's doll in the other. She simply smiled as Eliza talked, clearly not understanding everything.

"Be a good girl." Eliza kissed the top of her head. "Patrick and I will be back soon."

Maura walked beside her through the room and out the door. "I'm so glad you've come to Hope Springs. I wish I could have sent for you sooner. The idea of you still stuck in that awful Tower weighed so heavily on me."

"We're here now," Eliza said. "And this is going to be a perfect home for both of us. For all of us."

Patrick peeked around the back of a pony cart. "Ready when you are, Eliza."

Maura waved her off, and Eliza moved quickly to the cart, anxious to have the site assessed. Patrick handed her up into the cart, then walked around to the other side and sat himself. They rode at a leisurely pace down the road.

"How far from town is the proposed site?" Patrick asked.

"It's close to where the stage dropped us off all those weeks ago. A bit of a walk from town, but not terribly far."

He nodded. "Does the river pass close by?"

"Farther away than I'd prefer, but it's not miles and miles."

He made a sound of pondering. "We may have to dig a canal. Having water nearby would be helpful for construction."

"Could a well be dug, do you think?"

He tipped his head a bit, as if thinking. "That would be ideal. We'll have to ask around to see what luck the families here about have had reaching ground water."

"I don't know as many of them as you do," she said. "Would you mind asking your brothers and sisters?"

He laughed humorlessly. "You saw for your own self the state of things with my family. I'd do better asking strangers."

"The 'state of things,' Patrick, is awkward, not cold. With a bit of effort, that could be overcome."

"I suspect you would believe Cain and Abel could set aside their differences 'with a bit of effort.'"

"Are you planning to murder your brother?" she asked.

"How do you know one of them's not planning to murder *me*?"

She shrugged. "I've known you for weeks, and I don't want to murder you. The feeling is bound to be universal."

He laughed. Oh, how she loved that sound. "You're a joy, Eliza."

"I see I'm not *Mrs. Porter* any longer."

"After the murderous glint in your eyes last night when I called you that?" He shook his head. "Not ever again."

He directed the cart over the hill they'd crested when they'd first arrived in Hope Springs. "Ought I to turn the cart toward the north or south?"

"South," she said.

As they rolled in that direction, she let her gaze take in the view. Mountains sat in the distance, tall and majestic and snowcapped. The nearer mountains were smaller and more barren, but still beautiful in their own way. Rolling land spread out ahead of her, unbroken, unmarred by anything but the slight wear in the ground left by the twice-weekly roundtrip of the stagecoach. This was the very opposite of the tightly packed buildings and paved streets of New York.

She loved it.

"Stop here," she said as they reached the spot she was aiming for. "This is it."

She didn't wait for Patrick to come around the cart but scrambled down on her own. She moved to the edge of the road and turned to face where soon, she prayed, her inn would stand.

"This would be the inn yard. Right here"—she motioned a bit to the right—"would be the inn itself, with the front windows facing those mountains." She spun around to motion at the gorgeous purple peaks she'd come to love. "One wing of the inn would be an infirmary and living quarters for Dr. Jones, and the other would be living quarters for Lydia and me. The middle would be the inn itself."

Patrick nodded, his eyes darting all around the spot. "Would all the wings need windows facing your mountains?"

My mountains. She liked the sound of that. "I'd like a bed-chamber in my wing to have windows in that direction so I could see my mountains every day. But the rest can face whichever way makes most sense to the person building the place."

He quirked her a dazzling, theatrically arrogant smile. "That would be me."

She passed him again, snatching hold of his hand as she went, pulling him along with her. "Over here is where I'm imagining the stable. It would need to be large enough for four stage horses and Dr. Jones's horse."

"And yours," Patrick added.

"I don't have a horse." At this point, she didn't even have an inn.

"You likely will someday, though. It'd be easier to build big enough now than to add on later. Besides, it'd simplify things for me to be building an even number of stalls." He eyed her proposed stable location, then looked over her shoulder to where the inn was meant to be, then looked the other way at the road. "This is a good spot. The land is level. The road is accessible. You'd be near enough to town that the locals could come by for a bite now and then."

"Do you truly think so?" She could hardly contain her excitement. From the moment Mr. Archer had brought her here after services that morning to suggest it be the location of the inn, she'd been fighting the urge to let herself simply believe her dreams were within reach.

"I truly think so. I can't imagine a better spot."

"Oh, I knew it. I knew it." She threw her arms around him. "I'm going to have my inn, Patrick. I'm going to have my dreams."

His arms wrapped around her in return. "You've waited long enough. It's time you claimed the happiness you deserve."

She looked up at him, unable to hold back the emotion rising inside her. "The original Mrs. Porter told me I was a weight and a leech."

"Sounds to me like a muttonhead."

A tug of mischief pulled her smile ever wider. "A fancy lady like her? A lambchop-head, more like."

"You're a jewel, you know that? I've spent ten years unable to laugh at anything at all, and you somehow manage to make me laugh nearly every time I see you." He brushed his thumb along her jaw.

Her heart leaped to her throat, lodging there in a thick, wonderful lump of anticipation. "Maura said I was a witch."

"Hmm." His hand slid to her shoulder, then down her back, pulling her into a warm embrace. "Have you considered calling your inn The Witch's Broom?"

She smiled up at him. "What about The Crown Jewel?"

"Mrs. Porter's Lambchops?"

They both laughed at that. How good it felt to be so easily happy with another person. "I'm so glad you came to Hope Springs, Patrick."

"In this moment, so am I."

They held each other's gaze, neither looking away, both breathing slow and shallow. Her pulse pounded from her chest to her head in that telltale rhythm that told a woman she was likely about to be kissed. She ought to have been nervous or scandalized or something. Silently she begged him to make good on the unspoken promise in his eyes. And for just a moment, she thought he might.

But then his expression clouded over, and he stepped away. "We should likely get back. Ian'll be wanting his cart."

"Are you . . . upset?"

He gave her a quick, sincere smile. "I'm not. Simply doing what's best for you and Ian, and, at that, for me."

"And if I think you're wrong?"

He shook his head, leading the way back to the cart. "We'll simply have to live in disagreement on that score."

For the time being, Patrick O'Connor. For the time being.

Chapter Eighteen

Eliza walked at Katie's side up the walk to Tavish and Cecily O'Connor's home, not at all certain of the wisdom of this undertaking. She'd asked Katie about the sewing circle she'd unintentionally interrupted a couple of weeks earlier, hoping to inquire about the possibility of joining in now and then. Instead, she'd found herself happily excused from work for the remainder of the day and brought along for what was, apparently, an annual tradition: turning Tavish O'Connor's berry harvest into preserves.

"And this is how he makes his living?" Eliza asked as they approached the door.

Katie nodded. "He's the only berry farmer in most of the territory. And his berries are utter perfection. He sells them and the products he makes from them all over."

Maura's husband had a business selling hay to the local ranches. Katie had once made her living selling baked goods. Cecily oversaw an organized effort to create raised-type books for the blind. Was there any other town in this remote area of the world where so many people took risks and pursued their dreams?

Luck had not generally been on Eliza's side. Perhaps that was beginning to change.

Tavish answered Katie's knock and, with a smile all the O'Connors could claim, motioned them inside. He looked so very much like Patrick, a fact that shocked her anew every time she saw him. If Patrick ever shaved his close-cropped beard, the two would be nearly identical.

"Eliza!" Maura rushed over and threw her arms around her and Lydia. "I didn't know you were coming."

"Katie invited me." She looked at Tavish. "I hope that's fine with you."

"I never turn down help on berry day."

Maura guided Eliza inside, where several tables were pushed together to form one very long one. Both O'Connor sisters, plus Cecily, Biddy, and Mrs. O'Connor, stood gathered around. No one seemed unhappy to have her there.

"Biddy's Mary is keeping an eye on the little ones." Maura nodded toward the corner of the room where a blanket was spread out and a couple of children about Lydia's age played with Mary. "Lydia'll be out of your hair without being out of sight, pleased as a mouse in the cheese with the wee ones."

Katie had already set Sean among the children. Eliza did the same with Lydia. The girl was small for her age, but even so, she was getting too big to be carried all the time. She simply had to find the girl some shoes or resign herself to be tending cuts and splinters and other injuries if she continued to run around barefooted.

Lydia watched her with that look of betrayal she always wore when Eliza left her anywhere.

"Play with your doll and your hankie," Eliza said. "Mary'll look after you."

Lydia stayed put but pouted enough for everyone in the room to know she was none too happy about the arrangement. Eliza returned to the table. She was given a wooden pestle and a large metal bowl filled with berries. Her task wasn't difficult to guess. And, fortunately for her, mashing berries was also not difficult to *do.* The other women had jobs, as did Tavish. They worked quite well together. This was obviously something they'd done many times before.

Maura worked beside her, also enlisted as a berry masher. "Lydia finally has a doll. I know you've been wanting one for her."

Though there was nothing untoward or truly embarrassing in the doll having come from Patrick, she found herself hesitant to explain. She tried to clamp down the blush she suspected was deepening on her face.

"She loves it. She didn't even know how to play with it at first, but she warmed to it." In large part because Patrick had shown her how, bless him. "It and her hankie are never out of her hands now, even when she's sleeping."

"What a sweetheart." Maura smiled over at the little girl. "I suspect if our new addition is a girl, Ryan will simply smother her. He has such a soft spot for children."

The women and Tavish laughed and teased, shared stories from years past. They worked easily together, and she was readily and immediately welcomed among them.

She pretended she wasn't listening even more closely any time Patrick's name came up, but she was. The way he'd held her and caressed her face told her that he felt something more than indifference, something more even than friendship. But he'd held back and closed himself off. There had to be a way to get past his fortified walls.

"Did Patrick grumble your ear off during your outing on Sunday?" Biddy asked.

"He was perfectly pleasant."

"We're speaking of Patrick *O'Connor*?" Tavish's look of confusion was too exaggerated to be anything but jesting.

"I told Eliza already that I suspect she may be a witch, seeing the way that porcupine becomes all soft fur and smiles when she's nearby." Maura tossed Eliza a teasing look.

"Oh, there's a spell being cast," Tavish said, "but it hasn't a thing to do with witches."

The rest of the family at least attempted to hide their amusement.

"You be nice, lad," Mrs. O'Connor said. "Eliza's helping you, and you're teasing her mercilessly."

Tavish met her eye. "Patrick used to do that. The funniest of us all, he was. Teased everyone. I don't suppose you've seen *that* Patrick lazing about."

She continued with her mashing, though her arm was getting sore. "He makes an appearance now and then."

"Truly?" Mrs. O'Connor's shock was mirrored on the others' faces.

"Even in the stagecoach, he had moments of humor—dry as a desert, but humor all the same."

Mrs. O'Connor handed her wooden spoon to Mary, her oldest daughter, and moved beside Eliza. "Have you any idea why he's so aloof? Feels like none of us can get through to him."

"He's told me some things in confidence," she said. "I'll not break that trust."

"Please." Mrs. O'Connor set her hand imploringly on hers. "We've lost him once before. I feel like we're losing him all over again."

Eliza knew in her very bones that sharing the secrets Patrick had told her would send him into permanent isolation. They were all watching her, hope and expectation hanging heavy on their expressions. If they knew his burdens, they'd be far more likely to get through to him. But she couldn't violate his trust.

"I can tell you only this," she said, "when I burned my hand, he was nowhere nearby, but he apologized. When Lydia didn't know how to play with a doll because she'd never had one in the time before we met him, he apologized. When the Archer girls were bickering a bit with each other when he dropped by a few days ago, *he* apologized."

"But none of those things had the least to do with him," Ciara, the youngest of the O'Connor sisters, said.

Eliza kept her gaze on her work. She couldn't tell them more than she had.

It was Cecily who pieced things together quickest. "He's blaming himself for things that aren't his fault, *or* he is convinced the rest of us blame him for those things."

A heavy silence fell over the room. Eliza didn't dare allow any opportunity for more questions she couldn't answer.

"Mr. Archer sent word to the stage company about my inn." It was as good a change of topic as she could manage. "If they agree to make it an end-of-the-day stop, we'll be able to start building."

"How soon is that likely to be?" Cecily asked.

The group apparently accepted the new subject.

Eliza looked to Katie. "Do you know?"

"Joseph expects to hear from them within a week or two."

A week or two. So close.

"I heard talk of your inn at the *céilí*," Mrs. O'Connor said. "Word of your project has spread."

"And are people excited?" Eliza asked.

"The feeling is mixed."

Eliza's heart dropped. She'd fully expected enthusiasm.

"What has the town concerned?" Katie asked.

"Having an inn would change Hope Springs," Mrs. O'Connor said. "The worry is *how* it might change." She returned to stirring a pot on the stove. "Our valley has always been quiet and private. If stage passengers begin staying here, it won't be so hidden. That worries people."

"The place we want to build on is out by the existing stage road," Eliza said. "The town and valley can't be seen from there; the hill hides it."

That seemed to reassure the room. The O'Connors, apparently, had shared some of their neighbors' concerns.

"Would the stage passengers and drivers come into town often, do you suppose?" Ciara asked. "Having strangers wandering in and out all the time would be a bit uncomfortable."

"I can't say that none would ever venture over the hill," Eliza said. "But they'd have no need to."

"What if they're in need of something at the mercantile or from the blacksmith?" Biddy asked.

Eliza didn't have an answer for that.

"A great many roadside accommodations, especially out west, are taverns and saloons," Mrs. O'Connor said. "There's a lot of worry about that." But she was quick to add, "I can't imagine you'd run a questionable establishment, of course, but we've not had much liquor here in Hope Springs. Having it so easily bought and drunk would— *could* lead to trouble."

Here was another complication Eliza hadn't considered.

The Charred Oak had always served beer and ale, though never anything stronger. Not doing the same hadn't occurred to her.

If doing so would turn the town against her inn, then perhaps hers should be a dry establishment. On the other hand, travelers and drivers would most certainly expect that option. Disappointing them wasn't good business; travelers mightn't stay at her inn at all.

But if the town resented her inn . . .

She had to come up with a solution. She knew all too well the devastating impact of resentment—what it did to people and connections—and she couldn't bear to be a source of regret in the lives of people she cared about.

Not again.

Chapter Nineteen

"I think you'd best give the orders, Da," Patrick said. "I'm not certain everyone'll take direction from me."

Ian wouldn't, at least. And Patrick had his doubts about his sister's husband, Thomas. His other brothers-in-law were still virtual strangers to him. He also doubted that Finbarr and Aidan would pick a different approach from the rest of the family.

"'Tis your project, son. They'll listen to you."

"And if they don't?" He'd managed to not say *when* they don't, but that would've been the more accurate question.

"I'll knock a bit o' sense into their thick skulls. I've done it before." The years had aged Da, but he still held himself with the strength and confidence Patrick had depended on so much as a boy. "Life's taken a lot from Finbarr; it's well and past time it gave a little back." That was the determined and optimistic Da he remembered.

"You're talking as if life were fair. I've not found that to be the case."

"Aye, sure seems the lot of us are in the field when luck comes walking down the road. But together, we can snag a bit for one or the other of us. Often takes a bit of work, a bit of sacrifice."

Patrick watched the others chatting and gathering up their tools. "You'd work and sacrifice for Finbarr, to give him a spot of good fortune?"

"For any of m'children."

Patrick forced down a lump in his throat. His voice emerged a little quiet, a little broken. "Would you do that for me?"

Da's eyes were on the others, but there wasn't a doubt all his focus was on Patrick. "Would you let me?"

"That's a taller ask than you likely realize."

Da rocked back and forth from his toes to his heels. "I left Ireland for the sake of my children. I toiled in New York for the good of my children. I came here and helped build this town from the ground up to give my children a future." He turned and looked directly at Patrick. "And if I'd known the past ten years that you were in Canada, I'd've gone there and found you and done whatever you needed, Patrick, and I'd've begged you to come home if you'd been willing. There's nothing I wouldn't do for you, but you have to let me."

What he needed was for his da to know what he'd been through, to see the person he was and the person he was trying to be, but that meant sharing truths he didn't think he could; that meant betraying confidences he hadn't any right to betray. And yet, the weight of it all was crushing him. He was going through his bottles of whiskey, his need for it growing the past days. He woke up every morning lately feeling the guilt that always accompanied the next-day headache. The thought of running out of his liquid escape had him starting to panic.

He needed help, but he couldn't ask that of Da. The man loved his children too much for Patrick to even risk casting doubt and shadow over Grady's memory.

"There's one thing I'll let you do," Patrick said, affecting his most unconcerned tone and posture, one he knew Da didn't believe for a moment. "I'll let you round up those lazy bums over there and set them to work on this roof."

Da let him hide behind the shield he'd put up. With no more than a simple nod, Da crossed to the others. Patrick truly breathed for the first time in minutes. He'd come to Hope Springs looking for exactly what Da was offering, but what if he couldn't ever accept it? How long could he live his life so close to what he needed but unable to cross the chasm?

All these men, except Aidan, he imagined, had built soddies

before. They didn't need him to tell them what to do, which was likely for the best. The few times they sought out direction, the lot of them turned instinctively to Da, who tried, at first, to defer to Patrick, but in the end bowed to the unavoidable: Patrick hadn't any real sway with this group.

In the end, though, he found he didn't truly mind. Working alongside his brothers and brothers-in-law felt more natural than giving them orders.

By midday, they'd assembled a good amount of the roof. Patrick, Tavish, Thomas, Keefe—Ciara's husband—and Ryan stood on ladders and, as the roof took shape and could hold weight, they stood on the roof itself. Da, Finbarr, Aidan, and Ian kept their feet on the ground, bringing supplies and steadying the ladders. Everyone seemed content with the arrangement . . . except Ian.

When he suggested, again, that he could be more useful off the ground, Da said, "Biddy'd kill the lot of us."

"She worries more than she needs to," Ian insisted. "I've not had a dizzy spell in months. And I'm not so stubborn or thickheaded that I'd insist on staying up there if I found it to be too much. But that colleen has it in her head that I oughtn't ever even try."

"We promised her," Tavish said. "None of us is going back on our word. All the women would slaughter us if we did. We'd none of us hear the end of it."

The brothers tossed in their agreement. Patrick watched as Ian's tiny glimmer of hope faded and defeat pulled at his shoulders. He knew that posture. Ian had worn it before. Patrick saw it often in the mirror as well. He couldn't bear seeing it now.

"*I* didn't promise her," he said from the top of his ladder.

Everyone looked at him. Even Finbarr turned in his direction.

"Biddy told me her reasons for your not being up on your own roof, but she didn't make me promise anything." He began climbing down. "You can use my ladder. I'll hand you what you need."

Ian hesitated, but there was no mistaking the renewed life in his eyes, and even a shimmer of gratitude. "She really will kill you."

Patrick reached the ground. "The entire Confederate Army tried to kill me, and they didn't manage it. I think I like my odds better in this battle." He stopped right in front of Ian. "And if Biddy does decide to do away with me, I'll accept my fate with dignity and weep and beg only when there aren't any witnesses. You know, for the sake of the family's dignity and all."

"We may do better to pin our hopes of dignity on Biddy, then." Just enough cheek lay in Ian's words to bring a smile to Patrick's face. They used to joke like this easily and regularly. To have even a hint of it back was doing him a great deal of good.

"Oh, I've always pinned a lot of hopes on Biddy. She made something of you, didn't she?"

"That she did." Ian never looked happier than he did when talking about his wife. "And for her sake"—he looked out over his gathered family—"none of you'd better run off and tattle about this."

Chuckles and amused shakes of the head answered his threat, but no one objected.

Patrick hooked his thumb toward his abandoned ladder. "Up with you, then. Just tell me what you need."

Ian hesitated. He watched Patrick for a drawn-out minute, a question in his expression,. After a moment, he simply nodded and took up his new position. Work resumed, but with a lot of curious glances in Ian's direction. If he noticed them, he didn't let on.

As Patrick crossed paths with Da in their role of fetching and delivering, Da stopped him with a hand on his arm. Voice lowered, he said, "We've been holding him back. I didn't even see it until now. He needed someone who'd let him try to move forward."

Patrick shrugged. "I tossed Finbarr up on a roof a few weeks ago and kept him from accidentally killing himself. I think I can manage the same with Ian."

Da grinned. "Cecily's been singing your praises ever since she heard about you tying the lad to the chimney and all the work you've had him do on this house. The one thing she snips at the lot of us about is babying Finbarr."

"Does anyone snip at you for babying Ian?"

"Ian."

Patrick gave him a pointed look. "Maybe we oughta start listening to him. Now and then, at least."

"He always was quieter than the rest of us. But you were always the one telling us to listen when we sometimes forgot to." Da gave him a nod as he resumed his path toward the pile of cut shingles. "It'll be good for him to have you doing that again."

"Do you think he'll let me?"

Da looked back over his shoulder. "After today, I think you've a growing chance he will."

Ian proved himself more than capable of doing the work he'd insisted he could. Within the first half hour, the brothers all stopped watching him with worry and simply settled into the rhythm of their work. Laughter flowed as easily as water to the sea. Though Patrick's place was firmly at the edges of the group, he felt increasingly part of it.

He especially appreciated seeing Aidan interact with Ryan. The lad had lost his father at too young an age. To see him have a father-son bond with someone who clearly loved him did Patrick's guilt-burdened heart a great deal of good. He'd worried about the boy from the moment Grady had declared his intention to join the war effort. That anxiety hadn't eased at all over the years.

He remembered all too well Aidan's little five-year-old voice telling him, in tones of awe and pride, "My da was a hero. He went to save the country, and he went to save his brother. That makes him brave."

If there was a chance that explaining what really happened would change how this lad, who'd had so much snatched away in his short life, thought of his father, Patrick wouldn't risk it. The truth was not the most comforting of companions, and it had kept him constant company these past years.

Patrick sat beside Finbarr during a lull in their work. "Once the roof's sound, I'd be happy to tie you to the chimney."

Finbarr laughed a little. His scars tugged at things when he smiled and talked and laughed, but not in a grotesque or unsettling way. The disfigurement added a poignancy to his expressions. "Feels good doing something no one, including me, thought I could do. I confess, it was terrifying. I'd do it again if I had to, but whenever I have the option, I'll keep my feet on the ground."

"Can't say I blame you." Patrick leaned back on his elbows, enjoying a minute to breathe. "This'll be a fine house for you, Finbarr. I know it will be. And I built it as solidly as I could. It should withstand nearly anything this ol' world throws at it. I'll be plastering and whitewashing the inside. That'll brighten it up."

"I appreciate all the windows," he said. "I like that."

"The glass is meant to arrive with Mr. Johnson's son next week. I'll be making your door before then. After that, there won't be much left before it's ready for you to move in."

Nervousness filled the lad's posture, though he didn't say anything.

"To move in whenever you *want* to," Patrick clarified. "It's not going anywhere."

Finbarr's relief was palpable. Why was he so hesitant to strike out on his own? Patrick had seen the lad's confidence and competence on display time and again at Archers'. He'd watched Finbarr navigate the path from the road to this house more than once. He'd seen him make his way all over town assisted only by his cane. He'd wager Cecily had taught Finbarr to cook, clean, and look after himself.

Why, then, did he not want to claim his life and his future?

"I'll likely stay where I am for now." Finbarr's casual tone fell a bit short of the mark. "But you could live here for a time. Then you could work on whatever needed doing whenever you could get to it. No need to rush."

An excuse. Finbarr likely suspected that Patrick could tell, but, being up to his eyes in uncertainty himself, he wasn't going to push the boy.

"I just might take you up on that. Living in our parents' house isn't an ideal arrangement. Makes a body feel like a child."

Finbarr nodded in immediate agreement.

"I will, though, have to find a way to buy food," Patrick said dryly. "Not having a paying job makes eating a bit trickier."

"Once Eliza's inn gets moving, you'll be paid for that work."

"Do you know if Joseph's heard anything more on that score?"

"I heard him telling Eliza that the stage company didn't like the location."

That was surprising. "'Tis the perfect spot for an inn."

"Apparently not for an overnight stop on the route."

That was a setback. "What'd Eliza have to say about that?"

"Do you think I'm an unabashed eavesdropper?" Finbarr asked.

"I'm paying you handsomely to be."

Finbarr's smile tipped unevenly. "You're paying me?"

"Did I not mention that?"

Finbarr laughed. Da looked in their direction, a look of happy relief on his face.

"So, what'd she say, lad?" Patrick pressed.

"She said maybe the inn could be moved farther south to make it a first-day stop. Joseph sent another telegram."

A logical solution, but Patrick couldn't help thinking of Eliza's joy over the original location. She was likely disappointed.

"Does Joseph think the stage company will accept the new proposal?"

"He didn't say, but I heard Maura say she's not certain Eliza would stay in Hope Springs if the inn doesn't get built." Finbarr shared the comment without seeming to realize the blow it dealt Patrick. "She doesn't like working as a housekeeper, even though she's willing. But how long can she keep doing that before her unhappiness becomes too much? Maura's fretting over it a lot."

Now Patrick would be fretting over it too, which made him every sort of a fool. He had nothing to offer a woman. And if she left, he'd miss her.

"Life is a difficult thing, Finbarr," he said.

"Cecily says the added difficulty comes with added joy. I'm counting on that being true."

The idea offered a tentative bit of hope, something he needed desperately just then. "So am I."

Chapter Twenty

Eliza had helped the Archer girls get ready to leave for the *céilí* and now stood with them in the front entry, buttoning up Ivy's coat.

"We need to be going, Joseph. We'll be late for the *céilí*." Katie's voice carried through the house. She didn't sound angry, only excited for the weekly outing.

The wind was blowing even more fiercely than usual, and the air held a hint of rain. The party might be cut short.

Joseph peeked his head around the doorway to the sitting room. "Do you have a minute, Eliza?"

She nodded, fastening Ivy's last coat button, then joined her employer in the more formal room. "Is something the matter?"

"Unfortunately, yes." He motioned to the papers on his desk near the front windows. "A telegram arrived from the stage company."

For perhaps the hundredth time since proposing her idea, Eliza's heart dropped to her feet, weighed down by yet another impending disappointment. "They didn't like our compromise?"

"They still think even a few miles outside of Hope Springs won't be an ideal stopping point."

She pushed out a deep, heavy breath, trying to will herself to be calm and confident. "If I move it as far away as the stage company wishes, I'll be hours and hours away from the nearest town or farm or anything else. Dr. Jones won't want his infirmary there. We'd be too far away for Mr. Johnson's mercantile to benefit, so I cannot imagine that he'd continue to be an investor."

"I can guarantee he wouldn't," Joseph said. "And I wouldn't own the land you'd be building on. You'd have no choice but to buy it yourself, assuming we could find the owner and that the owner isn't the United States government, which would make any transaction so complicated I can't imagine it being completed in your lifetime."

The obstacles kept piling higher and higher. How could she possibly overcome one of them, let alone a mountain of them?

Katie stepped into the room, little Sean in her arms. "Are you about ready, love?"

"I am." Joseph held his arms out for their son. After the transfer was made, he wrapped one arm around his wife. "I am sorry to have brought you bad news, Eliza."

She waved off his worry. It wasn't his fault, after all. "I will think on all of this and see if I can't dream up a solution."

"As will I."

The family was gone after a moment, leaving the house quiet and Eliza's thoughts spinning. She fed Lydia and herself and buttoned them both up in their coats, but she couldn't bring herself around to the idea of joining the *céilí*. If she'd thought Patrick would be there, she might have been tempted. But he hadn't attended the last two, having moved out of his parents' house. She'd heard enough from his sisters and sisters-in-law at their weekly sewing circle to know that things were a little better between Patrick and the rest of the O'Connors. Certainly not whole or even truly happy, but better. She longed to ask him about that change and longed to tell him of her frustrations with her inn. He'd listened before; surely he would again.

"Should we go visit Patrick?" Though she asked Lydia, she was really inquiring of herself. As soon as she asked the question, she knew the answer.

Five minutes later, they were making their way toward the river, not to cross at the bridge, but to turn and walk toward the house Patrick currently called home.

The wind blew something fierce. The sky was leaden, with fast-moving clouds. The *céilí* wasn't likely to last to its usual late hour. Here was yet another reason the town ought to have been excited about the possibility of a nearby inn: their weekly party could be held inside when the weather was uncooperative.

If she could just see it built, those who were still unconvinced would see that she was offering them something of value. She had Patrick add to his building plans, a little room in the inn with a few things that passengers might wish to purchase from the mercantile, so they could buy what they needed without going into town. She'd also spoken with Seamus Kelly, the local blacksmith, about the possibility of building a small forge near the inn, should his services be needed. While she still hadn't settled the matter of alcohol at the inn, she'd found answers to all of the town's other concerns.

Couldn't the stage company see that her inn was worth changing their schedule for? Building the inn would show Lydia that her mum could provide her a home and hope . . . and *shoes*, for heaven's sake.

It all felt so out of reach.

When Eliza and Lydia arrived, light flickered inside the house. Patrick was home, then. Her nervousness and excitement halted her a moment, but only a moment. She knocked at the door and waited.

The door opened. A very confused Patrick eyed her standing there.

She offered what was probably an awkward smile. "I had a feeling you wouldn't be at the *céilí.*"

"So you thought you'd join the party I must've been hostin' here?" Drier than a desert, that answer. Was he not at all happy to see her after two weeks? For heaven's sake, he'd embraced her the last time they were together. He'd nearly kissed her. Did he regret those things?

"Don't fret, Mr. Patrick. I'll make absolutely certain not to enjoy myself or smile or say anything that isn't strictly business. And"—she could feel emotion climbing her neck—"I certainly don't expect you to pretend like you are"—the emotion thickened—"at all happy to see me. But you could at least"—she choked a bit on the lump in her throat—"let me get out two words before—before—" Merciful heavens, tears were actually falling. "Oh, never mind, you grumpy, grumpy man." She spun and turned to go.

"Eliza." He spoke her name so quietly, so tenderly.

She stopped but didn't turn back. She kept Lydia close and tried in vain to stop her tears, but she was too tired, too worn down, too frustrated by life. Patrick left the doorway and stepped outside, over the threshold, facing her.

Eliza tried to look firm and unaffected, but her chin quivered, giving her away.

He put his arms around her and Lydia and held them gently. "I'm sorry. I'd not meant to make you feel unwelcome."

She leaned into his unexpected but very-needed embrace. "I've had a horrible day, Patrick. Absolutely horrible, and there was no one I could talk to about it."

"Is that why you came here?"

She took a shaky breath and nodded, though she wasn't sure he could tell.

"Come inside. Tell me why things've been so horrible."

This was precisely what she'd come hoping for, yet she hesitated. "You didn't seem too keen on that a minute ago."

"Lydia convinced me."

She could smile at that. "We mustn't disappoint her."

His arms dropped away, but he didn't leave her there on the stoop. Instead, he took her hand in his and led her across the threshold and inside the house.

She'd expected it to be more or less empty inside, knowing the state of his coffers. But it had a small table, a few chairs, and shelves to the side forming something of a makeshift kitchen. The blanket she'd sat on when she'd come visiting was now spread out like a rug in front of the fireplace. A quilt hung from the rafters, dividing off part of the room.

"The family made some donations," he said, motioning to the furniture.

"You have more furniture than I do," she pointed out.

"But Lydia has the best furniture of all."

"True." Smiling felt good. It drove away a bit of the misery she'd been feeling. "Her little bed is just perfect."

"A nod to the designer." Patrick motioned her over to the chairs near the fireplace.

Eliza set Lydia on the blanket, then sat beside her. She might eventually move to a chair, but the little girl looked a bit overwhelmed. Patrick sat on the blanket with her and her daughter.

"I-und!" Lydia scooted over to him, holding up her doll for his inspection.

"Patrick," he reminded her.

"Pa-ick."

He met Eliza's eye. "She's getting closer."

Lydia repositioned herself so she leaned a little against Patrick's leg while she played with her doll and handkerchief.

He looked at Eliza. "Tell me about your day."

"Joseph received another telegram from the stage company." She released a tight breath. "They rejected our proposal to move the inn ten miles south so it could be a first-day stopping point."

"Ten miles?" Patrick whistled low. "That's a good pace away from town."

"The stage company says it's too far to go the first day, but too soon to stop on the second. But if we build even farther away from Hope Springs as they suggest, the mercantile and Dr. Jones would have to withdraw from the project."

"Did Joseph have any ideas for how to proceed?"

She shook her head. "I don't know what to do," she whispered. "The inn is feeling more and more impossible."

He brushed his hand over Lydia's hair as naturally as if he'd been doing it all her life. The O'Connor women had said he'd always had a way with children, a statement that was proving comfortingly true.

"I wish I had some grand solution," he said.

"I do feel a little better just having talked to you about it. And knowing you'll be trying to think of an answer helps me feel less alone."

Was he blushing under those whiskers? She liked that, even being as grumpy and stand-offish as he could be, he was still tenderhearted enough to color up at a compliment.

Lydia looked up at him, her little face pulled in worry that faded to a smile of relief when she saw that he was still there.

"If you aren't careful," she said, "Lydia will grow so attached to you that you'll be forced to fill this house with dolls and handker-chiefs."

He smiled at that. Heavens, she enjoyed seeing his rare smiles. "That wouldn't be such a terrible thing."

"Do your nieces and nephews cuddle up to you as readily as Lydia does?"

He shook his head. "I don't see much of them. Even when I have dinners with the family, most of them keep their distance."

"Most of the children?" she asked.

"Most everyone." Sadness touched the words.

Eliza turned to face him more directly. "Have you told them any bit of what you told me a couple of weeks ago?"

She could see the answer in the stiffening of his posture and the tightening of his lips.

"I'd thought things were a bit better between you and your family. I thought perhaps you'd opened up a bit."

He accepted the handkerchief doll Lydia offered him. "Even if I'd told them any of what I shared with you, it wouldn't be enough. There's just too much between us. Too much I can't tell them."

She scooted closer, sitting almost as near to him as her daughter was. "Then tell *me* a tiny bit of it, just enough to lift some of the weight from your heart."

He eyed her. She felt certain she saw the tiniest bit of his walls weakening.

"I'll tell you something about me," Eliza said, "and then you can tell me something about you. Give and take."

"I don't know."

"Contrary to what you probably believe about me, I don't share confidences easily. It would be a far fairer exchange than you likely realize."

Lydia laid her head on his leg, still playing with her doll, but more slowly and droopily. He continued stroking her hair in a soothing rhythm. "I can choose which things I reveal?"

"Of course."

He hesitated for the length of a drawn-out breath before indicating she should go ahead.

"When I was five years old, I stole a peppermint from the sweetshop in our town."

He gasped theatrically. "I didn't know you were a criminal!"

She swatted at him. "Your turn."

"During the passage from Ireland, I snuck up to the first-class dining room and swiped a pastry."

"I assume they threw you overboard as punishment," she said.

With an amused smirk, he said, "They never caught me."

It was again her turn to share something. "I once told my mum that she looked beautiful in a yellow dress, but she looked awful."

He chuckled. "When I was twelve years old, I kissed two girls in one day and felt so horribly guilty that I ran—literally ran—to the chapel to confess to the priest."

She didn't bother hiding her amusement. "Was he horrified?"

"I am absolutely certain he was struggling not to laugh."

What else could she share with him? She wanted to maintain their lighter tone, but also hoped he would touch on the heavier things that weighed on him. "When I worked in the factory in New York the first time, I used to pray every morning that the men who repaired the machines when they broke down wouldn't show up to work so that there was a chance we'd be done for the day before lunch."

"I can do better than that." He leaned close. "I was one of the men who repaired the machines."

She laughed out loud. His eyes twinkled back at her. Their exchange of "secrets" was doing her burdened heart good, and it seemed to be offering the same to him.

"Lydia cried so constantly when she was an infant that, though I loved her even before she was born, I struggled a little to *like* her. That made me feel rather like a horrible mother. But Maura told me it was nothing to be ashamed of. 'Difficult babies make life difficult,' she would say."

He didn't look the least shocked or disgusted. He took her hand in his. "You and Maura were good friends."

"We became like sisters. I don't know what I would have done without her."

He rubbed her hand between his. The movement warmed more

than her fingers. "She took me in after the war," he said, "and never made me feel like a burden. She was family to me when I had no one. I don't know what *I* would have done without her."

Surely that history and connection could give him some hope that Maura, if no one else, wouldn't cut him off. "So what is it you're still not telling her?"

He stiffened a little but didn't release her hand. "That's a far more complicated thing than what we've been tossing around tonight, Eliza. Far bigger."

"You need a bigger confession in exchange for it?"

He shook his head. "That's not what I meant."

But she knew in her heart it would help. She had only one unspoken truth kept inside that was as big as the enormity of weight in his expression. She swallowed, breathed, and let the words fall from her mouth, words she never thought she'd say. "My husband told me he regretted marrying me."

Patrick's eyes pulled wide. His mouth hung a tad open. "What?"

All the ache of that long-ago moment returned, but amplified. "He was working in a bar, which he hated. We were struggling to house and feed and clothe ourselves, and had only just realized I was going to have a baby. He saw no light ahead. He missed his family and the life he'd lost. In a heated moment, he admitted that he regretted *us.* That his family had been right, that our origins created a chasm between him and me that was too wide to ever cross."

"Saints above," he whispered. His mouth hung a bit agape, shock pulling his features.

"When things were calmer, he apologized and insisted he hadn't meant it, but the regret was always there lurking in his face." She dropped her gaze to their entwined hands. "He died less than a month later, trying to break up a fight between two drunkards in the bar. Everyone, including Maura, thinks he and I had a fairy-tale love story, that he gave up everything for me and never once looked back. But that's not true. He was miserable, and he regretted the life he gave up. He resented me for being the reason he had to live the life we had."

"How could anyone regret having you in their life?"

"He said in marrying me, he'd burned the one bridge he

desperately wanted to cross back over, that he was stuck." She looked up at him. "The most difficult thing was that he was right."

"Eliza." He cupped her hand between his.

"Marrying me was the reason he was in that bar, and he wasn't happy there." She emptied her lungs once more before pushing ahead. "There. I shared the biggest secret I carry around with me. You owe me something equally heavy."

He looked away, his gaze on the low-burning fire. "You are a stiff bargainer, Eliza Porter."

"And I'm as unmovable as the snowcapped mountains." She wouldn't have pressed him if she didn't know that unburdening his mind would help him heal.

Lydia had fallen asleep with her head on his leg. He gently shifted her onto the blanket, her arm still draped over her beloved doll. Eliza waited patiently, knowing he would speak when he was ready.

After a moment, he faced her once more. His expression had turned nearly blank, except for the determined angle of his eyebrows. "Grady and I both fought with the Irish Regiment of New York. You can ask anyone in the O'Connor family, and they'll tell you the story they all know well. He and I stayed behind when the family went west. I did because, as they see it, I loved being in the city more than I loved being with my family. Grady stayed behind because he loved Maura too much to even consider talking her into leaving behind her parents and sister."

"Neither of which is entirely true," she said. He'd told her that much already.

"Right. After a time, war broke out, and the Irish in New York began signing up to fight and defend this new home of ours. I was so hotheaded and impulsive that I signed up immediately. Grady, being the loving soul he was, signed up as well to protect *me*. He put himself in harm's way for his brother, the act of a true hero and near-saint. Then he died in a battle he was fighting in only because of me. And I, the one who'd recruited the danger in the first place, survived. An act of cruel fate. He lives on in their memories as the saintly brother he was, and I am the one they love *anyway*, the one they love *even though*."

He didn't speak with bitterness, but with undeniable pain.

"How much of that family lore is true?" she asked

In a quiet voice, he said, "Only some."

He'd released her hand when he'd tended to Lydia. She took hold of his again. "I'm listening."

"I debated enlisting once the fighting began. I kept hesitating, going back to how much I wanted to be able to join my family out West. Fighting in a war meant, assuming I survived, it'd be years before that was even a possibility. One day while I was trying to decide what to do, Grady came home—I was living with him and Maura at the time—and he told me in confidence that he'd enlisted. He felt strongly about the cause, knew this was a country worth saving, but he also knew he had to get out of the city for a time. He felt as if it were closing in on him."

"That was an awful risk, going to war to escape New York."

"It wasn't his primary reason, but, yes, it was a little foolhardy. I think he realized that fairly quickly, but he was a man of his word and wouldn't go back on it. And he really did want to defend the country he'd come to love."

Patrick was growing stiffer, more distant. Eliza wrapped her arm around his, as she'd done weeks before in his parents' loft. She rested her head against his shoulder, hoping the silent show of support would bolster him.

"I wanted to defend the country, too. I'd wanted to from the first rumblings of war, but I'd hesitated. Grady taking that leap was what finally pushed me past my reluctance. I figured we'd fight together and look out for each other."

Eliza was beginning to piece together the rest of his confession, and her heart ached all the more for him. Still, she said nothing.

"So I went and signed up as well, vowing silently to the family that I'd keep him safe. He had a wife and child who needed him to return safe and whole."

"You followed him to battle, not the other way around," Eliza whispered.

"I hadn't realized until returning to Maura's house after the war, after Grady was killed, that she'd assumed the opposite. She thought, and so did all of the family, that I was the one who put Grady in danger, that my rash decision had cost his little family their husband and father. They believed Grady had sacrificed everything to protect me, and though I don't know that they'd ever say it, there's a feeling of his death being my fault."

"Oh, Patrick."

"He is the hero who gave all, and in a very real way that is true. He was the bravest of the soldiers I fought alongside. He gave everything he had to the very end."

"Which is likely part of why you are so reluctant to tell the family how things actually came to be, though doing so would likely heal some of the resentment between your family and yourself."

He didn't answer for a moment. She could feel his breathing grow shakier. "I can't tell them anything about those years of fighting. What if something I say makes them think less of him? I don't want them to. They shouldn't. But I feel like no one knows me, no one knows the burden I carry, or the weight that's crushing me."

She looked up at him. "*I* know."

A soft, subtle hint of a smile touched his face. "You do. And you were right: it helps to speak of it."

"Why did you leave New York for Canada? No one seems to have an answer for that."

He adjusted his position and, to her delight and comfort, set his arms around her, holding her in a warm and tender embrace. "Aidan talked a lot about how his father was extra brave because he fought to protect me even though he didn't want to go to war. He didn't remember anything about Grady, but that . . . that version of things gave him something of his father to cling to. I couldn't risk taking that away from him. I still can't." He breathed deeply, the way she often did when feeling burdened. "It's easier being the villain at a distance."

"But you aren't the villain."

He sat, quietly holding her. She looked up at him only to find his gaze had grown distant. "What if they won't believe that?"

"What if they will?"

A clap of thunder shook the air. It startled Lydia awake, sending her immediately into sobs. Natural as anything, Patrick picked her up and rocked her, cooing soothingly. Eliza looked to the windows. No rain pelted the glass.

"I think we'd best head back to Archers' so we don't get caught in the rain."

"Aye. That'd be wise." He stood and held his hand out to her.

She accepted the offer and got to her feet as well. They were all three soon bundled and following the river in the wrenching wind. Patrick pulled his coat around Lydia, shielding her against the onslaught.

"You'll both need warmer coats before winter." He spoke loudly enough to be heard over the cry of the wind as they approached the Archer home.

"And she'll need shoes," Eliza said. "Perhaps I would do best to abandon my idea of an inn and simply be grateful I have income as a housekeeper." She stepped up onto the porch and took Lydia from him. "Some dreams are just too grand to hold on to forever."

He stepped up with her, standing close enough for his ice-blue eyes to be visible even in the dark of approaching night. "The grandest of dreams don't die, Eliza. Don't let them go yet."

"It's difficult to hold on to things that feel impossible," she said.

His arm slowly wrapped around her waist and pulled her close to him. "Perhaps you're not holding on in the right way."

Her pulse, pounding in her neck, grew loud enough to drown out the howling wind. "You know the right way, do you?"

He lowered his voice. "I'm beginning to sort it out."

She breathed slowly, tensely. Prickles tiptoed over every inch of her. "I'm getting an inkling, myself," she whispered.

She could feel the warmth of him so nearby, could hear every breath he took.

"Does this feel impossible to you?" he asked, his lips a mere inch from hers.

"It feels perfect."

In the very next moment, wagon wheels sounded in the darkness. As quickly as it had begun, the spell between them was broken.

He took a step back. "Thank you for letting me spill my secrets."

"And me mine. It's good to feel like I really know you. Finally."

He stepped off the porch. "Good night, Eliza," he said. Then he disappeared into the night.

Chapter Twenty-one

The morning after Eliza had come to visit him, Patrick did something he'd not done even once since coming to Hope Springs: he drank during the day. He kept himself to a single, albeit generous, swallow, telling himself it was temporary liquid courage.

Eliza had such faith in him, far more than he had in himself. And she believed in his family's love for him—far more than he'd allowed himself to believe in it for years. He didn't want to disappoint her. So he'd concocted a plan during his long and sleepless night.

He grabbed the bundle he'd pulled from his traveling trunk. The one he was going to bring to Da and Ma's house at the weekly family dinner. The one he was terrified to show them but knew it was time he did.

Patrick rubbed at the back of his neck as he stood at his front door, willing himself to begin his long walk. "It's easier being the villain at a distance," he'd told Eliza. He'd been more truthful in that moment with her than he had been with anyone in years.

"But you aren't a villain," she'd said.

If she could believe that he wasn't, then maybe his family could, as well. He stepped over his threshold and set his feet determinedly in the direction of his parents' house. He paused, as he so often did, on the bridge spanning the river, letting the sound of the water soothe him. He closed his eyes and listened and breathed.

"You aren't the villain," he told himself. Even if only Eliza ever believed that of him, it was true to someone, and that mattered.

He repeated the reassurance a few times as he walked down the road. He had ample time to convince himself not to turn tail and run—as well as ample time to do precisely that.

In the end, he pushed himself all the way to the door of his parents' home without losing his nerve. That he'd needed whiskey to hold on to that courage didn't reflect well on him.

Drinking during the day. He was in deep trouble if that became a regular thing again.

Ma spotted him straight away and hugged him the moment he slipped inside. He was so used to coming and going unnoticed. Whichever house they met at was always chaotic, full near to bursting with people. No one had a table large enough for all of them, so O'Connors sat and stood scattered throughout, carrying plates of food around with them. How easy it'd be to drop himself in the corner and let the gathering happen without him. He very nearly did, but then he saw her.

Eliza.

She stood not more than ten feet away, chatting with Maura.

He'd come within a breath of kissing her last night. The wind had rustled her hair, bringing a tinge of pink to her cheeks. She'd looked at him in such a way . . . But the return of the Archer family had stopped things just in time.

He was living a lot of lies, and she deserved better than that. Last night, he'd been a heartbeat away from tossing back the first of many mouthfuls when she'd knocked at his door. She, who'd lost her husband to drunkards, had very nearly arrived at the home of one. She deserved so very, very much better.

One of Mary's children noticed the bundle he'd brought with him and asked the question he'd been both dreading and anticipating.

"What's that?"

Here it was: the moment of truth. "It's a haversack."

Ian's oldest boy hovered nearby. "What's a haversack?"

Patrick pushed ahead. "It's a bag carried by a soldier."

VALLEY OF DREAMS

"Like in the war you fought?" the boy asked.

Patrick nodded.

The boys gathered nearby, clearly intrigued by the beaten, faded, black bag. A few other family members took note, watching.

Ian's daughter broke the momentary silence. "Was it your bag when you were a soldier?"

Patrick's eye caught Maura's, and for a moment he almost lost his nerve. "It was Uncle Grady's."

That brought the entire house to a complete standstill. No one spoke or moved or ate—or likely breathed.

For his part, Patrick was actually shaking. Would they resent that he, of all people, had brought them a piece of their lost family member's wartime service? Would it make them only more resentful? Eliza pushed her way through the crowd closing in around him and took his hand. She led him to the long bench in the midst of the gathering, with room enough for them both. She sat beside him. Her presence made all the difference. Saints preserve him, in that moment he let her be his strength.

"Every soldier had a haversack to carry our things in," he told his gathered family. "These went everywhere with us. But when a soldier—" He swallowed. "A haversack without an owner"—that seemed a softer way of speaking about death in battle—"was given to the quartermaster to be redistributed. I couldn't let that happen to Grady's after he—" This was every bit as difficult as he'd feared it would be. "I gave them mine, and I carried his sack and his canteen and his bedroll."

For the first few weeks he'd used it, the bag had even smelled like Grady. That had been torture. "I carried it with me the rest of the war. And it has traveled with me all over Canada."

All eyes were on the bundle, but no one moved.

"Nothing is more important to a soldier than his haversack and equipment. And these were his." He pushed the words out. "This bag and its contents were with him from the moment he left home"—he met Maura's teary gaze—"until the day he died."

"If a haversack is so important to a soldier," Mary's son asked, "why did you give yours away?"

197

"Because I wanted something of Grady's to carry with me, something of his to bring back home. This was all I had. All *he* had."

"The tintypes were in this bag, then?" Ma asked.

Tintypes? He looked to Maura. "You kept them?"

"Both. Of course I did."

He shook his head. "I really didn't want you to keep mine."

"Well, I wanted to keep it. 'Something of you to carry with me.'"

Ma had slipped out and returned nearly too quickly to be noticed, holding something he recognized at a glance: the hinged leather frame held a glass-etched portrait of either Grady or himself.

"Which one is it?" he asked, afraid of the answer.

"Grady's is at Maura's house, of course," Ma said.

His, then. That was the last thing he wanted to look at. He turned, instead, to his nieces and nephews. He motioned to the haversack. "It's filled with a few things of your uncle Grady's, things you've likely not seen before. You can dig through it." To their parents, he said, "No weapons or dangerous things inside. I swear to it."

The children needed no more encouragement. The grownups joined in the exploration soon thereafter. Noticeably absent from the perusal were Maura and Aidan, though they watched closely.

Maybe he should have brought these things to Grady's wife and son first. Saints, he couldn't seem to do anything right.

Lydia crawled from her perch on Eliza's lap to his and curled into him as she often did and wrapped her arms around her doll.

Ma slipped closer. "Maura brought this to us when she moved here last year." Patrick's pulse pounded painfully in his head. "We've kept it here ever since, but now that you're here . . ." She held out the tintype.

"I don't want it, Ma." He tried to keep his tone casual but knew he didn't manage it. "I left it with Maura for a reason."

"Do you not even want to see it?" She tried again to give it to him.

He couldn't entirely stop himself from recoiling. "No."

It was Ian who asked the next question. "Why not?"

Patrick had braced himself for interrogations but still wasn't completely prepared for the question. "Those were the worst years of my life. I hated everything about that war. I don't want to have to look at myself living my own nightmare, and that's what I'd see in my face if I ever open that leather frame."

Ian looked confused. "When did you start hating the war?"

"The first time I saw someone die," he muttered, dropping his gaze to the younger ones still rummaging through the haversack. Thus far, they'd pulled out the tin coffee cup, the metal mess kit, Grady's canteen and compass. "Though I never was eager for battle, even before we left home."

Lydia's tiny hand reached up and touched his cheek. "Sad."

He smiled at her. "I'm happy you're sitting with me, *mo stóirín*."

She held up her doll for him, and he offered it a kiss on the head. She mimicked the gesture before returning to her quiet play.

Eliza leaned closer to him. "You aren't a villain," she whispered.

He turned his head toward her, hiding his mouth from any curious eyes. He dropped his voice to a near-silent whisper. "I haven't told them everything."

"But you've told me everything, and you've made a start with them."

He pulled a breath in through his nostrils then pushed it slowly past his lips. "I hope it helps."

Her expression changed. Her mouth and brows twisted in contemplative confusion. She studied his face.

"What is it?" he asked.

Nothing changed, and she didn't answer.

"Eliza?"

She waved him off but didn't look any less concerned or confused.

Patrick returned his attention to those looking through the haversack and eying the things inside. He explained to one of Mary's children how to use the compass. Ciara flipped almost reverently through pages of Grady's pocket-size book of Robert Burns's poems. Ian's son took up the folding mirror.

"That was used for shaving," Patrick said. "'Twouldn't do to take a razor to one's throat without a mirror at hand."

"It folds up so small," Ian said, opening and closing it a few times.

"We hadn't much room in our haversack." For the first time in ten years, Patrick was able to talk about the war without being crushed by the weight of guilt and regret. Ma didn't try to give him the tintype again. Ian didn't ask any further questions.

Patrick ought to have been entirely relieved. But Eliza was still watching him in that unsettling way. "Are you upset with me, lass?"

She shook her head, but then she rose to leave. *Leave?* The dinner hadn't even begun yet.

Patrick followed her and Lydia out the door, stopping her a few steps away from the house. "What happened? You seem displeased with me."

She faced him, still clearly confused and upset.

"What is it?" he pressed.

"All the times we've talked and planned, and you've held my hand or held *me* . . . how often were you drunk?"

"*Drunk?*"

Her expression hardened a little. "My husband was not the only one who worked in a bar during our leanest months, Patrick. I know the smell of whiskey on someone's breath, and I know the particular redness in the eyes of someone who's been drinking."

Oh, blessed fields. Panic began surging inside him.

"How many more of my secrets were you going to require before you shared this one with me?" She sounded both angry and hurt. "I told you things from my past I've not told anyone because I was so certain I could trust you. You made me think I could."

"You can," he said. "I want you to."

"If I hadn't sorted it out on my own, would you have ever told me?"

He wished he could say yes, but he didn't know. He'd come to get his family's help with this, and he still hadn't told *them*.

"Were you drinking last night?" she asked.

"Not before your visit."

That didn't seem to reassure her. "Have you ever held Lydia after you've been drinking?"

"I've never been drunk when holding her."

Eliza's expression remained sharp and hard. "That's not what I asked."

"I usually drink only at night," he said quickly.

"Usually?"

He pushed his hand through his hair. "This isn't an easy thing to overcome."

"Did you ever plan to tell me?" Her anger was giving way to hurt. "You told me heavy things from your past, weights that effect *you*. But this thing, this secret that impacts my safety, and my *child's* safety, you never bothered to do me the courtesy to tell me any bit of it."

"I'm not violent when I drink," he said. "It doesn't make me dangerous."

"No." She stepped away, holding Lydia in a protective embrace. "What it makes you is a liar."

He watched her walk away, taking his heart with her. The pull that whiskey had on him, the destructive role it played in his life, was claiming yet another casualty.

Two, in fact. It was pushing away Eliza and drying up the last drops of hope he had.

Chapter Twenty-two

Patrick knocked at the back door of the Archers' house every morning and afternoon for the next five days. Eliza never answered. A few times, Emma Archer did. She firmly but apologetically told him that Miss Eliza was busy and couldn't come talk with him. The rest of his knocks were simply ignored.

He spent his days building the interior walls of Finbarr's house. They, too, were made of sod, though Patrick had cut these bricks narrower. He'd be done with the house soon. He hadn't the first idea where his next job would come from.

And, heaven help him, he was struggling again with the same losing battle he'd been fighting for ten years. The progress he'd made in the short months he'd been in Hope Springs was disappearing fast.

Everything was falling apart. He hardly had enough strength left to even hope.

Friday evening, Patrick summoned what little remained of his resolve and returned once more to the Archer home and knocked once more. If he could just explain in a way that she would believe he hadn't meant to mislead her, hadn't meant to hurt her . . . He'd given the same speech before. To landladies, employers, friends, women who'd interested him but not come close to captivating him the way Eliza had. No one had ever believed his pleas, and he didn't blame them. But he needed Eliza to believe. He desperately needed her to.

Please, Eliza. Please answer the door.

The handle turned. Would it be Emma again? Maybe Ivy this time. The younger sister would likely be an even harsher doorman than the older had been. He wouldn't stand a chance.

But it wasn't a guard or sentinel who opened the door.

"Eliza." Her name fell from his lips as a plea. "Hear me out. Please."

She didn't slam the door, but she also didn't invite him in or say a word.

"I came to Hope Springs to get help," he said. "I came so my family could help me conquer this."

"And have they?" she asked. "Or do they not know, either?"

"Well, that takes me back to being a villain, doesn't it?"

Lydia peered around her ma's skirts. Eliza nudged her back into the kitchen and away from the door. Away from him. His little angel. He was losing her too.

"I'm trying," Patrick said. "But it's a demon I've wrestled with for a decade. I've lost that battle too many times to claim an easy victory now."

"I am well aware of the struggle some people have with alcohol. That is not what bothers me. What bothers me is that this was something affecting me in the very moments we were interacting. And it was affecting Lydia. And you kept it from me."

"Eliza—"

"No. You don't get to excuse this away. I know the ways drink changes people. I'm aware of the need for a little extra wariness and watching for warning signs. You didn't even do me the courtesy of telling me that I needed to be a little on guard. You didn't let me decide if I wanted to place myself in that situation. More than that, you spent time with my child, holding her and caring for her, after you'd been drinking. You robbed me of the ability to decide what was best for her."

Her words pummeled him mercilessly but deservedly. He kept silent as she delivered one blow after another.

"I cannot even look back on the time we've spent together without wondering if I ever saw you, the *real* you, or only the alcohol.

During those personal moments between us, were you ever sober?" The defensiveness in her posture didn't abate in the least. "Are you sober now?"

He couldn't bring himself to answer.

She released a breath, the tensest he'd heard from her yet. "You should leave, Patrick."

"Please, Eliza."

She shook her head. "I cannot allow myself to trust someone who has already broken that trust. Not again."

She closed the door, leaving him shattered on the other side of it. Alone. He leaned his head against the door.

"Eliza." Her whispered name broke as he spoke it.

She didn't come back; he knew she wouldn't. But he needed her. He needed her to return and to believe in him the way she had from the first moment on the stagecoach, and in countless moments since. He'd come to Hope Springs to try to save his own life. But what if his wasn't a life worth saving? What if no one wanted to be part of his life?

He knew one surefire way to escape the pain at least temporarily, but doing so would prove him to be precisely what he'd been trying to convince Eliza he wasn't. Yet, what else could he do?

He dragged himself off the porch. His mind grew heavier the farther he walked. With each step, his heart cracked deeper and deeper.

These past months, he'd held himself together, pushed forward through his growing struggle against the bottle. It was time he quit trying so blasted hard.

The house looming in front of him wasn't his, but it was the only destination that made sense. He was too torn down to be nervous at the possibility of further failure. He had very little left to lose.

He knocked on the door, misery hunching his shoulders. Yet again he waited for a door to open and a person to appear who could, with a word, crush what little hope he had left.

When the door opened, he looked up and saw precisely who he needed.

"I'm in trouble, Ian." Tears thickened his throat. "I need your help."

Ian's hardened animosity disappeared on the instant. "What's happened?"

Patrick could see Biddy inside the house, talking with their daughter. "Could we maybe go out to the barn, or somewhere else a little less . . ."

Ian gave a quick nod and stepped out, pulling the door closed behind him. They walked side by side toward Ian's fields. Patrick could feel despair creeping into the cracks of his heart. If Ian wouldn't help him, he was done for.

"What sort of trouble are you in?" Ian asked after a painfully long bout of silence between them.

"It'll take a while to fully explain."

"I've plenty of fields to walk through. They'll give you time enough to talk." The Ian he'd depended on so much had always been willing to listen. He needed *that* Ian now.

"I was injured at Gettysburg."

"You were?" Obviously he'd not been told that before.

Patrick nodded. "Likely the reason I was wrongly reported killed at first. The injury wasn't fatal or disfiguring, but it was painful, terribly so. The sawbones gave soldiers laudanum to ease the pain, but I'd seen too many men destroyed by it. They needed it even after their wounds were healed. They needed it enough to betray one another and desert their post in search of more. I was afraid of falling prey to it."

Ian kept his gaze on the path.

"So I wouldn't take the laudanum, but we were marching again soon, and I wasn't yet healed. The pain was too much. I couldn't keep up."

"What'd you do?"

He hated admitting to any of this, knowing where it had lead. "A little whiskey took the edge off. After a time, some helped me sleep. For the rest of the war, that was enough. But a few months back in New York with Maura and Aidan, and things changed. I needed more. I thought about it more. The grip grew tighter."

"Is that why you left? Because you were drinking?"

The weight of shame on his lungs made answering more and more difficult. "That's a big part of it. Seemed best for them if I stayed far away. I did better for a time, but then the pull of the liquor grabbed me again. It pushed people away, and I knew only one way to deal with the pain of losing them. The same thing happened in every town I tried to live in. And over the years it's gotten worse."

On they walked. Ian hadn't abandoned him yet. "And have you been drinking again?"

"'Again' isn't the right word."

"I've not seen you raging or violent."

Patrick shoved his hands in his trouser pockets. "Liquor numbs me. But it also makes me not arrive for work or do things I've promised to. It's a wall between me and everyone else. After a while, that wall becomes too much for me to get over or anyone else to see past. It gets harder and harder to tear down. I—don't think I can do it again."

Ian stopped and turned toward him but didn't speak. He was waiting, listening. Patrick stopped as well.

"I can't get out from under it. I've been trying for so long, and I can feel m'self giving up." He forced himself to hold his brother's gaze. "I've no right to ask anything of you, but I'm here begging. If I can't beat this, it's going to beat me for good this time. I know it."

Ian didn't turn away.

Patrick pushed ahead, a desperate variety of hope pulling the words from him. "I need the Ian who told me he wouldn't let our ship sink on the voyage from Ireland. I need the Ian I shared a corner of our New York flat with. The Ian who told me before anyone else that he'd met an angel and was desperate to learn her name. The Ian who, thirteen years ago, would've saved me from anything. The Ian I've missed ever since. I need *that* Ian. He's the only hope I have left."

"You have liquor here in Hope Springs, then?"

He nodded. "At Finbarr's house."

"So, we won't be going back there."

Did this mean Ian wouldn't abandon him?

"I don't think Jeremiah Johnson has any at the mercantile," Ian said.

"He doesn't."

"You've looked."

"Every time I'm in there." Patrick was finding honesty easier to manage. "I don't go in with that purpose, but I always check."

Ian's gaze narrowed. "When was the last time you were in a place where you couldn't get a drop to drink no matter how hard you tried?"

"Never, probably."

Ian motioned him back toward the house, but he hadn't given an answer to Patrick's pleading.

"What now?" Patrick asked.

"We're for Finbarr's place. We'll toss out your bottles and pack up some supplies. We'll head out at first light."

The first sprinkles of hope fell from the heavens. "And go where?"

"To the mountains." He pointed toward one in the distance. "It'll take a couple days to get there. But there's not a drop to drink outside of spring water, and nothing to do but sit around and not get drunk."

Patrick could almost smile a little. "Does that mean you're going to help me?"

"You're my brother, Patrick. And for most of my life, you were my best friend. You tell me you need help. There is no question that I'll be there, wherever 'there' may be."

Emotion pulled at his heart. "You're not going to let me die?"

"Better than that, Patrick. I'm going to make certain you *live*."

Chapter Twenty-three

Eliza might have been only twenty-two years old, but she'd lived plenty long enough to know the pangs of heartbreak. She also claimed an unfortunately vast acquaintance with disappointment. Both pressed painfully on her as she rode in the back of the Archers' wagon toward the *céilí* with Lydia on her lap.

She was looking forward to the party; she truly was. But Patrick sat heavily on her mind and heart. He hadn't told her he *wasn't* tipsy during their moments together. But he hadn't been forthright about his drinking in general. That bothered her more than anything. He hadn't told her a truth she needed—and had every right—to know.

He'd promised he was a good choice of builder for her inn, and she'd placed so much of her dream on him—believing in him. But a man who drank his nights away was far too likely to be unable to work the next day. And one who drank during the day was a danger.

He'd spent time with her daughter, held her daughter, looked after her daughter—and not once said when he was sober and when he wasn't. As Lydia's mother, Eliza had every right to determine whether to take such a risk with her daughter. He'd taken that choice from her.

He'd jeopardized everything she held dear, all while insisting she could trust him. Why was it she so often put her faith in the wrong people? She'd crossed the ocean in the company of a childhood friend who'd promised that they would forge their way in this new country together. But after a mere three months, she'd tossed Eliza aside in favor of newly made friends with a firmer foothold and deeper pockets.

The factory boss at her very first job in New York City had said she'd have a reliable job and the pay that went with it if she simply worked hard, which Eliza did. In the end, however, he had demanded favors and attentions she'd been unwilling to give, and had, despite her work ethic, fired her.

At the Porters' house, the housekeeper had said she treated all the maidservants as if they were her own daughters and would look after Eliza, too. Instead, after Terrence's affection for Eliza was discovered, the housekeeper delivered the swiftest, harshest blows of them all, dismissing her without references, withholding the pay she was owed, and sullying her name to all the fine houses in the area. In short, ensuring Eliza would not find a new position at any of them.

Terrence himself had sworn to his true and unwavering devotion, saying he'd gladly given up the comforts and luxuries of the life he'd always known to build a new one with her, that he would have no regrets.

That promise proved as empty as the rest.

With Patrick, her heart had found solace and comfort that warmed it in a way she hadn't felt in years. No longer could she let her heart override her head. Over the years, she'd trusted too many of the wrong people, but this time, she wasn't the only one who would be hurt.

Eliza pulled Lydia closer. This town was supposed to have been a fresh start for both of them. Instead it was simply more of the same: broken dreams and broken promises.

They reached the *céilí*. The sound of joyful voices lifted her spirits. She did like Hope Springs even with the difficulties she'd had here. Katie and Joseph helped their daughters alight from the wagon. Joseph remained to assist Eliza as well. He had proven a very pleasant surprise these past weeks: a wealthy man who was also an inherently good person.

"Pompah." Ivy tugged at Joseph's jacket. "I need to find Aidan, so I can tell him he has to dance with me."

"Don't you think you'd better ask him instead of demanding it of him?" Joseph never seemed closer to laughter than when he was speaking with Ivy.

"Aidan is my friend," his little girl said. "He will think dancing with me is grand."

Katie looked to Emma, who had her little brother on her hip. "Are we needing to rescue Aidan from being too ordered about?"

"He's known Ivy long enough to know what to expect," Emma said. "I think he likes that she's a bit bossy. He thinks she's funny."

"Does he think *you're* funny?" Katie asked.

Emma shook her head. "But he says I'm sweet. That seems almost as good."

"I think being sweet is a wonderful thing."

The girl rolled her eyes. "You're my mama. You *have* to think that."

"Emma." Katie whispered her name, the sound one of amazement. "You've not ever called me 'mama' before."

She colored up, her gaze dropping. "Do you not want me to?"

Katie pulled Emma into a tight and teary embrace. "I've wanted you to since before I married your papa. I love you, my sweet girl."

Eliza had to turn away. The love and tenderness between Katie and her sweet girl were beautiful and heartwarming, but the scene echoed as an ache in her own soul. Sometimes she let herself imagine moments just like this one, in which someone loved Lydia as his own child. Such a thing seemed more possible in this town of broken people and mended lives. It had, in fact, felt entirely within reach a few short days ago. But life, as it so often did, had snatched that dream away.

Maura rushed over. Her expanding belly grew more noticeable every time Eliza saw her. She offered Lydia a quick greeting before turning her attention to Eliza. "Mother Callaghan's made barmbrack, the tea bread I told you about at the sewing circle. Everyone's excited for you to try it."

They walked together toward a grouping of chairs where the other O'Connor women sat other than Mrs. O'Connor, who always spent the *céilís* rushing about and seeing to everything. Eliza didn't see Cecily O'Connor, either.

"Is Cecily not here?" she asked.

Maura shook her head. "She and Tavish are making their annual drive around the territory, selling his preserves and cordials and berries. They'll be back in a few weeks' time."

"The family must miss having them here." Eliza had seen for herself the closeness that existed amongst this large and growing clan.

"We're missing a few people just now." Maura sighed a little. "Ian is gone."

Eliza hadn't heard that. Before she could ask the reason for *that* brother's absence, Maura added to her list.

"We're missing Patrick again, as well."

"He had seemed to be getting on better with the family." Eliza hoped to hear there was a reason for his absence other than their falling out.

"Everyone was very hopeful. We don't know where the two of them have gone."

The two of them?

"He and Ian are together?" There'd always been such tension between those two brothers. Eliza would not have guessed that they, of all the family, would take any sort of journey together.

As they arrived at the circle of O'Connor women, Maura whispered, "Wherever they are, they're with each other. We're hopeful they're mending the rift between them."

"Eliza." Mrs. Callaghan grinned across at her. "We have barmbrack for you."

"I look forward to trying it after all of you have spoken so highly of it." She sat, setting Lydia on her lap.

Ciara joined them, handing Eliza a small plate with a thick slice of bread—a rich, golden brown with small pieces of dried fruit throughout. It smelled divine.

"I suspect if I eat this, I will crave it for the rest of my life."

Anne Scott, another local woman Eliza had come to know a little, said, "Eat enough of it, and you might accidentally turn yourself Irish."

"I'd blend in well, then, wouldn't I?"

"With half of the town, at least," Ciara said with a laugh.

They were fun to talk with, so happy and light and friendly. Maura had been that way, more or less, during their time together at the Widows' Tower. She'd always been friendly and loving and welcoming, and they'd had moments of happiness and lightness. But the atmosphere here was more than that. The lightness lasted longer and went deeper.

Emma and Aidan slipped in among them all. They approached Eliza, of all people.

"The little ones are playing Duck, Duck, Goose," Aidan said. "And they're all giggling and running around and having so much fun."

"May we take Lydia over to play with the others?" Emma asked.

Lydia would enjoy that. She could make some little friends, and Aidan and Emma were rather like an older brother and sister to her. And they wouldn't be far away. "You'll look after her?"

"Aidan is very careful of her," Emma said, a little quietly, and a lot sweetly. "He wouldn't let anything happen to her."

Aidan just laughed. "You make me sound like a saint."

Emma bumped him with her shoulder. Everything in her posture spoke of a girl in the throes of young love.

"We'll take care of Lydia," Aidan promised.

That was reassurance enough for Eliza. She leaned near enough to talk softly to her daughter. "Emma and Aidan are going to play games with you. Go on ahead with them. You'll have fun."

Lydia thought on it a moment, finger over her lip.

Aidan hunched down in front of her. "Come with us, sweet girl." He tugged softly on her dolly's dress. "You can bring your dolly with you."

That seemed to convince her. She climbed off Eliza's lap and took Aidan's hand with the one holding her handkerchief. Aidan looked over at Emma and smiled. Her answering smile was unmistakably besotted.

They'd not gone far when Maura spoke up. "Rather adorable, those two."

Everyone smiled and laughed and agreed.

"Does Aidan return her regard?" Eliza asked.

"I don't think so," Maura said. "But he's kind to her, and they get on well."

"Poor Emma," Katie said, having joined them. "She seems destined to lose her heart to O'Connor lads who think of her only as a friend."

Eliza hadn't heard the girl speak of anyone else in a way that made her suspect a tenderness. "Who else has she lost her heart to?"

"When she was tiny," Ciara said, "she was forever asking about and following after Tavish. It wasn't quite the same kind of attachment, but a deep, deep fondness. Then Finbarr started working at the Archer home. She was a little older then and fell more than a little in love with him."

Eliza was the only one smiling about that. Why?

Katie's expression was heaviest of all. "I don't know that her heart has ever recovered from the blow he dealt her. It's done Joseph's mind good to see her warming up to Aidan. While none of us expects anything to blossom between them other than friendship, we're hopeful their connection won't turn painful."

The other women offered their thoughts, the conversation pulling everyone's attention.

Eliza turned to Maura. Lowering her voice, she asked, "Do you know what she's talking about?"

"Not entirely, as it began before I came to Hope Springs. But I do know there is a lot of hurt between Emma and Finbarr, and it weighs on both of them."

"I can't imagine either of them being anything but kind to the other."

"Neither can I. But watch them. You'll see pain there."

This was, indeed, a town of broken people. Not everyone's lives, it seemed, had been mended. Could hers? Could Patrick's?

No sooner had he entered her thoughts than she pushed him out. That way lay misery. She wouldn't let her disappointment in him dampen her spirits. How she wished they'd sorted out the difficulty of her inn. If that had been moving forward, she wouldn't have had the least doubt about this place being where she was meant to raise her daughter. As it was, nothing felt certain.

"Mrs. Porter?"

Eliza turned at the sound of a man speaking her name. "Dr. Jones." He was always pleasant to spend time with.

"The musicians are striking up an air. Would you care to dance with me?"

The women around her all smiled a bit too broadly, eyes twinkling. Eliza hadn't the slightest doubt Dr. Jones would run for the hills if any of them made a comment. He was confident in himself as a man of medicine, but he was also shy in most any other interaction.

"I would like to dance with you." Eliza stood as she spoke.

They made good their escape, leaving before the attention pushed Dr. Jones to an embarrassed blush. They'd danced at previous *céilís*, and she'd always enjoyed it. He was easy to talk with, and he always listened.

Eliza was reluctant to raise the topic she most needed to discuss with him, but she couldn't avoid it forever. "I am sorry I haven't been able to move forward with your infirmary," she said as they spun about the dancing area. "I'm not certain we'll manage it in the end."

"I understand, I assure you. Life is seldom *less* complicated than we expect it to be."

That was the truth. "I haven't given up yet, but . . ." She offered him an apologetic look. "You must be frustrated."

"I don't get easily frustrated," he said. "At least, I don't *stay* that way."

"Where did you learn the trick of that?" she asked, feeling a little better.

"The Chicago Orphan Asylum."

The answer was so unexpected, she stumbled over the next steps. "I'm sorry."

"About the asylum or the dance steps?" He spoke with a tiny upward tip to his lips.

"Both."

"You needn't be sorry about either one," he said. "The orphanage was not ideal, and I was not particularly happy there. But I found my way, and I'm far from there now." A hint of mischief entered his expression. "And I've stumbled over my fair share of dance steps." His graciousness was more than welcome.

"You really don't stay frustrated, do you?"

"Frustration convinces a person to simply stop when a road isn't leading where he wants. I prefer to find the road that *does* lead there rather than curse the heavens about the road I've been walking."

There was wisdom in that. "Switching roads can be frightening."

He nodded. "But worth it."

Worth it.

What if she switched roads? Would that be worth it? Choosing a different path to walk?

That, she suspected, was the question she needed to answer most.

Chapter Twenty-four

"I can't drink any more tea." Patrick eyed the cup Ian held out to him. He'd been drowning in tea the last two days.

"'Tis tea or water I have for you," Ian said. "You said you were thirsty."

"Not for either of those."

"I know." Ian set the cup on the ground beside him and walked back to the stump he'd been using as a stool since they arrived.

Patrick rubbed at his forehead. "You've grown malicious in your old age."

"You didn't used to make so many jokes about how old I am." Ian took up his whittling.

"You didn't used to be so ancient." Patrick took up the cup of tea.

Far from offended, Ian smiled. He'd done that a few times since they'd made camp out here in the mountains. Patrick was seeing more and more glimpses of the brother he'd known and the connection they'd once had.

A sip of tea proved as unsatisfying as Patrick knew it would. "This isn't quite the same as a pull of whiskey."

"I know it. And I know it won't ever be." Ian, to his credit, sounded sympathetic. "Uncle Archibald had a weakness for whiskey as well. But when it started pulling harder than it ought, he swore off it."

It'd been two days since Patrick had confessed his struggle, and this was Ian's first mention of Uncle Archibald. Ian remembered far more of Ireland and the family they'd left there than Patrick did. He wasn't entirely certain which of Ma's brothers was his uncle Archibald. If he'd known a neediness for alcohol had clutched someone else in the family, Patrick might not've felt so hopeless.

"Whenever he felt the pull back to the bottle, he'd have tea instead." Ian shaved a long curl of wood from the block he was working on. "He said tea never was quite the same, and it didn't make him stop longing for whiskey, but it gave him something to do with his hands and mouth and something to put in his belly. That helped, he said." Ian kept his eye on his work as he spoke. "Uncle Archibald said that, after a time, when he'd get thirsty for liquor, he'd reach for tea without hardly having to think about it. He'd traded one habit for another, one that wouldn't be the death of him."

Patrick swallowed another mouthful. He didn't bother to hide his grimace. "Uncle Archibald wasn't drinking *your* tea, apparently."

"Watch yourself, lad. I'm the only friend you have right now."

"Well, there aren't a great many options nearby just now."

Again, Ian allowed the smallest bit of a smile. Patrick was glad to see it, even if he wasn't particularly pleased with being sobered up. The doing of it would only grow more miserable, he knew that. But he knew he'd never have managed this much without his brother helping him navigate it.

"How much tea do you reckon Uncle Archibald drank every day?"

"Gallons."

Patrick snorted out a laugh. "Saints, you're not comforting me in the least."

Ian sliced off another curly shave of wood. "He drank more tea than anyone I ever met, Patrick. That's what I remember about him most. I asked Ma once why he was forever drinking tea. She told me."

"She wasn't ashamed of having a brother who'd once been a drunkard?" Patrick had worried a great deal about what Ma would think of *him.*

Ian shook his head. "She said that, near as she knows, he never drank another drop of whiskey once he switched. I'd wager she was proud of him. For slipping free of that noose."

"And she and the rest of the family didn't hate him for having it around his neck to begin with?"

Ian lowered his whittling and looked Patrick in the eye. "Not anyone in this family will hate you, neither. They'll likely all be relieved."

"Relieved that I'm a drunkard?"

"Relieved that there's a reason you've been so far away, even since coming home."

If only whiskey were the only reason.

Patrick finished off his tea and stood. "What else did Uncle Archibald do when he was too thirsty to endure it?"

"Work. Da knew Uncle Archibald nearly as well as Ma did. He said staying busy kept our uncle from thinking too much about his thirst, and being out in the fields or up on his roof kept him away from the pub."

Patrick nodded. "I'm not afraid to work."

Ian set aside his whittling. "I thought while we were out here, we could get a jump on wood for the winter. It's easier to make this journey now than after the snow's come in."

"Is that why you chose such a far-off spot? So you could trick me into felling trees for you?"

"Aye." Ian crossed to the wagon and began hitching the horses. "No point doing it all by my lonesome."

"Malicious, grumpy old man."

"With old age comes wisdom. Now help me hitch these beasts."

They worked well together. That hadn't changed in the years they'd been apart.

"The factory in New York teamed me with a different fellow after you left." Patrick talked as he worked. "Decent at the job, but a miserable sort. Made me detest going to work. I hadn't realized how much of what I liked about that job was working with you."

Ian adjusted one of the horse's belly bands. "We were quite a team, weren't we?"

"That we were."

"Did this miserable fellow who replaced me sign up for the Irish Regiment as well?" Ian asked.

"No, thank the heavens. We'd've had a mutiny."

"I thought mutinies happened only on ships. What's it called when it happens on dry land?"

"If it'd tossed the likes of him out of our ranks, it would've been called a mercy."

Ian smiled—what shouldn't've been so relieving a sight. The Ian he'd grown up with had smiled often and easily. But Patrick had seen so little of that side of his brother the past months.

Soon the wagon was ready to go. Ian took up the reins. Patrick sat on the bench beside him. They drove father into the mountains, to a thicker collection of trees. The valley below had virtually none.

"Why is it you don't build your houses out of this wood rather than buying it at the depot?" Patrick asked.

"This wood is what keeps us from freezing in the winter. None of us is willing to risk decimating it."

That was sensible. "And why does everyone generally wait until winter to collect it? You said it's a lot harder to do then."

"'Tis usually the first chance we have. Summer is spent tending the crop. Autumn is filled with harvesting and selling it. Collecting wood is our very next task, but winter comes early here."

Ian, then, had never come up this way this time of year on account of his fields and his livelihood.

"You're neglecting your crop." *Begor.* Patrick hadn't even thought of that. What sort of selfish brother was he?

"Da and the lads'll watch over it." Ian guided the wagon into a small clearing. "That's what I asked Da when we passed him on the road heading up toward Finbarr's place. I told him you and I needed to make a trek."

He'd worried about the conversation he'd not overheard. Da might've asked any number of things Patrick wasn't ready for him to know. "Did he ask why we were undertaking a journey?"

"Aye. But I told him it was none of his never mind."

Surprise dropped Patrick's jaw. "You said that to Da? And he didn't take a switch to you?" An unexpected bubble of amusement swelled inside. "Being old and grumpy can be handy, it seems."

"'Tis a useful thing, indeed." Ian nodded toward the nearby trees. "Every fourth one, that's our rule." He brought the wagon to a stop.

"We had rules like that in the Canadian towns where I worked, and those forests are thick."

"This one will last if we can help it."

Ian climbed down. He pulled an axe from the wagon bed. Patrick did the same. They walked out among the trees.

"You said at Da and Ma's house that you hated everything about the war. You must've regretted signing up so readily."

"I didn't," Patrick said.

The trees weren't as plentiful as they'd been in Canada. But they were tall. Species of spruce and pine grew alongside ash. Thick trunks, strong branches. They'd get a good number of logs out of them.

"You didn't regret it?" Ian asked.

"I didn't 'sign up readily.'" Patrick stopped at the base of a good, thick pine tree with room enough around it for chopping it down.

"But you always wanted to enlist. You talked about it even before we all left New York."

He ought've put an end to the topic the moment Ian introduced it. Now he was in a bind. "It was complicated."

"I'm capable of understanding complicated things."

Patrick tapped the tree trunk. "Maybe let's see if we're capable of turning this tree into logs."

But no sooner had they felled it and cut it into lengths small enough for the two of them to carry back to the wagon, than Ian jumped right back to the topic.

"You don't talk about the war," he said, "but not in the way I've heard other men avoid it, with that impression that they're too haunted by it to endure hearing even themselves speaking the words. For you, it seems more like you think *we* don't want to hear about it, even though we ask you about the war."

"If you knew what I wasn't telling, you'd know you don't want to hear it."

Ian swung his axe into the stump they'd left, then stepped over to him. "Whatever this is, it's keeping you at a distance from us. Anytime the war comes up, you tiptoe close before running away from it and all the family at full speed. But 'tisn't anyone here but you and me just now, and we've a lot of days ahead of us up here on our lonesome. Best spill your budget and get it over with."

"I'm not keeping mum on my account. 'Tis someone else who'd be hurt by my explaining."

Ian took Patrick's axe and swung it into one of the logs. Apparently Ian didn't mean to allow Patrick to escape the discussion by chopping wood. "When you think about this thing you're hiding—whatever it is—does it make you even thirstier for whiskey?"

"*This conversation* is making me thirsty." Couldn't his brother see he really didn't want to talk about this?

"The whole reason we're up here is to help you loosen the grip the bottle has on you. You trusted me enough to tell me about the whiskey, and I didn't betray that trust to anyone. The family knows only that we needed to leave for a time, but not why. I didn't even tell Biddy the reason."

That was surprising. "You always used to tell her everything."

"I still do, but I kept your confidence about the reasons for this trek." Ian sat on one of the long, thick logs and motioned for Patrick to do the same. "Burdens are lighter when you're not carrying them by yourself. You have to lighten this load, Patrick, or nothing we do up here is going to last long after we go back down."

He was bang on the mark, of course. Sharing this burden would ease the weight of it.

Patrick sat on the log. Shoulders hunched and gaze on the tips of his own boots, he told Ian. About Grady not wanting to stay in New York. About how Grady hoped to convince Maura to leave the city. Told him about his own plans to come to Hope Springs as soon as Grady secured Maura's agreement.

"Why didn't you tell any of us you were planning to come west?" Ian asked.

"I did." He looked at Ian. "I told the family again and again before everyone left that I didn't mean to stay in New York forever, that I'd join you in time."

Ian's confusion was precisely what Patrick knew he'd see in response.

"No one listened." He set his gaze on the distant trees, pain and disappointment spinning around inside. "Those who made the journey were the good children. Grady was staying behind on account of his wife, so he was a good husband. I was just the heartless blackguard breaking Ma's heart. No one heard anything I said that didn't fit the role that'd been fashioned for me."

Ian didn't say anything. Patrick would've wagered his brother was struggling to believe the story, and Patrick hadn't gotten to the most drastic misunderstanding yet. Best get it over with.

"If Grady hadn't enlisted, we probably would've come to Hope Springs in a year or two."

That broke Ian's silence. "Grady wouldn't've enlisted if you hadn't. He was protecting you, trying to keep you safe."

Time to shatter a family legend. His lungs tightened, and his heart pounded painfully in his chest. But he'd avoided this truth long enough. So he pushed the words out.

"Grady joined up first."

"He *what?*" Ian's mouth hung agape.

"He signed up first," Patrick repeated. "*I* followed *him* to war. *I* was protecting *him*. *I* was keeping *him* safe. Not the other way around." The agony of keeping this secret for so many years spilled over into anger and frustration and the clog of tears as he finally spoke the truth out loud. "I didn't drag him to his eventual death. No rash decision on my part tore him from his family."

"But Maura told us—"

"Maura assumed," Patrick said. "And why should any of you believe it could've happened the other way 'round? Grady was the saintly one who sacrificed everything for the people he loved. I was the selfish one who didn't care what pain I caused my family, so long as I got to do what I wanted, right? Putting my brother in danger seemed entirely in character for me. Didn't it?"

Ian sat in frozen shock. His expression was far from blank. Denial warred with defensiveness in his eyes. Then he pushed out a breath and hung his head.

223

"Why didn't you correct us?" Ian's voice had grown quieter.

"I didn't realize what everyone thought until after the war was over. Telling Maura her husband had gone to fight on his own account rather than on mine would've hurt her. Aidan never stopped talking about his da being a hero. I knew all of you viewed him as the best of brothers, a selfless defender of his family. I wasn't going to mar that. He deserves to be remembered that way. He *was* that way. No matter the order of things that sent the two of us to war, he fought bravely and heroically, and we did look after each other."

Patrick stood and paced away. Telling Ian was harder than telling Eliza. Still, if Ian knew, then Patrick would have someone to help when the weight of his past and the family's view of him pushed him back toward the very escape he was trying to avoid.

"We were in the same regiment," Patrick said, "so we were always together. I was with him when he died. Some deaths in battle happen in an instant. Some are slow and agonizing—torturous."

"Which was his?" Ian asked.

Patrick couldn't look back at him. "You don't want to know." He wiped at the sweat rolling down his neck. "We'd both been injured, Grady worse than me. He made me promise that I'd make certain Maura and the rest of you knew he loved you. The family might've seen me as the villain, but I don't break my word to a dying man. Telling everyone that he'd not stayed behind with Maura entirely willingly, that he'd left Maura and Aidan to join the war effort because *he* wanted to, not because I'd forced his hand—that all ran a deep risk of undermining my promise to him. I couldn't risk it."

"But when you left New York after the war, why didn't you come to us?" Ian asked. "Or at least tell us you were alive?"

"All of you believed I'd led my brother to his death in pursuit of my own vainglory. I knew from Maura's telling of things that none of you paid the least heed to my promise to rejoin you, insisting instead that I didn't care enough about my family to leave the siren call of the city. Add to that the fact that I'd become a drunkard." He shrugged, still not looking at his brother. "'Twas better to stay dead. You'd all think better of me that way."

Ian walked up and stopped beside him. "You're loved by this

family, Patrick. You always have been. So has Grady. And none of what you've told me changes either of those facts. Ma never stopped loving her brother even through Uncle Archibald's struggles against the bottle. None of us stopped loving you because you stayed in New York or because we thought you were the reason Grady enlisted."

"Grady deserves to be remembered the way he's thought of now."

"Don't you deserve to be thought better of than you are now?" Ian asked.

"I'm a jobless, homeless drunkard. You tell me."

Ian stepped around him and set his hands on Patrick's shoulders. "You're my brother. The rest is just distractions."

Emotion clogged his throat, but he swallowed it down. "I've missed you, Ian."

"I've missed you too," Ian said. "M'life hasn't been the same without you in it."

He'd needed that assurance all these years. "Eliza insisted I wasn't the villain. She also called me all sorts of a fool for not telling any of you."

"Wise woman."

"She'd be pleased to know I've finally told you. If she were still speaking to me, that is."

Ian turned him so they stood side by side, one of his arms around Patrick's shoulders. "Let's keep at the trees while you tell me about your troublesome colleen."

His connection to Ian wasn't entirely healed. It'd be a long time before it was. But they'd made a start. A long sought-after, reassuring, heart-lightening start.

Chapter Twenty-five

Eliza came to a conclusion in the days following her dance with the doctor: she would search out the path in life she wanted to walk rather than fretting over the paths she'd been on. Hope Springs had become home to her, and she meant to do all she could to make it the home she wanted.

Being a housekeeper wasn't a terrible arrangement, and while it wouldn't be her first choice of profession, if it meant she could stay where she had friends, where her daughter was loved, then she would be happy to keep toiling there for as long as the Archers would allow. And if it took ten, fifteen, twenty years of proposing new variations on her inn to finally get it built, then she would spend those ten, fifteen, twenty years, holding fast to that dream.

She would pick her path, beginning with tossing another idea at Joseph Archer.

As she was working on the laundry one morning, he approached the house. Seeing her opportunity, she snatched up Lydia and rushed toward the porch, despite her wet apron and sleeves rolled to her elbows. When she'd first come to work for the Archers, she would have been horrified at the thought of her well-to-do employer seeing her even the slightest bit harried. She wasn't afraid of him any longer.

"Might I bend your ear a moment?" she asked, reaching the porch just as he did.

"Of course."

She bounced Lydia in her arms, hoping to keep her quiet while they had this discussion. "I've given more thought to the inn. The stage company suggested we move it quite far south so it could be the first night's stop, but that doesn't work for us. What if, instead, we move it north so it can be the second night's stop? I don't think we'd have to go too far from town. Passengers are always more tired on the second day of travel than the first. They, the driver, and the outrider will all be eager for a stop sooner than the day before."

"That is certainly true." He assumed the expression he wore when he was intrigued by an idea. That he hadn't had an immediate objection or reason why it wouldn't work was encouraging.

"Do you own any land to the north of town?" she asked.

"I do," he said, "but not directly on the stage road. Still, it might be near enough to be worth a bit of an adjustment in their trail."

"And would it be near enough to town for Dr. Jones to still use it for an infirmary?"

Joseph rubbed at his chin, thinking. Lydia began loudly fussing, squirming in an attempt to be put down. With the laundry pot still simmering nearby, Eliza didn't dare risk putting her down. Like an armored knight of old, Finbarr stepped up beside her.

"Come sit with me, Lydia." He held his arms out for her, though not quite in the right direction.

Eliza set the girl in them. "The laundry fire's burning not far off, and the water's terribly hot."

He nodded. "I'll keep her near to the house."

"Thank you."

Finbarr set Lydia on her feet and took her hand, holding his cane in the other. "Let's go for a walk, lass."

Joseph watched the two move slowly around the side of the house. "He was that way with my girls, an absolute godsend when they were little, and we didn't have Katie with us yet. I don't know what I would have done without him. We don't see that side of him much anymore."

"Katie told me he and Emma had something of a falling out," Eliza said.

Joseph nodded. "He struggled a lot after the fire that took his sight. He pushed a lot of people away. She took the brunt of that a few too many times."

"Harrowing experiences cause ripples of pain." She'd experienced far too many of them herself. "A lot of people can get caught in them."

"Indeed." He spoke with the regret of one who knew those ripples all too well.

It was odd having something in common with a rich man. She'd not have believed that possible before coming here. Everything was different in Hope Springs. Making this valley her home brought her greater hope than she'd had in some time.

"I'll talk with Dr. Jones," he said. "If he's comfortable with the spot I'm thinking of to the north, then I'll send a telegram to the stage company to see if *this* proposal satisfies them. With a little luck, we may get this inn built after all."

"I have every faith that we will."

Finbarr came around the other side of the house, still holding Lydia's hand and walking at a pace she could keep up with. He held his cane in his other hand, sweeping the ground with it as he walked. Lydia's other hand held her doll, as always. Did Patrick realize what a perfect gift that had been? He'd given her unending joy. No matter the current difficulty between herself and that man, she was grateful to him for that bit of thoughtfulness.

"Finbarr," Joseph called out. "Ian's oldest is coming to help tomorrow since Aidan is needed at home. We're getting an early start."

"I'll be here," Finbarr answered.

Joseph looked to Eliza, dipping his head in a very gentlemanly gesture of departure. "I will keep you informed."

"Thank you."

He slipped into the house. Eliza met up with Finbarr as they reached the porch steps.

"Thank you for walking around with her. Watching her and having an adult conversation is difficult when she's being cooperative. It's nearly impossible when she's impatient."

"Ivy was even more that way than Lydia when she was tiny. That girl couldn't have held still if her life depended on it."

Eliza grinned. "She still can't."

Finbarr laughed a little. "I do like that lass. I think everyone does."

"Thank you again for looking after Lydia. I won't keep you from heading home."

"Actually, I wouldn't mind staying and playing with her while you finish the laundry. There's no one at Tavish and Cecily's other than me. It's a little . . ."

"Lonely?" Eliza guessed.

"I was going to say quiet."

She suspected, no matter what he was going to say, that "lonely" was what he meant. She wouldn't force him to confess as much.

"I will happily accept your offer. She's been sitting on a blanket just over this way. I imagine she'll sit there with you if you show ample interest in her doll."

"Ivy made me an expert in that."

They were soon situated. Eliza scrubbed the laundry, able to truly focus on her task for the first time in weeks. Usually she was too worried about Lydia wandering off or toddling too near the fire.

"Memma!" Lydia called.

Eliza looked up. Sure enough, Emma had joined them. She stood near the blanket, watching Finbarr with uncertainty. After a moment, Emma's gaze shifted to Eliza. "Mama wanted me to tell you the sewing circle is moving to Maura's house tomorrow on account of Mrs. Callaghan feeling a little poorly."

"She's not seriously ill, I hope."

"I don't think so," Emma said. "But Dr. Jones lives on their land, so he's nearby if she needs him."

The pain in Emma's expression when she looked at Finbarr tugged at Eliza's heart. She suspected the two needed only a little nudge to get them talking.

"Finbarr's looking after Lydia while I finish up."

"'Looking' after might be the wrong word," Finbarr muttered.

"Why do you do that?" Emma asked.

"Do what?"

She sat on the blanket, facing him. "People speak kindly of you, and you contradict them. I don't understand why. Do you think they're wrong, or do you simply not like hearing compliments?"

"I don't know. It . . . It seems like the right thing to say."

"It isn't." She spoke firmly.

Eliza pinned a sheet on the clothesline, watching and listening to the young people while trying not to be obvious about her eavesdropping.

"You, of all people, should be pleased to know I have a low opinion of myself," Finbarr said to Emma.

Emma didn't appear the least convinced. Indeed, her expression turned ever more determined. "And you, of all people, should know why *that* is utter rot."

Finbarr couldn't have looked more surprised. "You've a bit of fire in you, Miss Emma."

"I'm growing up," she said. "And I'm learning to be strong and firm. I suppose you don't approve."

He shook his head. "On the contrary, I think it's brilliant."

Finbarr's words of approval softened the young girl's edges of wariness. Eliza wished he could see how quickly and entirely he made a change in his friend, how very much he obviously still meant to Emma Archer. The girl might not still feel the sweet little-girl love she had when they were both younger, but anyone seeing her now would know in an instant that she cared deeply about what he thought of her.

"Lydia reminds me a little of Ivy." Emma scooted closer to the two of them. "Although she doesn't run away as often."

"I don't think anyone runs away as often as Ivy did. That lass sure loves to run. It's fortunate she's old enough now to find her way back."

"Assuming she wants to come back," Emma said with a little laugh. "She's stubborn, too, you know."

"Oh, I know."

They talked as they played with Lydia. Nothing they said was of deep significance, but Eliza felt she was watching something more important than it appeared to be on the surface. Hope Springs was a place of healing.

Was Patrick finding his needed measure of healing? She hoped so. No matter that he'd given her ample cause to be wary, she wanted him to do better, to feel better. He deserved to. His family deserved to have him back. Perhaps while he was gone with Ian, he'd find the strength to tell his brother what weighed on him.

She wanted to believe that she'd be able to face him with relative indifference when he returned. But he jumped often and easily into her thoughts, and when he did, her heart responded immediately with an aching thrum. When he returned, she would struggle. But difficult paths hadn't broken her before, and neither would this one now. This was the path she was choosing, and she would walk it.

"Mrs. Porter?" Emma's voice cut into her thoughts. "I think Lydia has something in her foot."

Eliza pinned Ivy's dress to the clothesline. "What is it?"

"A little splinter, I would guess." Emma eyed the sole of Lydia's left foot. "It looks sore."

Lydia whimpered a little, trying to pull her foot free of Emma's hold. Finbarr whispered something to her, and she stopped squirming for a moment.

Eliza hung up the last few bits of laundry then crossed to the blanket. She sat next to Emma and made her own study of Lydia's foot. There was no need to point out what had caused Emma's concern. A good-sized red blotch marred the girl's foot. Right in the middle was a dark spot, precisely what an irritated splinter would look like.

The girl still had no shoes. That she'd gone as long as she had walking about barefoot without getting a splinter was nearly miraculous. Of course, Eliza carried her around a great deal of the time, trying to avoid precisely this.

"I wonder how long her foot's been sore." Eliza turned toward Finbarr. "Did she seem to be in pain while you were walking around the house?"

"I can't see well enough to know if she was limping or anything." He sounded so disappointed in himself.

"But she didn't whimper or try to get you to pick her up?" There were, after all, clues that weren't visual.

"She did stop and start a lot. I assumed she was looking at flowers or something."

The spot was too red and puffy to be a new splinter and might be difficult to get out. "Let's take her inside and see if we can't remove it. Will you stay and hold her, Finbarr? That would make it easier."

"Whatever you need from me."

"I can help, too," Emma said.

By the time a needle had been procured, cleaned by a flame, and cooled, Finbarr was sitting on Eliza's bed with Lydia held in his arms. There wasn't the slightest bit of discomfort in his posture. Despite being the youngest in his family, he was entirely comfortable in the role of older brother. Emma sat next to him, facing Lydia. She had the doll giving kisses to all three of them, earning giggles of approval.

"This is going to hurt," Eliza warned her two helpers. "So give the poor dear as much love as you can manage."

Oh, how she hated the sound of her daughter's cries of pain. Emma clearly did, as well. Finbarr was solid as the earth itself. He whispered soothingly and rubbed Lydia's arms in slow, gentle movements.

The rest of the Archer family were soon at the door, obviously worried.

"She has a splinter in her foot," Emma explained, her voice tight with worry.

"All will be well, Miss Emma," Finbarr said. "You'll see."

Eliza dug again, praying fervently that she'd get the splinter out this time. She was so close.

Lydia's yelps of pain turned to sobs. Finbarr held her more closely. Emma rested her head against his arm, clearly trying to keep her own emotions in check.

A quick flick of the needle, and the splinter popped out. "I got it." Eliza pressed a rag to Lydia's foot, soaking up the little trickle of blood.

Ivy tiptoed up beside her. She leaned against Eliza much the way Emma did with Finbarr. "Is Lydia's foot going to get better?"

"Her foot will be grand altogether."

Ivy smiled up at her. "Mama says that. A lot of the Irish families do."

"I learned it from Maura Callaghan," Eliza said. "It's very useful, isn't it?"

Ivy nodded. "Is Emma going to be sad because of Lydia's foot?"

Finbarr answered. "She'll be grand altogether too."

Emma sat up a bit straighter, swiping quickly at telltale moisture in her eyes. But she didn't appear upset or offended at being talked about. "I don't like when people are hurting," she said.

"You have a good heart, Miss Emma," Finbarr said. "Don't ever be embarrassed about that."

Joseph and Katie, holding Sean, watched their daughters with love and pride. Emma appeared more at peace with Finbarr now, and he with her. Ivy was curious but kind. Lydia was clearly comforted by the embrace from her "big brother."

No, being housekeeper for this family hadn't been Eliza's first choice. But she was discovering the position to be a blessing in disguise. A blessing she was more grateful for every day.

Chapter Twenty-six

Patrick had spent two weeks in the mountains. He'd drunk more tea in that fortnight than he had in his entire life, it seemed. But in doing so, he'd found a way to face the pull of a master he no longer wished to serve.

And he'd found his brother again.

"Do you have a plan yet?" Ian asked, driving the wagon in the direction of town. They weren't near enough yet to see even a glimpse of the Hope Springs valley, but it oughtn't be long now.

"A plan for what?"

Ian tossed him a look of doubt in his intelligence. "Winning your lass's heart, you dunderhead."

"All I have," Patrick said, "is some advice I once got—long before this sobering-up trip—from a fellow who was more or less reliable."

"*I* gave you advice *during* this sobering-up trip," Ian said. "Do I not lean toward more reliable instead of less?"

Patrick pushed a needle through several layers of thick canvas. He was nearly done with a project he'd begun at the start of their two weeks away. He'd had to pause his efforts a few days in, when the need for whiskey had set his hands trembling and his head pounding fiercely. The worst seemed to have passed. "You're reliable enough, but this fellow . . . he was wise."

"What did this scholar tell you, then?"

"He, in his very wise way, said that when a colleen captured my heart, I needed to say what needed saying, take risks, and do what needed doing. He also said something about not being a coward, but since I was so very brave at the time, I didn't worry too much about that bit."

Ian tossed him a dry look. "*I* told you that, before we left New York."

"Couldn't be." Patrick twisted his face into an expression of confused disbelief. "This fellow was much, much younger than you are."

"You were much, much younger then, too."

"Aye, but I was and always will be younger than you."

"There was a time, Patrick, when I missed having you around." Ian adjusted his hat on his head. "That was back when you were nice to me."

"You're happy I'm back. Admit it."

"I'm happy *you're* back, not the shell of you that stumbled into town months ago." Ian kept his gaze on the road. "*He* was infuriating."

Patrick laughed, keeping at his sewing project. "Eliza liked him."

"And now Eliza's not speaking with him."

With a sigh, Patrick said, "If only that wise young fellow from all those years ago were nearby with some advice."

"That wise young—"

Patrick cleared his throat.

"—young*ish* fellow has been giving you advice for two weeks now."

"And tea," Patrick added. "He's been giving me far too much tea."

"It's helped, though, hasn't it?"

"It—and *you*—have likely saved m'life, Ian. And you did it even though I didn't deserve a bit of your help. You'd every reason to tell me *again* to keep the devil away from you."

They kept rolling down the road. "You weren't so far gone as all that, Patrick. Though whiskey had a greater pull on you than you'd like—and I'm not denyin' it's caused you no end of trouble—I've seen men shackled to it. Destroyed entirely. They couldn't've gone hours without it, and you've just gone two weeks. I don't think you were as

236

near to destruction as you feared. And I suspect that means you're going to be able to keep winning your battle with it."

"Provided I don't run out of tea."

Ian guided the horses over a small rise. "If you ever run low, come to my place. And if we don't have any, we'll go beg a bit of Ma. And if she's out, Mary. And if not Mary, Ciara. And if we get desperate enough, we might even talk to Tavish."

"I don't know if I'll ever be *that* desperate."

Ian laughed. That was a sound Patrick would never grow tired of hearing. "Do you know the worst part about your being halfway across the country these past thirteen years? I've had to be friendly with Tavish. Pure torture, that's been."

"Well, I'm here now, brother. We can ignore him together."

Their plot proved doomed to failure. Not thirty minutes later, Tavish, Cecily, and their nearly one-year-old boy, Matthew, turned onto the very road they were driving on in their own wagon. They waved and pulled their wagons to a stop alongside each other.

"How'd your sales do?" Ian asked.

"Grand. And I had better company than in years past, I'll tell you that."

Ian leaned a little closer to Patrick. "*I* have gone with him in years past."

"Ah."

"Where've the two of you been?" Tavish asked.

"Up in the mountains," Patrick said. "Ian's been torturing me."

His brothers exchanged looks: eyes a little widened, brows twitching upward, mouth twists that seemed to say, "Isn't this intriguing?" Silent conversations were the specialty of brothers who were particularly close. Patrick and Ian used to have such conversations all the time. He had hope they would again.

"Our brother, here, has made a mull of things with the lass who's claimed his heart," Ian said. "Any words of advice for him, Cecily?"

From behind her green-tinted spectacles her brows pulled low. "Is Eliza upset with you?"

Ian and Tavish laughed. Even Patrick found he could smile. Obviously he hadn't kept his preference for Eliza a secret.

"She's decidedly upset," Patrick said. "I don't know how to fix it."

"Bribery?" Tavish suggested. "How much money do you have?"

"Stop it," Cecily said, amusement filling her tone.

"Poor as a church mouse, this one," Ian said. "And he's every bit as ugly as you are, so we can't depend on him wooing her over with his handsome gob."

"And he's not very funny," Tavish said, "so we can't count on charm."

Patrick managed to sneak into the back-and-forth. "I sure have missed the two of you," he said dryly.

"You also won't win her over with a show of brotherly devotion," Tavish said. "She'll sort out that deception straight off."

"The only person here I'm likely to get any actual help from is Cecily, but the two of you won't stop flapping your gums long enough for me to discuss this with her."

"I think I'm offended," Ian said. "Are you offended, Tavish?"

"Deeply."

Cecily shook her head. "The two of you are utterly impossible. Patrick, switch places with Tavish. We'll let these ridiculous brothers of yours drive ahead, and we can follow behind."

'Twas the most intelligence anyone had displayed since the two wagons stopped.

"Brilliant," Patrick said, and climbed down.

"We're really doing this?" Tavish clearly hadn't expected that.

"Outta the wagon, old man." Patrick ushered him out. "Go sit with that other antiquity over there. Cecily and I are going to solve a problem."

"And is Matthew coming with me?" Tavish asked.

"Of course not." Patrick gave him a look of exasperation. "He's too bright to ride in the dullard wagon."

Tavish held a hand up in a show of surrender. "I'll ride with Ian if only to shut your gob."

"Odd, the reason I'm riding with Cecily is so that you'll shut yours."

Patrick was in Tavish's seat, his horses' leads in hand a moment later. "Is now the right time to tell you that I don't actually know the way home?" he said under his breath to Cecily.

She didn't look concerned. "Just follow the boys. They've made this trek many times."

Patrick did precisely that.

Cecily wasted no time addressing the topic at hand. "How difficult are things between you and Eliza?"

"Horrible. Honestly, horrible."

She patted her baby's back as they rode along. "What reason did she give you for this rift?"

"I kept something from her I shouldn't have," he said. "Now she's worried I'm not trustworthy."

"Are you?"

"I try to be. I'm determined to be."

She looked in his direction as they spoke, though Patrick knew she was entirely blind. Did she do so out of habit or a sense of expectation?

"If keeping secrets is what caused her concern, then being forthright is most likely to counter that," Cecily said. "Are there other things about yourself you haven't told her?"

"We've known each other only a few months. There's a lifetime of things I could share with her." He would enjoy doing so, in fact. And hoped she would tell him about herself in return. "But I don't know if I have things to share that are . . . 'important' enough to overcome this chasm between us."

"You must have kept something quite significant from her." Cecily, bless her, sounded more empathetic than judgmental.

"Aye." He'd made a right mull of it all. "And it affected her daughter."

"Mercy, Patrick. *That* will make regaining her trust very, very difficult."

"What should I do? I have to at least try."

Cecily didn't say anything as they rolled down the road. Patrick kept his gaze on the wagon ahead, trying to convince himself that his heart wasn't dropping to his boots. What if he couldn't fix things with Eliza? What if he'd ruined everything?

"Secrecy put you in this fix," Cecily said. "Vulnerability seems your only chance of overcoming it."

"You have my attention."

"It'll likely be very uncomfortable, and there's no guarantee it will prove effective," she warned him.

"Eliza is the most extraordinary person I know. She saw value in me when I didn't see it in myself. She loved me when no one else did. No amount of discomfort will convince me not to do anything and everything I can to try to prove myself worthy of her regard."

Cecily nodded in apparent approval. "Then let's make good use of the remainder of our drive and sort this out."

Patrick's arrival at the *céilí* that night did not go unnoticed. He'd worried a little about his family's reception, considering he'd dragged Ian away, giving them all extra work to do without explaining his reason for being gone. Far from rejection, he was hugged and welcomed every bit as much as Ian, Tavish, Cecily, and Matthew were. It was comforting and reassuring, especially in light of the plan he and his golden-haired sister-in-law had concocted as they'd driven toward Hope Springs. Their plot might go terribly wrong, but at least *something* had gone right.

He found Cecily. "Have you heard anything encouraging?"

She nodded. "Tavish tells me Eliza is sitting with Maura near the musicians. A rather perfect position."

"What do I do if this doesn't work?"

"You'll be no worse off than you are now," she said. "But if Eliza is at all receptive to the possibility of second chances, then it will have been worth the risk, don't you think?"

"She's worth any risk," he said.

"Then go take it."

Cecily was often quiet, but she had shown herself time and again to be fearless. Patrick liked her more every time he was with her. And, heavens, he hoped she was right about this.

Patrick moved toward the musicians. Eliza was right where Cecily had said she would be. Maura welcomed him warmly, but she watched Eliza, no doubt wanting to make certain her friend approved of him joining them.

"You've been gone for a while," Eliza said.

"I took your advice."

Her gaze narrowed on him, not in disapproval but in confusion.

He answered the question he was certain hovered in her mind. "I told Ian what I told you, and what you sorted about me."

"Oh." She watched him, hope in her eyes. "And did he denounce you as you assumed he would?"

"No. He *helped* me."

A tender and joyful smile touched her face. No matter that she was put out with him, she was compassionate enough to be happy for him.

Maura looked from one of them to the other a couple of times, brow creased in confusion.

"I'm an awful lying liar, Maura," he said. "I think you probably ought to know that. Everyone likely should."

Laughter filled Maura's eyes. How easy it would be to play this off as a grand joke. But he owed Eliza vulnerability and honesty. He owed those things to all of them.

"I didn't tell the family I was still alive. I didn't tell them I was in Canada. I didn't tell you I had Grady's haversack. And I didn't tell you the real reason I left the Widows' Tower."

Maura set her hand on Patrick's arm. "I have always wondered about that. We tried to make a happy home for you there."

"You did. And after years of warfare, it was a godsend."

Quietly, Maura asked, "What drove you away, then?"

"Aidan asked so many questions about his da's time in the war. He wanted to hear heroic things, and I wanted to be able to *tell* him heroic things, because Grady really was brave and unwavering and noble. But war is nothing short of a walk through the corridors of hell, Maura, and I was still so close to it. I was afraid I'd say something that would dim Aidan's precious little light, and I couldn't risk that."

"He missed you when you left," Maura said.

"I missed him. I missed you. All of you."

She leaned closer and pressed a very sisterly kiss to his whiskered cheek. "We've missed you too, Patrick. It seems you're finally coming back to us."

She rose to her feet, the movement made a little more difficult by her quickly expanding middle. Patrick helped her. She smiled once more before moving in the direction of both her mothers-in-law.

"I'd wager that's the most honest you've been with her about your flight from New York," Eliza said.

"I'm working to be more trustworthy."

She watched him but didn't reach out, didn't touch his hand as she'd sometimes done. "Are you meaning to be more honest with me, as well?"

"Aye. Starting with something I've not told even m'family." Saints above, he could hardly believe what he was about to do. "During the thirteen years I was away from them, I learned to play the fiddle. I played it around the campfire during the war, then on m'own while working in Canada. I've not played it in front of anyone since Grady died. It's always felt too personal, too vulnerable."

"I can appreciate that." She was still guarded, but she wasn't sending him away.

"You told me you needed me to be more open about m'self and who I am. So, I'm no longer hiding the parts of me I think might earn me dismissal or laughter. And I'm starting now." He rose.

"You're going to play? In front of everyone?"

"I'll have to borrow an instrument—I sold mine to buy whiskey." He tossed her a chagrined look. "It's feeling good to be a little less under that spell. I'm hopeful that'll get better and better."

She pressed her open palm to her heart, watching him with wide eyes. Now was the moment of truth.

He approached the musicians just as they were finishing a tune. A dozen pairs of eyes turned to him. Seamus Kelly, who always served as the voice of these evenings, moved to stand next to him.

"What's your policy on guest musicians?" Patrick asked.

"We encourage 'em, provided they can keep a tune."

"I'm a bit out of practice," he admitted, "but I'd like a chance to try."

Seamus nodded, eying him. "I don't spot an instrument."

"I'd be needing to borrow one." He looked back at the musicians. "A fiddle."

Mary's husband, Thomas, was among them, he being quite the penny whistler. "You didn't used to fiddle."

"I picked it up during the years I've been away."

"Your da and ma haven't mentioned it."

Patrick's nerves were growing more raw by the moment, but he wouldn't back out now. He needed Eliza to see that he was sincere. "Da and Ma are about to be surprised, I'll tell you that."

"A debut performance, is it?" Seamus sounded excited at the prospect.

"Something of."

That seemed to satisfy them all. Rowan O'Donaghue stepped to him from among the others and held out his fiddle.

"I'll be careful of it," Patrick promised.

The lender didn't seem overly worried.

Seamus called the gathering to attention. "We've a new musician among us. Let's give him a listen, shall we?"

And with that, Patrick prepared to share with a town of near strangers, and a family he was barely coming to know again, a bit of his carefully hidden self. He did a quick check of the strings, making certain the instrument wasn't in need of tuning. Satisfied, he took a breath, then pulled the bow and began a tune he knew all too well.

The strains of "Irish Washerwoman" echoed around him. He knew he wasn't the most expert player, but he felt he did the song justice. Ma drew nearer, delight on her face. Da popped his arm around her and listened at her side. All the family were there, except Finbarr, who never attended the weekly parties. And they all appeared pleased.

He hadn't looked at Eliza. Not yet.

Only when he'd finished, and the crowd applauded, did he hazard a glance in her direction. He couldn't entirely make out her expression.

He returned the fiddle to Rowan with a word of gratitude. The musicians offered myriad invitations to join them again at future *céilís*. He didn't know if he'd take them up on the offer. That hadn't been the purpose of the song.

Patrick accepted compliments as he determinedly made his way back to Eliza. It took a little doing to get there. By the time he arrived at the seats where she'd been sitting, she was gone.

He sat, deflated and discouraged.

Maura passed behind him. She leaned close and whispered. "Don't lose hope. She saw and she listened. You're making more progress than you think."

If there was any mercy to be found, his sisters-in-law—*both* of them—would be proven as wise and correct as he hoped they were. As he needed them to be.

Chapter Twenty-seven

Eliza bounced Lydia in her arms as she paced inside Mr. and Mrs. O'Connor's home. Outside, the *céilí* continued. Laughter and music floated in. Was Patrick still playing with the musicians? She hoped so. Sharing important aspects of himself with the people around him would help him heal.

Lydia whimpered.

"Doc will be back any moment, sweetie. He'll make your foot feel better."

That didn't stop Lydia's tears. She wasn't feverish, which set Eliza's mind a little at ease. An infection had taken hold in the girl's foot, but the warmth was limited. They'd not left it too late.

Footsteps sounded from the doorway. Dr. Jones at last.

"You'll feel better now," Eliza said.

"What's the matter with her?"

She spun back. It wasn't Dr. Jones at all, but Patrick who'd stepped inside. No matter that she hadn't entirely sorted out him or the role she was open to him playing in her life; she was surprisingly happy to see him there.

"She got a splinter in her foot about a week ago. I pulled it out and thought that was the end of it. But Emma brought her to me at the very end of your tune because she was crying and fretting over her foot. I peeked at it and"—worry tugged at her heart—"it's turned a bit putrid."

"Has Dr. Jones seen it?"

She nodded. "He rushed back to his soddie to fetch his doctor's bag. I'm just waiting for him."

Lydia cried more miserably. Eliza didn't know how to ease her girl's suffering.

"Come here, *mo stóirín*." Patrick held his hands out for Lydia. "Let's give your ma a chance to breathe."

Eliza hesitated.

"I've not had a drink in more than two weeks," he said. "I'll understand if that's not enough to set your mind at ease, and I'll always be honest with you on that score. I swear to you."

He *was* being very honest. And he'd been such a comfort to Lydia in the past. She could let herself trust him enough to hold her little girl, especially since she herself would be nearby. She set Lydia in his arms.

Patrick gently kissed Lydia's cheek and whispered reassurances to her. The poor dear was so miserable that she'd even abandoned her doll. But she held fast to Patrick. She held the lapel of his coat in one fist. Her other hand brushed over his neatly trimmed beard, something she did nearly every time she was with Patrick. He never seemed to mind.

Eliza sat in a chair nearby and just breathed. It was nice to have someone sharing the care of her daughter, even if only for a moment. She often felt inadequate. And she was nearly always exhausted. Patrick's tender kindness was soothing Lydia and slowing her tears. He was helping both of them.

Dr. Jones soon arrived, leather satchel in hand. He motioned Patrick and Lydia over to where Eliza sat, indicating he should sit in the chair next to hers. The doctor pulled over an oil lamp. He turned up the wick.

Lydia folded herself into Patrick, clearly not pleased at this new arrival. Poor Dr. Jones. It must be hard caring for people who were afraid of his help.

The doctor set out a vial and a few instruments, along with a couple of rags and some strips of linen. He then took hold of Lydia's leg and carefully straightened it enough for the sole of her foot to be accessible.

Patrick held her in an embrace, her back against his chest, his arms wrapped around her. Eliza reached over and took the little girl's hand. It broke her heart to hear Lydia cry as the doctor worked on her wound. The infection had to be drained out and treated, but the doing of it was so painful.

"She'll be grand," Patrick said. "You'll see."

"She will." Dr. Jones spoke as he worked. "But she'll also be a bit sore. You'll struggle to get her to walk for the next day or two. Little ones are resilient, though. She'll be back to running around in no time."

"Until she picks up another splinter." She kissed Lydia's little hand, hoping to provide some comfort as she endured the misery. "I may have to get her shoes before winter after all. I'd hoped to wait a bit longer, so I could have more on hand if the stage company gives their nod to the new inn location. But I can't have Lydia's feet full of splinters."

Dr. Jones wrapped Lydia's foot in the long strips of bandaging. "I've given some thought to your new idea."

"And?"

He met her eye. She recognized the apology in them, and her spirits fell. "I can't set my practice so far away from all of my patients. Even the time it took to get from here to my soddie and back made me nervous."

She could appreciate that, though it was disappointing.

"I hope that won't cause too many difficulties for you," he said.

Eliza shook her head. "The stage company and the funds are far bigger obstacles. I do hope you can build yourself a proper infirmary, though, and a proper home."

"So do I." He tied off the bandaging. Before putting his supplies away, Dr. Jones took Lydia's free hand and smiled softly at her. "I'm sorry that hurt. Your foot will feel better soon, I promise."

When he was ready to go, Eliza followed him back to the door, receiving instructions on how to care for Lydia's foot as it healed.

"I do hope you're able to get your inn built," he said, standing in the doorway.

"As someone once told me, if the path I'm on doesn't lead to what I'm looking for, I'll find the path that does."

He blushed a little. "That is good advice."

"I thought so, as well."

He dipped his head and slipped back outside to the party. He was a good man, their doctor.

Mrs. O'Connor stepped inside in almost that exact moment. "Oh, Eliza. How is Lydia's foot?"

"Doc says she'll be fine in a few days."

"Oh, what a relief." Her gaze moved to Patrick, holding Lydia in his arms. "Patrick always was so sweet with the little ones. He used to call Finbarr 'bean sprout' and they were such good little friends."

"He's very loving to Lydia. That speaks well of his heart."

Mrs. O'Connor crossed to her son and his precious armful. Patrick smiled up at his ma, a lightness in the expression Eliza hadn't seen before with his family.

"Poor girl has the sniffle hiccups," she said to her son.

He rubbed Lydia's back. She was curled into his chest. "She feels terrible poorly, Ma."

"Well." Mrs. O'Connor stroked Lydia's hair. "She'll likely be sleeping in a moment, now that Doc's done digging around and she has you keeping her warm and safe."

"Rest'll do her good," Patrick said.

"Rest'd do her worn-thin ma good as well." Though Mrs. O'Connor had lowered her voice, Eliza heard. Far from offended, she agreed.

As his ma made her way to the nearby table and snatched up a bowl of scones to take back out to the party, Patrick got to his feet, taking care not to jostle Lydia. Mrs. O'Connor stepped out once more. Patrick carried Lydia over to Eliza.

She reached for the girl, intending to make the exchange.

Patrick shook his head. "I'll keep holding her. I meant only to ask if you'd like to lie down. Lydia'll do grandly with me while you rest."

It was a kindhearted offer but one she couldn't accept. "I should take her home. She'll rest better if she's able to sleep in her own bed."

"Let me walk back with you," he said. "She can rest on m'shoulder as we go. Then the both of you can go to sleep straight off once you're home."

"You'd do that? Even though I tossed you out last time I saw you?"

He colored up a little. "I deserved it. And so there's no misunderstanding between us, I'm not offering to walk with you because I'm expecting you to have forgiven me, or to forgive me now. I just want Lydia to be able to heal, and I want you to be able to rest."

The sincerity of his tone and compassion in his words warmed her. "I'd be grateful to you if you'd walk us home."

As they wove through the partygoers, Patrick received a lot of compliments on his fiddle playing. He accepted them with obvious embarrassment.

Once they were free of the gathering, Eliza tossed in her own observation. "You play the fiddle very well. I hope you don't regret sharing your music with everyone. You said it was very personal."

"I'm learning to be more vulnerable," he said. "And more authentic."

"Because of what I said?" She wasn't sure what she wanted the answer to be.

"Because you were right. I've been hiding a long time. I'm ready to step into the light."

She was glad to hear it, yet she wasn't fully reassured. "I want to believe that, to believe *you*, but . . ."

"I don't for a moment expect you to have faith in me after only one evening's evidence."

"Does this mean you're going to provide me with more proof?" she asked.

"That is precisely what this means." He adjusted Lydia in his arm, so her head lay on his shoulder. She was limp enough to be asleep. "I plan to tell you about my time in the army, if you ask. I'll tell you the good and the bad of our voyage from Ireland. I'll tell you how many lasses I've kissed."

"That last won't be necessary."

She adored the sound of his laugh.

"And I vow I'll be honest with you about the drinking. I should've been before."

"Have you gone a full fortnight without a drink before now?" she asked.

"Not in years."

Even in the dim light of fast-approaching night, she could see pride in his expression. "Every time I said I was thirsty, Ian plied me with tea."

"I like tea," she said. "I might even have you over for tea now and then."

"I would like that."

They walked on a bit, an easy silence settling between them, which he broke after a while. "Dr. Jones said you have a new location for the inn?"

"A *proposed* location. I thought perhaps the stage company would be in favor of a spot as far north of town as we proposed south of town."

"That seems a good solution."

"I hope they agree." She emptied her lungs. "Joseph sent a telegram, but he hasn't received an answer yet."

Patrick put his free arm around her shoulders and tucked her in, a kind and reassuring embrace. She needed that more than she'd realized.

"I'll work as the Archers' housekeeper for as long as I need to, but I'm holding out hope for my inn."

"If you're accepting votes, Eliza, mine'd be cast for you staying as nearby as you can manage for as long as possible."

They reached the Archers' house. While Eliza lit a lantern, Patrick carefully laid Lydia in her bed, tucking her in. He turned to Eliza, a look of uncertainty in his eyes.

"I have something for you," he said. "It's nothing fine or fancy, but I hope it'll be of use to you." He pulled from his pocket what looked like two very stiff child's socks. "They ought to be about the right size. I remembered how big her feet were in my hand."

"For Lydia?"

"The soles are six layers of canvas sewn together. They're not as good as a real pair of shoes would be, but they'll make it far harder to get splinters in her feet."

"Oh, Patrick." She took the precious little hand-sewn shoes from his hand, amazed that he'd made something like this.

"They'll not do once winter arrives, but they should get you by until then. And it'll save the little lass's feet from a repeat of tonight's business."

"Oh, Patrick," she said again.

"I made 'em while I was in the mountains sobering up. I thought of the two of you a lot while I was there, wishing I hadn't caused you pain." He rubbed at the back of his neck. "I don't want you to think this is a bribe or anything. It's not. I was just worried about her feet and wanted her to be able to run around and not get hurt."

She held the little canvas shoes to her heart, so moved by the offering. "These and her doll. Your kindness to her . . ."

"I mean them to be kindnesses to you, too," he said.

Throwing caution to the wind, she wrapped her arms around him. "Thank you, Patrick O'Connor."

He held her for a long, drawn-out moment. And though she still had questions and worries, she found peace in his embrace to match what she'd felt weeks ago in his parents' loft, and before that, when they'd looked after Lydia together.

She wanted to trust him. She wanted to believe in him again. She wanted to feel this warmth and safety once more.

She wanted him to stay.

But reality intervened as it often did. He offered his farewells long before she was ready. After he left, she sat in the quiet of her room, longing for him to return. Her heart was running far, far ahead of her wary mind.

Chapter Twenty-eight

For thirteen years, there'd been a hole in Patrick's life. Working alongside his family in their fields at harvest over the next weeks, he came to truly recognize the shape of it. He was no farmer and didn't want to make a lifelong pursuit of it, but he'd've given near anything to have spent any of the past harvest seasons with them.

"That oldest boy of yours is a hard worker," he told Ian as they brought in the last of his grain on an autumn afternoon. "Is he wanting to farm as well?"

"He has more interest in horses. 'Twoudn't be surprising in the least if he worked out at one of the ranches."

"He'd still be nearby, though." Patrick knew that would matter to Ian.

"Biddy's particularly happy about that."

"Which," Patrick said, "I'd wager makes you particularly happy."

Tavish came up even with them on their walk to the house. "Eliza's here sewing with the womenfolk. I'd wager that'll make *Patrick* 'particularly happy.'"

The rest of the men were, apparently, near enough to overhear, as the laughter and jesting that followed was immediate and thorough.

Ian tossed Patrick a look that was equal parts amusement and sympathy. "Tavish told them."

"Didn't have to," Tavish said. "'Twasn't precisely a mystery."

Patrick knew his family too well to trust they'd not embarrass him in front of Eliza. To all the group, Patrick said, "I'd be beholden to all of you if you'd keep your jesting to your own selves. I've made a wee bit of progress with the lass these past couple of weeks, but she's skittish still. You'll frighten her off."

"If your ugly mug hasn't already done that," Finbarr said, "I don't think anything will."

"I'll have you know," Tavish tossed back, "Patrick looks almost exactly like me."

Finbarr wasn't deterred. "As I said . . ."

All the O'Connor men, those born to the family and those who'd married in, laughed heartily. Patrick's attention, though, remained on Finbarr. He often kept to himself, a little distanced from his brothers and da. But in that moment, he grinned and laughed right along with them.

Ian slapped a hand on Patrick's shoulder. "You'll never have the appeal of us ginger lads, but Finbarr and I'll try not to mock you too much for your homeliness."

"How generous of you and the bean sprout," Patrick said dryly.

He'd missed his brothers these past years. A fellow's spirits couldn't be low for long with them nearby. He oughtn't to have stayed away so long.

They reached Ian's house, having been working his fields that day, and the whole lot of them poured inside.

"You're done earlier than I'd expected," Biddy said as she approached Ian.

"We've extra hands this year." He set his arm around his wife and held her to his side.

Biddy turned her sights on Patrick. "You've made them more efficient. Impressive for a man who's not ever been a farmer."

"'Tisn't true," Da said, passing by. "He worked the land in Ireland."

"Da, I was eight years old when we left." Patrick had more vivid memories of the boat journey to America than he did of Ireland herself. "I can't say even a bit of those skills crossed the Atlantic with me."

254

"It's in your blood, lad. We belong to the land no matter where we live. It calls to us."

Patrick did like being in a place with more land than buildings. He'd liked that about Canada, as well. But farming didn't call to him in the way it did the others. He wanted to stay in Hope Springs, but it'd be a struggle to support himself in a valley of farms.

"Pa-ick!" Lydia was getting better and better at saying his name. He loved hearing it.

She rushed to him, her little canvas shoes on and her beloved doll in her hand. Patrick scooped her up and spun her around.

"You're walking so much better, *mo stóirín*. Makes me happy as a cat in the cream."

"Happy cat."

Patrick looked over at Eliza. "Two words." He was both amazed and delighted. "I don't think I've heard that from her before."

She joined him, smiling softly at her daughter. "Lydia's finding her voice."

"You and me both, sweet pea." He kissed the little girl's soft cheek. She giggled. So, he kissed her again, and she giggled louder. The game continued until he was laughing too hard to continue.

Eliza watched them, amusement dancing in her eyes. "I believe Lydia has won your little game."

"That she has." He bounced Lydia in his arms but kept his gaze on her ma. "Thank you for letting me be in her life again."

"You're good to her. I'm grateful for that."

Her faith in him did his heart a world of good. He'd made some headway these past weeks showing her she didn't need to be wary of him. He was close to undoing the damage he'd done; he felt certain of it.

Eliza wiped a smudge off Lydia's chin. "Your ma said that the men in the family will be making a trek to the train depot in the next couple of days." She looked to him once more. "Are you going with them?"

He nodded. "Da said I would be. He tossed that out like nothing else made sense."

She smiled at him. "They like having you around."

255

He held Lydia closer and lowered his voice. "I always assumed I'd have to convince them to love me again."

"And did you have to?"

Gratitude swelled inside him. "Turns out I didn't need to. Ian told me they'd never stopped loving me, but I couldn't believe it."

"*I* told you, too," Eliza pointed out.

He smiled. "I really should start listening to you."

"Yes, you should."

Lydia wiggled, pointing at the floor. "Down."

He set her on her feet, and she toddled away toward the other children.

Eliza motioned him over to the door, away from all the others. "How much have you told them?" She kept her voice low, barely above a whisper.

He slipped his hand around hers and walked with her out onto the porch. He liked the feel of her hand in his, the warm strength of this surprising woman. He closed the door, quietly so it wouldn't draw attention.

"Ian knows all of it," he said. "Da asked me a few things while we were working the fields, so I told him. But he thought it best not to lay it all bare to Maura or Aidan unless they ask."

"Is that a weight you can bear?"

"It doesn't feel like a weight anymore. I'm being myself with them now. I talk about the places I lived and the people I knew in the war. I play music for them when I can borrow a fiddle. We sing together. We laugh. And they like me and *love* me."

"Of course they do." She hadn't pulled her hand out of his. That was encouraging.

"You tossed that 'of course' out real easy. Am I right to hope that means you're thinking more highly of me yourself?"

"I may be starting to."

"Did your da say how long you all will be gone?" Eliza asked.

"A little more than a week. The grain'll get sold. The men'll buy some supplies they can't get at the mercantile."

She turned wide eyes on him. "I didn't realize this was a trek to the shops." Her tone was light and teasing. "How very exciting for you to do a bit of shopping."

"We've not fooled you. This'll be nothing but a pleasure jaunt." That brought to mind something he'd meant to ask her. "Are you needing anything you've not been able to find at the mercantile? I can fetch it and bring it back for you. I'd be happy to."

The thinnest sheen of worry tugged at her mouth. "We need winter coats, and Lydia needs proper shoes. Do you suppose those could be purchased there?"

"I can't imagine they couldn't be. A bigger town like that'd be more likely to carry ready-to-wear coats and shoes in all sizes."

She pressed her lips together, brow pulled low. "I wonder how much it all would cost. Saving to pay part of the inn myself is my new plan. I have to be careful of my coins."

"Your new plan for the inn." He rubbed her hands between his, hoping to keep them warm in the chill autumn air. "Did Joseph Archer hear from the stage company?"

"No, and he doesn't think that's likely a good omen." She slipped her hand free and moved to sit on the steps. "I'm trying not to lose hope entirely, but I've been chasing this dream for so long—even before I came here—and it's become more of a struggle to be optimistic."

Patrick sat beside her. "And are you thinking you'll leave if the inn doesn't get built?"

"It *will* get built," she said, "even if the stage company won't agree to make it a stop. I'm determined not to lose this dream."

"Will you have enough business, do you think, if stage passengers aren't stopping?"

She sighed and leaned her head against him. "That's why I need to save money first. If I have some put aside, then I'll be able to stay open even if I don't have as many guests as I need. But I can't be certain Joseph or Jeremiah would still invest in the inn with that much risk involved."

He put his arm around her. "I wish I had answers for you, darlin'."

"Building the inn was meant to be your next job, and your livelihood," she said. "If it's not built, will *you* leave Hope Springs?"

He honestly didn't know quite what he'd do. Finbarr might let him work his land in exchange for a roof over his head and a bit of the profits. But he wouldn't enjoy it. Still, Eliza didn't enjoy housekeeping, and *she* wasn't rushing off to the next opportunity. Learning to like work he'd not prefer to do was a small price to pay for staying in Hope Springs and staying with her.

"I've been running long enough," he said. "I think it's time I put down some roots."

"And you'll be putting them down here?"

He leaned his head against hers. "Provided no one objects."

"They'd better not."

Patrick grinned. "And what'll you do if someone disapproves of my staying?"

"I would give *them* reason and plenty for leaving."

He laughed long and deep. She was a delight.

"I was so certain during our stage ride that you were a happier person than you seemed," she said. "I'm so glad I was right."

He squeezed her shoulders and pressed a kiss to the top of her head. "I'm glad, too."

The door opened behind them, and quick steps crossed the porch.

"Enough sparking, you two," Tavish said as he sped down the steps beside Patrick. "We're for Thomas's fields now."

The rest of the brothers and Da were hot on his heels.

"What about lunch?" Patrick asked. "That's what we came in for."

"Already ate," Ciara's husband, Keefe, tossed back. "You nap through a meal, you go hungry."

Thomas flipped around, walking backwards so he could face Patrick as he said, "I'd wager he wasn't napping."

"You had best go," Eliza said. "The teasing will only get worse if you don't."

"It'll get worse either way." He stood, reluctant to go, but also eager to be with his brothers and da.

"I think you like it." She reached out, and he took her hand, helping her to her feet.

"It's good to be with them again." He pulled her into an embrace.

"And it's good to be with you, even if only for the length of a quick lunch."

"A lunch you didn't eat."

He bent to kiss her forehead but paused, watching her, wondering. She brushed her fingertips along his cheek just above his beard.

"They'll tease you if you take too long."

"And well worth it, it'd be," he whispered.

He brushed the lightest of kisses over her lips. Such a simple, brief touch, but it set his mind spinning and his heart pounding. "I'll miss you while we're at the depot," he whispered. "I'll miss not seeing you every day."

"You'll simply have to come back, I suppose." Her lighthearted response stood in direct contrast to the harsh dismissal she'd dealt him weeks earlier. They'd come so far.

He kissed her once more, the effort cut even shorter by the sound of his brothers whooping and whistling.

Patrick stepped back, letting his arms fall away from her. "Remind me again why I wanted to reconcile with those troublemakers."

"Because you were alone far too long," she said, "and you ought never be alone again."

Two days later, Patrick sat on a wagon bench up beside Joseph Archer with Finbarr standing behind, leaning against the bench back. Wagons from Hope Springs rolled along in front of and behind theirs, all headed for the depot. Patrick was enjoying the company, but he'd far prefer to have been sitting on Ian's front stoop with Eliza. He'd seen her briefly before the exodus for the depot, but with all the Archer family hovering about, they'd been limited to words of parting when he'd far rather have kissed her again.

He required every ounce of constraint he had to keep his expression neutral every time he thought about that brief kiss. His brothers would've asked too many questions and come up with too many answers if they'd caught him making cow eyes to himself. He liked their teasing, generally. It was how a person knew he'd been accepted by the O'Connor family. But he wasn't fully ready to be teased about *this*.

"Does the town always leave together?" Patrick asked.

Joseph nodded. "We've found that selling our crops in bulk is easier, and we're more likely to get a good price banding together."

"This town looks after each other."

"*Now*," Finbarr said.

Patrick had heard bits and pieces of the town's past feuding. While he heard regret in the voices of others who spoke of it, none held the hint of bitterness Finbarr's did. There was pain there, Patrick would wager. Deeply buried pain. Maybe that was why he didn't want to move out to his new house. Maybe he didn't actually want to stay in Hope Springs. Patrick hoped that wasn't true. He'd only just gotten his family back; he didn't want to lose any of them.

Eliza's future in Hope Springs was also a little uncertain. Patrick couldn't be easy on that school. "Have you had any further word from the stage company about Eliza's inn?"

"I'm going to stop in at the stage office while we're at the depot," Joseph said. "One way or the other, I need an answer from the company."

"Do you think they'll agree to change their schedule to include a stop at the new proposed location?"

"No." Joseph gave him an apologetic look. "I hated having to tell Eliza that, and I won't be much happier to give her the final news if it's bad, as I expect."

"She'll be heartbroken." Patrick couldn't like the thought of that. "She'd love to run an inn again."

Joseph nodded. "And you would enjoy building it."

"I do like building, but there aren't many chances to do much of it around Hope Springs."

"What are your plans, then?" Joseph had a way of asking personal questions without sounding prying.

"I'll pick up odd work where and when I can. Outside of that, I thought I'd see if Finbarr here would take me on as a farmhand out at his place."

Finbarr leaned evermore forward, his arms hooked around the bench back. "What do you know about farming?"

He shrugged. "Practically nothing, but I'm a quick study in most things."

"You trained Aidan in a summer to be one of the best farmhands I've seen," Joseph said. "You could teach Patrick."

Finbarr pulled his hat down further, hiding more of his face. Did he realize it did that? Is that why he so often wore his hat tilted forward that way? "There's too much to do for me to talk him through it."

"It's farm work," Patrick said. "You've been doing it almost all your life."

Finbarr turned and slid down, sitting in the wagon bed. "It's never been planted. The fields haven't been chosen or laid out. The irrigation ditches haven't been dug. I can't do any of that."

"I've worked digging ditches," Patrick said. "I'm good at it."

"I can't see the land," Finbarr said. "I couldn't tell you where to dig or how to lay out the fields."

"You and I have five brothers and brothers-in-law who take great delight in bossing me. Da enjoys it too. You can sit on a rocker under the overhang and enjoy listening to them bark orders at me."

"Grannies sit in rockers under overhangs," Finbarr grumbled.

"Given the choice, *I'd* sit in a rocker under an overhang." Patrick kept his tone light, not caring for the turn in Finbarr's mood.

"No, you wouldn't. You'd be *building* the rocker, and the overhang, and the house it was attached to." He slumped a little lower. "You wouldn't want to be useless."

Useless? Patrick shot a look at Joseph. The worry and sadness in the man's face matched what must have been on his own. Finbarr had seemed at home and at ease in their brothers' and da's fields the last couple of weeks. For months, Finbarr had moved about confidently with Aidan's assistance. Why did doing the same on his own land deal him such a felling blow? Whatever the answer, there was no mistaking that Finbarr didn't want to discuss the matter further.

Patrick jumped back to the earlier topic with Joseph, hoping to give the lad a chance to regain his footing. "If the stage company gives you the answer you're expecting, is there any hope of moving forward with the inn?"

"They weren't going to make any monetary contributions. The funds would still be sufficient, but the overnight guests wouldn't be."

So it could still be built. "'Tis a shame, that. Having so large a building would be a boon to the town. We could have *céilís* no matter the weather. Wedding suppers could be held without limiting the guest list to those who'd fit in a small house. The doctor could have his infirmary."

"Only if we build closer to town, like Eliza had wanted to begin with," Joseph said. "But we know the stage won't stop for the night just outside Hope Springs. They pass us closer to midday. And, with the stage running each direction only twice a week, staying afloat would have been difficult even with their business. Without it . . ."

"In one of the Canadian towns I lived in, a woman took in boarders, but only in the summer. 'Tweren't enough visitors passing through in the winter months. She said that made things mighty lean half the year."

Joseph glanced back at Finbarr. The man cared a lot about Patrick's little brother, there was no mistaking that. He liked him all the more for it.

"Eliza would likely have had to close the kitchen a couple of days a week even with reliable business from stage passengers." Joseph slowed his wagon as those in front of them slowed as well. "She is certainly in a difficult position."

The first inklings of an idea began forming in Patrick's mind.

Open only in the summer. Close the kitchen a couple of days a week. The stage passes midday.

He needed to think longer, sort out the details, but he had the entirety of this run to the depot to do so. And, better still, he had Joseph's mind for business at his disposal.

An answer was tucked just out of reach; he knew there was. And he was going to find it.

Chapter Twenty-nine

Eliza stood near the stage road, her eyes on the distant mountains. How easily she could picture the inn here, where she'd first dreamed of it being. Patrick had sketched plans back when they thought this was to be the spot. He'd framed that view in what would have been her bedroom window. She would have loved that. And the large public room had a large picture window with a grand vista as well. The weekly *céilís* could have been held in the winter with the beauty of snow falling on the other side of the glass.

She and Lydia could have spent Christmas beside the fireplace in their very own home. And Patrick—

She stopped that thought before it fully formed. Her worries over him had eased tremendously over the previous weeks, replaced by the tenderness that had been growing for months. But she'd best not get ahead of herself. So much was still unsettled between them.

The wind blew, as always, swirling the dust in the road and rustling the tall grass around her. What a peaceful spot this would have been to make a home. The location farther north was likely nice as well. If the stage company would agree to stop there on their twice-weekly journeys, giving up this one would be worth it.

She wrapped her arms around herself, breathing in the moment and attempting to breathe out the dream. The path that led to what she wanted wasn't the one she'd been treading. She needed to be ready and willing to change direction. She simply wasn't yet.

Maura arrived while Eliza was contemplating. She drove a little pony cart and parked it almost exactly where Eliza had envisioned the stables. "Ryan was bang on the mark, it seems."

"What was he correct about? *This time,* I mean."

Maura's eyes crinkled with a smile. "He said you'd be out here at your 'inn' and that I ought to drive out and fetch you, so you needn't walk back."

Ryan had remained behind when the other Hope Springs men made the southbound trek. As it had been explained to her, a few men always remained behind to help tend to their neighbors' animals and land. With Maura due to have her baby soon, Ryan had volunteered to be one of those who stayed in town.

"This would have been the perfect place for it, you know," Eliza said.

"It would, indeed."

Eliza pressed her hand to the back of her bonnet, holding it fast against the wind. "And you would've come and eaten dinner here now and then, wouldn't you? I'd have asked very reasonable prices."

"We would've come, for sure and certain. I think most folks in town would've, now and then. A real treat, it would've been. And the ranchers, well, they've a fair bit of coin to rub together. They'd likely have come, too. And their hands would've enjoyed splurging, especially after getting paid."

Maura's words were cold comfort, but comfort just the same.

"It might have worked." Eliza sighed. "And it would have been wonderful."

"Are you giving up, Eliza?"

She turned back to face her friend, hoping that her determination showed despite her flagging spirits. "Not at all, simply setting my sights on a different path."

"Tonight, let's set our sights on the road that leads back to my house," Maura said. "We've dinner ready, and your Lydia'll be pleased to have you back."

Eliza climbed into the cart. "Thank you, again, for watching her today."

"Of course. We love having her with us."

"I would offer to do the same when your new one arrives, but I have all I can manage at Archers'."

Maura guided the horses around and drove back toward town. Eliza couldn't help one last backward glance at the site she would always think of as the place where her inn ought to have been. Being farther away wouldn't be terrible if it meant actually getting an inn of her own after all these years. Not perfect, not ideal. But also not terrible.

She forced her focus forward, in more ways than one. "How are you feeling?" she asked Maura.

"Quite well, really. My cough hasn't grown worse, which Dr. Jones is both surprised and pleased with."

That was good news. "Is he optimistic about your lungs enduring the strain of delivery?"

"More than before, but he's still not shrugging away the possibility of complications. But, it is what it is. We'll face what'll be and do what needs done." Maura was always determined and unshakable. It was hardly surprising that she was facing the prospect of a difficult delivery with the same stalwartness.

"You'll send for me, I hope, to be there with you, as you were there with me when Lydia was born."

Maura shook her head in amusement. "Thus far, I have been requested to send for both my mothers-in-law, all of my sisters-in-law, Dr. Jones, and you. We will be having a regular *céilí* right there in my bedroom."

Eliza couldn't help a small laugh. "Would you have ever guessed during our years at the Widows' Tower that there'd be a time when you were so surrounded by family that you'd be concerned about overcrowding?"

"I could not have even imagined it. But, once I got here, I couldn't stop imagining this town with you in it."

"I will be forever grateful that you sent for us. I love Hope Springs. I love it so very much."

They rolled over the rise behind which the Hope Springs valley hid. "Would a certain bearded Irishman be part of the reason you love it?"

"Might be."

Maura looked over at her for just a moment. "Is he being good to you, Eliza? I know things were difficult between you for a bit there."

"Yes, but we're better now. I feel that I'm finally seeing the true Patrick, the man he is beneath the caution and reserve." A peaceful sort of warmth spread from her heart at the thought of him the past couple of weeks. He'd been the kind and thoughtful man she'd seen so many times, but without the wall between them. "What was he like before?"

"I first met him when he was about my Aidan's age. He was light and happy, and, heavens, he was funny. I don't know that I've ever met anyone as quick-witted as he was. And he and Ian were inseparable. They brought out the best in each other. Patrick was the light of his family; he had a knack for giving them hope because he was overflowing with it himself."

She tried to imagine that younger version of him. "He struggles to be hopeful now."

"Something that weighs on all of us. But there's more hope in him lately. Does us all good."

"He told me a story not long after we arrived here about filching pastries during the voyage from Ireland." She grinned at the memory. "We were telling each other things in our lives no one else knew. It was the lightest I'd seen him since I met him. I knew then he wasn't supposed to be so burdened and heavy. It broke my heart seeing him that way afterward."

"You've been good for him, Eliza."

"Then why does that declaration sound so hesitant?"

The wagon rolled over the bridge heading toward Maura's home.

"You're a sister to me. I'd not see you unhappy for anything, not even for someone I love as much as Patrick."

Eliza clasped her hands on her lap. Thinking of Patrick made her heart leap around a bit. "He's been good for me, too, Maura. He loves my Lydia. He's thoughtful and hardworking. He listens when I talk to him. He doesn't make light of the things I worry about. And he's funny, like you said he used to be. And I'm happier when he's nearby."

Maura brought the cart to a stop outside the barn. Ryan stood in the open doorway, leaning against the frame and smiling at his wife in a way that could only be described as besotted.

"I think he's rather fond of you, Maura."

"Well, I'm rather fond of him, so 'tis a good arrangement all around."

Ryan helped her down, then kissed her sweetly. "How're you feeling, sweetheart?"

"Grand altogether."

Eliza climbed down and made her way to the house, giving the couple a bit of privacy. The moment she stepped inside, Lydia hopped up off the floor.

"Mama!" She ran to her and threw her arms around Eliza's leg. Her doll hit Eliza's other leg on the way around.

Eliza set her hand on Lydia's curly head. "Have you been a good girl?"

Mrs. Callaghan answered. "She's been an angel."

"That's my sweet pea." She held Lydia in her arms. The girl had blossomed in this valley. Patrick had begun that transformation in her, showing her love and kindness and caring. He'd taught her cautious heart to trust.

Perhaps it was time Eliza more fully learned that lesson herself.

Chapter Thirty

Eliza sat on the floor of the Archers' sitting room with Katie, the Archer children, and Lydia, a quarter of an hour into what was likely to be a very long game of Duck, Duck, Goose. Ever since playing it at a *céilí* weeks earlier, both Lydia and little Sean wanted to play nothing else. Eliza and Katie had put them off all day with the promise of a game once the girls were home from school.

"Why do we have to play this every day, Mama?" Ivy asked, flopping around dramatically while still remaining in her spot in the circle. They usually played this game out of doors, but the weather was a bit too cold for comfort that day.

"The little ones enjoy it," Katie answered, as calm as ever. "I'm full certain Emma played many games with you when you were younger that she'd've rather not."

"Scads of them," Emma said as she walked around the outside of the circle. She set her hand on Katie's head. "Duck." Then Sean's. "Duck."

Lydia bounced, watching her approach.

Emma paused and, with intentionally slow movement, moved her hand toward Lydia's head. She pulled her eyes wide. Lydia giggled.

"Goose."

For just a moment, Lydia didn't remember what to do.

Eliza helped her to her feet. "Goose. Go."

Lydia ran after Emma, her steps awkward and teetering but her face split in a broad grin. Good sport that she was, Emma made a show of running but didn't move very fast at all. One of Lydia's feet bumped into the other, and she toppled into a heap on the wood floor. Before anyone in the circle could react, Lydia was scooped up and set on her feet by Joseph Archer.

"Pompah!" Ivy was on her feet with all the speed of a young and limber child. She ran to her father and threw her arms around his legs. "Pompah!"

Emma rushed to him as well, her more subdued but equally sincere greeting characteristically different from her sister's. Little Sean didn't arrive quite as quickly, but neither did he hesitate. Joseph picked him up and held his son in one arm.

Katie stood a few paces off, watching her family. Joseph met her gaze. No one seeing them in that moment could ever doubt how deeply they loved each other.

"My Katie," he said softly.

She closed the gap between them and was immediately enfolded in her husband's embrace, their children pulled close as well.

Eliza took hold of Lydia's hand and slipped from the room. The menfolk hadn't been expected to return for another day or two. Their early arrival was, no doubt, a pleasant surprise for Joseph's family.

She paused in the dining room a moment, her thoughts on those long-ago days when she had greetings such as that to look forward to; first, in her childhood family, then Terrence during their brief marriage. The regret and strain between them hadn't made their marriage a miserable one. She missed the days when things had been good and happy between them. She missed having someone to greet, and someone to greet her. She missed having a family to come home to.

Lydia's hand sat softly in hers, easing the sadness.

"We're family," she said to her little girl. "And I have you with me every day. That's reason and plenty to be joyful."

Eliza was determined to keep her spirits up. They walked hand in hand into the kitchen. It wasn't empty.

Patrick sat at the work table, a stub of a pencil in his hand as he scratched out some sort of note.

"Pa-ck!" Lydia's latest—admittedly odd—version of his name pulled his attention away from his writing.

The look of utter adoration on his face melted Eliza's heart. "*Mo stóirín!*" He moved quickly around the table and held his arms open as Lydia rushed into his waiting embrace. "I've missed you, *mo chailín beag.*"

That last was an Irish phrase Eliza hadn't heard before. But there was no mistaking his tone. Patrick loved her little girl. Lydia leaned her head against him and scratched her fingers in his beard.

"It's longer, isn't it? I've not trimmed it since I left."

Lydia just smiled at him, and he, kneeling on the ground, held her. He looked up and met Eliza's eyes.

"She's missed you," Eliza said.

"Has *she?*"

A little flip of the heart delayed her response a moment. "She has. And she has hoped that you spent some time with your brothers and father while you were away. And she hopes your connection to them has deepened."

"For a wee girl who's not spoken more than two words at once in all the months I've known her, she's had a lot to say while I was away."

Heat touched Eliza's cheeks. Was he laughing at her?

She clung to what dignity she could and moved to the stove. The family would want their dinner soon enough.

"Eliza?"

"Did you have a good journey?" She tried to sound casual.

He slipped up next to her. "Oh, 'twas a terrible thing I've endured. Suffering. Torture. I've not eaten in two weeks. Have pity on me, dearie. I'm begging you."

His teasing lifted her spirits. "I suppose I can let you stay, but only if you tell me what is in that note you were writing."

Patrick picked up Lydia, who was tugging at the leg of his trousers. "I didn't want to disrupt your work, so I was leaving a note explaining that your two coats and Lydia's shoes are on your bed."

Her excitement was tempered by nerves. "Did they come terribly dear?"

He shook his head. "In fact, the money you sent me with is on your bed as well."

"You didn't pay for them yourself, did you?" He hadn't money enough for such things.

"I didn't. A man who lives near the depot was desperate to finish up his new barn before winter arrives. I spent the couple of days we were all there working on it with him in exchange for a very warm woolen lady's coat, an equally warm little girl's coat, and a pair of child's shoes."

"You might have been paid for that labor, Patrick. I know you haven't had work. You need the money."

He set his unoccupied arm around her waist and pulled her up to him. Eliza's heart nearly jumped out of her chest. It was the scene she'd seen play out in the sitting room, but with herself part of it.

"My sweet Eliza," he said. "I'd not've suggested the trade if I'd been at all opposed to it. The man also tossed in a tremendous amount of tea as part of the exchange."

"Did you drink a lot of tea while you were there?" She'd worried about him being in a place that had saloons and liquor to be bought with ease.

"Gallons of it," he said.

That was a relief.

"Between the tea and the barn, I didn't struggle as much as I feared I would," he said. "And trading for labor wasn't too much of a worry. I'm not needing money in m'pocket just now."

"You aren't?"

He smiled warmly. Even the growth in his beard couldn't hide his beautiful, heart-flipping smile.

"I'll be working Finbarr's land until he's ready to take it over. He'll be letting me keep a good bit of the profits on the harvest as well as whatever food I grow in the kitchen garden. I'll not starve."

She leaned against him, much as Lydia was doing. "But you won't have any profits or crops for an entire year. What will you do until then?"

He pulled her in a touch closer. "According to Joseph, I'll be building an inn."

She all but jumped. "You'll *what?*"

His chest shook a little with a silent laugh. "We had ample time for tossing ideas around, and we managed to come up with one that he's confident will work. The stage company has already given their approval."

She pulled back, watching him closely. Her breaths came faster, more eager. "What is it? What's the plan? Where are we building?"

"I'll not keep you from your work, Eli—"

"And I'll not be able to summon the least focus if you don't explain, Patrick. Truly, I'm struggling to even form words at the moment."

He stepped away and set Lydia on a chair at the table. Eliza followed him, trying not to be too hopeful all the while finding less and less reason not to be. Oh, if this hope broke her heart . . . How would she ever recover? "Please tell me, Patrick. I can't bear it."

Joseph and Katie stepped into the kitchen in the very next instant. Katie pressed her palms together with a look of excitement. "Joseph just told me about the inn."

"I've been trying to get Patrick to do that."

Joseph spoke to Patrick. "Borrow my buggy and drive her out to the building site. You can explain it all there."

"What about dinner?" Eliza asked. "I've not even begun it."

Katie gave her a quick hug. "I'll cook tonight."

"And Lydia?" she pressed.

"The girls will be delighted to look after her." Katie gave her a nudge toward the door. "You go with Patrick. Let him tell you what they've concocted."

The buggy rolled past the mercantile without Patrick having offered even a clue about their destination, the plan for the inn, or the likelihood of the plan succeeding.

"Will you not at least tell me *something?*" She heard the pleading quality in her voice; he couldn't possibly miss it. "I am trying not to let myself fully hope—my dreams have been dashed on this matter too many times—but I also don't want to be discouraged if I needn't be."

He adjusted so he held the horse's lead in one hand, freeing the other to take hold of hers. He raised it to his lips and lightly kissed the back of her fingers. "Allow yourself to hope, darling. You've ample reason to."

She slipped her fingers from his so he could drive more easily, but threaded her arm through his, leaning against him with her head on his shoulder.

"The days of driving to and from the depot were not nearly this cozy," he said with a laugh.

"The last two weeks around here haven't been either."

They made the climb up the hill that hid Hope Springs from passersby.

"Will the inn have to be built terribly far away?" She was willing to go wherever she needed to for this dream to come true, but she worried that she'd be lonely so far from the friends she'd made. She felt certain Patrick would come visit regularly, but he'd not be able to do so every day. She'd miss him most of all.

"I think you'll be pleased with the location."

"You won't even give me a hint?"

He pulled the buggy to a stop at the top of the hill. "Your hint is this: were the inn already complete, you would be able to see it now."

They were well within sight of the original location, the one she'd had to abandon weeks earlier, the one she still longed for and wished for. She looked to Patrick, not daring to believe what she was beginning to suspect.

He smiled broadly. "There was never a better place for it."

"The original site? Truly?"

He nodded.

"How is that possible?"

He set the horse to a walk once more, the buggy aiming directly for her future inn. Her inn. Merciful heavens, it actually seemed within reach.

"Joseph and I tossed around every scenario we could come up with for making your inn an overnight stop for the stage company.

Even Finbarr added his thoughts. We couldn't find an answer that didn't pull you too far from Hope Springs."

"That's been my conclusion as well."

"But then, sweetie, I realized maybe we were asking ourselves the wrong question."

She hadn't the first idea what he meant. "Which question ought we to have been asking?"

He smiled at her, the look one of adorably self-satisfied excitement. "Instead of 'How do we make a Hope Springs inn fit an overnight stop?' we should've wondered 'What kind of stop fits Hope Springs?'"

What kind of stop? An overnight stop didn't work because the stage passed Hope Springs at approximately midday. Midday. "A lunch stop?"

He nodded. "A lunch stop."

Her mind spun. A lunch stop. The stage would pass at the opportune time for that, but how could that possibly be a solution? An inn without overnight guests wouldn't be an inn for long.

"I can see you're trying to sort it all out. Let me fill in a few of the gaps." He slowed the buggy as they approached the site. "Joseph suggested to the stage company that they take a midday stop in Hope Springs. The passengers can get themselves a bite to eat. The drivers can, as well, and their horses can rest for a spell. The stage makes the roundtrip twice a week."

"So I would have customers four days a week."

"A predictable four days a week," he said. "You can plan your days and supplies accordingly."

"Can I stay afloat on only four days of midday meals?"

"Dr. Jones would have his infirmary and would pay rent. That will help."

She would far prefer he'd said, "make all the difference" rather than "help."

Patrick stopped the buggy and climbed down. He gently patted the horse as he walked around to Eliza's side of the buggy. He held his arms out to her. She accepted the assistance and was soon walking beside him.

"Joseph believes that the stage company will come to realize the benefit of an established inn, one with food at the ready and protection from the elements. He's confident they'll make it a priority to sort out a means of making your inn an overnight stop."

"That would be perfect," she said.

Patrick took her hand. "You would likely still need to do some work at Archers' to make ends meet the first little while. Joseph means to talk with Katie about it, but he's confident something can be arranged."

"Katie's certainly capable of doing the work and more than willing," Eliza said, "but I see how much she loves having the freedom to be with her children and play her violin. I would always worry that she'd agreed to the arrangement out of compassion but wasn't truly happy with it."

Patrick kissed the back of her hand. "Even if you did nothing more than the laundry once a week, it would bring in a bit of extra money to stretch further."

"When the stage passes," Eliza said, "would the horses simply be resting while the driver had a bite to eat, or would horses be changed here?"

Patrick's head tipped and his brow pulled in thought. "A change of horses would be invaluable to the stage. They could travel so much farther on fresh horses."

"I don't have horses to lend them, though. And I certainly couldn't afford to purchase any."

He released her hand and paced away. "The stage company can drop an extra team here to be stabled and cared for. When the northbound stage stops for a midday meal, they'd trade their team for the rested one, leaving the weary horses to be stabled and cared for until the southbound stage stopped the next day for lunch, trading their team for the one here. And so on and so on."

"And the stage company would pay for the stabling?"

Patrick nodded, turning to face her with eagerness in his eyes. "That would bring in more funds *and* increase your inn's value to the stage."

Eliza pressed her palms together, resting her fingertips to her chin. "I'd have to hire someone to look after the animals; I haven't the first idea how to care for horses."

"I've worked as a stable hand," he said. "Did a fine job of it. Enjoyed it, too."

"You want to be my employee?" The idea made her laugh.

"Oh, love." He slipped closer. "That's not at all what I have in mind."

She pretended to be confused. "You want to be *the stage company's* employee?"

Patrick put his arms around her, holding her as they stood on the very spot where so many of her dreams had resided these past months. "I can see I have more work to do."

"Building the inn?"

Laughter shook his chest. "You're trouble, you are."

She leaned into his embrace. "I've been a source of trouble to many people. I do try not to be."

"Oh, sweetie, I was only teasing."

"I know." She wrapped her arms around his middle. "And I'm glad of it. You never make me feel like a weight or a leech."

"You're never either one. And if ever you doubt that, you need only ask. I'll tell you the truth of it."

The wind whipped around them, swirling and tugging. She felt very little of it, shielded and warmed by his embrace.

"I'll likely not be able to pay you very much to tend the horses."

"I will have income from Finbarr's farm," he said.

"You won't resent that I'm the reason you're working two jobs?"

He kissed her forehead. "I've never been afraid of hard work, and I like being busy."

"So do I." She looked up into his eyes. "It seems we're birds of a feather."

"It seems we're a lot more than that." He leaned his forehead against hers. "I never did get to kiss you goodbye before leaving for the depot."

"You didn't kiss me 'good to be back,' either."

"Hmm." He somehow drew closer despite already being so close. "Seems to me we ought to be able to sort that out."

"I should hope so."

When he'd kissed her on the front step of Ian's house, it had been soft and hesitant, like the brush of a feather. There, on the spot of land where her dreams had been planted, he kissed her again, but this time, his lips were fervent, and his embrace was ardent.

She bent her arms around his neck and returned his kiss with every ounce of feeling she had.

This was truly a place for dreams to come true.

Chapter Thirty-one

"Canada is not exactly a temperate clime. I'm keenly aware of the difficulties of building in the harshness of winter." Patrick looked over his gathered family, grateful for the acceptance he'd found among them. He needed a favor, and even a month earlier he'd not have dared ask for it. "But if the exterior of the inn can be up and complete before winter truly and fully arrives, I can work on the inside no matter the weather. And if I can do that, we'll have an inn ready to open come spring."

"Why's this inn so important to you, then?" Tavish asked with his usual teasing glint.

His wife set her hand on his, effectively shushing him but not wiping the grin of amusement from his face.

"This is a big project, more daunting than Finbarr's house. I can't get the framing up entirely on my own. Getting the exterior walls boarded, sealed, and plastered would likely take me longer than I have." He was keeping calm, but only just. Eliza's heart was so set on this; he couldn't bear the thought of letting her down. "If the inn can't open in the spring, we're sunk."

" *We* ?" Tavish, it seemed, couldn't help himself.

"Continue on that way, Tavish," Ma warned, "and I will beat you like a rug after a dust storm." She turned to Patrick once more. "Tell us what you need, *mo buachaill álainn.*"

"He's your lovely boy, and I'm the rug you beat?" Tavish made quite a show of being offended, but they all knew him far too well to think he was anything but amused.

"*He* is behaving," Ma said.

Ian jumped in. "Patrick, you see what you left me with the last decade? It's a miracle I've any ability to converse like a human being. Thank the heavens for Finbarr, or I'd've been rendered a mess of a person."

Saints, it was good to laugh with his family again. Patrick had needed it for years.

Da, though clearly enjoying the banter, brought things back 'round to the subject at hand. "Are you needing us to hold a barn raising?"

"An *inn* raising, but aye. If I can get the inn framed and most of the outside walls boarded as soon as possible, I might have a fighting chance."

"You'll want the fireplaces in and functioning as well," Thomas tossed out. "You'll not be able to do a lick of work inside in the dead of winter if you can't heat the place."

Patrick had been so focused on the walls, he'd not even thought of that.

"Karl Kester is a dab hand at rockwork," Keefe said. "And Matthew Scott isn't shabby, either. Between the two of them and a few more willing workers, they could have the fireplaces you need built quickly."

"That would help tremendously. How much do you think they'd ask for their work? We haven't a lot to spend, but we'll pay what's fair." He was taking some liberties using "us" and "we" when referring to the inn. Yet he had every reason to believe those would soon enough be the correct words.

Biddy, with her little boy bouncing in her lap, joined the discussion. "If the exterior walls are completed and the fireplaces are working, could we hold *céilís* inside the unfinished inn this winter, even with your ongoing work?"

"There'd be space enough, certainly. And I don't think Eliza would object."

Biddy looked to the lot of them. "If finishing this inn means we won't all have to descend into isolation for the winter, I'd wager the entire town would be willing to help get the walls up. They did for Joseph after the fire. They built Ryan's hay shed. They'd help build the inn."

The entire town. With that much help, Patrick would be far ahead of schedule rather than in a desperate race with the calendar. "Do you think they would?"

"You leave it to us, son," Da said. "We'll rally the entire valley."

Patrick wasn't so optimistic. "They aren't all in favor of the inn, worrying about the town being overrun, or the inn turning in to something too much like a saloon."

"Placing it on the other side of our hill will set most minds at ease," Da said. "Jeremiah Johnson is eager to open the tiny mercantile inside the inn that Eliza proposed. That will address the town's worries about strangers coming into town looking for items to purchase. And Eliza's said she doesn't mean to serve liquor, which answers the remaining worries. Letting the town use the inn for gatherings and winter parties will take them from acceptance to enthusiasm."

The family was already getting to their feet.

"We'll begin getting the word out," Mary said. "We can schedule the raising for this Saturday and end with the *céilí*—outside, if need be."

Patrick's brothers and Da, as well as Joseph, had brought the building supplies back from the depot. Work could begin immediately.

Ma didn't head out with the others but crossed to him instead. "*Mo buachaill álainn.*"

"You used to call me that all the time. I haven't felt very 'lovely' in a lot of years."

She touched his cheek softly and affectionately. "And, yet, I'm full certain you've been precisely that. Not perfect, not saintly—who among us is?—but lovely. And kind. And lonely."

"I've missed you."

"And I've missed you, my sweet, darling Patrick. Having you here with me is a miracle. Not a day goes by in which I don't thank the heavens for you."

"Being back with this family has saved my life," he said. "And it's given me a future and a reason to hope."

"And it's given you Eliza," Ma added.

"Almost," he corrected.

"Oh, son. Not nearly as 'almost' as you think. There's no mistaking what I see between the two of you." She slipped her arm through his. "I suspect you need only ask her."

They walked toward the front door of Da and Ma's house.

"What if she says no?" Patrick's heart dropped at the thought.

"Then I will eat my bonnet."

He could not hold back the laugh that comment summoned. "I adore you, Ma."

"And I love you, my Patrick. Be brave, son. You had courage enough to come here and reclaim your life. It is time you begin fully living it."

Saturday morning dawned a little colder than expected, but with clear skies and only a light breeze: the perfect day for building. Patrick stood in the midst of the piles of lumber and burlap sacks of nails, looking out over the gathering. He'd hoped his family could round up a few extra hands to help. The crowd gathered to help exceeded his wildest hopes.

At least as many people were gathered around the inn site as attended the weekly parties. They'd arrived with hammers and saws and friendly greetings. The spread of food was impressive. The excitement in their faces was encouraging.

"Best get them started, son," Da said.

"Me?"

"'Tis your inn, lad."

He shook his head. "'Tis Eliza's."

"I'll grant you that, but they're here to help *you* build it. Direct 'em so we can get started."

Patrick climbed onto the back of a nearby wagon. He let forth a shrill whistle, pulling the crowd's attention. "Thank you all for coming out to help this morning. We're to have an inn near enough for gatherings like this, and for *céilís,* and for having a place to store unwanted family members when they come for a visit."

That earned him the expected smiles and eyerolls.

"We'll divide into four teams," he told them. "The plans have a few bends and corners, which complicates things for three of the four teams, but the fourth team will be building the long back wall and the interior load-bearing wall. That should even things up." He pointed to the simplified building plans nailed to a makeshift easel he'd constructed. "This is what we're needing. I've marked where the windows, doors, and fireplaces are meant to be. Frame up accordingly. I've a prize for the first team to finish their portion."

"And what would that be?" Seamus Kelly called out.

"I will fell, cut, and deliver a wagon full of logs to be divided amongst the winning team."

That brought a murmur of excitement. Obtaining wood was a time-consuming thing, and winter tended to sneak up on the people of this valley.

"Put together your teams. We'll break in a couple hours' time for a bite to eat, then push through 'til we're done. And we've a *céilí* awaiting us at the end of the day, though that means listening to Seamus yammering all night."

Seamus took the taunting in stride; he always did. The group wove about, forming their teams.

Patrick spotted Eliza not far distant, sitting with Maura at one of the tables hauled over for the day. Lydia sat on the table, clutching her doll and handkerchief and wearing the shoes Patrick had brought back for her from the depot. They were building more than just an inn that day. They were building a home for two people who meant the world to him. They were building a fresh start and a brand-new future. Patrick felt more and more certain that he'd be granted a place in that future. He couldn't believe Eliza would kiss him the way she had if she didn't care for him as much as he did for her.

Quickly enough, four teams were assembled. The appointed heads of each approached Patrick for their assignments. He answered their questions, gave some further instructions, then declared the competition started.

Everyone there had helped build homes throughout the valley. They wouldn't need much input from him. He'd keep an eye on it all, walk around to make certain everything was as it ought to be. Overall, there wasn't much for him to do. He didn't dare join his family's team, as he was meant to be impartial. He'd help anywhere he was needed, though.

Not long after the inn raising began, Eliza found him. "I cannot believe everyone came to help with this. So many people didn't even like the idea of an inn when it was first presented."

"You heard their worries and didn't brush them aside."

"I care about this town. I would never do anything to hurt the people here."

"Is that why you've decided not to serve liquor at the inn? Not every stage passenger or driver will be happy about that."

She slipped her hand in his. "I'll serve them all the tea they want. I mean to have plenty on hand."

Tea. That word stirred emotion in his heart; he knew what she was telling him. She'd made the decision for his sake.

"I don't want you to ever feel anything other than at home here," she said.

He raised their entwined hands and kissed the back of hers. "This will be home to you and Lydia. Finbarr's house isn't so far from here, plenty near enough for visiting regularly. That'll make this one of my favorite places."

"You will come visit, then? You'll not be so close as you are to the Archers. I'll miss seeing you every day."

He leaned near her ear and whispered, "I believe we can sort out a solution to that difficulty, love."

Someone shouted his name from the building site. He pressed an all-too-brief kiss to her all-too-tempting lips before moving to see what was needed.

As the day went on, there was no opportunity for anything more between him and the woman he loved than smiles and quick words in passing. While the building was going on, he was in constant demand. During the lunch break, she was.

Through it all, Ma's words echoed in his mind. *Be brave. You need only ask her.*

Be brave.

By the time the inn was framed and the winning team declared— the O'Connors, Callaghans, and Scotts, despite having chosen one of the more difficult sections of the inn—Patrick's resolve to be brave had evolved into a plan.

The tables were gathered together and laden with foodstuffs for the *céilí*. The chairs were moved to form the usual groupings, with room for dancing and a spot for a fire and tale telling. The musicians gathered, chatting and laughing.

Patrick snagged Ryan and Thomas from among them, then pulled Ian, Tavish, and Keefe aside as well. "I'm needing a favor from the lot of you."

"You still owe us a wagon of wood," Tavish said. "Are you truly wanting to add to that debt?"

"I'll risk it," Patrick answered dryly. "Besides, Ma'd skin you if you turned me down on this. 'Twas her idea, in a way."

"What is it you're needing?" Ian asked.

"A song. I know you know it. We've sung it before, ages ago." He looked to his newer brothers-in-law. "I actually don't know if you lot know it, seeing as I didn't know *you* ages ago. But it ain't a tricky one. Even if you're new to it, the chorus is the same thing again and again, and that's the bit I need your backing on."

"We're quick studies," Keefe said. "Get on with you; we'll join in."

He next had a quick word with Seamus, explaining briefly what he needed, and secured that man's cooperation.

As soon as most of the gathering had settled in, Seamus cued Ryan on the pipes to catch everyone's attention with the usual trill of notes.

"Welcome, friends!" Seamus called out. "We've something a bit different to begin tonight's *céilí*. Our host for the inn raising will be playing host of the music for the length of a song." He motioned his green derby hat toward Patrick, then stepped back, giving him leave to do his business.

Be brave.

Patrick traded places with Seamus and addressed the crowd. "When I first arrived here, you sang a welcome song, a tradition, I was told. But, there's something in the offering that's not sat well on m'mind ever since. While I was honored to share the moment with Eliza Porter, she deserves a song of her own."

Eliza watched him from her seat at the edge of the dancing area, curiosity in her expression, but, to his relief, no sign of panic or worry. Lydia watched him as well, with the sweetest smile he'd nearly ever seen from her.

"I've not done a vast deal of singing," Patrick warned them all, "so I've enlisted a bit of help."

His brothers knew their cue, though he'd not specified it. From amongst the crowd and the musicians, they made their way toward him. Ma looked like she might cry with excitement. How long had it been since her boys had sung together? Not since Patrick's arrival, at least. If only Finbarr had come.

"Eliza." Patrick met her eye. "A song for you."

Maura nudged her to stand, which she did. She looked around the gathering, uncertain. Lydia sat on her hip, clinging to her, clearly unsure what was happening.

"You needn't search out a dancing partner," Patrick said. "I don't hold to that part of the tradition."

She smiled at him. Just enough amusement lay in her expression to tell him she suspected he had something mischievous in mind.

He looked to his brothers. "Lads?"

They gave him nods.

His heart thrummed in his neck and head. *Be brave.* He swallowed down his nerves, and dove in.

"*I'm tired now of single life.*
"*My mind's made up to take a wife*

"To help me through this world of strife,
"And keep me out of danger."

Right on cue, his brothers joined him in the chorus, striking just the right harmonies and trills.

"Love, won't you marry me,
"O, marry me, marry me?
"Love, won't you marry me
"And keep me out of danger?"

They stepped back, allowing him full ownership of the next verse, which he'd reworked a bit for the occasion.

"My heart belongs to Eliza P.
"She is the only lass for me.
"I know our lives will happy be,
"If she'll agree to marry me."

His brothers rejoined for the chorus, though a few laughs and grins and elbows to the ribs made it more raucous than before.

"Love won't you marry me,
"O, marry me, marry me?
"Love, won't you marry me
"And keep me out of danger?"

Patrick stepped toward his love while singing, on his own this time, the chorus once more. The crowd parted as he drew nearer her.

"Love, won't you marry me,
"O, marry me, marry me?
"Love, won't you marry me—"

He took a breath and took her hand.

"And build a life together?"

Silence fell over the gathering, all eyes on the three of them. Patrick tapped Lydia's little button nose. He offered the little girl a reassuring smile before looking fully to Eliza once more.

You need only ask her. Time to discover how wise his ma truly was.

"Build a life with me, Eliza," he said softly. "I'm far from perfect and nowhere near ideal, but I love you, darlin'. And I love our Lydia. And I'll spend all m'life doing all I can to prove that to you, if you'll let me."

She reached up and brushed her fingers along his cheek. "I'll give you an answer under one condition."

He hadn't expected that. "What is your condition?"

"That your brothers sing the chorus again and sing it with gusto."

He didn't even have to make the request. The lot of them burst immediately into the most enthusiastic version of "Love, Won't You Marry Me" that he'd ever heard or could possibly have imagined.

She laughed, and he couldn't help but do so as well. The townspeople picked up the tune, and the two of them were soon being serenaded by the entire town.

"What's your answer, darling?" he asked as the crowd posed the question again and again in song.

"Of course I'll marry you, my love. I've been hoping you'd ask me for ages."

Patrick kissed her and kissed her thoroughly. The musicians began playing, joining the enthusiastic voices. Dancing broke out all around them. Still, he kissed her. He'd come to Hope Springs looking for mere survival, but he'd found so much more. He'd found hope. He'd found a future.

He'd found love.

Chapter Thirty-two

Maura straightened the ribbon in Eliza's hair. She stepped back and gave her a quick inspection. "Beautiful. Though the baby is an odd accessory for a wedding day."

"You have an angel in this one, Maura." Eliza cherished every ounce of happiness she saw in her friend; it had been in such short supply during their time together in the Widows' Tower. She carefully set the tiny, sleeping bundle back in Maura's arms.

"An angel and a miracle." Maura brushed her cheek along her infant daughter's. The miracle had arrived only a week earlier. The strain on Maura's factory-damaged lungs had been significant, but she'd emerged whole and healthy and more joyous than Eliza had ever known her to be. The baby had been named Grace, a fitting choice.

"Could you have believed during those difficult, lean years of suffering in New York that this was the life that awaited us just down the road?"

"Never." She slowly rocked her daughter in her arms. "I can't imagine being more grateful to have been wrong."

"I like your Ryan," Eliza said.

"And I like your Patrick, the Patrick he has grown to be since knowing you. He's a good man getting closer to deserving you."

Eliza smoothed the front of her dress. She only ever wore it on Sundays, and it was decidedly the nicest thing she owned. "I wish I had something new and truly beautiful."

Maura tucked her baby girl into the crook of one arm, freeing the other, which she wrapped around Eliza's shoulders. "You are beautiful, and I promise you Patrick will think so as well. He is well aware how fortunate he is to be marrying you today. You'd be a vision to him even if you showed up in beggar's threads."

A memory of Ivy declaring him a beggar man flashed through Eliza's mind, and her heart warmed. How far he'd come, and how very much better she knew him now.

"Shall I go marry my beggar man, then?"

"I think you had best."

Maura walked with her from the Archers' home, down the road to the church. Wagons and buggies surrounded the building. They were not having a large wedding—only Patrick's family, the Archers, and the preacher, and his wife—but the church wouldn't be anywhere near empty.

Though far from conventional, Maura would be walking with Eliza to the front of the church. Her father was in England, and she hadn't anyone else in her life as much like family to her as the woman who'd been like a sister to her these past years.

Patrick stood at the front of the chapel, Ian beside him, and the preacher waiting with his Bible in hand. Mrs. O'Connor sat on the frontmost pew with Lydia on her lap. Patrick's family had fully adopted Eliza and her daughter, treating Lydia no differently from their own grandchildren. They were part of a family now.

Any nervousness she'd felt melted away at the sight of Patrick smiling at her, his eyes never leaving her face. She kept her gaze on him as she and Maura closed the distance. Ryan slipped Grace from her mum's arms as they passed, freeing Maura to give Eliza a loving, sisterly hug before stepping aside.

Patrick held his hand out to her. Eliza set hers in his, and together they stood in front of the preacher.

"Dearly beloved . . ."

Eliza held fast to Patrick's hand as the ceremony proceeded. Such strength existed in this man, but such tenderness as well. Emotion broke a little in his voice as he spoke his vows, and her heart was evermore his. Without any hesitancy or uncertainty, she spoke hers.

The preacher declared them married. Their gathered family and friends cheered as Patrick pulled her into a fierce and earnest embrace.

"I love you," he whispered.

"I love you," she answered.

He kissed her as tradition dictated, but there was nothing solemn about it. There was warmth and love and affection. Lydia tugged at her dress and his trousers, interrupting the moment in a most welcome and perfect way. Patrick scooped her up, and the three of them, now a truly official family, turned to receive the well wishes of their guests.

After a great many hugs and handshakes, they managed to maneuver their way out of the church.

"Joseph has lent us his buggy," Patrick said. "We won't have to walk all the way to Finbarr's house."

He handed her up, then set Lydia in her arms. After another quick kiss, he hitched the buggy up, climbed inside, and set the horse to a gentle trot. Eliza laid her head on his shoulder.

"I was so nervous during the stage ride to Hope Springs," she said. "I knew only Maura and Aidan, and I worried I'd never find a home. I could not have imagined that my home was right there in the stagecoach with me."

"I know I didn't show it at the time, but your determination to befriend me during the journey meant the world to me. I needed it more than I can say even now."

As they drove on, she began humming the tune that refused to leave her thoughts, a tune that had made a home in her heart these past weeks. She knew the moment Patrick recognized it; he laughed.

"A catchy little ditty, isn't it? 'Love, won't you marry me? O, marry me, marry me?'"

He continued singing as they wound their way toward the home that would be theirs until the inn was finished. Finbarr had made a point of telling them he wanted them to live there. Though it was inarguably kind of him, she knew with certainty that more than generosity was at play in his prolonged absence from the home his brother had built him. He never attended the *céilís*. He didn't consistently make an appearance at family dinners. The young man was struggling with something; she only hoped this family she was now so fully part of could find the means of helping him navigate it.

They arrived at their temporary home only moments before the rest of the family did. Soon, the house was full to bursting with O'Connors. Food was nearly as abundant as the laughter and music.

Patrick and Eliza sat near the fireplace, hand in hand. He was no longer uncomfortable when surrounded by his family. She cherished that change in him. He'd found peace. With efficiency borne of many years' practice, Mrs. O'Connor and her daughters and daughters-in-law had the entire clan fed. The children ran about, happily playing. The adults took obvious delight in one another's company.

As the evening wore on, Ian and Biddy came and sat beside Eliza and Patrick. Ian held a paper-wrapped bundle out to his brother. "A present for you."

Patrick took it, curiosity and amused wariness in his eyes. He untied the twine holding the paper and slowly, cautiously began unwrapping it.

"'Tisn't anything dangerous," Ian said with a laugh.

Patrick pulled the paper back entirely, revealing a dark green tin. "Tea?"

"I told you in the mountains that I'd see to it you never ran out of tea. I'm making certain you start this new life with a plentiful supply."

"You must like me, at least a little."

"A very little."

Eliza exchanged a theatrical eyeroll with Biddy. "These two. What will we do with them?"

"Love them, probably."

Eliza nodded. "Sounds like heaven."

Patrick rose and crossed to the cupboards by the stove, then set the tin on a shelf.

"Thank you for that," Eliza said low and quick to her new brother- and sister-in-law. "He's so much better now than he was, and not merely because he has something else to drink when he's . . . thirsty. You've helped him to see that he's loved and wanted by all of you. He needed to hear that from more than just me."

"Thank *you*," Ian answered. "I'm convinced your friendship and your kindness kept him here, and you kept him trying. You saved him, and you'll be my favorite sister for that." He said the last bit with a mischievous glint in his eye. "Just don't tell the others."

"It will be our secret."

Patrick returned a moment later, having acquired a sleeping Lydia on his way back. "*Mo stóirín* has had all the fun she can handle for one day, I'd wager."

"You never have told me what *mo stóirín* means."

"My little darling," he said.

He'd called Lydia that from the beginning. He'd cherished her from the very first. How could he possibly have doubted his goodness?

"We'd best let your sweet girl sleep," Biddy said, getting to her feet.

In a surprisingly short amount of time, the large O'Connor clan gathered their things, their children, and themselves, and with hugs and words of happiness, slipped out. And the house was sweetly, peacefully quiet.

Patrick carried Lydia through the door to the room they'd decided would be hers and set her in the bed they'd made for her months ago when they'd been little more than acquaintances working at being friends. She didn't wake, hardly stirred.

They tucked her blankets comfortably around her and each gently kissed her soft little cheek.

"I love you, *mo stóirín*," Patrick whispered to Lydia before standing once more.

He wrapped his arm around Eliza's waist and walked with her from the room, carefully closing the door behind them. A low fire burned in the fireplace, casting a gentle glow and lending a soothing crackle to the silence around them.

"I used to sit here in this empty house by myself and imagine what it would be like if you were here with me," he said. "I missed you every moment we were apart but was too afraid to let myself believe there was reason to hope."

"There was always hope, Patrick O'Connor. Even in our lowest moments, there was always hope."

"And there was always you." He lightly kissed her forehead. "And now there will always be *us*."

"Forever," she whispered.

"Forever and ever."

He kissed her in their new home on this, the first night of their new life together.

Hope had brought them to this town. Love had built a life for them here. Beautiful, powerful, miraculous love.

Acknowledgments

With gratitude for information and insights . . .

- Rideau Hall, Ottaway, Canada
- The Manitoba Museum's collections database, Winnipeg, Canada
- The Oklahoma Sod House Museum
- Utah Humanities, for information on stagecoaches of the western United States
- Yellowstone Heritage and Research Center

A heartfelt Thank You to . . .

- Annette Lyon, whose deeply detailed edits make me look smarter and more talented than I actually am. I could not do this without you.
- Heather Moore, who continues to believe in the value of this series and the stories it tells
- My own Irish ancestors for continually speaking to my heart words of love for our culture, our heritage, our history, and our ancestral homeland

About the Author

Photograph © Annalisa Rosenvall

SARAH M. EDEN is the *USA Today* bestselling author of multiple historical romances, including Foreword Review's 2013 "IndieFab Book of the Year" gold medal winner for Best Romance, *Longing for Home*, and two-time Whitney Award Winner *Longing for Home: Hope Springs*. Combining her obsession with history and affinity for tender love stories, Sarah loves crafting witty characters and heartfelt romances. She has thrice served as the Master of Ceremonies for the Storymakers Writers Conference and acted as the Writer in Residence at the Northwest Writers Retreat. Sarah is represented by Pam Victorio at D4EO Literary Agency.

Visit Sarah at www.sarahmeden.com